Midcentury

was originally published by the
Houghton Mifflin Company at $5.95.

Other books by John Dos Passos

Chosen Country

District of Columbia

The Great Days

The Men Who Made the Nation

Prospects of a Golden Age

Three Soldiers

U.S.A.

  *The 42nd Parallel

  *1919

  *The Big Money

*Published in a WASHINGTON SQUARE PRESS edition.

MIDCENTURY

JOHN DOS PASSOS

POCKET BOOKS, INC. • NEW YORK

Midcentury

Houghton Mifflin edition published February, 1961

GIANT CARDINAL edition published July, 1962

1st printing...May, 1962

This GIANT CARDINAL edition includes every word contained in the original, higher-priced edition. It is printed from brand-new plates made from completely reset, clear, easy-to-read type.

•

GIANT CARDINAL editions are distributed in the U.S. by Affiliated Publishers, a division of Pocket Books, Inc., 630 Fifth Avenue, New York 20, N.Y.

•

Notice: GIANT CARDINAL editions are published by Pocket Books, Inc. Trademark registered in the United States and other countries.

L

Contents

3. *Systems of Enterprise*

What man can contemplate the aardvark without astonishment?

Acknowledgments

The profile of James Dean on pages 468–475 originally appeared in *Esquire* in October 1958; the profile of Eleanor Roosevelt, pages 178–186, in the December 1960 issue of *Esquire*. *True* magazine first published, in February 1961, the profile of General William F. Dean appearing on pages 405–415. "Analyst," pages 24–30, appeared in *The National Review* for December 17, 1960. Grateful acknowledgment is also made to *The Reader's Digest* and *This Week Magazine*, in which other passages from this book have previously appeared, usually in somewhat different form.

1.
Your Place in the World

Walking the earth under the stars,
musing midnight in midcentury,
a man treads the road with his dog;
the dog, less timebound in her universe of stench and
shrill, trots eager ahead.

The man too senses smells:
the frosted pasture and the cold loblollies,
the warmsweet of cows, and perhaps a hint of the passing of
a skunk; hears
the hoot, hoot, hoot-hoot of the horned owl,
as full of faraway foreboding as the hoot of a
woodburning locomotive heard across the plains as a child
long ago; sees
Orion overhead sporting glistening Rigel
and Betelgeuse, and the three belt buttons
that point out Sirius, and Belletrix that indicates
smoldering Aldebaran.

Eyes sweep
the bluedomed planetarium pivoting on the
polestar which the meditative Greeks and the Bedouin
dreamed
engraved with the quaint creatures of the
zodiac; the spheres spun to music
and cherubim, benign to man,
with halcyon voices chanted
glory to God.

The dog stops short, paw poised, sniffs deep
and takes off yelping after some scuttle in the underbrush.

3

The man walks on alone.

Thoughts swarm; braincells, as multitudinous as the wan starpoints that merge into the Milky Way overhead, trigger notions; tonight,

in the century's decline,

new fantasies prevail. Photoelectric calculators

giddy the mind with numbers mechanically multiplying immensities by billions of lightyears.

A million hostile Chinamen a month; a hundred and thirty thousand miscellaneous manmouths a day added to the population of the planet Earth.

But rockets successfully soar and satellites trundle on their punctual trails above the stratosphere. Sam the Rhesus returns in his space capsule, his little face as inscrutable as when he went up. An aeronaut from a twelvemilehigh balloon spies moisture in the Venusian atmosphere. Norbert Wiener says his calculators are hep; watch out if they get a will of their own. A certain Dr. Otto Struve has predicated the possibility of ten million lifebreeding planets among the island galaxies, and, at Green Bank, West Virginia

(far from the sins of the world)

they are building a radio telescope the size of a baseballfield, tipped sixty stories up in the air, where the physicists of project Osma plan to listen for messages emitted with intelligent intent

from tau Ceti or epsilon Eridani.

A million men on a million nights, heirs of a

million generations, ponder the proliferation of their millions to the millionth power till

multitude bursts into nothingness,

and numbers fail.

I feel the gravel underfoot, the starlit night about me. The nose smells, the ears hear, the eyes see. "Willfully living?" "Why not?" Having survived up to now at least the death-dealing hail of cosmic particles, the interpreting mind says "I am here."

In the underbrush under the pines my dog yelps in hot chase. Furry bodies jostle in the dark among the broken twigs. Fangs snap, claws tear; barks, growls, snarls, panting

breath as jaws close on the soft hairs under the throat. A
shriek, not animal not human, a shriek of unembodied agony
rips the night.

In the silence my dog panting drags a thick carcass
through the brambles out on the road
    and places at her master's feet
    in the starlight
    a beautiful raccoon
    that was alive and is dead.

This much is true.

Documentary (1)

HOW TO MAKE A LEFT TURN IN OUTER SPACE

BECAUSE MAN TODAY MUST SPEAK TO MORE MEN, FASTER,
THE SHOUT MUST BECOME A CHORUS THAT REACHES TO
THE STARS

you get specific directions showing smart ways to
handle details of your income, savings, job, business, investments, retirement . . . smart money-
making money-saving plans for people on fixed
incomes, small business men, investors, heads of
families . . . everything you need to know to come
out of the boom with your future secure

SUN SAID TO ROAR AS MOON RUSTLES

Inflated Rubber Plane Crashes After Blowout

the Astronaut will be strapped in a reclining position, on a couch inside a one-ton space capsule.
The mushroom-shaped capsule will have insulated
double-thick walls—so thick that no meteorite can
puncture the vessel. The bottom of the capsule will
have a blunt rounded nose to absorb the intense
heat on re-entering the earth's atmosphere

SPACE AGE STOCKS GAIN; OTHER PRICES
IRREGULAR

happy men with happy family lives are the "go-do-it-ers"
of American Business. Nearly every company can use more of

6

them. It's easy; use the top men you have more frequently, farther, faster

MECHANICAL BOY ASTOUNDS PSYCHIATRISTS

In the current issue of a national magazine a University of Chicago scientist describes the case of "Joey," nine-year-old who is so convinced he is a machine that he is unable to eat unless he first plugs himself in. The boy, who is being treated for schizophrenia in an institution, stretches an imaginary electric wire from an imaginary outlet to the table. There he "insulates" himself with paper napkins before he dares switch on his eating machinery. His pantomime is so impressive that the attendants and the other young patients step carefully over his imaginary wires. Joey believes he can't breathe without an elaborate contraption of tubes and straws he calls his carburetor. He says he will die if his current is interrupted. Even the maids who do the cleaning are so impressed that they try not to disturb the "Rube Goldberg" construction made of wires and old radio tubes and bits of old clockwork and cardboard and masking tape around his bed. When he is not plugged in he sits absolutely still. From time to time he will suddenly turn himself on and shift noisily from gear to gear until he explodes. He starts screaming "Crash, crash," and throwing his apparatus around until something breaks. Then he'll stop yelling and jumping and sink back into what is described as "mute motionless nonexistence."

When the individual escapes into a world of delusions, explain the psychiatrists, these delusions are usually made up of fragments of the real world nearest at hand. Joey's story, they add, has relevance to the understanding of emotional development in the machine age.

Proconsul

In the unmilitary United States there flourished during the nineteenth century a number of families who raised their children to the sound of bugles; among the most dashing were the MacArthurs.

The first general, Arthur MacArthur, was the son of a Scottish lawyer who had become City Attorney in Milwaukee and Lieutenant Governor of the state. At seventeen he joined the 24th Wisconsin Regiment to help quench the rebellion. He carried the regimental colors through the smoke and slaughter of Missionary Ridge and became known as "the Boy Colonel of the West." He continued in the army after Appomattox, married the daughter of a North Carolina physician and went to fight Indians. It was a life of jingling spurs and sweated saddles and trailbreaking;

reveille and taps on the parade grounds of dusty outposts.

On January 26, 1880 at the Little Rock Barracks there was born to the MacArthurs a son who was to fulfill their fondest hopes. "I think there is material for a soldier in the boy," said the father when he took young Douglas, wearing a mass of golden curls and bearing a toy musket over his shoulder, to be photographed in San Antonio. While his father was stationed at Fort Sam Houston, young Douglas attended the West Texas Military Academy. There he won a gold medal for "extraordinary excellence" in sports, deportment and scholarship.

While the son was astonishing the schoolmasters the father was earning a Congressional Medal and climbing promotion's ladder to Lieutenant General (American generals were scarce in those days) and Chief of Staff.

When the short summer war against Spain almost by accident catapulted the American dream into the sweltering Orient the elder MacArthur received the assignment of straightening out the Filipinos. The Insurrectos had been all for American help to throw out the Spaniards, but when the Americans decided to stay they turned recalcitrant. The five year pacification proved an ugly business.

> *Underneath the starry flag*
> *Civilize them with a Krag*

went the soldier's song. (There was more to it than that: with the rifle and the flag went the old copybook maxims; life, liberty and the pursuit of happiness; devoted missionaries and teachers, effective administrators and the new science of sanitation. For better or worse after Aguinaldo's surrender the conglomerate populations of those distant scattered islands began to see their future as American.) Arthur MacArthur was our first proconsul.

He looked the part. He acted the part. His arbitrary behavior caused misgivings among the Washington civilians. When a civilian commissioner arrived to install due process he was treated with scant respect. In 1901 General MacArthur was summarily relieved of his command.

Meanwhile young Douglas, with his mother in Milwaukee, was tutoring for the West Point examinations. A brother was already at Annapolis. Needless to say Douglas MacArthur passed with an extraordinary score. A tall handsome deadly serious young man with impeccable manners, in spite of a little rougher than the usual hazing by upperclassmen, in spite of the indefatigable supervision of an ubiquitous mother who insisted on renting a house near the Military Academy to be near him, he broke all records of scholastic and military deportment. He made the baseball team. As senior he was First Captain. He graduated at the top of his class.

He chose the unpopular Corps of Engineers because advancement was rapidest there.

He saw his first service in the Philippines but soon he was detailed to Tokyo as his father's aide on a spit and polish

mission to the Orient. He accompanied General Arthur Mac-
Arthur as an observer during the Russo-Japanese War.

When in 1912 the father died suddenly of a heart
attack at a Grand Army reunion of his old Wisconsin regiment the son was already well on his way to succeed him.
He held various staff jobs in Washington. When Woodrow
Wilson began to apply the Big Stick to the tumultuous Mexicans, the youthful Captain MacArthur in the company of a
young German observer named Fritz von Papen scouted hostile positions outside of Vera Cruz, disguised, his biographers
tell us, as "a Mexican bum."

World War I found him in France as chief of General
Menoker's staff. It was MacArthur's idea to assemble a Rainbow Division made up from units of twentyseven different
state militias. He believed in the citizen soldier.

Preux chevalier sans peur et sans reproche, already he had
a reputation for never perspiring. His uniform didn't wilt in
the hottest weather. He seemed without fear. He went into
combat without sidearms or gasmask or helmet. He'd taken
to pulling the wire lining out of the stiff uniform cap and
wearing it at a rakish angle. Newspapermen called him
d'Artagnan of the AEF.

He won his promotion to colonel on the battlefield.
He was gassed, twice wounded, decorated thirteen times, cited
seven times for extreme bravery under fire. Pershing promoted
him to brigadier general and put him in command of the
Rainbow Division he had helped create.

After the war he was for three years Superintendent at West
Point. It was MacArthur who first gave the cadets a complete
college curriculum and introduced compulsory athletics. Of
course he was the youngest superintendent on record, as he'd
been the youngest brigadier general, and the youngest di-
visional commander.

He married late (assuredly the dowager Mrs. MacArthur
had kept the girls at bay); even then it seemed more an affair
of the Social Register than of the heart. Louise Cromwell
Brooks was a rich grass widow who had queened it over the
social doings of the higher echelons of the AEF in Paris after
the armistice. General Pershing, himself a widower, is said to

have suffered from her charms. The society columns hailed the affair as *The Marriage of Mars and Millions.*

The union was shortlived. After the splendors of New York and Paris the lady is said to have found Manila, where Mac-Arthur was appointed to his father's old post as American commander, quite unamusing. It is admitted that the general lacked humor.

These were trying years. When General MacArthur became Chief of Staff in 1930 the army was unpopular. Disarmament was the obsession. Because MacArthur saw dangers ahead from the rising dictatorships of Germany and Japan he was labeled a warmonger. His trips abroad were described as medal hunts.

MacArthur had a bad press.

When President Hoover ordered him to disperse the bonus marchers the Communists were stirring up to sedition in their poor Hooverville on Anacostia Flats, he superintended the job —which he could well have foisted off on a subordinate—himself, and saw that it was done efficiently and with a minimum of bloodletting. For that public service he was denounced as a "man on a white horse" by the wet-eyed journalists who were heralding the New Deal revolution.

It was noised against him that seven years before he'd sat on the courtmartial that dismissed his friend Billy Mitchell from the service for expressing too soon his conviction of the wartime ascendancy of the airplane. The vote was secret. Not till years later did the story leak out that MacArthur had voted for acquittal.

All the same Franklin Roosevelt put through his appointment as Chief of Staff for an unheard of second term. What little combat readiness there was in the army the day of Pearl Harbor was largely due to MacArthur's interest in motorized warfare.

In 1935 Manuel Quezon, who as a boy Insurrecto had surrendered to MacArthur's father, became the President of the independent Philippine Commonwealth. Alarmed by the advance of the Japanese Co-prosperity Sphere, he asked Washington for the loan of the American general best versed in Far Eastern affairs to help plan the islands' defense.

At the age of fifty-seven Douglas MacArthur retired from

the United States Army to become Field Marshall in the Army
of the Philippines.

In the course of the long steamship trips between the West
coast and Manila he met, besieged and soon married an agree-
able young woman from Tennessee.

This time it was for keeps. The dowager Mrs. MacArthur,
now a very old lady indomitably bent on following her son's
career, reached Manila only in time to take to her bed and die.

The MacArthurs were raising their small son at their pent-
house on the roof of the Manila Hotel when they had news of
Pearl Harbor.

MacArthur had been twenty-three years a general
officer. According to the hymenopterous punctilio of military
stratification the general officer lives in a sealed world. A
proper brass hat doesn't know whether it's raining or sunshine
until he's briefed by his staff. Like the queen bee he's fed on
royal jelly.

MacArthur in the Philippines was the brass hat of brass
hats. A man of brilliant intelligence with the real strategic
bent, he must have been strangely cut off from the real world
to allow his Flying Fortresses, after eight hours warning, to be
smashed in rows on Clark Field by Japanese planes flying all
the way from Formosa. He hadn't enough planes or PT boats
to begin with. Now he had nothing.

He declared Manila an open city to save the lives of the
puzzled Filipinos who had trusted him as they would trust the
Virgin Mary.

The retreat to Bataan was a routine performance plotted
long ahead. It certainly was not lack of physical courage that
kept him so long in the tunnel under Corregidor. The doomed
troops never saw hide or hair of him. "Dugout Doug" they
shouted after him when he fled (under direct orders from
Washington) by PT boat, through infested seas to Mindanao.
He took his wife and the little boy and the little boy's Chinese
nurse along with him. There was just time to snatch them in a
fourmotor plane off the Del Monte strip before the Japs closed
in.

It was the old MacArthur who stepped out of the
plane on his first Australian airstrip. The American collapse,
Rommel in Africa, the loss of the British battleships off Singa-

pore had scared the Australians out of a year's growth. Their military men were talking grimly of holding the Brisbane line. MacArthur showed no interest at all in the Brisbane line. He talked of invading the Philippines. He would only plan for victory.

Fresh from humiliations and defeats that would have ruined any lesser general's career, the Aussies saw MacArthur sit cool and unwilted in his headquarters in Brisbane smoking his corncob pipe—a folksy touch that gave an edge to his starched uniform and punctilious manner—plotting the strategy of victory. "I came through and I shall return," he broadcast to the Filipinos to let them know he'd escaped through the Japanese lines. The Aussies caught fire from MacArthur.

He couldn't have done it without the Navy, or the Marines who squandered their lives on forgotten reefs and coral-strewn beaches. He couldn't have done it without the Aussie prospectors' early knowledge of the Owen Stanley Mountains and the stinking Kokoda trail in New Guinea; or without the amphibian techniques developed in the Central Pacific or the erosion of the Japanese airforce or the floating bases and the incredible supplylines that girdled the globe;

but he knew how to seize the right moment,

he knew that attack was defense;

with a chessplayer's skill he kept four moves ahead of the Japs; where they were he wasn't. Where their defense was spread thin he was landing in force;

until, leaving wellarmed Japanese troops frustrated and starving on a score of islands,

MacArthur, having darkened the sky over the Philippines with little books of matches bearing his picture "Rely on me: I shall return,"

waded nonchalantly ashore

amid the whirring of motion picture cameras

on Lingayen Beach.

"I have returned. Rally to me. Let no heart be faint."

"Boldness and disdain of the enemy" he explained to the correspondents at his headquarters at San Miguel the day his troops got their first toehold in the suburbs of Manila. He was proclaiming the city's capture. . . .

(Press releases. Army and Navy and Marines; their brass

fought the Japs allright, but they fought each other for headlines in the stateside press. MacArthur's PRO beat everything.
God and the general were so often linked in the news people
could hardly tell which was which.)

. . . there was mighty little left of Manila when after weeks
of block by block fighting the last Jap threw up his hands.
"Boldness and disdain of the enemy."

The Manhattan Project. Iwo Jima. Okinawa. The
mushroomshaped cloud over cities become heaps. In spite of
pulling and hauling in Washington by adherents of the various
services it was to MacArthur that Harry Truman awarded the
palm of victory. As General of the Army he took the Japanese
surrender in Tokyo Bay.

Supreme Ruler of Japan.
Douglas MacArthur was as inaccessible as he'd been in that
desperate tunnel under Corregidor, but somehow he managed,
decking them out in terms of the hour, to promulgate the old
copybook maxims that had Americanized the Filipinos in his
father's time:
  civil liberties,
    freedom of the press,
      land ownership for the peasant who worked the
soil, unhampered trade unions, the rules of fair play. He kept
the Communists off base and foiled the best spy-diplomats
that Moscow could train.

When the Emperor Hirohito renounced his divinity, the
displaced godhead seemed to hover for a while over the GHQ
of the Supreme Commander, Allied Powers; Commander-in-
Chief, United Nations Command; Commander-in-Chief, Far
East; and Commanding General U.S. Army, Far East.

A movement to nominate him for the Presidency in 1948
seemed an anticlimax. No American before him had ever occupied such a pinnacle of power.

In spite of the five stars and the gold braided caps
and the chest banded with rainbow after rainbow of ribbons
Douglas MacArthur, as an old man at seventy-one, was to
look once more
into the grinning skull of defeat.

When through a series of wrong moves, so maladroit that historians will be puzzling over them for a hundred years, the managers of America's destiny managed to leave the friendly republic they'd been fostering south of the 38th parallel in Korea

wide open to attack by the vigorous army the Russians trained in the north,

war broke out overnight.

Again as in Manila, it was MacArthur the unready. (All the brass hat knows is his briefing from his staff.) Early reverses were wiped out by a skillful amphibious landing at Inchon. MacArthur ordered the advance to the Yalu. In spite of the fact that the first Chinese thrust had been with difficulty repulsed, MacArthur's PRO's were filling the press with accounts of his troops eating Thanksgiving Dinner, victorious,

in sight of the Yalu River.

The mighty MacArthur would clear the peninsula and get the boys home by Christmas. A few days later the boys were on the run, or dead, or prisoners dripping with dysentery in stinking stockades.

"Boldness and disdain of the enemy." Every reader of *The New York Times* knew that the Chinese were massing an army on the Yalu; they announced it themselves. (A brass hat lives like a queen bee, sealed off from the world, dependent on his staff to feed him the royal jelly.)

In spite of the retreat conducted in the best War College style by the troops in the northern mountains (flying boxcars flew in a whole suspensionbridge for a rivercrossing by the First Marine Division)

the Chinese inflicted a smashing defeat

on the forces under MacArthur's command.

The rest was the facesaving diplomacy of failure.

When Douglas MacArthur was, like his father before him, summarily relieved of his proconsular post, the little ward-heeler from Independence Missouri who occupied the White House

made the dismissal as curt as he could,

but somehow he managed to give the impression that the general's crime had not been his defeat

but his insistence on planning to win;
"There is no substitute for victory."

Win or lose MacArthur had grandeur. Perhaps most Americans agreed with Harry Truman that grandeur was for the birds,
all the same they greeted him as no defeated general has ever been greeted before. In New York City the streetcleaners figured that sixteen million tons of paper and ticker tape were dumped out of office windows by the frenzied inhabitants during the MacArthur parade. Clearly a record. In Washington the members of both houses of Congress listened in awe
as the old general offered his ritual submission to the civil government, and pulled about him the nostalgic toga of the old soldiers of the Republic (Washington too made his farewell):

"I am closing my fifty-two years of military service. When I joined the army, even before the turn of the century it was the fulfillment of all my boyish hopes and dreams. . . .
". . . The world has turned over many times since I took the oath on the plain at West Point and the hopes and dreams have long since vanished. . . . 'Old soldiers never die, they just fade away.' "

He set the whole nation to humming the old song.

The Beginning of Home

Terry Bryant is the first man off the transport.
As he jumps out he has a whirling glimpse of ranked planes and hangars and tugs and carferries on the bay and the piled up buildings of San Francisco dimshining through the mist. Overhead through bright tatters of mist the sky shines blue blue blue.
Not home but the beginning of home.
For a moment Terry thinks of throwing himself flat on his face and kissing the concrete runway.

What he does is to squat on his heels and give the concrete three quick pats. Getting to his feet with a queasy grin on his face he notices that the man behind him has the same idea. This is a stocky serious dark fellow who makes the gesture slowly and deliberately. He kisses the palm of his hand and presses it lovingly on the ground.

Terry catches his eye and they laugh and nod in each other's faces like a couple of jackasses.

The rest of the men come crowding behind them in mussed and varied battle dress: leather jackets with Chinese and American flags on the back, sheepskins, mottled brown and green ponchos. Nobody says anything. They look about them with big shining eyes, like children's eyes Christmas morning, eyes big enough to take in all America. After the warmth of Pearl the chilly misty morning makes them shiver. With quaking fingers they start to light cigarettes.

"No smoking boys," intones the airport officer in a weary voice. They stamp out their cigarettes with eager obedience and crowd after him as he leads the way with the papers fluttering in the breeze off the board in his hand.

Inside the reception center it was all desks and counters round the walls, and long lines of men waiting under numbers and lettering, dragging barracksbags and duffle as they moved.

The biggest crowd was round a milk bar attended by two cute girls in some sort of USO uniform. Terry couldn't keep his eyes off them as he waited his turn. One was blond. The dark one had eyes as blue as the sky over San Francisco. Both girls had a clean laundered look. Their slender pink fingers moved deftly among the glasses, never spilled a drop of the yellow milk.

Prettiest sight he'd seen in four years, Terry was telling himself as he waited his turn. He couldn't find a word to say. All he could do was give them the Asiatic stare. "By God," the man next to him muttered as they were pushed away from the stand by guys edging in behind them, "they talk English."

Terry had to waste those first delicious stateside hours standing in line and checking in, standing in line and checking in. It took forever. Still he had a lucky break. His service ribbons and the fact that they were short of sergeants that day earned him a detail to ride herd on a bunch of men scheduled

to depart at 13:45. "Direct flight to Noo York," whispered
the wiseguy who stamped his orders.

It wasn't so direct as all that. The takeoff was two hours
late. There were long waits in Salt Lake City and Omaha and
at some weathered-in airfield out in the boondocks in the
Middle West. Too much coffee, too many cigarettes. Bumpy
as hell over the Alleghenies. Holloweyed and desperate they
ended up the second evening in a wet snowstorm on an empty
airstrip near Allentown, Pennsylvania. Flight terminated.

"What do we do now?" the guys asked each other. The
sleepy lieutenant in the transportation hut didn't have an idea
in the world. After a lot of trudging about in the wet driving
snow—and this was only October, the guys told each other,
supposed to be Indian summer in this man's country—a bunch
of them chipped in on a taxi into Philadelphia. Haggard and
jangled after all those hours in the air and the waiting and the
uncertainty, what they needed was a drink.

Just no place a man could get a drink in Pennsylvania not
on a Sunday night, said the driver.

It wasn't the homecoming any of them had planned.

Ridgefield looks about the same. The house hasn't changed,
except that it needs painting. There's the privet hedge
Pop used to try to get the boys to help him clip and the
bay window and the brick steps they built themselves up to
the narrow porch that faces the street, and the colored glass
on either side of the front door. Old torn sheets of newspaper
and rags and dirt have piled up behind the hedge. The little
strip of grass has a straggly look it never would have had if
Pop had lived.

The front door is locked. Leaving his duffle piled on the
porch Terry tiptoes around to the back. The boards of the
kitchen stoop creak and give. As soon as he has his hand on
the knob he smells the warm vinegar. So long as he can remember the house has smelt of pickles in the fall. His mother's
square shoulders and the starched bow she's tied in her apron-
strings are just as he remembered them. When she turns from
the crock she's fussing over her eyes look as blue to him as
that girl's eyes at the milkstand in Oakland.

Mom hasn't changed any more than her house, except that
her hair is all white. In the old days before Pearl Harbor
Terry used to worry about how gray it was getting.

"Terence," she says, in that unexcited way she has, as if she had seen him the night before and he hadn't been away at all. She takes hold of his elbows and looks him critically up and down. "Terence you're two jumps ahead of a fit. . . . I got to feed you up. . . . Feeding up my boys is about the only pleasure left to an old woman like me."

She lets out one of her little gruff sudden laughs.

He hears himself explaining haltingly that Okinawa left them all jumpy.

"But that was months and months ago."

She changes the subject abruptly.

"Buddy's home on leave. Of course I never see him except when he's asleep." She's trying to hammer some sense of responsibility into his head, especially now that he's an uncle.

"You're an uncle too, Terence." Mom gives him one of her sharp straight looks. "Your sister made me a grandmother in the shape of a bouncing boy about six weeks ago," Mom rattles on cheerfully. "I guess you never got our letters. . . . Buddy's asleep in there."

She opens the door of the downstairs bedroom a crack and makes Terry look in. All he can see is a body muffled up under the bedclothes about four times as large as the fifteen-year-old Buddy last seen four years ago. A gob's uniform is neatly hung over the chair. Mom closes the door softly and they tiptoe back to the kitchen.

"If your poor father had only lived to see this day," she starts to say, but her voice dries up. She starts making a great clatter with the breakfast things over the electric stove.

Terry finds himself following her around the kitchen getting in her way like he used to when he was a young fellow. He doesn't want to look so glum. He has to think of something to make her laugh. "What do you suppose they called me, Mom? Joisey . . . I can't imagine why that was."

Mom starts in on the neighbors. They fall to laughing easily together over funny things that happened like they used to. It's only when Terry finds he can't eat the fine breakfast she's cooked for him that Mom begins to look worried again. Muttering that what the boy needs is a good rest she helps him get his things upstairs to the room under the eaves with the twin beds that used to be his and Buddy's in the old days. He stretches himself out without even taking off his shoes and falls into a dead sleep.

When they woke him to come down to dinner the whole family was assembled. Terry didn't know which of the women to kiss first. There was Francine and her husband, heavylipped Fred Dirks, and the baby looking up out of a bassinet with his tiny pink face just like his father's. There was Mom's sister Aunt Lillian, and her husband and their daughter Jane, eighteen already and a goodlooker and there was Buddy with that long smooth brown face of his and the slit eyes and a smirk on his mouth.

Mom made Terry sit at the head of the table in the chair with arms where he remembered Pop sitting with his glasses pushed up on his forehead to read the evening paper. Her eyes were shining when she came out of the kitchen with a steak for her returned serviceman. Mr. Snider the butcher had been saving it for when Terence came home. She'd been saving up coupons for three months. The rest of them would have to eat hamburger, she said.

The steak must have been three inches thick, done to a turn just the way he liked it. They all watched the juice run out when he cut into it. Their eyes were all on his face. He put a piece of steak in his mouth and chewed and chewed but he couldn't taste a thing. His stomach felt like a rock. He managed to swallow that piece, but he knew that if he took another he'd throw up. He was in a cold sweat.

"Think nothing of it, Mom," he said. "I'll make Buddy my deputy. All those K rations shrink a guy's stomach."

"Tell me the Air Force had the best chow in the service," Buddy said as he reached over with his fork and speared the steak off Terry's plate. "I need the strength," he added with that smirk on his mouth. "I've lost ten pounds since I been home, just havin' a time."

An indulgent titter went round the table. Aunt Lillian's husband let out a guffaw.

Mom hadn't touched the food on her plate. She sat looking into Terry's face. All the blue sparkle had gone out of her eyes. The skin round them looked old and crinkled. "But it was months ago," she said again.

"Why bring that up?"

Terry felt the nasty snarl in his voice. It wasn't his fault. To hell with it.

When the women went into the kitchen to help Mom with

the dishes Terry found himself out in the front hall with Buddy. Fred Dirks and Aunt Lillian's husband were smoking cigars in the living-room and arguing about what kind of a President Jimmy Byrnes would have made if he'd been Vice-President instead of Truman. Buddy came up to Terry and pulled at the lapel of his tunic. He still had that smirk on his face that rubbed Terry the wrong way while they ate.

"How about comin' out on a double date, Terry," Buddy whispered as he pushed a cigarette at him out of his pack. "I know some pretty hot numbers." He gave Terry a wink. "It's a sailor's privilege."

Terry pushed away the cigarette. He felt the frown wrinkling his forehead. He wanted to wipe that damn smirk off the kid's face.

"You need what you ain't been gettin' in the worst way, Terry."

"None of your goddam business what I need." Terry didn't want his voice to sound so nasty, but he couldn't help it. "You young punks think you're the only man ever slept with a woman."

Buddy gave his shoulders an exaggerated shrug.

Terry's fists were clenched so tight his nails cut into his hands. He was breathing hard.

"Well I guess I'll scram," said Buddy.

"No you don't. Not till you've put on the gloves with me." Terry's voice sounded nasty to his own ears. "Remember how Pop used to make us put on the gloves if we had a fallin' out?"

Buddy shook his closecropped narrow head. "No Terry no." Terry plunged down the basement stairs. Buddy followed him pleading into his ear. "Easy does it Terry. Easy does it."

The gloves were hanging from their old place on a nail across from the furnace.

The sight of them brought back Pop's red round face smiling under his mustache and the way he would snap his suspenders while he told the boys tales of Kelly's gymnasium and the bareknuckled brawlers before Fitzsimmons. Pop used to make them settle it like gentlemen if they had a falling out. "Never go to bed in anger against your fellow man," Pop used to say. The warm memory of good old Pop was like a picture suddenly glanced at on the wall. It had nothing to do with the way Terry felt now.

Buddy stood between Terry and the gloves still arguing.
"Look at the dust on 'em. I'm all cleaned up to go out." There
was a childish whine in his voice. "Terry let's take it easy tonight. Mom wants us to be with her. Easy does it." He didn't
want to stand up that date. "Never disappoint a woman."
That smirk was back on his mouth.

"You put on those gloves before I slam you one with my
bare fist."

Buddy pulled off his navy blouse and hung it carefully on a
clotheshorse. The boy sure had developed a pair of shoulders.
Terry caught himself feeling a sudden gush of pride in his kid
brother, but it was lost in the nastiness seething up inside him.

He started sparring before Buddy had time to tie his gloves.
Buddy was light on his feet. He kept his gloves up and parried
and ducked. Terry could see he was pulling his punches. That
made him all the madder.

He swung at Buddy and Buddy came back with a tap on
his jaw. There was the black taste of blood in his mouth. He
dove at Buddy with both fists. Buddy came back a little
harder.

Terry couldn't stop that left. He had a cut on his lip. He
wanted to kill him. He started swinging.

Mom's voice brought him up sharp. "Terence." Buddy had
backed off and lifted his gloves above his head. "Have a heart,
Terry. . . . I'm not fightin' you."

Their mother was standing on the stairs behind them. Terry
could see the whites all around her eyes. Her mouth made an
"O." "Terence," she cried again in a voice like breaking glass.

He shook his hands free of the gloves. "Someday I'll kill the
little smart alec," he hissed out of the corner of his mouth as
he brushed past her. He stamped up the two flights to his
room and slammed the door behind him and locked it on the
inside like he used to when he had a tantrum as a little kid.
Then he let himself drop down on the bed.

He couldn't sleep. He couldn't even stay on the bed. He
spent the night pacing up and down the room.

Next morning before anybody was up he got a few things
together in an overnight bag.

He wrote a note to leave on the kitchen table:

Mom tell Buddy I'm sorry. It's what they call battle

fatigue. I've seen the symptoms often enough to know what they are. I figured I'd better get fixed up before I got separated from the service. I'll write and call up. Don't worry.

Documentary (2)

MAN'S BARK FRIGHTENS COMMUTERS

Mildew damage? Extra laundry and tailor bills caused by perspiration? Extra cleaning bills caused by summer dirt?

Add to this lack of energy, poor appetites, lost sleep. If you are an allergy-sufferer you are paying for lack of clean filtered air.

SOLAR SAILING

This "brain" is a fully integrated guidance system, almost entirely land-based. Only the vital signal-receiving apparatus is expendable within the missile itself. It defies "jamming," is completely mobile, is designed in separate "building-block" units which are replaceable in seconds—and is deadly accurate.

SOPHISTICATED MISSION TRAINING

whether you're interested in mass-production cleaning or degreasing of mechanical, electronic, optical or horological parts or assemblies

CALCULATIONS EASILY SOLVED

at a few degrees above absolute zero the application even of a small electric field to a sample of germanium will grossly affect equilibrium of the conduction of electrons and increase their average energy by a factor of twentyfive or more

The case of a man who barked at people was placed in the annals of human behavior Wednesday by a British psychiatrist.

The man, now 65, barked like a dog every ten minutes for a year and a half.

His bark was so loud it could be heard several hundred yards. It frightened his more timid fellow commuters when he was waiting for a bus.

Until he was 65 he barked only occasionally. But then the urge became uncontrollable and he took to barking six times an hour.

THE PERFECT SOLUTION
(*can save you money*)

It would have been far less difficult to have made merely a statue of the human figure, instead we set ourselves the ambitious task of making it demountable with an articulated skeleton with each of its 206 bones sharply delineated. An ingenious parts within parts system permits examination of the respiratory complex, the chambers of the heart, the interior of the kidneys, the viscera, the brain and optic nerves inside the skull, the bronchial branches inside the lungs. With the cover of the chest cavity removed internal members can be demounted at will and easily replaced without disturbing the stability of the figure.

Analyst

They were our guests for dinner in our small dining-room on a quiet street in an obscure suburb of the somewhat obsolete city where we lived. We had roast beef and baked potatoes and bourbon whiskey in wide glasses. We talked of the old days. It was a pleasant meal.

Our friends brought one of their sons with them, a dark-eyed young man with untidy hair and an irregular face who sat sprawled in his chair eating and drinking without saying a

word until all at once his voice tears the sociable smiling
prandial mood apart,
    like the screech of chalk on a blackboard.
    "You gave me a hard time."
His eyes stare black with hate in his mother's face.
    "Yes you"
His voice is a whip lashing in his mother's face.
    "But when?"
    "Before I was born. The birth trauma was bad enough but
the damage was done before. Too busy with causes, Dad's
dogooding, my sisters and brothers. You never understood me.
And now
    here I lie tracing resentment back to the womb
    on the analyst's couch."

    (And they thought he was there to go to college.)

    In twenty thousand doctors' offices, in great cities,
in small towns, in complacent exurbia,
    the thaumaturge,
    seated out of sight at the head of the couch,
    prods the prone patient endlessly to associate
    words with words,
    by an occasional ejaculation or a grunt or a cough or a
query, directs the selfprobe of neuroses, hysterias, compul-
sions, anxieties, repressions, inversions, resentments;
    deep
    into the quivering primordial protoplasmic unconscious;
    peels the skins off the onion,
    dream by dream, fantasy by fantasy, recollection by recol-
lection,
    tracing resentment back to the womb,
    on the analyst's couch.

    Man the misunderstood,
    incestuous, polymorphously perverse, narcist, masochist,
sadist, exhibitionist, homosexual,
    has descended into neurosis,
    but through free association at twentyfive dollars an hour
may seek redemption by total recall of that first prime talis-
manic wish—*In the beginning was the Word*—
    that he may rise again

into the paradise of scientific psychoanalysis
where Ego sits at the right hand of Superego in the sub-
limation of the Id,
and transference is complete.

*Three Essays on the Theory of Sexuality . . . The In-
terpretation of Dreams . . . The Psychopathology of Every
Day Life . . . Civilization and Its Discontents . . . Beyond
the Pleasure Principle . . .*

Amid the scientific ruminations of the late nineteenth
century, Dr. Sigmund Freud, a talented Viennese neurologist,
who was an avid reader of folklore and drama,
discovered that to treat neurasthenics
he had to listen very carefully to their fantasies, and their
dreams and their anxious misstatements and their slips of the
tongue and their grammatical errors. Among the disturbed
nothing was what it seemed on the surface. "Neurasthenic
anxiety," Freud declared, "is transmuted sexual libido."
The psyche was sex.

Out of Sophocles and Shakespeare and Goethe and
Frazer and Darwin,
and out of the ramblings of sexstarved intellectuals who
thronged to his office—the strong enjoy their sex, the weak
talk about it—out of the free association of words jostling each
other in the mouths of the frustrated, the prurient, the unfit,
the illadjusted, the lame, the halt, unsatisfied rich matrons
with too much time on their hands,
Freud, who like so many men of intellect of Jewish upbringing felt the horns of Moses on his brow—
Joseph interpreting dreams for the Egyptians—
believed he'd had revealed to him
Man's psychic origin in the form of a myth.

Probably at the base was Darwin's hypothesis:

*"If we therefore look back far enough into the stream
of time . . . the most probable view is that he originally
lived in communities, each with a single wife, or if
powerful with several, whom he jealously defended
against all other men. Or he may have been a social ani-*

*mal and yet have lived with several wives like the gorilla,
for all the natives agree that only the adult male is seen
in a band, when the young male grows up a contest is
held for mastery, and the strongest killing and driving
out the others, establishes himself as head of the community";*

so Oedipus,
　as the old Hellenic playwrights put it,
killed the old man and had his mother in his
father's bed; hence the curse,
　　the complex that only total recall can cure.

　　　　As the fetus recapitulates the mammalian rise (from
mudpuppy to president) so every man in infancy re-enacts the
primordial crime, in fancy slays the old man, rapes the
matriarch, and lords it over the apish horde.
"Happiness is the deferred fulfillment of a prehistoric wish."

　　　　Sigmund Freud was a poet;
　　(poets are the makers of myth;)
　　but Dr. X and Dr. Y
　　who have draped themselves in Freud's cast-off prophecies
are practitioners:

　　　　Dr. X sports a beard, perhaps to emphasize some
slight fancied resemblance to the Master. His speech has an
Oxford lisp picked up while he was being psychoanalyzed in
London. A bust of Plato faces the inevitable portrait of Dr.
Freud in the outer office.
Within, Tanagra figurines and etchings of the great cathe-
drals and tiers of books in tooled bindings emit a faint scent
of morocco leather reminiscent of the storied past. His patients imagine themselves in Vienna.
Dr. X, whose own lovelife has been fretful and somewhat
intermittent,
has a sharp nose for incompatibility between husband and
wife,
so that he is in great demand among the divorcing set. He'll
root the father image out of his female patients' dreams if it
takes him five years of daily sessions to do it:

—except for vacations. Dr. X is a great vacationer—he's
fond of talking about verve and zest;

and with time and talk enough he'll find that naughty house-
maid little Johnny transferred to from Mama at the age of
three and thence will deduce the wellsprings of incompatibility between Mr. and Mrs.

that gives them a thin time in bed.

They had better find transferences afresh. Dr. X sets up the
specifications and sends them forth, insatiably cured,

to winnow the cocktail parties for new mates.

Dr. Y gives his patients a racier ride. He's a small
man, light on his feet, his red face glows with health. He has
a guttural way of pronouncing the word Eros that stirs his
women patients to their depths. His English has a touch of
the Danube (indeed his detractors claim that instead of medical school his preparation was as a masseur in a Turkish bath
in Bucharest; be that as it may the parchment diplomas of
European universities line the walls of his waiting room).

In his inner sanctum he sits at a birchwood desk gleefully
writing with a scratchy pen. The light is diffused. The walls
are pearly white. The couch is upholstered in oystercolored
corduroy. As he lies on his back the patient can discern the
red white and black kidneyshapes of a mobile stirring in an
unfelt breeze.

Dr. Y takes the patient's whole life for his province;

proscribes pictures or mountainclimbing or the production
of a novel.

For the very rich he'll recommend starting a newspaper or
backing a musical or subsidizing a season of concerts,

along with a new wife

to overcome that tired feeling

and the desire to jump from tall buildings.

Eros, erotic, erogenous zones: Dr. Y's patients find
their subconscious an Ali Baba's cave full of an oriental pro-
fusion of erogenous whimsies, only to be sublimated

at considerable expense,

by art

or a beautiful redhead.

Dr. Y's own libido, stimulated perhaps by years of

groping amid the labyrinthine symbolism of the neurotic
dream,

has shown remarkable manifestations:

a respectable colored maid,

married and the mother of four,

complains that he presented himself, stark naked, and
wearing a purple silk turban on his head, and started making
passes at her (hypnotic and in the interests of science he
explained)

while she was trying to clean his room at a summer hotel;

and two young girls, one the daughter of an eminent friend,
had to run like turkeys when he pounced on them on an
excursion boat,

to escape

having their little fannies pinched black and blue.

. . . Of course there's more to the story. Explorers
stake their lives to skindive in the foul deep pools of madness; there was Dr. L

who, sick of the routine heartbreak of his work as
a prison psychologist, snatched at salvation by Freud.
Through pentothal interviews and the hypnotic trance he
groped his way amid thickets of misery and hate

to find the key to crackup in the primordial crime. One
likely lad

with a fresh complexion and gentle blue eyes

imprisoned for a peccadillo involving murder and rape

nearly did him in. Just at the moment when they reached
after many suggestive hours of treatment

the mother's wedding ring

which symbolized the frustration of incestuous desire that
had caused it all,

shrieking Kill Kill Kill the gentle lad leapt on the therapist
and would have throttled him to death if guards hadn't
stumbled into the office in the nick of time. Dr. L died young.

(They tell us inhibition breeds neurosis: the insane lack
inhibition to a startling degree)

By crying up inhibition as the ultimate ill Freud
disposed of thou shalt not. God

is a father image to be talked out of the system. The Marxists at least
made transcendent their anti-God principle;
for Paraclete read Dialectic; Man worships History,
Thesis, Antithesis, Synthesis
form another new Trinity: by scrupulous adherence to the Party Line a man may be assured of salvation
by dialectical materialism;
these are the brainwashers, the twin myths of Marx and Freud, opposed yet interlocking, as victory interlocks with defeat, which soared out of the scientific ruminations of the late nineteenth century
to hover like scavenger birds
over the disintegration of the Western will.

We tried to question our friends' son about his analysis. All he would say was his parents had driven him to it.
Blessed be the weak for they have inherited the earth.

Documentary (3)

STEALTHY VIRUSES AT LARGE

The sergeant's letter was written in longhand and addressed "To whom it may concern."

There was no date on it.

It read:

At 1705 hours (5:05 P.M.) my plane went down 400 kilometers out at 035 to 050 degrees. I was one mile northeast of here at 5000 feet when my engine went quite dead. I tried to make it in but landed in the water. At that time there were large open areas of water. I did not try to land on the ice as it did not look thick enough. Also I wanted to get as close to this light as possible.

The plane went down in about two minutes after it landed. Before it did it floated close enough to a floe for me to jump. The ice was not over two inches thick. Another large body of water separated me from the light so I waited.

Suddenly the wind shifted to the northeast. The ice I was on started to move. My ice floe broke up fast so I ran for the light. I got ashore but was wet from falling in. My clothes froze before I could get the door open.

Once inside I used your towels and overshoes to keep from freezing.

About 2100 (9 p.m.) I got your stove lit. I hooked up the batteries and lit your warning lamp. The radio receiver worked but the transmitter was dead. I didn't know enough about it to make it work. I have used the batteries until they are going dead. I sat up last night sending out S O S calls by blinking the main light.

Right now I am deliberating whether to stay here or cross the ice. From the chart I will have eleven miles to travel. The ice looks very bad. There are large water holes, thin ice which had been broken into pieces by the wind yesterday. There is hardly any wind today. We have had two freezing nights, so I ought to make it in about four hours. I want to go now because it is nice weather.

"TO MARKET, TO MARKET . . ." BY TRUCK ON A TRAIN

Because Man Could Communicate the Whisper of a Pen Became a Mighty Shout

How so? Through two lines of beautiful precoated steel in coils. One: steel with enamel coatings in almost every color imaginable. The other: steel with laminated vinyl coating in an almost limitless variety of colors, patterns and textures—every one with high resistance to abrasion, fire, scratching and strain.

TORTURE A CAT-CRACKER

you'll understand why we can say little here about
our products except that they are advanced elec-
tronic, electro-mechanical devices, designed and
manufactured to extremely high levels of reliability.
We can fully utilize your talents, be they in design,
production or supervision. All roads lead up

The Beginning of Home
(*concluded*)

At the rehabilitation center Terry checked off the questionnaire.

He had had a touch of Malaria (1) but not Dengue (2) Severe Diarrhoea (3) maybe yes, but not Amoebic Dysentery (4) or Sleeping Sickness (5) or Relapsing Fever or Lympho-granuloma (7) or Dhobie Itch (A) or Jaundice (B) or Pneumonia (C) or Blastomycosis (G) or Filariasis (J) or Maduromycosis (K) or Gonorrhoea (M) or Syphilis (N) or Chancre (P) (my God how had he gotten by?) He was free from Yaws (S) or Typhus (T) or Kala-Azar (U) or Pinta (V) or Favus (W) or Trachoma (Y). But when, under caption 19, he was told to describe his present feelings he checked the whole list:

Very tired, tense, worried, nervous, restless, irritable, not sleeping well, having bad dreams, feeling very blue, persistent headaches and heart often pounds.

"I'd be in perfect health if it weren't for the items I checked," Terry told the sergeant as he handed him the questionnaire.

When he reached the psychologist who wore the uniform of a lieutenant and looked like a high school kid, Terry tried to explain: "I thought I could handle it on my own," he said "until I found myself tryin' to kill my kid brother." He talked very slowly to keep his voice from shaking. "If I'd had a gun I'd have killed him."

He sat in a leather easy chair staring out of the window at a bright green lawn that sloped under tall trees red and yellow with autumn. The place had been some kind of cushy private school. They were alone in a study lined with books. The reflections from an open fire flickered on the brass ashtrays on a hammered copper smoking table beside him. There was a deep rug under his feet. Terry felt out of place there. Inside him his heart pounded with a rasping sound like a defective waterpump.

The psychologist was too young. His crew cut and his mild bulging eyes, set far apart behind round steelrimmed spectacles, gave him the air of an astonished rabbit.

The psychologist was laughing.

"How come?" Terry sat frowning on the edge of the deep chair.

"But there are times," spluttered the psychologist as he tried to stop laughing, "when we all want to kill our kid brothers, nothing peculiar about that, the peculiar thing is that you are so worried about it. That's our problem, now isn't it?"

The psychologist's laugh was catching. Terry almost started laughing himself until something inside him closed like a trap and he felt himself frowning again.

"It's not like us, our family has always been close."

The psychologist got to his feet and started walking back and forth behind his desk. "Sergeant Bryant," he said tapping his pencil on the wad of papers he held in his hand, "you've got an excellent service record. I don't understand why you never got a commission."

"Why bring that up?"

"May well be part of the clinical picture," interrupted the psychologist. He dropped back into his seat behind the desk and stared at Terry with his chin on his cupped hands. "Just let yourself lie back in the chair. I know you can't relax just at the moment but it helps to go through the motions." He smiled soothingly. "Sergeant Bryant, one thing we've learned in this war is that every man has a breaking point."

"What the hell if you're put to maintainin' planes you've got to maintain 'em," interrupted Terry.

The psychologist pointed an accusing finger at him. "You held on a little too long. . . . No wonder you felt let down when you got home on leave. We all do."

"I figured that out for myself." Terry couldn't keep the nastiness out of his voice. "What I couldn't figure out was how to snap out of it."

"Ever thought of hobbies, cabinet work, watercolor painting, golf?"

"If you're goin' to set me to weavin' baskets . . . Go ahead, but I'll tell you right now it won't do me no good."

The psychologist pulled his rank. "Take your records to Captain Wilkins in the next room, Sergeant Bryant," he said severely. "He's the medical officer. He'll put you on sedatives for a few days so that you can catch up on your sleep. My recommendation is going to be that you be attached to this rehabilitation center as personnel, not as a patient. Sergeant Bryant," his voice was cordial again, "you look like the kind of personnel we need around here."

It turned out that they needed Sergeant Bryant so badly it was six months before Terry could get his discharge. But maybe taking care of the other guys was the right therapy for him after all. He didn't mind the work once he caught on. Dealing with all these disturbed kids, he wrote Mom, brought out the scoutmaster in him.

As a relief from the Rehabilitation Center, Terry got permission to take evening classes in a New Haven high school for his diploma. That was half an hour on the bus. He just didn't dare go out drinking on the town with the enlisted personnel. He was still too tight inside. He figured if he took a drink something might snap like that night back home when he started slugging Buddy.

They had a lecture course in Postwar Problems and Prospects advertised for Friday evenings at the high school. Terry took to sitting in on the lectures just to be among normal people for a while. He still was tight as a spring inside but he guessed he looked natural enough. The audience was mostly women, schoolteachers, but here and there a real goodlooker. All Terry dared to do was give them a catfish kind of a smile. If a girl smiled back he'd just knot up tight like those fellows that wouldn't move their arms and legs.

One night it didn't work that way.

The lecturer had been real interesting. He was a short baldheaded man with a purring voice. His story was that we weren't to believe all this crapehanging about how a depression must necessarily follow the end of a war. He talked about a built-in boom. There was need for housing. People hadn't been able to buy new cars or refrigerators or washing machines or electric irons during the war and now they had the money saved up from wartime wages and a big crop of babies demanding an ever higher standard of living. Babies were great consumers, the man said. He talked about the coming of television and airconditioning and increased airplane transport. He seemed to feel very good about everything. America was entering the most marvelous era in the history of the human race.

Terry left the hall in such a glow that before he knew it he found himself keeping step with a girl as they walked down the stairs. She was short, maybe a little too stocky. Her eyes were large and a light brown with curved black lashes. She was excited too. She spoke with some sort of a slight accent. She said the man had made her feel like when she visited the Futurama at the New York World's Fair.

"That future sure went down the drain."

She had to tilt her head back to look up in his face.

"How do you mean?" she asked.

He found himself looking down into brown pools, losing himself. It was hard to keep from grabbing her in his arms right then. He gave his head a shake.

"The goddam war," he snarled. He didn't mean that nasty tone. "It's been four years," he tried to explain. "It was an experience all right."

"Not regular army?" she asked hastily as if that might worry her.

"I'm on a special detail. . . . I can get my discharge any time I want."

People pouring out from the school were crowding them off the sidewalk.

She gave him a smile. There was a deep purr to her voice that pleased his ears. "Comin' next week?"

"Sure. You comin'?"

She nodded, gave him another hasty smile, ducked her head and was gone into the crowd.

On the bus, sitting on his cot to take his shoes off, shaving in the washroom, typing out report cards at his desk, he kept remembering her eyes and the curved lashes and the serious brows. He thought about her all week.

When next Friday came he went into the lecture hall all of a fluster. "Don't get excited, she won't be there," he kept telling himself.

He stood against the wall with his fingers twitching and watched the people file in. Trying to remember what she looked like gave him a tense blank feeling. Her hair must be dark to go with those eyes or had she worn a scarf on her head? He couldn't remember. Just for a second he couldn't remember his own name. "Now I really am going nuts." Terry let himself drop into a seat.

The lecturer had popped up from behind the desk and started talking in a flat dogmatic voice. Terry couldn't follow him.

All at once he saw her. Her eyes were looking into his from across the room. She had been trying to find him. Something thawed inside his head. A great lightness ran through his veins. Terry was so busy thinking up things to tell her afterwards he never heard a word of the lecture.

When they met on the stairs her hand clasped his like an old friend's. It was a hard dry capable hand. As she smiled up at him he stared hard in her face so that he'd be sure to remember it. He still couldn't see anything but her eyes.

He started talking all in a rush: "I been kickin' myself all week I didn't ask you last time to have a soda or somethin'. Let's go someplace. There are some things I didn't get about the lecture. You wouldn't mind helping a feller a little . . . How about a cup of coffee?"

It was bright and warm in the lunchroom. They opened up their coats. In the warmth of the lunchroom the dark smell of her hair made him dizzy.

"I sure hoped you'd come," Terry said.

"I did too," she answered in that low quiet voice.

Terry had never seen a lunchroom that looked so pretty. Around the glass tub of the orange drink there were cutouts of oranges and orangeblossoms. Printed purple grapes as big as peaches advertised grape juice. The clean marble counter had a kind of a sparkle to it. Ferns in pots stood up beautifully green against the steamy glass. The Coca-Cola signs and the stainless steel spigots and the containers that held the paper straws were shiny and gay.

When the girl ordered a hamburger roll and hot chocolate he thought it was the cleverest combination he had ever heard of. "I'll take the same," he said. The darkskinned counterman showed even teeth in an approving smile. "Catsup?" he asked.

"Sure, plenty of catsup."

This time it was easy talking to her. Outside of the friendly counterman they were the only people there. Her name was Tasha. Her people were Slavish. She was born in Bridgeport but she worked in New Haven as inspector at the Leamington plant.

"You must be a pretty smart girl," he said.

He explained how he'd held down some good jobs himself right from the time he'd had to leave high school. He'd worked in a rubber shop for a dollar and a quarter an hour when he was only seventeen. He'd gotten to wish he'd never seen a rubber shop. They'd kept him in rubber; maintenance, repairs, airplane tires all through his tour of duty in the Southwest Pacific.

At the words Southwest Pacific her eyes got wet. How come? Somebody, somebody she knew quite well went down on the *Galveston*. When he asked if it was a brother she shook her head. She flickered her long eyelashes to shake out the tears.

"Rudy was my friend," she said. She gave a little gulp. They had decided not even to get engaged until he came out of the service, so that they would both feel free. "Well," she shrugged—"that was that."

"I'm free too," said Terry. "Too goddam free."

She didn't say anything to that, just munched on her hamburger and looked up at him out of understanding eyes. They finished all too soon. No sense just standing there. He couldn't think of anything more to say. His head was full of wool.

It had suddenly gotten late. He just had time to walk her to the end of the street where she lived before he had to run to catch the last bus. On the bus and all week he was kicking himself because he hadn't tried to kiss her good night.

At the next lecture they sat side by side. The lecture was about modern housing. He just sat there not hearing a thing and watching her take notes in a small slanting hand on a pad she'd brought out of her handbag. He liked the way she used her hands. All he could think about was he had his pay and an overnight pass in his pocket. His heart was beating so he was afraid she would hear it sitting next to him.

At last the man was through. Seats slammed. Feet scraped on the floor. This was the final lecture. "Let's celebrate," Terry said.

This time the streets were full of slush. The snow was turning into rain. Terry declared he was starving, he had to have a real meal. He took her into an Italian restaurant. They sat in a booth and ate spaghetti. She said she liked wine. With her he wasn't scared to drink. He ordered dago red. He could see her whole face now; broad cheekbones under the big sorry for him eyes, firm thin lips, a pointed chin with a little cleft in it.

Sitting across the table from her in the tight little booth in the warm restaurant that smelt of grated cheese and sizzling oil from the kitchen, drinking the smooth red wine, things began loosening up inside of him. The wine warmed him. Through the close smell of wop food he was breathing her hair.

Hell he was talking her ear off, he couldn't help it. He was telling her what an experience the war had been, on account of the guys he served with. They met up in New Caledonia; right from the first they'd formed a team. Maynard's Marvels: maintenance of fighter planes.

Captain Maynard was an oldtime stunt flyer; only man he'd ever met with two silver kneecaps; too old and banged up for a pilot but there wasn't an airship in the world he couldn't make sit up and say "Uncle." Joe Heinz and Jim Bates were the boss mechanics. They ended up lieutenants. When they found out Terry had worked in a rubber shop they handed over the tires to him. As far back as Tinian they knew the war would soon be over. What they were planning to do was to pitch together when they got back stateside. Captain Maynard was rigging a company to service planes. He could raise all the capital he wanted through old buddies he had in the airlines. It would have been a marvelous opportunity.

She sat looking at him with those wide brown eyes until he wanted to dive into them like into a pool. Their knees were touching under the table. Tasha didn't pull her knees away.

"What went wrong, Terry?"

"Okinawa. Goddam kamikaze hit us ridin' ashore on an LST. They never found enough of the rest of the gang to put in a coffin. I was standin' out on the landin' ramp. Knocked out cold. Somebody fished me out of the drink."

He went on to explain at great length how he'd turned and looked over his shoulder and seen this little jimcrack plane coming in for a perfect three point landing and the little goddam Jap sitting inside the plexiglas with his little face all waxy smooth like one of these here Japanese dolls. He wanted her to see it as he'd seen it, but he couldn't find the words.

Terry had his hand on the table. She slipped her hand over his.

"So that was why you said your future had gone down the drain?"

"Did I say that? It's losing all your friends just in a minute like that . . . It's always the good guys get theirs."

He had hold of her hand now. He was afraid if he stopped talking she would pull her hand back. He had her knee between his knees and was pressing on it very gently. He hadn't meant to tell her about the rehabilitation center for fear she'd think he was a nut, but he couldn't stop talking, he had to explain how Okinawa broke him all up and he went on and on about the doctor and the psychologist and the psychosomatics and the therapy and how he couldn't eat that steak his mother fixed for him the first night he was home. "What worries these guys most," he said, "is that they think they are impotent."

She flushed and pulled her hand away and straightened herself up in the booth. It was getting late, she remarked in that practical tone of hers, hadn't they better get a move on before the waiters swept them out with the sawdust.

He managed to give her shoulders a hug when he helped her on with her coat. It had come on to rain. Down the street where it was dark she tilted her face to let him kiss her. Her lips were wet with the rain.

"If we just had some place to go," Terry groaned.

In her deep quiet matter of fact voice she said he could

come to her place. She explained that her mother and sister had gone to Bridgeport to visit the relatives. Her father was dead.

"Mine is too," said Terry. It made him feel good that they had something like that in common.

The rain poured down. They walked hand in hand. It was a long way.

As they trudged through puddles and slush she explained, without looking up at him, like she was talking out loud to herself, that she was taking a chance. She knew she was taking a chance. Maybe he wouldn't turn out the right guy she thought he was but she didn't like it the way some girls got men all stirred up and then held out on them. Maybe it was wicked but she'd always thanked God she hadn't held out on poor Rudy. They had loved each other all the way right from the beginning.

She had been lonesome these years without Rudy. It was as bad now as when he was first listed missing. She'd tried picking up an occasional serviceman and pretending it was Rudy but it had never been right somehow. Maybe it was the precautions.

Her voice was so expressionless she might have been talking about somebody else. "Maybe this won't be right either."

Terry didn't dare say a word.

She lived in a four story frame house. There were no lights in the windows. The street was dark. The rain poured down.

While she fished in her purse for her latchkey he stood shivering beside her. His toes squdged in his wet shoes. His shirt collar was wet. His teeth were chattering. When she opened the door he pretty near turned and ran.

Instead of switching on the light she took his hand and led him up the stairs in the dark. The first thing he noticed was the vinegar smell.

"Is your mother crazy about puttin' up pickles?"

When she switched on the light he could see that she was smiling. Water dripped from her red scarf. The wet hair stuck to her forehead. She nodded.

"Mine too." He grinned into her face. Again he had that feeling of thawing inside.

The furniture was freshpainted. The lamps had pretty lamp-shades. The floor was waxed.

"Your folks like a clean house," he said. "Mine do too."

She told him to take his wet things off and went into the other room. His hands were still shaking. As he sat there unlacing his boots he found himself praying: "Oh God, please God, please." He stripped the drenched socks off his feet.

When she came back her hair was combed. She had freshened her face up. She was wearing a pink flannel dressing gown. She carried a bottle with two small glasses on a tray. "Plum brandy from the old country," she explained. "My mother keeps it for holidays."

A look of concern came over her face when she noticed he was still shivering. She set the tray on the table and crouched down to light the gas heater. There was something unbearably attractive about the shape of her hips as she crouched there on the floor at his feet. He pulled her up towards him.

He pressed his face into her neck. "Be, you know, patient with me kid," he whispered in her ear through chattering teeth. "You know what those others all think."

She pulled away from him and burst out laughing. "A great hulk like you." She mussed up his hair. The plum brandy warmed him. He held his bare feet up to the gas heater. He was beginning to feel at home. She was his kind of folks.

"When I was a young kid back home I was quite the ladies' man," he stammered. "And in Brisbane with those good-lookin' Aussies . . . but now . . . I'm a goddam mess, Tasha."

"Poor baby." She pressed her cheek against his. "You have been worrying yourself sick about it."

He held her face up between his two cold hands and looked into her eyes. "Remember Tasha." His voice was firm now. "It's for keeps . . . This time I'm playin' for keeps."

"Me too Terry."

When he pressed her to him their mouths fitted, their bodies fitted.

When he got up in the middle of the night, he stood a while looking at himself in the bathroom mirror. At the Center he had been scared to look at himself. Now he smiled at himself in the mirror. He looked good to himself. "Hello feller," he said and hurried back to her warm bed. She reached for him sleepily as he snuggled up to her.

He never could have gotten up to catch that goddam bus if Tasha hadn't hopped out of bed first to get him his breakfast. He just had to follow her around wherever she went. They made plans hurriedly while he wolfed the bacon and eggs and drank the hot coffee.

He wanted them to get married right away, tonight, tomorrow, as soon as he could get a license, but she said she'd need time to break it to her folks. She bet his mother would take some talking around too. Women were in more of a hurry to marry off their daughters. It was different about their sons. "If you were mine, Terry, and some girl tried to marry you, I'd scratch her eyes out."

She had to push him out of the house.

As soon as he'd checked in at the Center, he had her on the phone. What was her full name? Natalie Stepanich. Age? Twentyfour. It was for the marriage license. He'd get one right away to have it ready. She said dearest she couldn't talk now she had to go to work. She'd need that job so he could go to college maybe on the GI bill. Her voice faded in his ear. It would be days before he'd see her again.

Tasha was right. Getting married wasn't as easy as all that. Mom wrote back by return mail to ask if the girl was a Catholic. If she wasn't would she be willing to take the necessary instruction and join the church? Tasha's people were just as bad. They were Greek Orthodox. They wanted Terry to join their church.

Terry would have gone off his rocker what with the waiting and the red tape about his discharge and the uncertainty and the delay if he hadn't been able to cash a war bond and buy himself a '39 Ford one of the doctors at the Center wanted to sell. It was getting to be spring. Every evening he waited for Tasha a block from the plant when she got out of work and drove her off into some secluded lane or other where they could be alone together and huddle in each other's arms listening to the spring peepers and the sound of water swirling down the stony brooks. They planned and planned what they were going to do when they got married. He was losing his nervousness. Every time he was out with Tasha he came away feeling more like a man.

It was a Friday afternoon in May that he was finally shut of the uniform. He had already been carrying his marriage license around for two weeks. He had his pockets stuffed with money from accrued back pay and separation allowances. He'd had a motor job done on the car and she was running sweetly. He felt on top of the world.

Tasha was late coming out of the plant. Terry went through the usual tortures thinking that she'd been hurt, that there had been an accident in the plant, that something had gone wrong at home, until suddenly there she was climbing into the car beside him.

She did act a little quiet. Right away he got so busy telling her about how good he felt to be a free man again, and how he was going to buy her an eight dollar steak at a famous old restaurant he'd heard of downtown where the wealthy college boys ate, that he forgot to ask her what the trouble was. She said she didn't want an expensive dinner but he insisted. It worried him a little that she wouldn't eat, but he was feeling so good he ate the whole steak up himself. It wasn't until they were parked in their favorite spot out near West Rock that she loosened up and told him that she wasn't quite sure, she wouldn't know for sure until she had been to a doctor, but she thought maybe she was going to have a baby.

Terry slapped her on the back and bounced up and down in the seat of the car. "Tasha, that's the best news I ever heard in my life. Now I'd like to see our damn relatives try to stop us from gettin' married."

They were waiting at City Hall when the office opened next morning. An old man who was county clerk or something read the marriage service. He had sandy gray soupstrainer mustaches and a lascivious twinkle in his eye and Tasha whispered with her lips touching Terry's ear that he looked just like her Uncle Ossip. They hadn't brought any witnesses so they had to ask two of the girls who worked in the office. They were the bachelor type and smirked and tittered like they'd never heard of a couple's getting married before.

They all had a big laugh when the time came to produce the ring. Terry hauled a fourteen carat gold wedding ring out of his vest pocket and it turned out Tasha had brought one too. She'd bought one that morning for fear Terry would forget. Tasha gave her chin a toss and carried it off by saying that her folks used the two ring ceremony anyway.

When he kissed her out in the hall it was as if he had never kissed her before. Terry always said it was the greatest moment of his life when they walked out of that office Mr. and Mrs. William Terence Bryant.

The relatives on both sides of the family were plenty sore about their running off and getting married. Mom wrote that as far as she was concerned they would be living in sin until they were married in church. Just to keep them from counting on their fingers Terry and Tasha moved to New Brunswick. Terry had been corresponding with the personnel director of the Raritan Hard Rubber Company there. It was a small concern and they would only pay a dollar thirteen an hour—less than he'd made as a kid, but he figured he'd better take the job and see what came of it.

Tasha had planned to go to work herself, but the doctor told her that she might lose the baby if she did anything but rest during the first three months.

"They call it morning sickness," she said bitterly, "but it lasts all day."

They both had to dig into their wartime savings to fix up the apartment and buy furniture and dishpans and china. Everything they had was new and glossy. His life was like that, all new and glossy, Terry kept telling himself.

Terry babied her as much as he could. He turned out a pretty good hand at cooking and cleaning. He got her breakfast before he went to work and supper after he came home. The guys he got to know at the plant would have kidded the pants off him if they'd known, but he loved it. She lay propped up on the bed sewing baby clothes. She had never in her life been waited on before. Her eyes were all smiles. She loved it, too.

The plant was something else again. The scorched spicy smell of cooking rubber brought up Terry's memories of how the Swede foreman had ridden him when he was an ignorant kid at that rubber shop in Passaic before he'd enlisted. Catch 'em young, tell 'em nothing and treat 'em rough had been that foreman's attitude.

At Raritan Hard it was worse. Since Terry had experience they put him to work on one of the Banbury mixers that chopped up the raw rubber and mixed the compounds. It was hot dirty hazardous work. He threw everything he had into it. He was sweating and sooty and half choked with the fumes all day but the thought of Tasha waiting for him at home with his little baby growing inside her made him feel so strong and wonderful he felt he could handle anything. He worked considerable overtime. He could have sworn he worked more time than showed up on his pay check.

A peculiar thing about that shop was that no man would let another man see his pay check. Hardly any of them spoke English. They were DP's from eastern Europe, Polacks, Sudetens, Slovaks, and Slovenes, quiet hardworking people like Tasha's folks, donkeys the strawbosses called them.

They'd taken such a beating in their homelands anything' that happened in America seemed like heaven. Not even the foreman spoke English. The foremen were arrogant as hell. The way those workers let the foremen ride them got Terry Bryant's Irish up. He was boiling most of the time from more than the heat of the Banbury.

"We got to do something to help these people," Terry would be talking over his shoulder to Tasha who would be lying on the couch while he washed the dishes after supper. "Pop brought us up to hate injustice more than anything in the world. Pop's old man brought that with him from the old country."

Tasha would try to soothe him down. "Wait and see," she would tell him. He couldn't tell what was really going on in that plant until he'd been there six months. "Now Terry don't you go off half cocked." She didn't want him sassing the foremen and getting fired before the baby was born. "No use sticking your neck out till you know what the score is. I'm only a girl but I've worked in a lot of factories."

She would kid him about being such an idealist and get him to laughing. "Mom used to tell me I was a natural scoutmaster," he would admit. "I had to do my good deed every day and make damn sure the other boys did theirs too."

"That's why you are going to get to be a foreman."

"If I don't bust one of those johnnies in the jaw some fine day."

"You ought to have a union," said Tasha, "to take the responsibility off your shoulders."

They did have a halfass company union. There was a safety committee and a labor-management committee left over from wartime but they never met. Terry had been talking union with the boys in his department so when an election came up, he found himself elected shopsteward. The older men on his shift told him it was because they wanted somebody who could talk English good. They slapped him on the back: "Attaboy Terry."

Hurrying home he noticed a smell of cooking as he climbed the stairs. Tasha's eyes were big as the house. She stood waiting for him in front of the table all set with a white tablecloth. He could see she had been listening for his feet on the stairs.

"I could smell you cookin' paprika chicken halfway down the street. Tasha, you oughtn't to."

She gave a quiet chuckling laugh. "Dr. Crosby told me he wanted me to do a little housework from now on. He checked me this morning. Everything's fine."

As soon as Terry had washed up he ran to the corner saloon for a carton of beer. Tasha's chicken sure did taste good after eating his own cooking all these weeks.

"Well Tasha meet the shopsteward," he said with his mouth full. He'd been spoiling to get the lead out of that safety committee. They had a meeting today. George Slansky—he was the management representative—had a brother Steve worked in the plant, seemed a pretty good guy. This George he used to work in the plant too but he got into the labor-management racket during the war, a big curly haired slab-sided slob, looked like one of them tenor opera singers. It was hot in the conference room. The boys just sat there yawning and stretching their legs and trying to take as much time as they could about everything so that the meeting would last till the whistle blew and they wouldn't have to go back to work. "What the hell can you do with a bunch like that?"

There they were sitting in their workclothes, and this George in his business suit, just blowing smoke out of ten cent cigars furnished by the management and not accomplishing a thing. Terry brought up that leaky steampipe and George roared him down. "Competition to meet . . . prices goin' down . . . costs have to be cut." A lot of horsefeathers.

Then Terry brought up that elevator that didn't meet state specifications . . . He'd been studying them out of the book . . . and how they didn't have proper guardrails in his department.

"The war's over," roared this George, and started talking Polish, an' the union president, a guy they called Shorty, just sat there with his mouth open like a fish, without saying anything and then the whistle blows and this George shovels out the rest of the cigars and they all go out scraping their feet. "Thank you George. Thank you sir, Mr. Slansky."

"This George he saved the company thousands of dollars with a few lousy ten cent cigars. . . . What we need's a real union like you said Tasha."

She nodded with wry smile. "But please Terry, not till the baby's born."

Terry ate drank and slept union from that safety committee meeting on. To save the trouble of fixing himself sandwiches, he'd taken to eating his lunch at the diner across the highway from the front gate. There were always guys in there from the big Consolidated Tire plant down the road. They had money to spend. While Terry had to make do on a sandwich and a cup of coffee their Banbury operators ate steak and French fries for lunch.

Terry got to be real friendly with a longlegged black-browed lanternjawed Southern hillbilly named Earl Fagan who worked in the other shop. He was a shopsteward too. Terry asked him about safety conditions. There were just too damn many men getting hurt over at Raritan Hard.

Earl said it would be as bad at their shop if it wasn't that they had an International Union. The way he said these words really made them sound good. Earl was a talker.

One noon hour Earl got to telling about how he'd gone into organizing: He was a farm boy raised on Sand Mountain. Never knew nothing about unions nor nothing like that till in July 1936 he got married. He was running a little crop on halves and soon he'd have a family to feed.

"Just my predicament," said Terry—but Earl didn't stop.

There had been nothing for him to do but go down to work in a rubber shop in Gadsden. His daddy told him he had better not but times was bad and he was desperate so he went to work. A man couldn't hardly get in that plant unless somebody recommended him. There was a highway patrolman who was a friend of his and when he carried him over there he said he wanted him to promise he wouldn't mess with no union . . . Well he went to work there but conditions was terrible. He hired out at thirtytwo cents an hour. There was a bunch from the International talking union already. Management had gunthugs. Every day they'd run some man out of the plant. They'd come down the aisle kicking his ass as fast as his feet hit the ground. Well Earl had made that promise and he just kept his mouth shut. "I kep' a big blackjack in my toolbag just for selfprotection. I was caught between a shit an' a sweat."

He gulped the last of his coffee and wiped his mouth with the back of a long hairy hand.

"When Clinch Rodgers who'd been elected president of the union in the big Akron rubber shops came down to Gadsden, those gunthugs beat him nearly to death."

Earl stopped talking with a jerk and sat staring out at the cars passing on the fourlane highway beside the diner.

"Well?" asked Terry.

"When the war came on some other organizers came down. By that time I'd had enough. It was bondage, that's what it was. They'd fire a man for bein' late twice. Every time a man seemed to be making a little money they'd lower the piecework rates. Ah found out the hotel the organizers was stayin' at. 'Boys,' Ah said, 'Ah'm not sure Ah want to join a union but Ah sure do want to talk about it.' They talked pretty good. Next night Ah had seventeen signed up off my night shift out of twentythree. It only took eighteen to form a local. Them organizers nearly went crazy. We held an election under the War Labor Board and from then on things started hummin'. We set up grievance committees to handle the problems of the people. If we had a gripe we could take it to the War Labor Board. . . . To tell the truth Terry Ah'm just a country boy. . . . Ah didn't know I was a citizen of the United States until Ah joined a International Union."

Documentary (4)

with the help of better medicine and drugs your doctor has today—anesthetics, antibiotics, anti-histamines, diuretics, vitamins

LIVE LONGER

The socalled "big bang" theory holds that the present chemical constitution of the universe was decided in half an hour five billion years ago.

WHAT IS THIS BLENDED WHISKEY EASTERNERS CALL RYE?

Get set, here comes the commercial! Never let prices fool you. Just remember the old saying *"the bigger you are, the less it costs to do business."*

This saves money all along the line—a lot of money.

These crisp green folding dollars—all of them—land in our customers' pockets.

WAGE RISE SPURS STEEL COST FIGHT

No picture of the honest thrifty savers, whose life savings shrank today as surely as though a thief had stolen part of them. No picture of the little boy who won't go to college in years ahead, because his father's life insurance can't pay swollen prices. No pictures of them. They're just Americans who pay the taxes and fight the wars and try to do what's right.

IT PAYS TO PLAY FAIR

But You Don't Know These Surprising Facts

49

a powerful transmitter is the Crab Nebula, a star
that exploded violently 900 years ago and is now a
rapidly expanding blob of gas. Even more spectacular is Cygnus A the scene of a stupendous collision
of galaxies, each a mighty system of stars and gases.
The stars are bypassing each other with minor dis-
turbances but the gases are colliding violently and
producing radio waves

CREATION STILL GOING ON?

*wherever the truth lies it is sure to seem fabulous
to laymen*

The Promised Land (new style)

The Marxian
man worships History.
Thesis, antithesis, synthesis
form a new Trinity; by scrupulous adherence to the Party
Line a man may be assured of salvation
through dialectical materialism.

On July 28 1901 there was born in a respectable
suburb of Melbourne, Australia, to a highly respectable Eng-
lish-Irish family a baby,
named Alfred Bryant Renton Bridges,
whose career,
was to be notably successful.

Thesis: The father, described as a John Bull type,
was a professional landlord and manager of rental property.
The mother had Irish republican antecedents. There are
rumors of uncles who were labor politicians. (Labor politics
flowered early in the English-speaking Antipodes,
flowered and went to seed.)
Young Bridges was brought up a Catholic, attended the

better parochial schools, and St. Brendan's Academy. Graduating at about sixteen,

he was found respectable employment clerking in a retail store. In his spare time he helped his father collect rents in what are described as the poorer districts of Melbourne.

Antithesis: To hell with it! He ran away to sea.

We are told the lad read too much Jack London; no need to read. Those were the years dyed bloody by October. The reasonable nineteenth century European hegemony had shattered in a burst of lyddite. Europe's best brains and warmest hearts had strangled in muddy death in Flanders or the Argonne hills.

The October Days in Petrograd: like fallout from an exploded volcano bolshevism was blanketing the earth. No need for an adventurous Aussie growing cagily into young manhood to find pretexts in Jack London for throwing over his father's suburb

or the dreary selling of threepenny bars of soap

across the counter

or the badgering of poor proletarians over last week's rent.

In red Petrograd the proletarians had shot their landlords down; they were murdering their little fathers in cellars in holy Russia.

Young Bridges shipped on a Tasmanian schooner, was wrecked; shipped again, sailed the South Seas and turned up as deckhand on a barkentine in a California port,

Along the way he'd picked up Harry for a moniker.

A new name helped dim the memory of the bourgeois past.

(Politicos of the hammer and sickle prefer to think of themselves as fatherless, motherless,

spontaneous spawning of the Marxian proletariat.)

Smarter than his shipmates, Harry Bridges signed on an American coastwise freighter, where pay and conditions were better. In port in New Orleans he saw his first strike. There he found the trade union leaders were selling out the rank and file. A close-mouthed wiry fellow with a crooked hawk nose and a cocky curl to his hair, he found he could stand on his feet and convince his shipmates with his cagey talk. His Aussie twang gave a special tone to the occasional

remark he dropped out of the corner of his mouth. "The rank
and file gets rooked, of course." He was rank and file. He
joined the IWW.

The IWW turned out a gone goose. Though he'd risen to
quartermaster on a Coast Guard cutter he threw up the drifting seaman's life and went to work as a stevedore on the San
Francisco waterfront.

He made good money; worked on the star gang.

The longshoremen had a union—they called it the blue book
—but they groused that even when racketeers weren't horning
in the blue book benefited principally the employers. "Of
course," said Harry Bridges.

Rank and file had no say in the hiring halls. "Of course,"
said Harry Bridges.

In the shapeup the dockwallopers stood around all day with
their handhooks dangling from the back pockets of their jeans
waiting to be hired.

Half the time they had to kick back to the foreman to get
work.

They felt the pinch of the depression. The business agents
of the AF of L weren't interested. Not enough money on the
waterfront. With the wobblies gone it was the commies who
interested themselves in the woes of rank and file.

Rank and file became Harry Bridges' trademark as a labor
organizer. Marxism appeals to the systematic mind and gives
vent to impacted resentments against the established order.
Can those men have hated their fathers that much?

"There can be nothing in common between the working
class and the employing class," the wobblies had taught. "Of
course," said Harry Bridges. Marxism was building an empire
on that dogma. Bridges had class war in his blood. Marxism
offered a program for strategy and tactics.

In 1932 he took over a mimeographed sheet called *The
Waterfront Worker*. In the bloody longshoremen's strike in
1934 Harry Bridges was a man his mates could rely on. Dogma furnished every answer. In his battles with the police he
organized his "red guards" with military precision to give protection to his rank and file.

By the end of the strike Harry Bridges ran the San Francisco waterfront. He ran it well. Even the hostile press had to
admit that.

He improved wages and working conditions. He took advantage of every hand up Roosevelt's New Deal had for the labor organizer. He was a Roosevelt booster in those days. He organized the International Longshoremen's union and the Maritime Federation into a Pacific Conference which extended its sway over the docks and sugar and pineapple plantations in Hawaii. If you weren't a Bridges man you were hard put to it to find work in those waters.

On the mainland he fought the Teamsters as to who should organize the warehouses. In 1937 he led his longshoremen under John L. Lewis's wing into the CIO.

His enthusiasm for the New Deal so some bilious commentators pointed out only lasted till the Stalin-Hitler pact. Then Bridges denounced Franklin Roosevelt as a warmonger. It was war to the knife with the administration in Washington. Bridges showed himself a master of legal infighting. The union funds furnished him with plenty of money to hire lawyers. Even so the Attorney General was about to have him deported as a Communist alien when Hitler's stormtroopers invaded Soviet territory.

and Bridges once more became a patriotic American.

After Pearl Harbor no labor leader in the country was more enthusiastic for the war effort. Bridges allowed no strikes. He was for the speedup, for doubling the longshoreman's load of cement. He was so keen for the herding into concentration camps of the Pacific coast Japanese that he fired one of his smartest attorneys—a Civil Liberties man—who opposed it.

The Supreme Court threw out the deportation ruling. "I'm the only guy in the U.S. who has a Supreme Court ruling that he isn't a Communist," said Bridges with that special twang.

Eagerly sworn in as a naturalized citizen he was appointed joint chairman of the Pacific Coast Labor Management panel.

With the collapse of Germany and Japan the honeymoon with Washington cooled, but Bridges was one of the most powerful men in America. In 1946 he shut down the Pacific Coast and Hawaii for eleven weeks. Labor must stand up for its rights, the California liberals crooned.

In '49 he was indicted for making false statements in his naturalization proceedings. The jury found him guilty. Five years in jail. His lawyers appealed.

At the time of the Korean War Bridges tried to put through a resolution condemning American resistance to the Communist invasion, which, even in his own local 10 in San Francisco, caused such an uproar a riot call was made to the police. His longshoremen were not buying the Party Line that day.

Three years later the Supreme Court reversed his conviction in the naturalization case on the grounds of the statute of limitations. Charges brought too late.

In May 1959, appearing before the House Un-American Activities Committee, Harry Bridges took the Fifth Amendment all down the line. "If I'd taken the Fifth over twenty years ago," he was quoted as saying, "I'd have saved my union a lot of money and myself a lot of trouble . . . I'd have been better off if I'd kept my yap shut."

Harry Bridges keeps his yap shut and smiles a twisted smile. Silence has served him most evidently well; that and a canny knack for institution building. In America he is feared only by reactionaries we are told. Behind the widening frontiers

of the proletariat's Promised Land
where every man owns everything
except his own life, he is said to have many admirers:
the elected of History.
Thesis, antithesis . . .

Synthesis: when Nikita Khrushchev visited San Francisco he made quite a point of attending a meeting at the longshoremen's hall. Bridges staged an ovation for him. K. came away wearing a longshoreman's cap
and an unusually satisfied smile.

Documentary (5)

THIS IS THE RAMJET

. . . most efficient propulsion system
ever devised by man

a precise jet of abrasive particles, gas-propelled
through a small easy to use nozzle; cuts or abrades a
wide variety of materials, such as germanium, fragile
crystals, glass, oxides, ceramics

GARDEN FOR MOON GROWN IN L. I. TEST

Nothing could be further from the truth. We do
sell tens of thousands of pairs of these height-in-
creasing shoes every year. We don't think there's
anything especially funny about them . . . any more
than there is about women's lipstick or eye makeup
. . . or anything else that makes people look better.

BLAST IN THE GROUND AN ATOM INFERNO

Wearing dark clothes and a tiny rosebud in his
lapel, Lewis alternately sat erect and slouched in his
chair, driving home points with a wagging finger,
sometimes with a pounding fist:
"I believe that when you tamper with the liberties
of 70,000,000 workers you are tampering with the
liberties of all Americans. Damn the chains and
those who advocate them."

TONIGHT YOU WILL SLEEP IN LONDON

and every moment between now and then
will be pleasure filled

Two workers can operate the machine at near top
capacity. The grading and packing line incorporates
the newly developed electronic bloodspot detector
with the latest in egg handling equipment.

Ungraded eggs are first examined for dirty or
cracked shells. Eggs containing bloodspots are removed automatically. Clear eggs move onto a line of
scales where they are individually weighed and
channeled to the packing units.

The latter automatically position the eggs with the
small ends down. For quality reasons, eggs must be
packed in this position.

Blackie Bowman Speaking

(Scene: a bed in a Veterans' Hospital)

Rest time, hell. It's always rest time. I know that this is one
of the best goddam hospitals in the country, but why does the
nurse have to try to put the light out as soon as I get started
writing a letter? Some people can't stop gabbing no matter
what happens to them. I guess that's me—can't stop gabbing.
When I get a pencil in my hand my fingers just keep wriggling trying to put down all the things I'd like to be saying if
I had some guy here to say them to.

At that most of my energy goes into just pulling the air into
my lungs. A tough fate for a man who's led an active life to be
stuck to a bed like a fly on flypaper, and no better chance of
getting off either. The mind goes buzzing on and on like the
poor damn fly's wings. And here I go pulling the breath into
my stiff lungs just to keep alive. I know death's a gift like life.
I'm not scared of the gift of death any more than I been
scared of life. I've tried to stop breathing but I can't and all
the time I think I'm going to choke. That's where the agony is.

I just lie here flat on my back and remember. Can't even sit up to eat, have to shove a little food into my mouth with my fingers and still I stay alive month after month remembering. It's all clear, especially the early part.

Where it's dim is the last days. Ablebodied seaman during the war. Sure I was ablebodied. I went on dishing it out at an age when most men are getting ready to crawl into a wheel chair. But that last brawl was an assault.

It was when we got paid off from the *Pacific Wanderer*. I can still remember the sunny dusty look everything had, the piles of lumber and scrap behind a long wooden fence with billboards on it and up at the end across the streetcar tracks the Rolling Stone Bar and Café. A nice little brick building all painted up with fresh green paint and white trim. I was attracted. Slim Jackson and I were attracted and we went in there, just to get the young punks out of our hair.

It had been an unhappy ship. They had a Communist cell, stiff selfrighteous kind of guys always making trouble and the rest of us all broken up into factions. Smitty's friends and Joe Ingram's friends. A few of us oldtimers tried to tell 'em about workers of the world unite and the brotherhood of man but the Commies they'd stir up first one faction then another until everybody was at everybody else's throat. Angels of hate. You were a damn stoolpigeon reactionary capitalist if you didn't say everything exactly like they said it in the *Daily Worker*.

Joe Ingram's friends were jailbait like you get on a ship sometimes. Smitty was the union delegate, a nice clean little guy who tried to do right by everybody. The Ingram gang hated his guts because he wouldn't fall for their crooked crap games and the Commies hated him because he wouldn't go their way.

It was one brawl that I wasn't even drunk. Slim and I were sitting in the Rolling Stone having a beer and a ham sandwich before we went on into town to do some real eating and drinking when who should come in but Smitty. Smitty with a crewcut and honest dog's eyes. We couldn't turn him away like a stray pup so he sits down to drink a beer with us. I'd just caught sight of a yellow cab on the street outside and I was saying let's mosey along downtown when out of the backroom comes Ingram's gang, all drunk and mean and snarling. Ingram he calls Smitty a dirty name and Slim he gets mad and before I could get my fists up they were swarming all over us. They

were ten and we were three. Tell me that place looked like it
had been hit by an airraid when the cops came.

There was so many of them a man didn't hardly have to look
where his fists flew. I just closed my eyes and punched, right
left, right left. In those days I still liked fighting. It was terrific. Every punch connected with the point of a chin or
crunched on a guy's nose until some joker came up behind
and felled me to the floor with a piece of lead pipe. I was out
with a fractured skull. One of the gang, maybe it was Joe
Ingram himself, was considerate enough to gouge out my right
eye with his heel. That's how I wear a glass eye to this day.

The cops had me in a cell for drunk and disorderly, not that
I knew anything about it. Nora the nightnurse told me when I
started to come to all wrapped in bandages like one of those
mummies I saw in the museum in Alexandria, Egypt.

I'd have been dead as a mackerel if some nosy little medical
student pinch hitting for the police doctor who was out on a
four day drunk hadn't made the sergeant open up the cell so's
he could take a look at me. Then they put me in the hurry up
wagon to the hospital.

That Nora was a nice woman. All my life I've attracted nice
women, but the only ones I've stuck with have been bums.
She told me all her troubles and they were plenty and I told
her mine right back. Never would have made it if it hadn't
been for Nora. When the ward was quiet after midnight she'd
come and stand by my bed and let me hold her hand for a bit.
Gave me strength.

Poor Nora had two children in school to support and a husband who'd walked out on her. The usual story. She reminded
me of my mother, dark Irish eyes and a face full of weary lines
and black hair parted in the middle. Only my old man never
did walk out, been better if he had, a big bullheaded Saxon
type, stupid as an ox, made Mother's life a hell and I
didn't help any. Thank God some of my brothers turned out
decent citizens. Did you know one of them was a Monsignor?
And me an atheistic rebel. If it hadn't been that Nora was a
Catholic and that I'd never taken the trouble to divorce Eileen
—I didn't know where she was to serve papers on her even if
I'd had the money to pay the lawyer—Nora and I might have
made a go of it and I might have spent my last days in happiness and peace, instead of a helpless derelict stranded in a
veterans' hospital. Just wasn't in the cards.

I forgot about Smitty. When they started to get me to walk round a little and I was sitting up in a chair by the bed, there he was one day, standing beside me all pink and clean and smiling in a new blue business suit. What he'd done was crawl in behind the bar when he saw me go down. Smitty's a little shrimp of a fellow. Those damn mugs were so drunk they started slugging each other when they didn't have me to beat up on. Nobody ever knew how they got drunk so quick. Just the bestial meanness welling up inside 'em I guess. When the cops came Smitty walked out the back door like nothing had happened. Came out without a scratch, but no more following the sea for him.

He walked right off the waterfront and he's never been back. Got himself a job in a filling station to learn the business and now he owns a big automobile service station right there in San Pedro. He'd been putting money in the bank all through the war. No more proletariat for Smitty. I had plenty of chances to do like Smitty but I had my convictions.

Nora and me might have worked out something, but to tell the truth after I got out of that hospital I didn't have the manhood left to make the effort. Too damn shaken. The skull fracture left me with horrible headaches, but for some reason it didn't damage the brain. Before they discharged me the psychologist put me through a whole battery of tests and I came out with flying colors. My brain's clear as a bell right now. It's the old carcass that's about to founder.

Frankly I guess I like it this way. I've been too much of a rebel all my life to settle down to bourgeois felicity. There's no place left in this world for a philosophical anarchist. If I weren't in this here hospital I'd be a hermit in a shack in the mountains. And I never did learn to cook, lazy as a hound about housework.

It's scary how clear things come back. While I just lie here looking back over the years it's as if it was all still happening to me.

Ablebodied seaman. The great sea and air war. I seen the first war from behind the wheel of a Mack truck, that's why I'm in this here veterans' hospital now, but all I saw of World War II was sea and sky and a lot of mugs chipping rust off steel plates. At sea eight months of the year. I guess I swabbed on enough paint in my time to paint a fourteen foot band clear around the equator. Way back I began to figure out some kind

of a coating that really would resist rust. I had the ideas and
other guys had the laboratories. I understand one of the big
paint companies is at last ready to put a preparation on the
market to resist the corrosion from petroleum products that
eats away the steel on tankers. Should have been done twentyfive years ago. Just like radar. Any fool who knew how radio
waves bounce should have been able to dope out radar but it
took a war that turned the world upside down to do it.

Damn fool business that it should take a war to shake loose
the stranglehold the interests got on men's brains.

And my God the wartime wages. If I hadn't blown it all in
I'd have been able to start a business like Smitty or settle
down as a remittance man in St. Petersburg Florida. It just
wasn't in the cards.

All my life I been waiting for the Promised Land. We used
to call it the revolution but all that means now is firing squads
and jails. That's why I never accomplished anything in my life.
Waiting for pie in the sky made nothing ever worth bearing
down on.

Then the organizations began to take over. Opened up the
Promised Land to dues paying members only, and then only
so long as you keep your trap shut.

The great success of the Commies was because they were
smart enough to take advantage of the trend. They took all
the hopes of mankind and turned them into a concentration
camp. If it hadn't been them it would have been some other
goddam dogma. Everybody's got to wait till they get the word.
We wobblies used to think every man ought to think his own
up for himself.

It's mass organization that turns man into a louse. Organized charity. What I don't know about organized charity. It
was this home for disabled seamen. I'd been trying it on my
own but I really was too sick to work. I thought it was just the
results of that skull fracture but it really was the old TB I developed after I got discharged from World War I. Spent a
year in a state sanitarium. That's where I got my education,
really started reading and trying to figure things out. The doctors told me I was cured. Go young man and be sick no more.
Now they've got all kinds of drugs for TB. They've got the
disease checked again but they've got me checked too. Check-
mate I guess.

When I first landed in this home, The Haven they called it,

I thought it was the prettiest place in the world. I was always ready to fall for that Promised Land. Lovely trees and nicely kept flower beds and fat robins hopping about the green lawns. What a sink of corruption. And there I was ready to think it was all wonderful. If I'd been a kid of nineteen I couldn't have been more had.

Mr. Ainsworth the Superintendent, a little shrewfaced man with a pointed nose and buck teeth who dressed like an undertaker, had me into his office. He talked down in his boots, confidential, like undertakers talk. He handed me a cigarette and treated me like I was an elderly millionaire about to endow the joint. It was an English cigarette at that, one of those limey cigarettes that taste like straw. The little man sat there at a mahogany desk with girls' faces carved on the corners, puffing cigarette smoke up at the ceiling. "The Haven, Mr. Bowman, is based on mutual trust, we lay our faith in togetherness. . . ."

Damned if it wasn't the first time I heard the word. I was going to learn about togetherness during the next six months. Right then I thought the guy was nuts, but I didn't know there would be so much method in his madness. I sat there coughing and sneezing from the cigarette trying not to listen to the guy sounding off because that kind of guff gives me a pain right in the pit of my stomach, until he took pity on me and called in Captain Timmons to show me to my room and walk me around the grounds and introduce me to the folks.

Captain Timmons was Ainsworth's pet seacaptain; hell they said he was a seacaptain, I never saw his master's papers. If he was ever captain of anything bigger than a towboat, I'm an admiral of the fleet. Syd Timmons didn't seem too bad till you got to know him. He was a redfaced old man with a laugh like bollocky Bill. He wore blue glasses and stumped around on a peg leg, the bluff old seadog, just like something out of a book. The only thing real about him was his wooden leg.

I hadn't had a square meal for two weeks and all I could think of was when do we eat? but the damned old hypocrite had to walk me all over the estate. He showed me the bandstand and the rose garden and the electric light plant and the vegetable garden and the laundry. There he went stump stump stump down the gravel paths on his peg leg and I stumbled along after him sick at my stomach from hunger while he introduced me to the damndest bunch of sharpies and high-

binders I ever saw gathered together on God's green earth.
They were sitting on benches in twos and threes in the sun
waiting for their chow.

I was so tired when I finally got my duffle up to the little
cubicle they called a private room that when the dinnerbell
rang I just couldn't get on my feet to go down to the messhall.
It was supper before I got a bellyful of the slumgullion. Time
enough I guess. I just lay there on my lumpy old cot smelling
that disinfectant smell they have in cheap boardinghouses
when they've tried to get rid of the bedbugs and haven't quite
succeeded. I lay with my eyes half-closed fighting for breath.
Every now and then there was a creaking on the floor outside
and I'd let the lid on my good eye drop open and see some
mug sticking his dirty snout in through the crack in the door.
Nothing friendly in those looks. They weren't looking at me.
They were looking at my things.

That Haven was a sink. An honest man couldn't live. The
first night while I was down eating supper somebody stole my
only good shirt. After that I locked my door but it didn't do no
good. Somebody, I always thought it was Syd Timmons himself, had a passkey. Little by little everything went, some nice
handkerchiefs my nieces sent, the books my brothers mailed
me, my hairbrush, my wornout blue denim shirts: I never was
very good at keeping track of possessions. None of them would
have been worth more than fifty cents in a hockshop. They
even stole my glasses. Can you think of a meaner thing than
that? The place was heavily endowed, everything found, we
even got pocketmoney. They seemed to just steal for the pleasure of it. Togetherness.

It took me a couple of months before I found out what the
racket was. Liquor. The Haven was temperance, strict prohibition under the terms of the endowment. And those old stum-
blebums spent their time dreaming of a drink of whiskey.
Whiskey came high.

What they did was steal stuff and take it to the crosseyed
Chinaman who ran the laundry and he took it out and hocked
it, for a cut, naturally. Then they took the money and gave it
to Syd Timmons to buy them liquor with. Syd Timmons had
the use of the superintendent's car. The place was four miles
from town and no way of getting to the local saloon for a decent drink without special permission, and it was too far away
anyway for most of us old wrecks to walk, so the management

had us by the short hairs. Syd Timmons bought the cheapest old bar whiskey and he and the chink cut it with water and you paid four dollars a pint for it and took it back to your room when you went down to fetch your laundry. And you guzzled it in a corner to make sure nobody would swipe it. Togetherness. Can't tell me that Ainsworth didn't get a cut on it.

Of course some of us made a few honest dollars playing craps on Saturdays when the cigarette money was doled out. And some cash came in from remittances, pensions and that sort of thing. Gambling was strictly forbidden but the attendant didn't say anything if he got his dollar from the winner. Attendants they called them, they looked more like the turnkeys in a rundown country jail. We played craps and reddog and rummy. Some of them even played cribbage. The dudes made up tables of bridge. But mostly we stole.

We stole from each other. If a new man came in with a watch or a fountain pen or any kind of little knickknack or some keepsake he'd saved from the wreck it was rare sport to see who would get it first. When there was nothing left to steal from each other we stole from the foundation. We stole the cups and saucers out of the pantry and knives and forks and the blankets off the beds and the electric light bulbs out of the halls. Even the knobs off the doors. Ainsworth made money on that too, so he could afford to act big and close his eyes to the stealing.

His racket was that he got a cut from the dealers that sold him replacements. The more he bought the more he made. The more stealing the better, see! No wonder the Haven was costly to run. Those trustees must have been a bunch of dopes or most likely they didn't take the trouble to add up the figures. No skin off their ass.

What did we used to say about the cooperative commonwealth? From each according to his means to each according to his needs. There wasn't a man in the whole place who wouldn't steal the pennies off a dead man's eyes. But it was so damned unpleasant. The lying and the backbiting and the hard feelings. I been on some thievish ships but the Haven was the worst. When somebody stole my shoes from under my bed one night I got my Irish up.

I went in to complain to Mr. Ainsworth and when all he'd say was a man ought to adjust and not be a troublemaker, that same old broken record about mutual trust and togetherness, I decided I'd write the trustees. I looked up their addresses in the telephone directory and wrote them all personal letters. No answers naturally. I wrote the newspapers. I wrote the DA. I believe I even wrote the President of the United States. A lot of good it did.

Ainsworth spread the word I was touched in the head. When I stomped into his office to ask him how come, he called up the cops to hurry he had a crazy man loose. He must have been tipped off I was coming because he was hanging up the phone just as I pulled open the door. Ought to have seen him cringing back in his chair pale and white, looking like a sick weasel, with his buck teeth and little greedy eyes. I had been planning to slam him one in the jaw but I didn't have the heart. I just stood there looking at him.

The cops sure did come quick that time. I did myself the satisfaction of roughing the cops up a bit. They had to slip a straitjacket on me before they could get me out of the office. Last I saw of Ainsworth he was rolling on the floor swivel chair and all in a pool of ink.

The cops took it out on me all right when they got me in the wagon. I was a sight for sore eyes when they dumped me out in the psycho ward.

Lucky for me the house physician was a real man who knew his stuff. He filed an information against the cops for beating me up and he had me in his office for two hours reading off charts and looking at little lights and all kinds of gadgets to test your nerves. He'd been in the war and around the world a bit. We had a real good time together. He said there wasn't a thing wrong with my brains, but he sent me to a medical doc who found out about my lung condition.

When I said I was a veteran that doc sent me over here and here I lie to this day with nothing to look at but gray blankets and a few cracks on the ceiling and the white enameled crosspiece at the foot of my bed and legs and feet and stupid old faces sticking out of hospital cots down the ward. And the babble of pain and the greasy smell, mealtimes. People are disgusting when they get old.

Isolation ward. All my life I'd wanted a chance just to go off in a corner and think. But now it's too late. That Haven had me worried. I always thought it was economic necessity made

people do wrong, but there they really did have pie in the sky
with everything free, gratis and they lied and stole worse than
ever. . . . Suppose I did come up with the answer who the hell
would know it? It's the isolation ward all right.

Now and then through the window I can look up in the sky
and see a seagull. Who'd have thought they'd fly over the city
like that? It catches me right in the throat to see the white
gulls skim overhead, bending their wings ever so little to take
advantage of the aircurrents, and something inside me casts
loose and soars. Who'd have thought an old fo'castle hand
would get all weteyed and bothered watching a goddam
screeching seagull?

Documentary (6)

*A Boy Can Now Hear Sounds that You Were Able to Hear
Only in Your Dreams*

PATTERNS FOR TOMORROW

among the accomplishments of this unusual organization are important contributions to ultra-high-
vacuum technology, electron-tube materials development, photo-electronics, ceramic and sapphire-on-
metal seal development, meg-awatt electronics, heat-
transfer analysis and applications, micro-wave theory

GIFTS OF THE FIREBIRD

a solid background in thermodynamics is required
with several years experience in fluid systems design

IF YOU KNOW THE WOMAN WHO SHOULD
HAVE THIS CAR . . .

. . . you must admire her very much. She never
tries to impress . . . it isn't necessary. She never

"makes an entrance," yet, somehow, people turn
when she comes into a room. If she's impatient, it's
only with pretension. If she's proud, it's mostly of
being a woman. She's gentle, durable . . . and in-
tensely feminine. . . .

THE BIGGEST ITEM IN THE TAPE TOTAL
PUTS NOTHING IN THE BAG

"Name one thing you have helped the skilled workers on,"
a woodworker writes his BA. "You have taken the craft away
from them. Perhaps you have been too busy on the seniority
racket.

"How can any young man go to a manager to learn a trade?
I shudder to think what might have happened to myself, and
my mother who was a widow with four daughters to support
if your organization had been in power at that time.

"Seniority is one thing but ability is another, and I don't
think that anyone no matter who he is should think that a
street sweeper is worth as much as a skilled man (at heart yes
we are all flesh and blood)". . . .

The Promised Land (old style)

Of course it's all a fairy story.

Once upon a time many many years ago there lived in a
crowded slum in a haggard horrible city under the leaden
skies of eastern Europe a poor little Jewish boy named Samuel.

It was a city full of mud and misery. The police wore great
heavy highleather boots just for the purpose of kicking poor
little boys and especially poor little Jewish boys around,

and the rich landowners and the intellectuals in their high
stiff collars passed by on the other side without a thought for
the hungry bellies and the hungry hearts of poor little Jewish
boys in the slums.

This was a little shrimp of a boy, very skinny and

very weak, but there burned in his heart so great an ambition
that he decided he'd run away.

Far to the west, beyond the Rhine and busy England, across
the ocean there was a country called America. "What did I
know about it?" he says now. "It was a dream."

All he knew was that poor people's eyes became bright
when they heard this word "America."

All he knew was if he could reach America he would make
his fortune.

He managed to beat his way across the channel to England.

He had a nice smile. People helped him; all his life he was
to have a knack of making the right friends.

(In those days, before the world wars began, once a man,
or even a boy, got west of the squalor and oppression and the
policemen in highleather boots along the Czar's frontiers he
could travel anywhere he liked;

all he needed was money.)

In England and America particularly they had something they called "Freedom." Although he hadn't learned the
language yet already in England freedom suited little Samuel.

In a smoky grimy city in the English midlands he found a
sister of his mother's. His relatives took him in and helped him
find work. As it was a city of metalworkers the work was in a
blacksmith's shop. He wasn't strong enough for the work so
they fired him; but he didn't care because what he wanted
was to go to America, just to be in America. It was the sound
of the word America.

Finally his relatives found the money for his steerage pas-
sage to New York.

When Samuel tried to tell the officials at Ellis Island
what his last name was they couldn't understand him so they
put it down as Goldfish. America was a land where everybody
picked new names. Freedom meant a man could pick the
name he liked the sound of. So it was Sam Goldfish who went
to work in a glove factory in Gloversville, New York.

The factory whistle blew every morning at ten to seven and
the winters were cold and they worked ten hours a day for
four dollars a week, but Sam had a knack for making the right
friends; so the story goes that he made friends with the boss's

son and before long he was selling gloves instead of making them.

" 'What do you know about selling?' they asked me," he says now. "But I knew I could sell gloves, 'Just give me a chance,' I said, 'don't pay me a salary . . . I'll travel on trolley-cars.' "

He believed so thoroughly that the gloves he was selling were the most wonderful gloves in the world that not many years passed before he was salesmanager of the concern and married and living in a nice brownstone house in a nice part of New York.

He wasn't satisfied. Ambition still burned in his heart. "I'm never satisfied," he says now. "I'm always worried. Any time you're completely satisfied you might as well go out and shoot yourself."

In those days, so the story goes, he had an office somewhere near Herald Square. On Herald Square there was a nickelodeon. For a nickel you could sit in a dark stuffy hall in back and see flickering on the screen something they called Vitascope.

Sam was a young man who never stopped working but when he did take a stroll on his lunch hour he couldn't keep away from the pictures that flickered on the screen.

They were short. They were violent. They were out of doors. They only cost a nickel.

Perhaps they recalled some adventurous dream of a sunlit wild west America that had buzzed inside the skulls of hungry little boys under the leaden skies of eastern Europe.

Up to then he'd only dreamed of being a glove manufacturer. Now he began to figure: the exhibitors were making big money on a nickel; suppose you charged a quarter instead of a nickel.

His brotherinlaw was in show business. Sam started to argue with him that he ought to put some money into making a motion picture. Take a real Broadway play, a real matinee idol, everything of the best.

As a glove salesman Sam was a snappy dresser; elegance, quality, that paid in the glove business: why wouldn't it pay in the motion picture business? There were poor people in America who couldn't afford the price David Belasco charged for seats in his theatres; suppose you gave them a real Broadway play, running an hour say, for twentyfive cents?

His friends all said he was crazy. In those days they used to show movies to clear the theatre for the next set of vaudeville turns. They called them chasers in showbusiness.

It was Sam's idea that quality would pay. If Sam was selling an idea it was the most wonderful idea in the world. The belief burned so bright in his heart that other people found themselves believing in it. After a couple of flops in operettas and music halls his brotherinlaw decided to try out Sam's idea; they produced *The Squaw Man* with Dustin Farnum. The word "feature" was born.

People crowded into the halls. (Of course it's all a fairy story.) At thirtyfour Sam Goldfish found himself a millionaire.

It turned out just as he had dreamed. He'd reached America and he'd made his fortune. It was what they called freedom.

"I just do what pleases me," he says today.

Sam was in at the start of a number of the most successful picturemaking concerns but he couldn't work with partners. If Sam had an idea it was just the most wonderful idea in the world. When he was selling an idea he was so busy selling it he just didn't have time for other people's notions. Partnerships broke in yelling matches.

It cost him a lawsuit and a lot of expense to pull the name of Goldwyn out of one of these corporations. (Now that he really knew English, Goldfish was getting to sound silly for the name of a great producer and a millionaire.) Goldwyn was a name he liked the sound of.

It was a composite of Goldfish and Selwyn.

The Selwyns were the theatrical producers who provided the stories and the plays while Sam produced the motion pictures. Their company was called the Goldwyn Pictures Corporation.

After Sam took the name for his own by due legal process (there was freedom in this country; a man was free to choose his own name) he used to speak of it as "the company that bears my name." The only Goldwyn was Sam. Sam Goldwyn Inc. Ltd. it has remained to this day.

The name is part of the fairy story. When you step

into the hotel elevator and ask the elevator boy what floor Mr. Goldwyn's suite is on, the boy's face melts. He wants to touch you for luck like a hunchback. A clerk in a black suit walking along the corridor, when he hears the name, rolls adoring eyes towards a creamcolored door to point out the apartment.

Mr. Sam Goldwyn sits at the telephone on a crimson damask armchair in a large salmoncolored French style parlor. When he puts down the telephone he looks up with a smile. (When he's not mad at you he'll give you the most genial smile in the world.) He's a slender slight grayhaired man with eyes somewhat close together and a determined chin, he's passed his seventieth birthday, but in his sharp glance and in his smile you can still see the little smiling shrimp of an immigrant with ambition burning in his heart who landed on these shores at the turn of the century.

Sam Goldwyn gets to his feet and says "I just finished a picture." He sings the words. The way he says it you know he thinks it's the most wonderful picture ever made in the world. "I spent four million dollars." He expects you to think its the most wonderful picture ever made in the world. The telephone rings again. The maid arrives with a message. "Just a minute I must finish what I was going to say . . . I've been dreaming about that thing for sixteen years."

When he's disposed of the message and put down the telephone again he goes on. "I don't make many pictures, one picture a year." His manner is almost modest when he talks of his work. The words are salestalk but there's a modesty in his manner. It's all too good to be true.

It's not his life, it's a fairy story.

"People tell me it's the greatest picture ever made . . . Here I have it written down what I am going to tell the ladies . . . over at the Plaza they are going to present an award. No he took it away . . . Excuse me . . ."

He reaches petulantly for the phone. "I always attend to everything just when I think of it." He's calling some publicity man for a copy of the missing release. There's a sting in his voice. "It'll be here in a minute," he says relaxing into a smile again.

"Mr. Goldwyn do you ever think of that little boy who ran away from Poland and landed in America? How many years ago?"

"I came all alone. I was thirteen or fourteen." His mouth

shapes that sweet sad smile. "Any time things don't run right I take a quick cutback to my childhood and say this isn't so bad after all . . . I went right to work. America's been very good to me. And I haven't stopped working one day since . . . Progress has just begun . . . America has been a heaven to all these people coming over from Europe."

His voice is suddenly bitter. His face goes glum: "And in the last fifteen years there come people who want to make a hell of it."

The maid hurries in with the missing release, Mr. Goldwyn gets to his feet explaining that he has to go now. He looks hurriedly through the sheets of thin white paper. "This is what I am going to tell the ladies, it is what Hans Christian Andersen told the children: "Let your heart tell your eyes what to believe . . .""

Fifth Avenue between the Sherry Netherlands and the Plaza remains the spot in New York that has the most cosmopolitan gloss. There's the corner of the park, Sherman in tarnished gilt and the hansom cabs along the curb and the nude lady in the fountain and the fluffy clipped poodles led along the sidewalks by tailored women who've just stepped out from under the permanent wave machine.

The Plaza itself retains a faint aroma of the Four Hundred like the smell of old leather. Down in the Rendezvous Room the ladies are gathering round tables set with heavily gilded menucards. In the blur of cigarettesmoke the gold chandeliers are reflected in the mirrors. A warm scent of orange peel and whiskey trails behind the trays of cocktails the waiters are handing around.

The ladies of the motion picture councils have all put on their best hats and brought their furpieces out of storage to hear Mr. Goldwyn. The sound of their chatter round the tables is like the sound of the aviary at the zoo.

Publicity men bustle round the edges. When Mr. Goldwyn comes in smiling and suave the ladies follow him with their eyes as if he were the pied piper of Hamelin.

A lady in a hat full of forgetmenots is making a speech tendering "a personal tribute to the producer who has supplied us with the high quality of entertainment which we do heartily endorse."

She introduces another lady with a hat wreathed in rosebuds who asks a third lady in a hat all bobbing with cherries to be good enough to bring out "the interesting symbol of our esteem" so that she can present it.

A large flat volume is presented to Mr. Goldwyn, who rises graciously and stands in front of a green garden vista painted on the wall behind the speakers' table. This is his moment. (Of course it happens every day: his publicity men see to it that it happens every day when there is a picture to be released.)

Today it's a testimonial volume; tomorrow it will be orchids. He stands there looking down into the ladies' faces and their clapping hands. When the applause subsides Sam Goldwyn tells the ladies how pleased he is that he's pleased these ladies, how pleased all the people will be who worked on this beautiful picture, how pleased all the little underprivileged children will be who he's going to see to it will see the beautiful picture free, gratis, and without charge because he can never forget he was an underprivileged child himself. . . . Of course there's a great deal more applause. "This is what I meant when I told myself, in the hungry days so long ago: 'I'll go to America and make my fortune.' "

Documentary (7)

INFORMATION RETRIEVAL

Fallout can threaten more people than blast or heat in a nuclear attack.

So Pure and Gentle, Use It to Beauty-Bathe All the Costly Fragile Lingerie You Wear Next to Your Skin

THE SLEEPWALKERS

High Fidelity Recordings of the Actual Voices of Great Minds

the incredible variety of vegetation, insects, fishes, reptiles and mammals; the evolution of man himself from primitive savagery to the complex civilizations of today

MAGNETIC MEMORY OF AN OIL RESERVOIR

important thermochemical data is now being obtained on substances not amenable to conventional oxidation bomb studies

HOW TO DEAL WITH YOUR TENSIONS

We advertise because we believe that it is good for people to own shares in American business—good for them because they may thereby improve their standard of living and good for the country because continuing investment of private capital makes possible continuing expansion of our economy.

One Out of Ten Americans Suffers from Mental Illness

A better standard of living is the consequence of economic progress, it is said, and this in turn depends on an adequate economic policy, friendly international co-operation, the efficient utilization of natural resources and the talent and capacity of the citizen.

Blackie Bowman Speaking

(Scene: a bed in a Veterans' Hospital)

Now that Joe Mangeone has stopped telling me his troubles maybe I can collect my thoughts again. That fellow's a menace to the peace of mind of the whole entire ward. He knows a man can't get away from him. He sneaks up behind you in his wheel chair and there he is mumbling his troubles through his mustache before you've seen him coming. Troubles hell. He's going to be discharged in two weeks and he's got a nice home to go to with his married daughter out in Hicksville and total disability. I got total disability too but the only pleasure I get out of it is being able to spend a little money on my nieces and nephews. Joe'll have to wear an aluminum foot but he'll be able to walk around with a cane not like me glued to this bed. The man don't know when he's well off. Talks like being discharged from the hospital was being thrown out to starve. He don't know what it is to starve.

Me, I've starved plenty. The time I came nearest to really truly starving was somewhere about the time Franklin D. Roosevelt was being sworn in as President of the United States. That was a winter.

There are times in a man's life when everything seems to come to an end. The Great Depression was one of those times. For me at least. Don't get me wrong. I wasn't worrying about black Friday on the stock exchange. It was deeper than that. I was on the beach high and dry way down inside. No job no money no wife no hope.

I was used to the outcast life. I was always more the hobo than the home guard. It was the degradation of the wobblies that was tearing me down. Ever since the old days of the Bridgemen and Structural Iron Workers I'd believed in myself because I was a wobbly. I'd believed in myself because I thought I was doing my little bit towards forming the structure of the new society in the shell of the old, the way it said in the grand old preamble. I was an I Won't Work, a wobbly, an IWW and I was proud of it. Just as much as any goddam cocksure Communist I thought I had history on my side. I was helping bring on the revolution, only the right way, the rank and file way, the American way.

We had a wobbly hall for the unemployed way west on Fourteenth Street. I put in a lot of time there. I didn't have a damn thing to do but tighten my belt. It wasn't the starving I minded. I've starved before and I've starved since. A certain amount of starving's good for a man, stimulates thinking. It's that kind of sharp thinking that divides the men from the scissorbills.

All those hall cats and spittoon philosophers over on Fourteenth Street were starving too. We were all in it together, share and share alike in good wobbly style. What began to eat into me was that no thinking came out of it. Turn the bread lines into picket lines was the only slogan we could think up. What the hell did that mean?

From organizing the whole cockeyed industrial system we'd

fallen to organizing a bunch of dead beats. We had the psychology of mission stiffs. Mister can you spare a dime?

We didn't do too bad that way once we got the hall organized. We sent out details of panhandlers to work the sidewalks. Another detail brought in old packing cases and stuff like that for firewood, or scrounged around the markets for soup bones and baskets of discarded vegetables. Our cook was a sawed-off little Romanian who'd been chef in a plush restaurant down in the financial district. Constantine something: we called him Con for short. Give Con a bone and a few old frozen carrots and spuds and a withered onion, and he'd cut out the spoiled parts and make you as fine a soup as you would want to eat. Not a man ever got sick off the slumgullion old Con cooked.

We lived off the waste of the city. The waste in the markets and restaurants of any big city is enough to make you sick, but in that depression time it broke your heart. The stuff was going to waste because nobody had any money to buy it.

We kept the hall clean and warm. We managed to provide the fellow workers with one decent meal a day. Half the time we even had coffee: don't ask me how we got it. Fellow workers hell, for the first time in my life I realized a man's worth comes from the work he does. It's not inherent in the animal if you get what I mean. That was why the better I ate the worse I felt. I wasn't no better than a goddam social worker.

I got so discouraged I kept haunting those coal wharves over on the East River trying to figure out what the best time would be to jump off so that the tiderip would sweep you up towards Hellgate and you'd be sure not to be able to make it to shore if you changed your mind. I'd have ended up unidentified on a slab in the morgue if it hadn't been for a woman. Every time it's been a woman that saved my life when it wasn't one that was driving me crazy.

Thelma Ulrich wasn't too goodlooking. She had a kind of wholesomelooking spudshaped face like she'd come right off the milking stool. She did come off a farm in Nebraska but that was many a weary year ago. Why she wanted to be a dancer I never could imagine.

We met up down in Macdougal Street in the Village.

It was a springlike late winter evening, just coming on to rain. I was squdging along with holes in my shoes, not looking to the right or left, just thinking about jumping in that cold East River when I bumped into a girl in a slicker. She stopped in front of me suddenly to look down an areaway where there was one of those basement coffee shops with checked curtains they used to have in the Village in those days. I backed off and said I was sorry and she gave me a nice straight friendly desperate look. The two of us just stood there. She kept staring down into that window with the checked curtains. I said, kinda low and sympathetic: "It looks like you couldn't make up your mind."

"Well I can't," she said.

"Why not?"

"I got my reasons."

She was holding me off, but she gave me the friendliest grin. She had a nice quiet voice. I was beginning to warm up to her.

She was saying it looked bad for a girl to be always going into places like that all alone. I told her I wished I could be her escort but they tended to like to see a man's money in those joints and money was just exactly what I didn't have.

Ten years before when I was living with Eileen I'd have had credit and welcome in any dump in Greenwich Village. But now all I saw was unfamiliar faces.

She seemed to like something about the way I told her about not having any dough, because she looked me right in the face and laughed. "That's my trouble stranger."

We couldn't stand there in the rain all day staring at each other. All at once she made up her mind. "Come along," she said without looking at me and started off down the street. I had to stretch my legs to catch up to her. She put her feet down neat and quick like a cat. From the way she moved her hips I guessed right away she was some kind of a dancer. She had me puffing before we reached one of those cold water tenements down on Fourth Street and then it was six flights up. "At least we can get out of the rain," she said as she trotted on ahead up the stairs. As she was scratching in her bag for her latchkey I told her it was supposed to be good for your wind to lose weight but I swore it hadn't been good for mine.

"I can make you some hot tea." She opened the door to let me in. Still she wouldn't look up at me. When she took off her wet kinda bucketshaped hat I could see her hair was dyed, auburn I guess you'd call it. I wasn't much over forty then but my hair had streaks of gray in it too. She took my coat and hat. She kept darting back and forth in the room with that little cat tread. It was a tiny room with an iron bed and a sink and gasburner behind a screen.

A pair of wardrobe trunks took up most of it. Theatrical trunks. You could read her whole career in the tags and labels and stickers. Vaudeville acts, names of theatrical companies on tour. None of them was very recent.

She made me sit in the battered pink easy chair, apologizing all the while that she hadn't time to mend a rip in the slipcover. Then she laid out two nice clean white cups and saucers and a loaf of rye bread and a little piece of cheese about as big as a minute. That was all she had for her supper. I could see right away that she wasn't no whore, just a theatre worker down on her uppers. Not that I'd have minded if she'd been a whore. I've known some whores who were pure gold, not many of 'em but one or two. What I mean is that right from the beginning we talked straight, like one fellow worker to another.

I nibbled slowly on those slices of bread and cheese. I desperately wanted to stay there as long as I could. The room was shabby and untidy but everything was clean and respectable. There was a nice homey smell about Thelma and her clothes and her things that you didn't expect in the Village. If Eileen had been housekeeping there the place would have been filthy.

Thelma noticed how slow I was eating and asked why. I told her right out that I was eating slow because I wanted that bread to last. The cheese was gone the first bite. I wanted it all to last. It was the first happy moment, sitting in that chair and drinking that tea and eating that bread, and talking to her; it was the first happy moment, sober that is, since I'd broken up with Eileen, and I wanted it to last. I didn't care if it lasted forever.

"I can't let you eat it all," she said. "I've got to save some for breakfast."

Did I feel like a piker?

Who was Eileen she asked abruptly. Eileen was my wife, I said. She flushed at that. I went on in a hurry to explain that we'd been separated for years now. I didn't even know where she was. One thing led to another and before I knew what had happened there I was telling her the story of my life like any old stumblebum hitting the sawdust trail for a plate of hash in a Bowery Mission.

Thelma got real excited when I told her about knowing Freddie Davis and Jack Reed and Eugene O'Neill and Art Young and fellows like that in the old days when Eileen and I lived in the Village. Her eyes got real big. It was that hick streak in her. "And here I've lived in New York fifteen years and never met a celebrity." She let out her breath in an amazed kind of way.

"Why celebrities were a dime a dozen in those days," I said. "I guess you were too young to remember the Paterson strike."

"What was that?"

I got to my feet.

"I'll tell you about that next time." And there I was scraping my wet dogs on the floor and looking at the window, and hoping she'd ask me to stay, but she didn't.

"Come and see me again Blackie," she said. "Tomorrow's the day I make the rounds of the agencies. An old trouper never gives up hope. Call me about six"—her gray eyes were right in mine—"if you feel like it."

She scribbled a number on a slip of paper. "It's the Italian grocery on the corner. They got a little boy named Tony. He's a friend of mine. Tony'll run upstairs and get me." "Sure," I said trying to sound bright and confident. I held her hand a little when I shook it.

As I went down the stairs I suddenly got mad. No damn woman was going to throw me out of doors like a cur dog into the rain. I crunched up the slip of paper that had the phone number on it into a pellet and let it drop down the stairwell. Thank God I found it again when I got to the ground floor because I hadn't gone a flight before I'd forgotten all about being mad and could only think of how wonderful it would be to see her again. I remembered what the number was anyway.

The northeaster was blowing rain in sheets over streets all shining with headlights and the red and green of the stop and go signs. I'd forgotten all about the East River and the riptide and my wet feet and the water running down my back through that threadbare overcoat. It was like being a kid again hitting the big city for the first time, the flicker and the crowds and the cars and the rain and the feeling of life and light spilling out of the big buildings.

After Thelma's nice cozy room it sure was a letdown to roll up wet and stinking in my blanket on the floor of that wobbly hall. It wasn't the hard floor I minded. A man can sleep right good on the floor if he takes the spot next the wall. It was the crowding, the guys laid out in rows like sardines in a box cursing and snoring and honking. These last weeks I'd been too hungry and miserable to worry about that sort of thing but now I couldn't sleep all night for wanting a woman.

Next morning I woke up coughing and feverish. All I could think of was how the hell could I raise a couple of dollars to take Thelma out to supper. I never did like to beg, but that day I worked the sidewalks clear up Broadway to 42nd Street and across to the Grand Central station and down Fifth Avenue and then back west to the garment district.

I sure did compete with the phony doughboys selling apples that day.

I hated myself for doing it but once you get started there's a technique to begging like everything else. You have to size up the guy you're touching. Some you plead with and some you have to bully just a bit. What I told 'em was I was coming down with the flu and had to get me a room and some victuals. It was God's truth, and it wasn't the usual line. People were conscious of flu that winter.

The nicest one was a bigshouldered black boy unloading cases from a truck on one of those cross streets.

"Mister you ought to check in at a hospital," he said with a roll of his big white eyeballs. I could see he was flattered because a white man had asked him for a dime. "I ain't got no cash," he said, "but I'll write an I O U," he said in his musical proud voice and he took me into a little lunchroom right there and made the counterman give me a doughnut and a cup of coffee. He signed on the check. It did me good to see the way he wrote his name on the back. He wrote real good. Marcus Jones, I've always remembered the name.

"He's good for it," said the little old counterman giving me a wink when Marcus Jones swaggered back to his truck. "That boy's a prince, a black prince."

I tried to cadge another cup of coffee off the counterman but nothing doing.

By the time it was six o'clock I was a mess. My clothes were soaked. It had been raining all day. I had a fever and a cough loud enough to rouse every undertaker in downtown Manhattan. But I had two dollars and fiftysix cents.

At six o'clock sharp I went into a booth to call Thelma. I got Tony all right and he said in his piping little voice he'd run and get her. Then I stood there with the receiver in my ear listening to my heart pounding in that goddam phone booth. I was in a sweat. I didn't believe she'd come. I couldn't have been more nervous if I'd been a sixteenyearold trying to make his first date. My heart was pumping so hard I could hardly hold the receiver.

God it took long. I was just about ready to hang up when there was that nice fellow worker voice right in my ear. I was hoarse as a crow by that time. I croaked something about setting her up for a feed. "Come on down, Blackie," she said. "I'll be waiting for you."

By that time I could just barely walk. When I finally made it up all those stairs to that cold water flat I was coughing like I'd tear my lungs out. She must have heard me through the door because she opened it before I had a chance to knock. "Blackie, you're soaked," she said.

When I took off my coat she could see my clothes were all wet underneath.

"I oughtn't to have turned you out . . . I almost cried my eyes out after you'd left and now you've gone and caught your death."

"Death hell," I said. "I've gone and caught enough jack for two spaghetti dinners and a glass of red ink."

She never asked how I got it. Afterwards she told me she thought I'd gone out and robbed some guy in the park.

Right away I told her I oughtn't to have come. I hadn't planned to be infectious. I'd go along right after supper so that she wouldn't catch my flu. Of course I didn't mean a word of it.

She said not to be silly I'd brought her luck. She had a promise of a job teaching ballet for the WPA. WPA what the hell was that? That was the first time I'd heard of WPA. Us old time radicals made a point of not reading the capitalist press and the wobbly papers tended to run behind on the news. WPA. Those letters got to sound wonderful to us. I know a lot of it was just boondoggling and votebuying by the politicians but it sure was a godsend to a pair of derelicts like Thelma and me. And we weren't the only ones. For many a young fellow WPA was the Promised Land.

Her job began Monday she said, all excited, she'd tell me about it while we were eating our supper. It was then I noticed the change in the woman. It wasn't that she was better looking. Her best friend wouldn't call Thelma a good-looker. But her happiness was shining inside her like a candle in a jackolantern.

She decided I was too sick to go out. She'd take the money and buy some groceries and cook them up there, in her room. She put on a slicker and that funny hat and out she went leaving me with a clean bath towel to rub myself down with and an old ulster coat of hers to put on while my clothes dried. I felt terrible taking off those clothes in her nice room. They were stinking and my shorts were filthy and all in rags. I must have been delirious, with the fever and the flu coming on because what I did when she'd gone was to roll them up in a ball and open the window and pitch them out into the alley. Except for the shoes. The shoes would go even if they did have holes in them.

Now she couldn't throw me out.

When she came back with a big bag of groceries all splattered with the rain she was too busy cooking spaghetti and meatballs to notice about my clothes. Sick as I was the smell of tomatopaste and garlic sizzling in olive oil sure made my mouth water.

As she worked she talked over her shoulder telling me about how her grandmother never would turn away a tramp. "The stranger may be God," was what her grandmother used to say.

And besides I'd brought her luck. This WPA job was going to pay twentyfive dollars a week. Nine months she'd been at liberty, that's what theatre people call it when they're out of work. She was down to her last dime. Well that was over. Water over the dam.

She gave me a look out of her big gray eyes that almost scared me, a look that bored right through into the back of my head. "Blackie, didn't you tell me you were a structural iron worker?"

"What's the matter don't you believe it?"

"Sure I believe it. All I was going to say was I saw something like that on the list of WPA job opportunities."

There was a knock on the door. She pushed me behind the screen. I didn't blame her. I must have been a sight with that towel around my neck and my long hairy legs coming out from under that old ulster of hers.

It was Tony bringing up a bottle of dago red. She was telling him she'd pay his father for it the first of the week and he was piping up that that wasn't going to worry them, the old man would be on easy street if everybody paid their bills like Miss Ulrich did. Tony was a nosy little squirt and Thelma had to give him a big sugar bun she'd bought for our dessert to get rid of him. He must have seen my bare feet under the screen but he didn't let on. Slum kids like that are wise beyond their years.

When I came out from behind the screen she asked me right out: "Blackie what on earth happened to your clothes?"

I didn't know what to say. I lied and said they were so foul I'd put them on the fire escape but I couldn't help blushing. I'm funny that way. I blush like a girl at the slightest thing.

She was craning her neck out of the window. "Well they are not there now." She began to laugh. I was red as a beet. Thank God she took it funny. "Wind musta taken 'em," I gasped. I was beginning to laugh myself. We were both laughing like fools. "Now you can't throw me out." I figured that was about the time I ought to put my arms around her.

She pushed me away. That girl really had muscles. "First things first," she said and brought out a bottle of aspirin tablets and made me take three of them. Then she poured us each a glass of wine.

She looked me straight in the eye. "Blackie," she said in that matter of fact way she had, "it looks like I was going to take up with you but you've got to let me do it in my own way. It's being in too much of a hurry that ruined my marriage and every affair I've tried to have."

I was so weak and feverish I didn't have the gumption anyway. I let her push me into a chair and sat there shoveling in the spaghetti and meatballs as fast as Thelma piled up my plate.

There weren't many things Thelma knew how to cook but

she sure did know how to cook Italian food. She told me later her husband had been a singer at the Met, one of those wops in the chorus I guess, and he'd taught her.

I was sick as a dog but I was happy. That was one of the happiest meals I ever ate.

The damn wine and the aspirin and all that unaccustomed grub made me sleepy. Couldn't keep my eyes open. That feeling that a woman is really going to take care of you. There's nothing like it in the world. Thelma made me a pallet out of blankets on the floor and before I knew it I was as dead as a drunken Dutchman.

She nursed me like a baby for three days.

Saturday morning I woke up feeling a whole lot better, but weak as a kitten. The place was all tidied up. The bed was made but no Thelma. I got to my feet and looked for her. I thought she'd gone to the john down the hall but when I put on my shoes and went to look, still no Thelma. Back in the room no Thelma.

"You damn fool she's walked out on you," I told myself. What if she didn't come back. What the hell was I going to do stark naked in a strange woman's apartment?

I did have the sense to shave with a safety razor I found on her bureau. It always surprises me that women have razors too. A lot of them shave their legs and their armpits and all sorts of odd places.

I must have still been a little lightheaded from the flu because I couldn't help chortling at my own predicament. Then I felt so weak I had to lay down in my blankets. I drifted off to sleep again.

When I opened my eyes there Thelma was bustling round the room fresh and rosy as a May morning. What she'd done was go out and hock her last bits of jewelry, her wedding ring and all, and bought me some clothes. I ought to have known she was up to something when she took my measurements with a tape the day before. The suit was secondhand but it was clean and neat. She buttoned up my new shirt and helped me tie my necktie.

Then she stood me up against the wall and took a look at me. "Now you look more like somebody I could learn to love," she said.

This time she let me hug her and love her up a little but she wouldn't let me kiss her on the mouth, not till I'd gotten that flu out of my system, she whispered with her mouth against my ear. I could feel her heart beating behind her little flat breasts. Mine was pounding for sure. There was something about that woman made me shy as a lad.

That was when I told her it was on purpose I'd thrown away my clothes. "You've thrown away your old life," she cried out in her theatre voice, "and I'm going to throw away mine."

All that afternoon we just sat there side by side on the little iron bed, drinking tea and telling each other about things that had happened to us. Usually I'm pretty impatient in a situation like that but for once I kept telling myself: Fellow you go slow.

The next day was Sunday. It was sunny outside. My strength was coming back and I woke up horny as a goat. I wanted to go out and walk around the block to cool off but she said that was how folks got pneumonia going out too soon after the flu. So I just sat there bolting down the bacon and eggs.

After breakfast I helped her wash the crockery. When we'd set the last plate on the rack I pulled her to me and said it was now or never. I had to be a little teeny bit rough with her and she whimpered I was hurting her but she didn't seen to take it too hard. She made me tell her about what it had been like loving other women and that set me to spinning yarns. To tell the truth I made up most of it. I never did like to tell about my private life—not till I got old and the whole thing was over.

Pork was cheap in those days. We had a pile of pork chops and a bottle of dago red for our Sunday dinner. I made her drink most of the wine and afterwards she let me spread her out on the bed and take her clothes off very gently. I really did make her happy that day. If I do say it myself one thing I've learned in my disreputable career is how to make love to women. She told me I made her feel like a wild creature of the forest; you know how they used to talk down in Greenwich Village in those days.

Monday morning bright and early she went off to her job and I went up to the address she'd given me to see what I could do. There must have been a thousand guys waiting in line in a big dark hallway. There were old men and Bowery bums and respectably dressed characters in business suits who might have been stockbrokers for all I knew and kids one jump ahead of the truant officer. There were a few heavy-handed stiffs who looked like sure enough construction workers but there were damn few.

It was noon before I got to a little window where a sour-faced woman was telling everybody to come back in two weeks. I was just about to let her turn me away when I caught sight of a pugnose and curly head that looked familiar behind a desk in the back office. It was Eileen's kid brother Jim. He always did have a knack for landing with his nose in the butter. All the O'Dwyers did. "Jim," I called, "Jim O'Dwyer."

I could see he recognized me but he didn't let on. He got up from his desk and pointed solemnly towards a door at the other end of the ground glass partition. I walked over and there he was good old Jim his face all smiles pulling me in through the door and beating me on the back and carrying on about how he hadn't seen me in a dog's age. "Blackie you old bastard you."

Then he put on that solemn government employee look and talked low and ponderous to make the others think he was giving me the usual runaround, but what he was saying was that WPA was the softest graft ever and here I was an experienced bridgeworker and a real literate guy and he was going to set me up as an instructor in a vocational school they were organizing just to keep the guys busy until they could get their project started. Once the project was under way he'd see if he couldn't wangle me a job as a supervisor.

Only I must keep my trap shut. No wobbly talk. The Commies were strong in the unemployed councils and the WPA workers unions and I knew what they thought of syndicalists.

It was the first time in his life—Jim went on talking low out of the corner of his mouth from behind that pokerface of his—that he'd gotten any good out of being Kate O'Dwyer's brother. Kate, that was Eileen's older sister, though she used to be an IWW or even an anarchist all those years when she was throwing herself at Alexander Berkman, had been a terrible Communist ever since the Mesabi Range strike. She went under the name of Kate Levine, but a lot of people knew she really was an O'Dwyer. She'd become one of the Party's great speakers. The O'Dwyers all had the gift of gab, but Kate especially. She could wring tears out of a stone. In this WPA racket having a sister high up in the Party had been a real help.

I always said Jim ought to be an actor. You would have thought from his expression and tone of voice he was filling me up with Washington gobbledygook, instead of handing me the lowdown as fast as he could. On the level too. That's what I liked about the O'Dwyers. They were honest crooks. He took me to his desk and helped me make out the forms and there I was hired at twentyfive dollars a week, which was good money for those days when seventeen-fifty was what most of them got. Jim gave me his phone number so that we could get together under less official circumstances and slipped me an enormous wink and I went out of that place walking on air.

My radical days were over. I never did go back to the wobbly hall. Thelma and I, we rented ourselves a couple of rooms on Eighth Street. A couple could live comfortably on fifty dollars a week in the depression years. Thelma had decided she ought to educate me, so we bought the latest books and went to plays and concerts and had a lot of gabby people in for drinks after supper. Thelma tried to run my life, but she wasn't getting very far with it and for once I didn't care. We were happy together.

Now and then we talked about divorcing our various spouses and really making it permanent. I guess it's just as well we didn't; I didn't have it in me; but Thelma sure would have been a comfort to my old age. As it was I was getting a paunch like an international banker.

Thelma didn't have the slightest sense of humor but she was good as gold. I really did work at trying to make her happy and in spite of her being so bossy I probably would have stuck with her to my dying day if Eileen hadn't come back into the picture. I guess Eileen couldn't stand it when she heard I was sunk in bourgeois respectability. Couldn't help breaking it up, not Eileen. I guess Eileen knew that no matter how much I hated her, I never could resist her.

Two or three years had gone by. Looking back at them I guess they were the happiest years of my life. Thelma had been invited to teach in a ballet school uptown. They taught Follies girls and debutantes and musical comedy stars. Really high class. Thelma was too homely for a performer but as a teacher she was outstanding. It wasn't long before she was making a hundred dollars a week.

She moved us uptown to a studio apartment in Carnegie Hall. She took to dressing real artistic with Navajo bracelets on her arms and mascara on her eyelashes. As success began to grow on her she got bossier than ever. The theatre people made a fuss over her. Her kind of dancing was coming into style. These young fruiter balletomanes buzzed around her like flies round a sugarbowl. She was just the right age to attract the theatrical pansies.

Now I can take some of this art stuff or I can leave it alone but by God I can't talk about it all day long. It was bad enough listening to it, but when they wanted me to get in the act my hackles began to rise. A couple of Thelma's young friends even made passes at me, imagine at my age. How I managed to keep from taking a poke at them I'll never know to this day. Rough trade. Proletarians were fashionable during the New Deal.

The boys and girls—thank God some of the girls were attractive and sweet—I'd have given any one of them a tumble and gladly, but I couldn't bring myself to do that to Thelma. Well they used to sit around on the floor in Thelma's studio evenings. Thelma would turn off the electricity and light up the candles and she would swish around with her bracelets jingling, passing Russian tea in glasses and plates of cookies she'd made herself.

Those cookies were terrible. All Thelma knew how to cook was spaghetti. All the time we were living together I had to bring in cooked meals from a restaurant for my own protection.

Anyway when the kids began to run out of conversation and to start billing and cooing in corners, you know how kids are, Thelma would make me do my act. I guess the idea was to take their minds off sex. Thelma didn't like loose behavior. Basically Thelma was as respectable as a set of Grand Rapids furniture.

She'd make me sit in an easy chair and they'd huddle around my knees and I'd tell them about Joe Hill and Hayward, Pettibone and Moyer and Tom Mooney and the free speech fights and Wesley Everest and the Seattle general strikes. At first I tried to tell it to them straight but they couldn't get it through their silly little noodles. They couldn't see any difference between totalitarian Communism and the free society the Industrial Workers of the World beat their brains out for. If people haven't had the experience in their own hides they don't have any way of knowing what it's all about. That's why we wobblies were right trying to educate the working class by direct action.

All these kids could understand was martyrs and bogeymen and pie in the sky. When the stories I told got close to their own experience they'd really sit up. I told 'em about Fitzie and Eugene O'Neill's early plays at the Provincetown Theatre and the old *Masses* cartoonists and the Village before the first World War when we really believed all this stuff about art and revolution; and about the pageant the literary and artistic folks put on in Madison Square Garden for the benefit of the Paterson strikers. They ate up Freddie Davis. One yarn led to another. Before I was through I was making out I was one of the engine room crew on that secret trip Freddie made to Finland in the bunkers of an old coalburning tramp freighter, me handing him sandwiches wrapped in oilcloth to keep the coal dust out. If I remember right he really crossed in a perfectly good bunk in the third mate's cabin, but what the hell, I was spinning yarns. Before I was through I was leading the sailor's revolt at Kronstadt and escaping in a rowboat across the Baltic in the company of a beautiful Polish countess. Eventually I got fed up. I was sick and tired of playing the rough diamond for that bunch of punks.

This much I will say for myself. It was loving me and having me love her gave Thelma the confidence she needed to get her show on the road. Having a working stiff for the boy friend made her a real romantic figure. Romance palls. Now instead of needling me about how we ought to get divorces so that we could marry and settle down Thelma was beginning to talk about how a career woman could never have any home life and the sacrifices she was going to have to make for her art.

When the Roosevelt administration began to cut down on the relief money, I was one of the first laid off. The Commies attended to that. I became a mouth to feed instead of a meal ticket and that made a difference. Probably we would have broken up sooner or later even if Eileen hadn't put her spoke in the wheel.

If I didn't get liquored up I could do a pretty good job

keeping my trap shut about the Commies, but there were times when I just had to bust loose. Franklin Roosevelt had made Earl Browder respectable. I always had hated that old phony and I couldn't help saying so. It made me sore to see these Johnny come latelies taking over the labor movement. Particularly in New York the Commies controlled hiring and firing on most of the federal make-work jobs. They held the balance of power in the New York City presidential vote. Why the hell shouldn't they get their share of the gravy? Naturally they took care of their own.

My troubles started when Jim O'Dwyer moved to a really important racket in Washington. Right under Harry Hopkins. Getting relief jobs was an art in itself. Without Jim to instruct me in the necessary doubletalk I didn't have the chance of a snowball in hell.

Looking back on it I always think of the Roosevelt New Deal as the great days of the O'Dwyers. Until he moved to Washington, Jim kept me posted over occasional drinks in one of those Second Avenue ginmills that came to life with the ending of prohibition. Old Man Pat O'Dwyer, the hellroaring bit of the old sod who had tried to bring the children up in the fear of God and Tammany Hall, had gone to his reward. Jim said it broke the old man's heart when Al Smith lost the election to Hoover in '28.

Jim's older brother Pat, whom I'd known as a wobbly and Irish Republican in the days when Woodrow Wilson was making the world safe for democracy, had served a jail term for extortion in some union racket and moved out to San Francisco where he was going great guns organizing the operating engineers. Jim spoke of him proudly as the business genius of the family. Pat's vice was Hollywood starlets, Jim said laughing like he'd bust a gut. Those operating engineers sure would have to work hard to keep him in spending money. And what about Benny? "Benny," snorted Jim, "Benny's just an honest bookmaker. He hasn't got what it takes."

Benedict was the baby of the family. He haunted the Belmont track. I always used to say he was the only one of the O'Dwyers who never gypped a soul. He ran a wire service. I took to going to place a small bet with him now and then in the back room of a cigarstore on 42nd Street, where he could be found after a couple of properly spaced knocks, just for the pleasure of exchanging a few words with

him. He was still the same nice quietspoken little guy with
his hair parted in the middle. He'd never thought of marrying.
The horses filled his whole life.

Jim hadn't been too communicative about Eileen. All
Benny would say was that she was as pretty as ever and
living in the Village. How about her poetry? Hadn't heard
about that for years, said Benny. Then he clammed up.

It was going to place a bet with Benny that I ran into
Eileen for the first time in eleven years. The Kentucky Derby
was being run next day. I had some pretty hot tips that some
damn racehorse, maybe it was Man o' War, I forget the
brute's name, was sure to win and I'd parleyed fifty bucks out
of Thelma—she always was the most generous creature—to
see if I couldn't make a killing. I wanted to lose that feeling
I had of being a kept man which was making me unhappy.
Benny was leaning over the counter moving his pencil over
the roster of horses when he suddenly looked up over my
shoulder smiling a particularly tender smile and there she was.

Eileen's hair was still red or maybe she dyed it. Anyway
it seemed just as silky. Her skin still had that transparent
look like eggshell china. Her eyes were the same greenish
blue color you never could quite make out. The prettiest
little straight nose between a pair of beautifully arched
eyebrows. There were dark bags under her eyes to be sure but
the slightly haggard look made her even more attractive. It
was only when she spoke to me that I realized what a
change there had been. Her voice had a rasp. Been hitting
the bottle I told myself.

"Francis Xavier," she said, putting her hand on my sleeve
and kinda brushing her shoulder against mine as if we had
never parted. "Who's going to win the Derby? I've got to
win. This time I've absolutely got to win."

She always used to call me by my full name instead of
Blackie. Something about the way she said the name melted
me up inside.

There was a line right out into the corridor. Benny was
busy as a one armed paperhanger. You could see he didn't
like the idea of his sister playing the ponies. He told her
quietly that his advice was to save her money and invest it
in good conservative stocks. It was probably to spite Benny
for being so officious that she threw herself at me with that
sudden imperious way she had.

"Francis Xavier will set me up to a drink and we'll see what advice we can get from Racing Form."

She glared at Benny and swept me out onto the street. I was so taken aback I forgot to place my bet. Before I knew what was happening there I was sitting with Eileen in a booth in a little dark bar on West 43rd Street. It never came to my mind that I'd promised myself that the first thing I'd do if I ever saw her again was smack her in the mouth.

I swear that, in spite of the barroom creak in her voice, Eileen at thirtysix was more attractive than she had been at twentyfive. She always could wrap me around her little finger. I might as well admit that.

We forgot all about the goddam race. With her second drink she started to carry on about how she was sick of being bossed by her brothers. Jim had offered her a Washington job and to get her an apartment and everything if she gave up Joseph Ballestre. "I call him Precious. All his friends call him Precious. Isn't that a scream?" And last time Pat went through town he'd threatened to have one of his mugs bump Precious off if she didn't shake him loose. She knew Precious was a jerk but sometimes a woman needed a jerk. And now little Benny was putting in his oar. She didn't dare see Kate. I knew the kind of tonguelashing Kate could administer.

With her third drink she got quiet and ladylike. I always used to say you had to watch out when Eileen got ladylike. She leaned back in her chair and looked across at me through the crinkly smoke of her cigarette out of her big bluegreen eyes as if I was the only man in the world. She began to talk in a husky gentle voice about how it wasn't because she didn't like me she'd walked out on me that day. She liked me very much. It was because I always sided with the O'Dwyers. Worse than having another brother in the house.

"Every one of you, you used to talk about the exploitation of women and how a girl ought to live her own life. All I did was act on it and then you all got mad at me. You were the ones who were always batting the breeze about free love."

She was getting real dramatic. I'd have been more impressed if I hadn't remembered that she'd played Hedda Gabler in her highschool dramatics course. I didn't want her back on that broken record.

"Nothing's free in the whole goddam world," was all I could think of to say. When I'd delivered myself of that gem there was nothing to do but order up another drink.

"I am," she said.

I'd forgotten all about Thelma and the Kentucky Derby and how it was Thelma's fifty dollars I was spending. It was just me and Eileen getting drunk together like we used to in the old days, and me staring at her across the table crazy to get my hands on her partly because I wanted to wring her neck because she was so ornery but mostly because she was so wonderful to touch. Drunk or sober she was the most attractive woman in the world for me. I was crazy about her all over again. It was the call of the wild all right.

That evening turned out to be hell like all the others. We moved down Broadway from ginmill to ginmill. It was the same old routine. Eileen got to dancing, just a little tiny dancing step to a hummed tune that you could hardly notice, and trying to pick up strange men, but each time I was ready to say to hell with it and walk out she'd pull herself together and talk so understandingly in that sweet husky voice about the good times and the happiness we'd had together and there I was back on the hook.

I did have the decency to call up Thelma and tell her I'd met old friends and would be home late.

"I could scratch her eyes out," Eileen cried and stamped her foot when I came back from the phone booth. "You know I don't like my men to have other women. I hate it. I hate it."

She got so drunk I had to take her home. It was a walk-up on Hudson Street. She just about made me carry her upstairs, and then she clung to me and wouldn't let me go.

There was a man's jacket on the chair and a straw hat on the table. The place smelt of some kind of hair lotion these pimplike characters use. "What about Ballestre?" I had to shake her to make her listen. "Precious. What about him?"

Suddenly she was very mysterious and dramatic. "Precious and I allow each other absolute freedom. We are above being jealous. He's used to me bringing home strange men. I'll just tell him you're my husband. He can't object to that."

"Well I object. If he pokes his nose in here I'll slug him."

"That really would be funny."

She began to laugh. She was still laughing when I grabbed

her and started rolling her on the bed. After all I'm made of flesh and blood. I'm not a plaster saint.

Waking up was horrible. Never in my life have I felt so remorseful about anything I've done as I did about spending that night with my own wife.

We both had hangovers. Eileen declared she couldn't lift her head from the pillow. She lay under the covers making jabbing motions with her forefinger telling me where to look for the coffeepot. I was stumbling in my undershirt trying to find my way around her damn kitchenette when I smelt that sickish sweet hairtonic smell. There was somebody else in the apartment.

I stiffened. Honest I could feel the hair stand up on the back of my neck like a dog's that is going to get into a fight. I turned around with the percolator in my hand. My eyes were so bleary I could barely see him but there he was, a little smooth olivefaced guy in a new spring overcoat and a taffy-colored fedora. Brown eyes, eyebrow mustache. Oval face without an expression in the world.

We didn't have time to speak before Eileen's voice was screeching at us from the bed. "Joseph Maria Ballestre meet Francis Xavier Bowman. Exboyfriend meet exhusband." She gave the nastiest laugh I ever heard. "And don't either of you forget that I'm not any man's property. If you want to fight, go down on the sidewalk." She was enjoying the situation. Imagine that.

Eileen was a psychologist all right. Instead of wanting to sock the poor bastard I found myself having a fellowfeeling for him. Maybe he felt the same way. I never felt such a lowdown hound in my life. First thing I knew he was in the kitchenette cooking up the breakfast and I was handing Eileen her coffeecup and she was lying there handsome as a queen among her courtiers.

I couldn't face Thelma after that night. I didn't even have the nerve to call her on the telephone. I wrote her that I'd met up with Eileen and that old bonds had proved too strong and asked her to send my clothes down by express. Of course I had to give her Eileen's address, but she never came near us. All she did was write me a pleasant little note about how it was beautiful while it lasted but that now life had parted our ways and it was goodbye forever. She never said a word about the fifty dollars. She added a postscript begging

me to be careful about drinking. I must know that that was
my greatest weakness, underlined three times.

Afterwards I learned that Eileen had called Thelma on
the telephone and made a big scene about Thelma trying
to take her husband away. That finished me with Thelma.
Trust Eileen to squeeze all the drama out of a situation.

And there I was shacked up with Eileen in that filthy
fourth floor attic on Hudson Street. I use the phrase advisedly
because there was something positively indecent about our
relationship. I felt it and it ate on me all the time, but I didn't
know how right I was till later.

What I did know was that Precious was always around.
He slept in the hall bedroom at the head of the stairs. "Who
do you think pays the rent? You wouldn't have me throw the
poor boy out on the street," Eileen said when I needled her
about it. I said sure that was what I wanted her to do but
she paid no attention. Eileen had a wonderful way of not
listening to things she didn't want to hear. Still I didn't
think she was twotiming me with Precious right then. To be
on the safe side I never let Eileen get out of my sight day
or night.

Precious had me worried. I couldn't make out what his
racket was. I'd thought him a pimp or procurer but he didn't
seem to be. He was smooth and civil spoken but it seemed to
me there was something tough under his selfeffacing manner.
Still he let Eileen treat him like a valet. Whenever the place
was cleaned or a meal served it was Precious who did the
work.

I never could find out what his business was. He always
seemed to have money in his pocket. The phone had been dis-
connected but telegrams came for him and notes by special
messenger. Now and then he would disappear for several days.
"Connections" was all he would say with that smooth hurt
smile when I put leading questions. "Oh he's just an international spy," Eileen would shout with her screechy laugh.

Poor devil he can't have been too happy either. He got no
relief from drink because, though sometimes Precious would
buy himself a drink if he went out with us in the evening, he'd
leave it on the table untouched.

When I was in liquor I rode him pretty hard I guess. Occasionally if I pushed him too far he'd give me a look out of
narrowed eyes and the hard cruel bony skull would show

through that smooth face of his. "Some day," I told Eileen, "that guy will kill us both." She just wouldn't listen.

Getting drunk every night was the only way I could handle the situation. Eileen seemed to feel the same way. We still had that much in common. The trouble was drinking cost money. The way Eileen and I were hitting it up, we needed ten or fifteen dollars an evening. Eileen must have wheedled a little out of Precious. I raised some kale by hocking the good clothes I had left over from my respectable uptown life, but when that was gone I didn't have a cent. I don't know what we would have done if Pat O'Dwyer hadn't come to town.

Pat O'Dwyer looked like a heavier Jim. He had the same bullet head of curly reddish hair but he didn't have Jim's pokerfaced humor or his brain or his charm. He was a big thick beefy violent man. Now Pat may have been a lecher and a plugugly, but he was a good churchgoing Catholic and he loved his little sister. Those O'Dwyers had that Irish clannishness that made them stick together in spite of politics and everything.

Pat took Eileen and me out to dinner at a swell steak house and told us with tears in his eyes how happy he was we had come together again, "Whom God hath joined" etcetera. The O'Dwyers were real religious people except for Kate. Now it would be up to me to keep the little girl out of mischief. Pat had been worried as hell ever since she'd lost her job on that fashion magazine. It had gone big with the Hollywood girls when he told them his sister was an editor of *Art and Apparel*. How about me trying to help her get her job back?

All evening Eileen had been as demure as a little girl getting ready for her first communion. It just about blew us both out of the water when Eileen suddenly came out with what she came out with. "But brother I can't take a job right now," she said with her eyes on her ice cream, "I'm going to have a baby, Francis Xavier's baby, my own husband's baby."

My first thought was how had it happened so soon, but I counted back on my fingers and sure enough we'd been living together six weeks. Pat meanwhile was bubbling over with sentiment. Greatest thing that ever happened. Now Eileen really would have to settle down to love honor and obey, and she'd have to quit drinking. He'd come East for the christening, by God he would. When we separated that evening Pat

pushed a hundred dollar bill into Eileen's hand to help towards
a layette.

Before he left town Pat saw to it that I was fixed up with a
job. Pat had contacts all over the labor movement. A friend of
Pat's named Frank Sposato had just muscled into the Portwatchers' Union.

The portwatchers were retired longshoremen and small time
seafarers off towboats and barges who acted as watchmen on
the wharves. Most of them were elderly men. It was responsible and sometimes dangerous work because the thieving is
awful in the port of New York. They weren't as well paid as
they should have been. One reason the portwatchers let
Sposato take them over was to get the protection of his muscle-
men.

Sposato needed a front, some labor stiff with a clean record
to act as business agent of the Redhook local. There I was a
retired wobbly and structural iron worker who'd never gouged
a cent off a fellow worker in my thirty years in the movement.
For once radicalism was a recommendation.

Sposato couldn't wait to get me hired. With my gray hair
and my weatherbeaten countenance I certainly looked the
honest working stiff. The things a man will do for a woman.
In spite of every principle I'd ever had in my life I let myself
be used as a front for labor racketeers. What broke my heart
was the way those honest old guys made a fuss over me. At
last, they kept saying, they had a working man for a business
agent, a man they could trust.

I tried to kid myself that it was just to find out what the
racketeers were up to so that I could expose them but I knew
damn well it was to get money for drink. Eileen and me we
couldn't stand ourselves sober. If it hadn't been for her gush
about how I had to make a living for my baby that was coming I never would have been able to look myself in the face.
That wasn't any excuse. It wasn't too long before I got my
comeuppance and believe me I deserved it.

My pay was twentyfive a week on the books and that was
all right because I had to see to keeping up the local and hiring lawyers for compensation cases and checking on the dues
every month; but Sposato had installed himself as treasurer
and he'd let drop a few extra tenspots or so for expense money
and no questions asked. He knew I'd go and get drunk with it.

That suited him all right. He wanted me keeping my nose out of union affairs.

Eileen and I stayed drunk enough to satisfy any goddam racketeer in the business. Eileen was a bottomless pit. There were times when I thought she was deliberately trying to provoke a miscarriage.

We sure drank ourselves into a cocked hat that summer. The nights were the old round of hell cruising from bar to bar with Eileen moving around the table picking up men it would be up to me to get rid of. Luckily I've always been pretty handy with my fists or I'd have been fighting every night. It got so I just followed her around like a professional bouncer warning the guys off. Most of them were pretty understanding about it. Now and then I hit an ugly one and had to give him a poke. Fortunately the really tough guys saw that I was in earnest and laid off. To tell the truth having to take care of her kept me from getting as drunk as I wanted to. Eileen complained I was spoiling her social life.

It was a hot summer. We'd wake up around noon with the screaming jeebies in that oven of an attic and there would be Precious mounting guard like a corpsman. Sometimes he went out and got us bromoseltzer or a hair of the dog. It wasn't any picnic for him either.

Everything came to a head the night Eileen gave us both the slip. It was in a Greenwich Village joint called Alfredo's on Eleventh Street. It was one of the nights Precious came along. Eileen had been wilder than usual all through dinner and we'd both been working on her to take it easy.

"You both act like my brothers." She suddenly blew up in our faces and went stalking off to the ladies' room. Next thing we knew Eileen was climbing into a cab with a college boy she'd picked up at the bar.

I ran out but they were already rounding the corner. I jumped into another hack and tried to get the driver to follow but the light caught him on Seventh Avenue. We couldn't tell whether the cab had gone uptown or down. Nothing to it but to go back to Alfredo's. I'd paid the check after dinner and when I got back I hadn't a cent in my pocket for the hackdriver.

Luckily Precious was still there sitting at the table staring straight ahead of him with his skull showing through his face. There wasn't any meanness in the look he gave me. There was

even a kind of a pained grin on his mouth when he ordered
me a martini. Eileen had insisted on martinis with dinner and
gotten me started on them though I'm a whiskey drinker myself. Right at that moment I wasn't drunk. I'd been sobered
like by a punch in the jaw.

It took me a while to make out what he was trying to tell
me. Of course I knew Eileen was going to have a child. Wasn't
I the father? But I didn't know that Precious knew.

Precious was spreading out a blue slip of paper on the table
in front of me. I remember his small neat feminine hands with
tapering fingers. It was a report from the maternity clinic of
St. Vincent's Hospital. Pregnancy test: positive. Something
like that. He was carefully pointing out the date with a neatly
clipped clean fingernail. May 15. The Kentucky Derby hadn't
been till the twentieth.

"It is my responsibility," Precious said stiffly. "That is why I
stay."

I opened my mouth but I couldn't find any words. It was
like once when I'd been in an earthquake in some damn little
jungle port in the Philippines and the whole damn house had
fallen on our heads; of course it was just wicker and bamboo
and thatch or I wouldn't have lived to tell the tale.

"Which of us is the worst sucker? Me or you, Precious?"

He shrugged instead of answering and his face took on that
smooth oval look. He ordered up some more martinis. I could
see he was deliberately getting me drunk, but I didn't give a
damn. When I get drunk enough I'll give Precious a poke in
the jaw was what I kept telling myself.

Meanwhile he was sitting there pumping me about what I
knew about Eileen's friends and Kate and Pat O'Dwyer and
Frank Sposato and the guys who worked in the local of the
portwatchers union—particularly Kate; he wanted everything
about Kate. What the hell, I can spin a yarn as quick as the
next man. I gave him an earful. I kept talking and talking trying to find out what the guy was driving at. I tried to set traps
for him but he was too smooth. He was some kind of stoolie or
spy, I was sure of that now, but I wanted to know what his
racket was.

Every time I finished a martini he'd order two more. When
I'd finished mine he'd shove me over his. I kept telling myself
I'd better go easy but I couldn't stop and the joint began to

spin and all at once I heard myself roaring at him "And now Mr. Ballestre it's about time you got off the earth."

I took a swing at him but the guy was light on his feet. It never connected. Faces, mirrors, bar kept spinning around. I couldn't keep my eye on Precious. Instead I was exchanging fisticuffs with Alfredo's bouncer, a big slob of a two hundred and fifty pound wop named Nicolo. I was too busy with Nicolo to see what happened to Precious. Next thing I knew I was riding in the paddy wagon with a big sweaty cop on either side. They treated me all right. One of 'em grumbled that my friend had told them to treat me like a gentleman. "Precious is a good friend to have," said the other cop. "If it hadn't been for him we'd have beaten the shit out of you."

I was getting sleepy and yawning. It was all very gentlemanlike. I could tell I was getting red carpet treatment. They booked me for drunk and disorderly and put me in one of the clean cells they kept for distinguished visitors and to show welfare workers and I was out like a light.

Next morning I'd hardly come to when there was Benny O'Dwyer standing over me with a bondsman to bail me out. When I asked him how the hell he knew he said Precious had called him last night.

"Who the hell's this Precious?" I asked Benny.

"Precious's an investigator."

"Who's he investigating for?"

"Why the hell should I know? He's an investigator like I'm a bookie. Why should I know who his customers are?"

Benny took me over to a lunchroom and filled me up with hot coffee.

"Blackie," he said, "it always seems to me you were a natural born seafaring man. Sailors on land are continually in trouble. Suppose you go down to a hiring hall and ship. You and her drinking yourselves to death isn't going to help Eileen any. Precious told me the whole story. He's got friends who'll fix up your little misdemeanor so I'll get my bail back."

"What business is it of his?"

"I'll tell you one thing," said Benny slowly. "His people are Sicilians and you know they're kind of vengeful. Precious could get you bumped off as easy as eating his breakfast. I don't know if I'd blame him much. It might be the simplest thing."

Benny said it in that nice affectionate way he had, but I

could see that he meant it. I began to think maybe he was
right. I was fed up with New York. I wouldn't have gone near
Eileen again if she'd been the last woman on earth. Thelma
was shut of me, and a good riddance I guess she was thinking.
I had a headache and a sick stomach and I didn't give a good
goddam what happened to me. If I cleared out of that union
racket and went back to work I could at least look myself in
the face as an honest man again.

Benny wasn't taking any chances. He took me down to the
hiring hall in a cab and didn't let me out of his sight until I'd
found my able seaman's papers in my wallet and signed on a
brand new Texaco tanker called the *Lonesome Star,* clearing
for Maracaibo.

Documentary (8)

AMAZING GROWTH

How Americans Reached a New High in Well-being in a Single Decade

"We may as well admit," a clothing worker wrote his congressman, "we are living in a labor autocracy. Graft, Rackets,
Intimidation, Stealing, Goons, etc. . . . For fear of being
bumped off, beaten, ostracized, or deprived of making a living
I'm afraid to sign my name. I know many others like me."

SHORT CUTS TO EXECUTIVE SKILLS

> *one by one you'll acquire the important skills that
> mark "the man on the way up"—skills in getting
> along with people—creating new ideas—understand-
> ing business figures—winning new friends wherever
> you go—speaking in public*

IF THE COMMUTER TRAINS STOP RUNNING

Called a geoscope, the globe will be suspended

inside a glass room. It is intended to provide a better comprehension of world geography to help architects plan their work in a larger perspective.

Dr. Fuller said the trouble with conventional globes was that they were built with latitudes and longitudes, which represent areas of the world by spherical squares. "However, you cannot put a square on a sphere," he pointed out.

THE AMAZING POTENTIALITIES OF MEMORY

through the combined volunteer services and facilities of American business, advertising agencies, publishers, broadcasting stations, millions of dollars have been spent to bring that message to millions of people

"We cannot help ourselves as our servants have become our masters."

INVESTIGATOR'S NOTES I

The small gray man pops into the hotel room and shuts the door sharply behind him. He shoots frightened glances around the walls, into the bathrom, through the halfopened door, under the bed even, and starts trotting back and forth like a hamster in a cage. His little clawlike hands have some brown stain on them.

The investigator sits behind the cardtable he's using for a desk.

"Would you give me your full name Mr . . . Mr?"

"Not now."

The little man pants out his words wheezily. He stops his pacing and faces the investigator. He bares his small yellow teeth, runs his stained fingers through his white mane of hair. "Bymby . . . If Congress gives protection, I can supply everything . . . names, photostats, records . . . for fiftyfive years I live in this city. Keep record see? . . . of racketeers . . . not even best frien' know. If somebody know someday squeal and

. . ." He makes a gesture with his thumbnail across his wind-pipe.

The investigator offers him a cigarette. He snatches it and starts puffing on it greedily.

"Fiftyfive years I live in this city and still I don't talk English good. You call me Nick. All Greeks called Nick." He pants out a tiny wheezy laugh. "I come from old country at seventeen. My heart full of liberty. In old country poor and hungry but we have liberty in the heart. At seventeen I come to this country. What a wonderful country for the working man! What a wonderful city!

"First I shine shoes. Kick back plenty nickels to wop boss but still I eat good. Wop he kick back dollar bills to a guy named Joe, padrone of that block, but still he eat good. Then I get job waiter. Kick back tips headwaiter. Headwaiter he pay protection to Gentleman Jim. I work in restaurant right near City Hall . . . protection cost plenty . . . but still I eat good. In 1916 I wanna get married. To better myself I take a job moving picture machine operator at twenty dollars a week. I marry in just one room with victrola . . . I remember only record we had: 'Gigolo, gigolo.'

"To better myself I join union. What a wonderful country for the working man I tell wife. Man can join union to better himself. For long time union OK but then come repeal of prohibition . . . bootleggers out of work, Capone gang, the syndicate . . . Kickback, shakedown, protection all the same. All the hoodlums making big money selling protection to theatre owners. Bomb twentyseven theatres in one winter. Owners fight back. Hire lawyers, bribe politicians, stir up district attorney, police. Big row in newspapers. Maybe you remember? Seven men went to pen for extorting a million dollars from theatre owners.

"Hoodlums make big discovery see? More money in shaking down the working man. Little man can't fight back. Already in 1927 with sound, new operators needed. At first they need one operator for projector and one operator for sound track. Invisible empire already muscled into International. Hoodlums start putting in relative, brother, son, nephew. Everybody else pays for permit. New men hired for sound had to kick back ten percent or more to union to work. If you ask for accounting of union funds they laugh in your face. Elections? Who's going to vote against the man with the club?"

"Why you take this lying down?" you say.

"That not true—me and my friends we fight. We have liberty in our hearts, see? That's how I lost my savings. We take it to court. Sue business agents and city officials in cahoots. Sending Capone to jail didn't change a thing. Hoodlums went respectable, got smart, see? Only much safer to extort money from union members. If you wanna work you gotta pay . . ."

The investigator is fiddling with his pencil. He's doodling on his pad instead of taking notes. A ridiculous little man; too emotional; maybe he's paranoid, maybe he's making it all up; won't make a good witness, the investigator is thinking.

"See what happen."

The whitehaired moving picture machine operator spreads his stained hands in front of him as if parting curtains on an invisible screen. He throws back his head of white hair. His talk becomes a torrent. He stumbles over words, repeats himself, keeps stopping to look up dates and figures in a little notebook. He reads the notebook inside his jacket so that the investigator shan't see it. What a ridiculous little man, thinks the investigator, but in spite of himself he's listening. In spite of himself, he himself is suffering, living, undergoing the little man's story.

The little Greek has a friend, another Nick. The two Nicks pool their savings to pay the retainer of a highclass lawyer. Two Nicks against the hoodlums.

Here the story gets tangled up in a long explanation. Couldn't have done it if their families weren't out of school, grown up, on their own, see? One of their griefs was they couldn't get their sons in the union. The hoodlums wanted all the jobs for their own. When this Nick's son came out of the army his war record didn't help him with that bunch. Already had an apprentice's permit. This Nick got the unanimous approval of the union local and the executive board. The son had passed an exam for a license but the higherups wanted too much money. He was scared even if he paid they'd find some excuse for taking the money and still not let him work.

The two Nicks decide they'll clean up the union. They got this highclass lawyer telling them what to do. You demand an accounting at the next business meeting, says the highclass lawyer. So Nick gets up and makes a motion: Union treasurer must make monthly statements of income, funds in bank, expenditure (at that time the members don't even know how much salary the business agents get paid) and the other Nick seconds it.

The BA is the quiet kind. "A motion has been made and seconded . . . Any discussion?" he asks. You can feel somebody staring down the back of your neck. Two squarefaced men in square double-breasted suits nobody has ever seen before come shuffling round the ends of the seats with their backs to the wall until they look you square in the face. Each one of these men, he's got his hand in his hip pocket.

"No discussion?" asks the BA, kind of joshing. "Then we'll put it to a rising vote. Those in favor will stand up and be counted."

The men nobody has ever seen before stand there, with their hands in their hip pockets, just looking.

You want to get to your feet but your legs won't work.

"All opposed," shouts the BA and you all get up. It feels all right when you all get up together.

"Meeting adjourned," shouts the BA. Going down the stairs everybody edges away from the two Nicks.

"Intimidation," says the highclass lawyer. "You've got a constitution and bylaws. We'll take it to court."

The case drags on for twentyseven months and then it's lost in the lower court, but the highclass lawyer appeals and the appellate court sends it back to the lower court.

The original judge must have been reached—looks like there wasn't a man in this man's town the syndicate couldn't reach —because he invites us all into chambers.

"What the hell are you trying to do?" he asks, "put the judge on trial?"

And the BA's lawyer starts sweet talk about how it's just a misunderstanding and how he's sure it will all be ironed out at the next union meeting and the highclass lawyer falls for it and says his clients of course will meet them halfway.

Halfway hell. Just listen now. Nick's friend, the other Nick, he gets a telephone call to go to the BA's office to talk about putting the union finances on a more satisfactory footing. This Nick goes to Tony the barber to get a shave and a haircut before his appointment. Wants to be all nice and cleaned up before he goes to talk to the high brass see?

You stay in the barbershop reading the *Police Gazette*.

The other Nick he ain't been gone ten minutes when a cop comes in to arrest you as a material witness. He says the other

Nick tried to shoot the BA and the BA shot him dead in self-defense. Sure enough. There Nick was lying in his blood with his gun in his hand. The only thing was he didn't have no gun.

Tony the barber was a good boy and he was ready to testify Nick didn't have no gun when he sat with his coat off in the barber-chair but down at the courthouse they didn't call no witnesses. They charged the BA with homicide and they didn't call no witnesses but the cop on the beat, and the BA pleaded selfdefense and walked out a free man.

The highclass lawyer lost interest in the case after that. Nick's money had run out anyway. All that happened was that you were thrown out of work and you hadn't worked since.

"Understand?" Nick points his finger in the investigator's face. "If they knew I'd come into this hotel to talk to you the same thing would happen to me that happened to my frien'."

"Would you come to Washington to testify if I requested?"

"I'm seventytwo years old. For thirty years I keep every record. Why should I worry? All I want is to get what's due me from the welfare fund so I can go back to old country to see the graves of my parents . . . Me, I still got liberty in my heart, but the old woman she scared . . . not well . . . all she wants is go back to old country to see the graves of our parents."

With stained shaking fingers he writes his name and address and telephone number on the investigator's pad.

When the little Greek had put on his frayed overcoat and shaken hands and gone, the investigator yawned. He lighted a cigarette and crushed it out in the ashtray. Smoking too much. Too damn hot in here. He pushed open the window and stood looking down at the neon signs in the street below and the slow traffic all jumbled light and dark by wet dancing snowflakes.

Got to watch out for nuts, he told himself. Even if he's straight he wouldn't be a good witness . . . Persecution complex . . . probably paranoid.

He yawned. His head ached. It had been a heavy day. He shoved his notes into his briefcase and stretched out for a nap before dinner on the bed.

At breakfast next morning an item in the morning paper caught his eye:

ELDERLY MAN SLAIN BY MUGGERS

> Michael N. Papadopoulos, 75, of 18567 N 63rd
> Street, was found dead on the snowy sidewalk out-
> side his home by Patrolman H. C. Connors of the
> 77th Precinct at a late hour last night . . .

The investigator dropped the paper and reached for his
briefcase. That was the name and address all right. Then he
called up the morgue. A son had claimed the body. No information forthcoming.

Explaining patiently that he was an investigator for a Congressional Committee he made call after call. At last he
reached a police captain with an intelligent voice.

Undoubtedly a robbery. No. No little notebook was found
in the inside pocket of the old man's jacket. All the pockets
had been rifled. It was possible that death had resulted from a
heart attack, though there were signs of a beating by his assailant.

How about the assailant? Any clews?

The investigator suggested that he might give them a lead:
union racketeers.

The police captain's voice became plaintive: Have a heart.
This was a big city. These things happened every night. . . . A
needle in a haystack. There was absolutely no doubt, no sir,
that robbery was the motive.

The investigator hung up.

Organizer

When John L. Lewis retired at eighty
as President of the United Mine Workers,
the heavyweight orator of American labor was universally
acclaimed as the mightiest organizer of them all.

Born in the shadow of a minetipple
in Lucas, a miners' shantytown in southeastern Iowa,
the eldest of eight,

son of a classconscious Welshman on the black books of the
coal companies for proselytizing for the Knights of Labor,
and an Iowa schoolteacher,
John L was raised on righteous indignation.

From the time he could toddle he was the leader of a
gang of burly brothers. At gradeschool in Des Moines, where
his father, barred from employment as a miner on account of
his radical utterances, eked out a living as nightwatchman at
the county jail, John L sold newspapers and did odd jobs to
help the family budget.

No chance for highschool. Too many mouths to feed at
home. At fifteen he went to work in a mine.

When he was seventeen the family moved back to Lucas.
Whether it was that the hearts of the coal operators had been
softened by the silvery trumpetings of William Jennings Bryan
against the vested interests in the past fall's presidential campaign, or whether the triumph of McKinley's "full dinner pail"
increased the demand for soft coal,
the black list was forgotten,
and Thomas Lewis and his two eldest sons went to work for
the Big Hill Coal and Mining Company.

Leadership came naturally as breathing to John L.
He got up debates among the young miners and managed a
baseball team. He read everything he could lay his hands on.
He interested the local physician's daughter, Myrta Bell, in
helping him get an education. With her he read Shakespeare
and Milton and practiced composition and public speaking.
He was damned if he'd wear out his life and his lungs digging
coal the way his father had. He thrashed around for better
paid employments. He tried managing the local operahouse,
running a mill. He lit out for the West.

For several years round the turn of the century he wandered from job to job:—through gold camps, silver mines, copper towns from Arizona to Utah to Wyoming—hoping to strike
it rich.

Those were the days when the Structural Iron Workers and the Western Federation of Miners waged the class war
Wild West style with sixshooters and dynamite.

John Lewis was tough as the next man.

Tall tales filled Lucas of how he'd swum the Big Horn River in full flood, how he had helped carry out the bodies after the mine disaster at Hannah, Wyoming, how he'd killed a balky mine mule with one blow of his fist, how he was training for the prize ring.

When he strode back through his hometown streets a burly curlyhaired young man of twentysix, full of muscle and beans and the gift of gab.

the miners elected him their delegate to the United Mineworkers convention,

and Dr. Bell gave him his daughter in marriage.

In 1909 John L moved the family (five brothers followed him) to the Montgomery coal field at Panama, Illinois. There the Lewises took over the local union (his brothers always did what John L said) and elected John L president. His wife helped with his speeches.

He became the state legislative agent of the Illinois miners; when a hundred and sixty miners were killed in a single accident in the Cherry mine, John L laid it on the line to the legislators at Springfield. By the sheer lungpower of his roaring indignation he pushed through a series of safety bills and a workman's compensation act.

At their Indianapolis convention in 1911 the craft unionists of the AF of L were balky about granting charters to the mineworkers' industrial unions. John L got next to Gompers. Wily old Gompers knew a good organizer when he saw one. John L got his charter and Gompers appointed him field representative and legislative representative

for the AF of L.

By 1916, with the world war looming, John L was serving as president pro tem of the UMW of A. His formal position was Chief Statistician. He moved his family to the Indianapolis headquarters. He was elected vice-president. The president was a drinking man. Evil tongues claimed that John L kept Frank Hays drunk on purpose so that he could run the presidency himself.

When the coalminers struck in 1919 John L, as acting president, had his first run in with the federal government. Woodrow Wilson claimed the strike was unlawful, and John L thundered back in his throaty voice:

"I am an American free born, with all the pride of my

heritage. I love my country with its institutions and traditions. With Abraham Lincoln I thank God that we have a country where men may strike. May the power of my government never be used to throttle or crush the efforts of the toilers to improve their material welfare and elevate the standards of their citizenship."

The power of the government was used to do just that. Judge Anderson issued an injunction in federal court and found the miners in contempt. John L and William Green hurried to Washington hat in hand and received a dressing down from schoolmaster Wilson.

John L took refuge in a cloud of righteousness: "I will not fight my government, the greatest government on earth." He called off the strike, but he had learned enough of Washington ways to manage to get a commission appointed which eventually awarded the miners a 14% increase in wages.

In 1920 John L took over the presidency of the United Mineworkers with a salary of $5000 a year in time to face the disastrous strike and lockout in the West Virginia coalfields.

Strikebreaking was a profession in those days. The operators hired gunmen;

fifty thousand miners were evicted from company houses. No help from the Red Cross. The miners had ammunition and rifles. It was fullfledged war with skirmishes and ambushings in the West Virginia hills until the army moved in.

The strike was broken.

In Pennsylvania the Coal and Iron Police enforced the open shop.

These were years of defeat. In 1921 John L. Lewis was beaten 2 to 1 when he tried to oust the aging Gompers as President of the AF of L. John L and Gompers weren't such good friends after that.

In the coalfields atrocity answered atrocity.

In Herrin, Illinois striking miners besieged a bunch of men whom they alleged were scabs working a stripmine. They bombarded them with dynamite from an airplane and demanded their surrender.

Governor Small might have averted the massacre by sending in the National Guard, but Governor Small was preoccupied that day, in court at Waukegan to respond to a charge that he'd misappropriated a million and a half dollars of the public funds.

When the men working the stripmine threw up their hands and came out

the people of Herrin shot them down with no more compunction

than if they'd been groundhogs,

(John L blamed the Communists). The coroner's jury found the man who hired the scabs

responsible for their deaths. Williamson County was miners' territory.

Inside his own union

John L. Lewis suppressed insurrections with a heavy hand. In district after district he suspended autonomy. A man who spoke out of turn would be tossed out of meeting. He exposed Frank Farrington as an agent of the Peabody Coal Company. John Brophy he threw out as a dreamy idealist. It wasn't till 1932 that he had thoroughly subjected the Illinois locals to his rule.

These were depression years. Labor unions were in retreat. Overproduction was strangling the coal industry. The market was shrinking. John L's union miners made $7.50 as against $3 in the nonunion mines but they didn't work every day. Operators who paid a fair wage found it hard to compete.

Franklin Roosevelt's first inaugural was followed by the hundred days of the adolescence of the New Deal. The Democrats were discovering the labor vote. John L hailed Section 7a of the National Recovery Act as Labor's Magna Carta. "The President wants you to join the union," was his word to the working man.

Membership in the United Mineworkers increased fourfold in one summer. John L negotiated the First Appalachian Agreement to cover the whole industry. Four hundred thousand miners paid dues. John L spent their money to organize the Committee for Industrial Organization.

His moment had come to organize all labor into industrial unions. What the wobblies had dreamed, John L's heavy-handed management began to put into effect. He knew what was good for the working people better than they knew it themselves. Come one come all. In his need for trained organizers he welcomed Communists, Socialists, bourgeois radicals, popeyed idealists.

The craft unions put up a resistance. John L and bullying Bill Hutcheson the carpenters' boss fought with their fists on the platform of the 1935 convention of the AF of L in Atlantic City. "Congratulations, sock him again," a delighted carpenter wired John L.

Franklin Roosevelt rode into office for his second term on a surge of trade union organization. John L saw to it that the organization he controlled contributed mightily to the Democrat campaign. "I see a third of the nation illhoused, illclad and illnourished," Roosevelt declared in his second inaugural. John L thought he had the President in his pocket.

John L. Lewis felt the equal of presidents. From Washington he directed the organization of American labor. He disposed of immense sums of money. He was wrapped in the folds of Old Glory. Wherever the class war raged he was there with his hoarse exhortations. Sitdown strikes in rubber in Akron, in automobiles in Flint and Detroit. Unrest in steel. The solution was industrywide unions. Labor was taking the offensive. The leader of insurgent Labor was the most powerful man in the country.

Too powerful for the President, Franklin Roosevelt, who began to remember that he was President of the nation entire. Sitdowns infringed the rights of private property. When industry fought back organizing meant riot and bloodshed. "A plague on both your houses," Roosevelt cried out in a speech in June 1937.

John L's righteous indignation was volcanic:

"It was in that winter," he confided in Saul Alinsky his biographer, "when we were gripped in fatal conflict with the organization of General Motors that I discovered the depths of deceit, the rank dishonesty and the doublecrossing character of Franklin Delano Roosevelt."

Labor Day he let the President have it: "It ill behooves one who has supped at Labor's table and who has been sheltered in Labor's house to curse with equal fervor and fine impartiality both labor and its adversaries when they become locked in deadly embrace."

In 1940 John L came out against a third term: "We want

no royal family"; Roosevelt was the warmonger. The Communists, bound by the Hitler-Stalin pact, flocked around to cheer. The tipsters said it was hope of the vice-presidency that brought him to endorse Wendell Willkie.

Meanwhile Franklin Roosevelt was hiring John L's industrial organizers right out from under him. Lee Pressman was high up in the New Deal. Sidney Hillman was the President's right hand. Hitler's invasion of the Soviet Union cut off support from the Communists. Stalin needed quick help. Warmonger Roosevelt became the Communists' god. Liberals, radicals, idealists all flocked in their trail. Warwork meant primarily help for the Soviets to many a Washington bureaucrat. Undermined in his own CIO John L. Lewis suffered a heart attack. He resigned as president the fall of Roosevelt's re-election.

Pearl Harbor found him moving his organizers into the steel companies' own private mines. He reached out again for Old Glory and tried to use the war emergency as a pretext for merging the AF of L with the CIO, under control of John L. Lewis of course. The Roosevelt men were too smart for him. Raging and ranting he led his own union out of the CIO. Lewis and his miners would go it alone.

It took courage to buck the liberal-communist propaganda machine and the wartime powers of the presidency. It took courage to go back to his pleasant eighteenth century frame house in Alexandria the day he buried his wife Myrta who had been the companion of his heart for thirtyfive years. Courage. John L. Lewis was a lonely man.

Dr. Win-the-War was taking the place of Dr. New Deal in Franklin Roosevelt's radio addresses. Alphabetical agencies multiplied in Washington. In 1943 the WLB froze coalminers' wages while the OPA awarded the coal operators a price raise of 23 cents a ton. The miners rebelled; wildcat strikes ran through the coalfields. Franklin Roosevelt ordered the men back to work. John L. Lewis raised his great bushy gray eyebrows and found the strikes quite regrettable.

Meeting the Appalachian soft coal operators in New York to negotiate a new contract he demanded portal to portal pay. When they balked he announced very quietly that war or no war his miners would refrain from trespassing on the mineowners' property until the mineowners signed a contract to his liking.

As Secretary of the Interior Harold Ickes seized the mines for the government. The miners went back to work. The operators refused to sign. The miners struck again. Back came Harold Ickes to run up the Stars and Stripes over the pitheads. In each skirmish John L gained ground. And so it went on. By the end of the war John L was the real boss of the coal industry. His miners were the best paid workers in America.

Under Truman the campaign continued. Now they were striking for fringe benefits, welfare and retirement funds, hospitalization. The press was against them. Washington was against them. In 1946 Judge Goldsborough levied a fine of three and a half million dollars against the United Mine Workers for disregarding his injunction and nicked John L personally for ten thousand. The Supreme Court supported the judge.

The union paid and John L paid. They could afford to. Through his control of the union funds John L had become a sizable figure in the financial world. He founded banks. He bailed out ailing coal companies. He used his influence with management to back modernization and laborsaving machinery. He ruled his unions with a heavy hand. To mine coal you had to mind John L. He reduced the size of the labor force engaged in mining by tens of thousands.

The remaining mineworkers thought what John L wanted them to think. He was boss. Before he gave his orders they were already doing what he told them to do. He priced his product out of many a market, but when,

weighed down by the years he retired,

his miners,

from being serfs of the mineowners forever in hock to the company store,

had become the top aristocracy

of the best paid working class in history.

2.
A Creature That Builds

Man is a creature that builds
institutions
  out of abnegation of lives linked for a purpose
  the way the flowerlike polyps, the coralmakers of the warm
salt seas
  build
  from incrusted layers of discarded careers:
  niggerheads, atolls, great barrier reefs
  and coquina benches forming the limestone basements of
peninsulas where civilizations flourish and flower and fall
frazzled to seed.

Man's institutions fashion his destiny,
  as the hive, the nest, the hill, the sixsided cellular comb of
the honeybee, serried, tiered,
  grouped according to impulses
  inherent in the genes,
  fashion the social insect, his castes and functional diversities:
  the winged males and females, the blind workers, the soldiers, the nasuti, the alternates of the "fourth caste"
  of the pale termites,
  dwellers in dark,
  whose complex society has so astonished the
naturalists.

Institutions, so the sociologists tell us,
shape man's course.
  as the comings and goings of the hardshelled ants—their
diligence since the dawn of philosophy has delighted the
makers of fables and the pointers of morals—are
  predetermined by instinct.

Institutional man,
like the termites and the social insects among the hymenop-
tera, must, we are told, sacrifice individual diversity for diversity of caste. (Already in his bureaucratic form, with a
diligence which would astonish any uncommitted naturalist,
institutional man accumulates
    in vaults and cabinets and files,—
    paper,
    the same paper the polistes wasp builds his
house of
    and the termites of the tropical uplands
    their towering castles.)

Lecturing on "Social Insects" the late Professor Wheeler of
Harvard used to point out with some malice to his students
    that the ants,
    too,
    in spite of the predestined perfection
of their institutions,
    suffered what he called "perversions of
appetite."
    Their underground galleries and storied
domes
    are infested by an array of lethal creatures, thieves and
predators, scavenger crickets, greedy roaches and rove beetles,
and one particular peculiarly plumed little bug
    which secretes in its hair an elixir so
delectable to antkind
    that the ants lose all sense of self- or
species-preservation
    and seek death in its embrace.

Documentary (9)

Sog Is an Element Released by Ice Cubes in Contact with Gin and Vermouth

BEYOND THE RIM

as a precaution however the peephole may be covered on the inside by a small piece of window glass which will plug the hole completely for electrons

NEW SPLIT SNAGS RACKETS HEARING

Dining well, like so many of the leisurely pleasures of life, calls for a relaxed and worryfree frame of mind. An organization like ours can make a surprisingly large contribution to this desirable mental state. How? By taking over major responsibility for the direction of your investment program, for example, and by providing sound guidance on many other phases of family financial planning.

HUSH HOUSE CUTS JETS' ROAR TO A WHISPER

and a complete line of silencers and acoustical systems for all industry, including silencers for gas turbines and snort valves

THE SEX GAS OF HYDRA
a wire and cable story

. . . for example boron carbide, a starting point for high energy rocket fuels . . . zirconium carbide,

119

today's highest melting point material available in
tonnage quantities . . . titanium and silicon carbide,
key metallurgical additives . . . They have gained
importance as rich chemical source materials . . .
as high temperature electrical conductors and re-
sistors . . . and as refractories and cermet com-
ponents . . .

WE HAVE MANY OPENINGS IN CHALLENGING AND REWARDING WORK

*The Story Behind Our Growth Is One of Total
Engineering—in Which We Tackle All Controlling
Factors to Produce Complete Systems or Single
Units Perfectly Mated to the Products They Control*

The Big Office

There were still little red schoolhouses in southern
Indiana when Frank Worthington was a boy.

Frank was an only child but his people raised him to work.
Neither his father or mother was idle a minute. His mother
was forever busy over the stove or setting hens or feeding the
ducks or caring for a weak calf or the wabblylegged lambs.
Even when she sat resting beside the student lamp after
putting away the last of the supperdishes there would be a
pile of mending at her feet and the needle would still go
flicking through the cloth while her eyes looked up blue and
loving through her spectacles at Frank or Dad tramping back
into the house after the chores.

Dad was a restless frowning lanky man, on the go from
morning till night. He farmed forty acres of sandy land. He
sold guano. He kept a small livery stable and was a partner
in the feed and grain business redfaced old jellybellied Josiah
Twig carried on at the gristmill on Still Creek back of the
Worthingtons' barn. They customground flour and corn and
retailed a series of feeds in bags labeled Worthington's Special.
There was never a month when Dad wasn't behind on his bills.

Dad was always trying something new to make ends meet, either raising broilers on some newfangled system or experimenting with a fresh way to feed hogs. Once he bought seven Guernseys at a sheriff's sale on the theory that he could feed them on corn cobs and molasses and tried to set up a milk route into sleepy little Clairmount four miles away.

Every day of his life Dad laid out more work than he could finish. He tried to do everything himself with no help except a rheumatic old colored man named Charley who slept on a cot in the harness room and what help Frank could give him after school. No matter how hard they tried there were always chores left undone when they staggered in dead tired to bed.

School was Frank's haven of refuge. He was as far ahead with his lessons as he was behind with his chores. By the time he was eleven he was helping Mrs. Straughan keep the other children in order and hearing their lessons and even teaching school himself days when Mrs. Straughan was laid up with one of her numerous colds.

Frank's real liberation came when he started highschool in Clairmount. The Worthingtons had acquired an old Model T roadster. After milking Frank would load the heavy can on the platform that replaced the rumble seat over the rear axle and go chugging off along the rutted roads to the Clairmount Dairy. After school he would pick up the empties and drop by the depot to collect any supplies that might be consigned to the mill or the farm. He'd get back home in time for the evening chores.

When Frank graduated at sixteen he was a skinny gangling youth who kept a close mouth in spite of being captain of the debating team. He wrote a good hand. He had learned double entry bookkeeping. He was secretary of his class and delivered a commencement day address on the subject of the Golden Rule.

Not long after that he enlisted in the state militia. This was the spring Woodrow Wilson declared war on the Central Powers. Frank thought the world of Woodrow Wilson. His mother tried to hide her tears but Dad wrote out his consent with a flourish; wouldn't have had any son of his do any different, he said. Frank hadn't been long at the training camp before he was promoted to corporal, then sergeant. He made himself so useful as an instructor he never did get to go overseas. When the armistice came he was on his way to an officers' training camp in Northern Ohio.

Ohio was Frank Worthington's favorite state because Lillian Johnson lived in Portage. Lillian was a serious plainfaced girl who wore her sandy hair in braids round her head. From the minute they met each of them felt there was something especially fitting about the other. It was at a rally in Indianapolis where Lillian was selling war bonds with a group from her local YWCA. Frank had been detailed to the guard of honor for a parade celebrating the Third Liberty Loan. They danced together at the Red Cross canteen. After that they wrote each other almost every day.

The peace put an end to any prospect of a commission. For Frank it was a bitter disappointment.

When Frank got his discharge he took the first train to Portage to see Lillian. They had agreed they wanted to study to be schoolteachers. The question was whether they ought to get married right away or wait until after they graduated. Lillian's folks wanted her to wait. While she tried to make up her mind Frank found himself a job in one of the rubber shops building tires.

News from Clairmount promptly settled that argument. In the slump that came with the peace Dad's feed and grain business failed. Josiah Twig pocketed what assets there were and left for parts unknown, leaving Dad to face the debts. The day the farm and mill were sold at auction Dad suffered a crippling heart attack. Frank's mother moved him into town to the Clairmount House where she had been offered the job of housekeeper. That paid their board and lodging but it didn't help with the doctor's bills or the druggist. Frank had to send most of his paycheck to Clairmount every week.

Lillian took it like a trump. If Frank wasn't going to normal school she wasn't either. They might as well get married right away. She talked her parents around to her way of thinking. Lillian was the baby of the family. The other children had married and moved away. The Johnsons insisted that the young couple move in and live with them. They were tired of rattling around in their big house. Instead of losing a daughter they would gain a son. Until the old people passed away Frank and Lillian lived with the Johnsons with never an unkind word.

It was from Lillian's father that Frank learned about the labor movement. Old man Johnson was a retired locomotive engineer. He'd been a Knight of Labor in his youth. Debs was his hero. The day President Harding pardoned Eugene V. Debs, Ephraim Johnson sent them both telegrams of congratulation. Because Debs was a Socialist old Johnson always voted the Socialist ticket.

Frank wasn't too hard to convince that production for use might be the answer. He had seen Dad wear himself to pieces trying to make a success of free enterprise. When people talked about free enterprise, Frank used to say, the words reminded him of getting up before day zero mornings to milk or carrying swill to the hogs late at night when he wanted to be doing his homework. Or old Josiah Twig walking out to leave his father holding the bag. Frank wanted no part in it. Dog eat dog surely wasn't what Christ meant when he laid down the Golden Rule.

Frank was a natural born administrator. With the first half-hearted efforts to organize unions in the rubber shops he became deeply interested in Labor.

The Worthington girls were nine, seven and five when the depression hit Portage. The Consolidated plant where Frank had been making good money as a supervisor dragged along for a while on two or three days a week; then it closed for retooling—so the men were told—and Frank was out on the street with the rest of them. At that he was better off than most because the Johnsons' house was free and clear and the old man had his pension and Lillian still kept her job as receptionist in the office of one of Portage's successful physicians.

Frank was no man to sponge on his wife or his wife's folks. He walked the streets until he found a small plant making rubber heels where they needed a laborer to replace a man crippled in an accident. Nobody else wanted that job. It only paid forty cents an hour.

All his life Frank had hated physical work. He and Lillian had been dreaming of a promotion into the personnel director's office at Consolidated. Now it was as bad as when the war's sudden end robbed him of his commission. Frank began to think of himself as a failure. Here he was at thirty right back where he started.

Frank's foreman in that operation was a Kentuckian named Clinch Rodgers. There was something not quite ordinary about Clinch. The two men eyed each other for a couple of weeks then one evening they fell into step walking home along the same sidewalk. They hit it off right away.

Clinch had been a captain in the Marine Corps during the war. He'd seen action and plenty. He was all hot under the collar at the treatment the men in the rubber shops got from management. "Hillbillies, hell. If they are hillibillies I'm a hillbilly. Those are the boys who would walk through hell and high water for you overseas."

Frank said he'd tried to see both sides, but since he'd been laid off there was only one side so far as he was concerned. The depression had taught him his lesson. After that they would talk union walking home every night after work.

Franklin Roosevelt was elected President. The Wagner Act was passed. As employment picked up in the rubber shops everybody began to talk union. Business agents turned up at the plant gates. Frank was back building tires at Consolidated. He wouldn't have taken his old supervisor's job back if they'd offered it. He'd thrown himself heart and soul into organizing.

His old pleasure in public speaking came back. He found he could hold the men's attention by his quiet businesslike little talks. When the AF of L organized Consolidated, William Green himself picked Frank to be president of the local.

Meanwhile, over at All Purpose Tires, Clinch Rodgers was setting the men on fire. His was the kind of speaking the men from the coves and the creeks were accustomed to hear at camp meeting. When William Green came back to set up the International Union he saw to it that Clinch Rodgers became president and Frank Worthington vice-president.

When he started organizing it had been Frank Worthington's opinion that union officials ought to keep on working in the shop. He soon had to admit the idea wasn't practical. There weren't enough hours in the day.

Clinch Rodgers didn't have an idea in the world of management or administration. He depended on Frank to set up the big office, to find men capable of handling finances; to start departments to handle research in the prevention of accidents, time study, compensation; to find lawyers to draw up sample contracts for negotiating committees.

Paperwork, paperwork, paperwork.

Frank loved it, but he was slow. He liked to give each problem full attention. Each day was a fight against time. Always there was a full basket of unanswered mail. It would be late at night back home in a warm corner of the kitchen before he got a chance to figure out what he wanted to say in his next day's speeches.

Clinch Rodgers dreaded overhead. Their first International office was over a corner grocery store, in two rooms behind the noisy hall of the All Purpose local, where chairs were always being folded and unfolded and streams of men with gripes and grievances shuffled and stamped around the vending machines and the soft drink bar. Afternoons you could hear the rumble of balls and the crack of falling pins from the bowling alley out back. If Frank needed to have a quiet talk with some man half the time he'd have to take him to the drugstore across the street.

Frank fell so behind in his mail that Lillian gave up her job and came in to pinch hit as a secretary. Frank didn't think it would look right to pay her a salary. For the first time in their lives they went into debt.

The companies were still trying to pretend the unions weren't there. Frank began getting his men ready for a showdown. When they struck the Big Five, Clinch Rodgers, who had been mooning around the office with his great heavily veined hands dangling on his knees, was in his element again. He organized the strike like a military campaign, with supply depots, intelligence, forces in reserve, the longest picket line in history. His speaking stirred men to their guts. The sitdowns put the strike over the top.

Frank worked around the clock. Happily he had every kind of support at home. Lillian organized coffeestands. The girls threw themselves into lettering placards and streamers. Lillian's parents contributed to the strike fund and Ephraim Johnson insisted on walking the picket line, carrying an enlarged photograph of Eugene V. Debs at the end of a stick. The old gentleman was quite a sight out in the zero cold in his oldtime locomotive engineer's outfit with his ruddy cheeks and white hair and hale blue eyes. All the outoftown reporters wrote him up. They printed his picture in the illustrated magazines.

In some ways the union leaders were as astonished as the employers that they put their strike over. It brought about a change in attitude among the townspeople. Storekeepers and fillingstation attendants and even the tellers at the bank began to treat union members with respect.

John L. Lewis who had been in and out of town all through the struggle wanted the International Union in the new CIO. The rubber workers were the vaunted vanguard of Labor's majestic march out of the brutal bestialities of bondage, he shouted at a crowded mass meeting.

The organization spread like a prairie fire. Dues kept coming in from new locals. For the new International offices they rented half a floor in the city's newest officebuilding right across the street from the Portage Hotel.

At last Frank had a professional secretary and the protection of a switchboard. He could make sure that no man could take up his time who didn't have something important to say.

Now he could really give his attention to searching out the right man for the comptroller's office and for the department he set up to advise the locals on compensation cases. He hired a researcher on industrial accidents right out of Consolidated's personnel office. He found an economist in an elderly Austrian refugee from the social-democratic regime in Vienna who worked at the public library. Just the way business did he began looking for bright young men out of the colleges.

Frank was a natural born executive. He had his eye on every administrative detail from the daily bankbalance of the International to the per capita paid by the smallest member union.

It was the kind of life he'd always dreamed of leading. Out of the ten thousand dollar salary the executive board voted him he and Lillian began to pay off the mortgage they'd had to put on the old people's house. They were a frugal couple. It was more money than they had ever dreamed of; they began to buy farmland as an investment; they had to think of the girls.

Clinch Rodgers wouldn't hear of a salary. He promptly returned the checks they sent him each month. All he would take was expenses for the constant trips he made to help organize new locals. He didn't feel right sitting in an office he told Frank with a laugh. He had to be out speaking in halls, leading picket lines. A leader's place was out front.

When Clinch Rodgers left the office to drive down to organize a local in southern Alabama he told Frank not to worry, the people down there were his folks. He'd been raised with boys like that.

He found himself in a ramshackle hall the rubber workers had somehow managed to hire. There were tense white faces as he strode to the speaker's stand. He was set upon before he could open his mouth to speak. "Run the rednecks out of town." Pluguglies crowded around Clinch. His bare fists were no match for brass knuckles and hunks of lead pipe. Men with baseball bats cleared the hall. They beat him to the floor and left him there with a broken collarbone and a fractured skull.

No doctor in town would treat him. Friends had to drive him a hundred miles north to Birmingham for medical attention.

Going to see Clinch Rodgers in the hospital was one of the worst moments of Frank Worthington's life.

The room was dark. Clinch was under heavy sedatives. A hoarse voice Frank didn't recognize rumbled from among the bandages. "My own folks, the kind of men I've been raised with. The kind of men I've led in battle, how could they do this to me?" The man was shaking with horrible raucous sobs. The nurse made Frank leave the room.

That beating broke Clinch Rodgers. When months later he hobbled back to the office on a cane he seemed ashamed to show himself. He refused to attend the convention over at the Kalon Hotel that was called after the International went into the CIO. Though the men still idolized him Clinch refused to have his name proposed. Frank Worthington was elected president. Frank Worthington was elected to the national executive board of the CIO.

At the big office Frank kept improving his personnel. Personnel was his fetish. Now when company representatives tried to talk over his head at the bargaining table he had the staff to brief him on the answers.

The Worthingtons came of respectable stock. They were happy in the new position of respectability the union enjoyed. Frank couldn't keep up with the requests to speak. A nearby university made him a doctor *honoris causa*.

When the old Johnsons died Lillian used her share out of the sale of their property to buy a lot out near the Country

Club. They built themselves a neat Cape Cod cottage on it, plain, roomy and unassuming. They had to think of the girls growing up. Lillian was president of the PTA. She was in the League of Women Voters and was invited to join the Ladies' Garden Club. The girls were asked to the really nice dances.

Roosevelt's war brought a boom time to the rubber shops. Wages were frozen but overtime soared. The companies were rich. The unions were rich. Everybody had more money than they could spend. The economists had all been clucking their tongues about the depression that would follow the end of wartime spending. Instead of a depression a boom. Everybody wanted everything that could be bought. Lightheartedly the voters were getting ready to elect Harry Truman to the Presidency.

All through the war the big office had run smooth as cream. Grievance committees and safety committees functioned in the locals. Labor and management cooperated. When peace came Frank Worthington's brain trust urged him to set a pattern for industry. Wage increases. Fringe benefits. First round. Second round. Third round. Frank couldn't complain of his popularity with the rank and file.

As wages rose employment slackened. Overproduction. Assembly line methods. There began to be an uneasy feeling in the rubber shops. Men were beginning to talk of a six hour day to spread employment. Grumbling was heard in the locals; the International president was too aloof from the local leadership. When the local officials got to him with their gripes he fixed his eyes on the ceiling and talked about the overall picture.

As a CIO union the organization was democratic. Democracy meant politics. Frank Worthington loathed politics. A clean honest administration, he told his friends, should stand on its own merits.

At the convention called while Truman was campaigning the delegates met in sullen mood.

After Frank had been re-elected by only a handful of votes Grant Graham, the International's organizational director, dragged Frank away from the convention hall for a conference in a private room in a Chinese restaurant five miles out of town.

Grant was a large expansive man who dressed and acted

like an automobile salesman. Only from the powerful grip of his large hands could you tell he had once built tires himself. "Get wise Frank," Grant began pleading as soon as he'd closed the door behind the Chinese waiter. "We got to trim our fences or we'll lose the organization to the crooks and the crackpots. You got to go after the key men. Most of 'em would be for you, Frank, if you gave 'em encouragement."

Frank glared through his glasses into Grant's bulging bloodshot eyes. "What do you want me to do? Distribute patronage like a politician?"

"Exactly," said Grant Graham.

Frank pulled his thin lips tight and got to his feet and walked out of the room.

Frank Worthington had won the presidency but the executive board had fallen to the opposition. His stormiest year was ahead of him.

All through that winter Grant Graham kept leaving little notes on Frank's desk. A certain Jed Starbright, who had backed the man Frank had defeated for International president, was busy stirring up discontent in the locals. As regularly as he read them Frank tore up Grant's little notes into very small pieces and watched them flutter down into his waste basket.

Jed Starbright was president of a local in Doylesville, Pennsylvania. Frank had discovered irregularities in his financial reports. He was preparing charges against Starbright before the executive board. To keep the whole thing aboveboard he went down to Doylesville to address a membership meeting.

When he started to lay it on the line the members shouted him down. Starbright's men rushed the speaker's platform. The group from the big office held their ground. Grant Graham proved handy with his fists. Clothes were mussed, eyes were blacked, noses bloodied. When somebody put in a riot call the state troopers and the local police arrived. They escorted the International officers to their cars. None of them felt very proud of themselves as they drove home to Portage that night.

It was Grant Graham who brought in the news that Frank Worthington was being tried behind closed doors by the executive board in session in Cleveland. Frank was being accused of slandering local officials, of conspiring to deprive them of their rights, of bringing the International into disrepute by wild and unproved charges.

"But Grant those guys are crooks. I've got the evidence right here in my safe." Grant shrugged. "What's the use of evidence if they won't let you present it? You're tryin' to run a labor union like a Sunday school picnic. Frank, you make me tired."

Grant was right. The Starbright faction took over the executive board and removed Frank Worthington from office. Not militant enough was the story they gave out to the rank and file.

That afternoon, leaving fat foulmouthed Joe Biggs, the vice-president they'd put over on him along with the opposition executive board, hunched like a lump over the desk in the president's office, Frank went home in a taxicab. His hands were shaking so he didn't trust himself to drive his own car. He was cut off from his files, from the dictaphone that recorded his every word, from the quiet deference of his secretaries, from all the little administrative details that had become his life. His head was a fog.

A gabble of voices came from the livingroom. Lillian and the girls were busy with some sort of teaparty for visiting Hindu labor men. Frank brushed through the hall and down into the basement.

He had to find something to keep him busy. He had a bench and some tools under the window back of the furnace. He set to work putting up some shelves he had been planning for months. He worked on doggedly with the sweat running into his eyes. In his airconditioned office he hadn't realized that the afternoon was so hot. When Lillian came down to try to get him to eat some supper he just stared at her without saying a word. About nine o'clock that night Grant Graham found him down there planing numbly on a board.

Grant shouted so loud the rafters rang with his deep voice. "If you are goin' to take this layin' down Frank I'll be damned if I will."

Frank went on planing down his board.

"If somebody had come up to me and told me Frank Worthington was a quitter, by God I'd have punched him in the jaw." The metal latches on the basement windows rattled,

Grant roared so. "You've got your organization behind you one hundred percent, Frank. The staff's getting ready to walk out. The girls in the office want to strike."

Frank set down his plane and pulling his rolled shirtsleeves down over his thin arms walked over to Grant. He gave him an embarrassed little tap on the shoulder. "All right, feller," he said. "Let's go to work."

Grant loaded Frank Worthington into his caramelcolored Chrysler and drove him over to the Consolidated local. At Consolidated they had been solid for Frank all along. Grant had already latched hold of an office to be used as headquarters for a "Reinstate Worthington" campaign. Frank's fighting spirit rose as the Consolidated boys poured in to shake his hand.

Grant conducted an informal reception in that Consolidated office all summer. Kiddingly he called it his back office campaign. Shop-stewards, trustees, members of executive boards, union presidents, he saw to it that no union leader visited the big office without being detoured past Frank Worthington's desk. Whether they came from San Diego or from Texas or from New Jersey or Pennsylvania or Portland, Maine, Grant saw to it that every man who came to town to do business with the International got to shake Frank Worthington's hand.

As Organizational Director he headed up the field representatives who saw to organizing new unions or supervised small unions in marginal industries. The Field Reps, he kept pounding it into Frank's head, were their first line of defense.

Grant knew them all. He knew the industries they dealt with. He knew their wives' first names. He knew who'd gotten drunk with whom at the state conventions. He knew the amount of per capita each one was responsible for. He made each one of them feel that Frank Worthington considered him the indispensable man.

At the convention held in Montreal during the following fall the delegates again were sullen and restless, but this time their peeve was directed against the Starbright faction. To prove how militant he was Joe Little had pushed the seven All Purpose locals into a strike for a twentyfive cent raise and a six hour day. They had failed to make the strike industrywide. After six weeks they settled for the ten cent package the company had originally offered. The Portage

Press in a box on the front page added up the wages lost to each individual union member. With the loss to the companies and to the local merchants they came out with a staggering figure. Joe Biggs's reply trying to disprove the newspaper statistics only made things look worse. Grant managed to get copies of both articles distributed to every convention member.

Grant Graham and his field reps had the convention in hand from the beginning of the keynote address. Joe Biggs's gavel had hardly rapped for order before Grant was on his feet introducing a motion to rescind the action of the executive board and to reinstate Frank Worthington with full pay and privileges as of the moment when he had been illegally removed from the presidency. Hundreds of voices seconded the motion. The ayes were so thunderous that Starbright's supporters didn't even ask for a show of hands.

One of the field reps from New Jersey, a foreignlooking man named Milan Slansky, had worked so hard all night lining up delegates as they arrived at their hotels that Grant arranged for him to have the honor of putting Frank Worthington's name in nomination for re-election as president for the coming year. The election was a landslide. When Frank walked stiffly out on the speaker's platform, men jumped to their feet and cheered.

Back in Portage the following Monday morning Frank was in his office at seven thirty as usual. The cleaning woman burst out crying when he opened the door. "God bless you Mr. Worthington," she sobbed. Frank crossed the room with his usual soft tread, took off his coat and hat and started groping for the coathanger that usually hung on the hook.

"What's happened to the coathangers Mrs. Shipley?"

"Oh everythin's been at sixes and sevens, Mr. Worthington. . . . I'll fetch you another."

Frank took off his jacket, adjusted the sleeve garters on his arms, polished his glasses with a clean handkerchief and started to clear Joe Biggs's accumulations out of his desk. He was so deep in his paperwork he never looked up when the office workers began to arrive. The girls all said it seemed as if he'd never been away.

Documentary (10)

AROUND THE WORLD ON ONE BATTERY

Perfect Getaway Wagon for Families on a Tight Budget

from shelf to shopping cart move millions of cans, bottles, jars, and packaged goods wearing provocative labels. Their bright shiny surfaces are designed for printability and scuff resistance. They make products eye-appealing for impulse sales as well as planned purchases

TEENAGERS IN SEARCH FOR ASSURANCE

studies of the absorption spectra of these unique solvents containing actinide, lanthanide, and other transition metal ions are yielding detailed information concerning oxidation states, oxidation-reduction reactions, complexion formation, coordination numbers and reaction rates

"Either we shall use our new machines and technology to help us create security and dignity in the construction of a brave new world," says Walter Reuther, "or the impact of our jet-propulsion technology upon a huffing and puffing model T distributive system will dig our economic graves . . ."

We Suggest You Send Us a Letter Outlining Your Corrosion Problems

"Is it freedom when a man cannot work at a job without paying a union for the benefit of doing so?" a group of

Sheboygan men wrote the *Chicago Tribune.* "Is it freedom
when a man cannot work when the union boss says "strike"?
Is it freedom when our streets are blocked, cars overturned,
windows broken, buildings and homes blown up by gangs
of hoodlums who call themselves pickets? . . . Is the right
to vote any more sacred than the right to work?"

Social Engineer

Walter Philip Reuther was born into the vanguard
of the labor movement. His father Val Reuther was president of the Ohio Valley Trades and Labor Assembly. His
grandfather helped organize the Brewery Workers.

Valentine Reuther was a sober literate German-American
working man. He preached responsibility. He made his children pay attention in school. He raised his boys to be leaders
of labor.

The mother was a devout Lutheran. Sunday mornings
they went to church. The father was a devout Socialist. Sunday afternoons they debated the issues. It was a close knit
family. They studied social problems together. Val Reuther
urged his boys to read. He sent them to the public library to
bone up on contested points.

The Reuther home was a warm seminar of the hopes of
a new world to come. The Reuthers were working people,
they were poor but they knew they were the salt of the earth.
A certain amount of poverty must be borne with pride, as
a badge. Under socialism they would come into their own.

That was what Debs told the working people crowding
into labor temples and union halls during his presidential
campaigns. When socialism won at the polls and the trade
unions took over the factories, the old Adam would slough
off meanness and greed. Freshfaced and rosy as on the sixth
day of creation mankind would inaugurate the cooperative
commonwealth. A vote for Debs was a vote for man's perfectibility. Val Reuther brought his boys up in reverence for
Eugene V. Debs.

The Reuther boys were all bright, but Walter was the

redhead. He had a winning way, and a knack with words.

At fifteen because money was short he left highschool and went to work for a corrugating plant. The plant went on a seven day week. Sunday work meant giving up the discussion sessions at home and it was a damned outrage besides. Walter had been raised to give vent to his opinions. He did.

Tried to talk up a union. Fired. No more jobs at home in Wheeling for radical young Walter Reuther.

The automobile industry was booming in Detroit. Ford's five dollars a day attracted up and coming metal workers like bees to a clover field. Walter left home for Detroit and got himself hired at the Briggs body shop. Then he switched to Ford's where he became foreman of a tool and die room. He studied nights to finish highschool and started a college course at Wayne University. He organized a Social Problems Club. He campaigned for Norman Thomas in 1932. The Young People's Socialist League. A vote for Norman Thomas was a vote for the perfectibility of man.

Agitators were no more tolerated at Ford's than at Wheeling Steel. Walter Reuther's radical talk caught up with him. He was asked to step up to the pay window. No more working at Ford's.

Jobs were hard to come by. It was the deep dark of the Depression. A third of the population of Detroit was out of work. American capitalism seemed on its beam ends.

The Reuther boys were frugal fellows. They'd saved up a little dough. Nothing doing at home: why not see the world? Walter and Victor pooled their savings and decided on a trip to the Soviet Union to see how the working class was doing in the only country governed in its name.

While they waited for the Russian bureaucracy to furnish them with a visa they toured Europe on bicycles. They stayed in youth hostels. They visited factories and union halls. They pedaled out to the village near Stuttgart where their mother was born. They turned up in Berlin the day of the Reichstag fire.

Nazism made Walter Reuther's hackles rise. He was still German enough to feel it close to. The Reuther boys were full of anti-fascist zeal when they climbed on the long slow dingy train to Moscow. The Soviet Union was the workers' republic, socialism in our time. Why wouldn't their blood tingle?

Walter got himself a job as diemaker in the truck factory Ford's people had designed for the Russians at Gorki on the Volga. He was made foreman, only there they called it "leader of a labor brigade."

The Russian language was a maze. Soviet life was confusing. "Who are we to criticize? The Russians have to do things their own way."

The people were full of cordial curiosity about their American comrades. The girls were caressing. Here was a great nation relentlessly pursuing the ideals the Reuther boys had been brought up in from the cradle. Why shouldn't they write enthusiastic letters home?

After sixteen months, before they'd had a chance to learn, through Stalin's purges, the bloody underside of Soviet-socialism, the Reuthers left by the Transsiberian for home. After all they were Americans. It was American socialism they were dedicated to build.

On the way home they peeked into China, had a glimpse of India, spent a few weeks in Japan.

Back in Detroit, since he was still blacklisted as a radical, Walter went to work for General Motors under an assumed name. He married a redheaded girl who had been active in the Teachers' Union and started seriously organizing the West Side local of the United Automobile Workers. When his local sent him to a convention in South Bend he had a time convincing the chair that Walter Reuther and the other guy were one and the same.

Never again was there any doubt who Walter Reuther was.

Elected to the International board he opened a tiny office at 5th and Michigan Avenue. He was a labor organizer now full time. He started with seventyeight members. After the sitdown at Kelsey Hayes there were thirty thousand paying dues. Unionization was an avalanche. The agitators found themselves trying to hold their workers back until they could train up the organizers to service them. Even the Communists had their hands full.

The Reuther boys were campaign strategists. The class war was developing military tactics: strike where the enemy least expects it.

The automobile workers fought Harry Bennett's Service Men and the local cops and threats of fine and imprisonment

and broken heads and bloody noses,

with organization and oratory at all night meetings, and soup kitchens and hospital units,

and baseball bats on the picket line: the battle of the Dearborn drawbridge.

This was the contest the Reuther boys had been training for all their lives.

Industrial Michigan was in insurrection. Good kind liberal Frank Murphy, who wanted to be the working man's friend, couldn't very well help calling out the state militia. From the Olympian heights of Washington, Franklin Roosevelt talked the national interest: a plague on both your houses.

John L. Lewis, institution-building in the CIO, bustled with beetling brows between the White House and the UAW, blustered, bullied; squeezed every last dribble of drama out of the scene when he ostentatiously boarded the night train for Detroit to take over the sitdowns:

"Let there be no moaning at the bar," he boomed somewhat out of context to the reporters, who dutifully copied out these sibylline words for the morning papers, "when I put out to sea."

Franklin Roosevelt and John L were working at cross purposes, but between them they convinced the automobile industry that unions were here to stay. Ford's reversed its policy overnight. Harry Bennett agreed to negotiate. The National Labor Relations Board held an election in which the UAW won 58,000 out of 80,000 votes cast. Ford's signed, agreed to the union shop, the checkoff, overtime pay, seniority, grievance machinery, everything all down the line.

Harry Bennett did have one last word: the pluguglies of Ford's Service Department had acted like "a lot of tough bastards," he admitted, "but every goddam one of them is a gentleman."

The United Automobile Workers became the largest union in the world. The local at Ford's #600 (dominated by the Communists to be sure) was the largest single local in the world.

Through years of strategy and strikes and long night sessions at the bargaining table, Walter Reuther gained influence in the UAW. His brothers backed him. Victor documented his theories and did his paperwork. For the Reuthers Walter was the front man, the sweetfaced redhead with the winning way.

First he had to team with the Communists against Homer Martin's AF of L administration. Factions in the union came and went. The UAW was a sure enough industrial democracy. Teaming now with one group, now with another, Walter Reuther forged ahead.

He never had much sympathy with the Communist bigots. He'd been raised a social-democrat. He had faith in self-government.

He liked to quote John Stuart Mill: "If all mankind, minus one, were of one opinion and only one person were of the contrary opinion, mankind would be no more justified in silencing that one person, than he, if he had the power, would be justified in silencing mankind." This didn't quite apply to scabs.

Walter Reuther was an idealist with an institution to build. Building institutions takes special skills. Walter was a quiet family man of blameless life who drank only milk and didn't gamble and never smoked and who didn't give a damn about money and style. He was so convinced of the probity of his own intentions that he never could believe in the probity of people who had other ideas.

Organizing the nation for global war Franklin Roosevelt took the laborleaders into camp. War Production Board, War Manpower Commission, Labor-Management Production Committees. Alphabet enough for everybody on Olympus except for John L. Lewis who sulked. Walter Reuther learned his Washington.

The truce with industry ended with the shooting. Now, their treasuries swollen with wartime dues, the labor unions demanded their place in the sun. Walter Reuther could debate with management on equal terms.

He had become famous for his coolness at the bargaining table. Always neat, his associates marveled that even in the hottest weather he had the look of just coming out from a cold shower. Where other men got drunk with power, Walter Reuther took it in sips, coolly, like a glass of milk.

At last at the national convention in Atlantic City in March of 1946 his long climb ended with his election as president of the UAW-CIO. His first act was to introduce his old father to the delegates. It was a great day for the Reuthers.

Although the Communists had been with Reuther at first they turned on him savagely. A man makes enemies when he climbs to power. His campaign against gambling in the plants had antagonized the gangsters and the fast buck boys. One night when, coming back tired from the office, he sat drinking a glass of milk in the kitchen of his "modest working-class home" someone shot at him through the window with a sawed off shotgun. He was dangerously hurt and carries the scars on one arm to this day.

A year later an almost identical attempt was made to kill his brother Victor. Vic came away with his life but lost an eye. In spite of rewards posted and hullabaloo from detectives and district attorneys no one was ever able to discover who arranged these shootings.

Violence.

Institutions are built on zeal.

They are also built on fear. The Reuthers came to feel that to question the UAW's mission to organize every bunch of metal-workers they could lay their hands on was treason to the working class and unAmerican besides. Democracy was when the men voted the way the Reuthers wanted them to vote in a union election.

When they struck Kohler's works that make bathtubs in Sheboygan the Reuthers were hurt and pained to discover that quite a large body of working people didn't want to be serviced by their organization.

This time the storm troops were on the union side. "No one has a right to scab," said the UAW officials the way Harry Bennett at Ford's in the old days used to say "No one has a right to strike."

When the Congressional Committee presided over by Senator McClellan questioned Walter Reuther about the fanatical boycott of Kohler products and the beatings of nonstrikers, the wrecking of automobiles, the throwing of acid, the spraying of paint into livingrooms, rocks thrown and foul vituperation of working men's wives and children over the telephone, he answered with his usual righteous coolness and a trace of his small winning smile: "I believe that when a company deliberately and willfully embarks upon a labor policy designed to break a strike and destroy a union, that it must assume the prime moral responsibility for anything that happens."

INVESTIGATOR'S NOTES II

This fellow Ruffin has beefy shoulders but his skin is dead white from indoor work. He is sitting in his undershirt slumped over an enameled table in the hot kitchen. Astonished brown eyes stare out of a round deadwhite face under a bush of wavy hair. He talks with a mild Ozark drawl: "Mister, maybe you can tell me why the company would rather give their money to a hoodlum than pay their employees."

The kitchen is much too hot. Mrs. Ruffin is wiping dishes at the sink. The children crowd bigeyed around. Mrs. Ruffin is a tired stringyhaired woman. Her face is lined with fatigue and fear. Her eyes are searching the investigator's face. "Mister, please help us," the eyes say.

Ruffin leans his aluminum chair back and stares up at the ceiling. "I ought to know because I been a union man since my daddy took me to work in the mines when I was fourteen. I've seen good unions and bad unions but I've never seen anything like what's been happenin' the last few years. Gangsters moving in and tying up with management . . . and here I've been on the committee ten years fightin' this Russo and the company too and still I don't understand why the managers of a respectable business like this here tobacco factory are willing to consort with hoods. I don't blame the workin' people so much. They are scared."

He yawns and stretches out his plump, pale arms.

"There are fifty percent women in the cigarette section where I work and most of the rest are colored boys or hillbilly characters who can't read and write so good. You know women, maybe it's the nicotine in the air, operatin' machines in a cigarette factory seems to make 'em more nervous and jumpy than the usual, and Russo keeps 'em half pleased and half scared, struts around with a big frown on his face. I guess it's sex, a big buck of a wop all dressed up with fancy vest and a diamond ring. Well this Russo, he's tied up with every hoodlum in South Chicago. He got in by pretendin' to organize an AF of L local. Even the AF of L wouldn't sponsor this Russo, but management did. He owns stock in the company. They'd rather pay goons than pay wages."

Mrs. Ruffin has finished her work. She sits down humbly in a corner. The investigator has to look straight in front of him to avoid her pleading eyes.

He can hear the alarm clock tick on the kitchen shelf. The children are tensely listening. The children hardly breathe. The house, set back of tenements in an alley in the middle of a block, is tensely quiet. The traffic noises come muffled from the rainy street. The investigator notices that the locks on the back door have been re-inforced by a stout twobyfour set in slots. Maybe it's the twobyfour that gives him the feeling of being under siege.

Ruffin yawns and stretches and starts talking again:

"All the time I was talkin' CIO but the women were nervous about the CIO. I tried to interest the local office of the Automobile Workers. Walter Reuther's a cleancut fellow. I could go for him. Tobacco was out of their field they told me. I knew the contract was runnin' out and this was our chance to switch to another union . . . anythin' ud be better than this Russo."

They are barricaded in the small hot kitchen far away in the middle of a block, but still Ruffin lets his voice drop to a whisper: "This Russo should have gone on trial for embezzlement April 7 from another union he runs out in Cicero. They claim he stole four hundred and twenty thousand dollars. He moved to Hollywood to get out of the state. A guy I know met him right on Hollywood Boulevard and Russo said wasn't it too bad he lost that money crossing the Rocky Mountains. Did the district attorney try to extradite him? Not a bit of it. And Russo's here most of the time, just uses Hollywood for an address. Those hoodlums are laughing at us . . . And why wouldn't they when people will sell out their country for a few free beers. He gives picnics with free beer to keep the

boys and girls feelin' good. At the state convention I'm damned
if they didn't come out with signs 'God Bless Russo.'

"When the contract expired it was a yellow dawg contract
if I ever saw one, not that I ever saw it; Russo attended to
that, but I judged by the results—I tried to get up a petition
to the NLRB for an election to choose some other union—any
union—but out of four hundred people working in my section
I could only get two colored boys to help collect signatures.
Nobody else had the nerve. The word had gone around
through the grapevine that every man who voted for a new
election would be taken care of by the union or fired by the
company. There's no defense for a man who stands up. So
far as freedom of speech goes we are worse off than Russia.

"At that we got a hundred and forty votes but the NLRB
turned us down. The whole thing is a crackedup mess but
what I'm most afraid of is the hoodlums will hurt my kids.
There is nothing they'll stop at."

The investigator puts down everything about the petition
for an election. He is careful to get the dates and figures
right so that he can check with the local NLRB. They are
fussy about dates and figures at the NLRB.

Ruffin has gotten to his feet. Standing he is a very large
man. He towers over the investigator. "We need men and
laws to penetrate this," he is saying. "I have no right to
carry a gun. Give me a little defense and I'll come right out
in the open and fight . . . The people workin' in this factory
would be with me if they dared. Didn't they elect me to the
executive board? Trouble is a feller dassent open his mouth."

He stands there, a pale giant of a man, rubbing his chin
with his big hand. "And we're supposed to be eddicated in
this country . . . I see the women getting more nervous and
jumpy every day. The bosses keep pressuring them, put
more work on them all the time . . . This Russo don't give
a damn. He gets his cut both ways. All he's out for is the
dollar. Looks like the bosses are tryin' to get people so
hungry they'd have to keep their mouths shut . . . We're
only pavin' the way for the Russians . . . I wouldn't be a
Communist," he drawled with a shake of his head. "It could
be so different. If the unions were run right they'd be the
backbone of the country. . . . I'm standing behind my fellow
workers and the company if they'll do the right thing. . . . I
want to see my country proud and strong."

The investigator is clearing his throat. "About time for that cab," he says hoarsely. "Well Mr. Ruffin this has been nice."

"You just wait till it comes," says Ruffin, "and you make a beeline down the alley and across the sidewalk."

He is talking with his eye to the crack in the venetian blind. "There's your cab. The cabby's waitin'. Now you walk fast. A man needs eyes in the back of his head. I wouldn't have them hoodlums take you for me," he let out a yelp of laughter, "and bash in your head, mister."

Documentary (11)

LABOR BILLS HIT BY LEWIS

*Vegetables in Pressurized Glass Jars May Be Key
to Diet of Space Men*

"Don't forget to investigate Management. It takes two to make a deal."

> The body was in a north-to-south position, with knees bent and head flat on chest. A wooden-handled knife was placed across the woman's heart and a necklace of stones about her neck. A brass bracelet was found among buffalo hides in the grave. A weasel's head, significant in Indian ceremonies, was also uncovered together with considerable jewelry. A brass ball bearing the letters G.H. and I. and the words "New York" was removed from a small bag.

HOODLUM SHOT SEVEN TIMES IN BROOKLYN

"When there is a hearing of any nature, or an investigation," a bulldozer operator wrote his congressman, "those called to speak for the working man are always union officials.

Did it ever occur to you that these union bosses do not speak for the working man, but for the union bosses?"

ADAMANT ON FARM SUPPORTS

All the ideal qualities for a moon vegetable are not contained in one plant yet, Mr. Stein said, but he noted that diet requirements could be met by either corn, roasted peanuts, soybean sprouts or lettuce.

Critical of Labor Laws

"Consequently the members of our local union find ourselves between the Devil and the deep blue sea. On one side the greedy and ruthless employers, on the other the racketeer-infested union with corrupt leadership."

Blackie Bowman Speaking

(Scene: a bed in a Veterans' Hospital)

You would think a man would get to know all the little stains and pockmarks on a hospital ceiling lying on his back like I do and staring up at it all day, but if you stare at a thing too long it gets to be a blank; even the gulls in the patch of sky out of the window and the dishrag faces and racked limbs of the other old wrecks in the beds down the ward get to be a blank and the only thing real and clear is the old times you carry in your head.

When they rolled me into this isolation ward it never occurred to me that I'd have to lie here while the years went by with nothing but my funny little thoughts to keep me busy. I'd expected I'd be alive one minute and dead the next, instead of all this good care I'm getting at the taxpayers' expense that keeps me hanging like Mohamet's coffin between heaven and hell. It sure don't fit into the picture of the exploited working staff that has been the basic conviction of my life.

Funny me being a veteran. According to my convictions I ought to have been a conscientious objector and gone to jail with the hundred and one they convicted in Chicago.

It was me registering for the draft that broke up my marriage with Eileen. Kate had a great influence on her in those days and Kate chewed my ear off for a nogood yellow bastard. Kate could scold like a Liverpool fishwife when she felt like it. I've figured out since it was my leaving for the army, with Eileen so young and her head so easily turned, that started her on the downward path. If I'd gone to jail it might have been different. It would have been harder for her to twotime a classwar martyr. In spite of our convictions as free lovers we'd been faithful as a pair of lovebirds until I got those greetings from the President of the United States. After that she couldn't drag in enough guys to sleep with just to spite me.

The joke of it was I did all right in the army. Somebody decided I wouldn't do for the infantry so I found myself driving a truck out at Camp Devens. The sergeant in charge of the first depot I was assigned to turned out to be a structural iron worker. Chuck Donovan was a South Boston lad. He was one of those genial harps with a glad hand for just the right folks. He knew exactly how to work the army red tape. When he found my mother was Irish and I had a brother a priest and was a bridgeman to boot, he took me under his wing. I didn't faze him when I admitted to being a revolutionary atheist. He just laughed and said, "Blackie when you hear the shriek of that first shell coming in you'll be right back in the arms of Mother Church."

Chuck Donovan's religion didn't keep him from sympathizing with Tom Mooney and being a hellroaring Irish republican. When he got himself transferred to the Engineers at Fort Belvoir he wangled me a corporal's chevron and took me along. Fort Belvoir was something. Army transport was still a packtrain of Missouri mules in the minds of some of the old field officers. The place was divided, ideologically as the Marxians would say, between the muleskinners and the truckdrivers.

Chuck got to be the indispensable man in the outfit of a Colonel Hogan who believed in Mack trucks and before we knew what happened he had us over in France driving along those much too narrow roads lined with those beautiful tall poplars. Mostly we shuttled between the SOS at Tours and the Ardennes Forest. Donovan's traveling circus. Chuck saw to it we were good. We kept our trucks in repair. No drinking on duty. Every detail accomplished on schedule. We were cited in the orders of the day and the old man got a medal.

To tell the truth I never heard a shot fired in anger, if you don't count a few booms and bangs beyond the distant hills that might very well have been blasting. The squareheads were already on the run. The war for me was riding the roads and seeing the sights and *beaucoup vin rouge* and omelettes and mademoiselles and a few of those red plush French fancyhouses with mirrors over the beds. France was still a damn pretty country in World War I.

Après la guerre finie I found myself driving up Fifth Avenue in a squall of tickertape with the rest of the bloody heroes. Trust Chuck Donovan to wangle us that detail. When the parade was over we all got leave. Nobody could deny the returned doughboy anything. Hadn't he made the world safe for democracy? It was to laugh.

First thing I did was to try to find Eileen. I hadn't a word from her in the whole eight months I had been overseas. None of the O'Dwyers in the telephone book were the ones I was looking for, so I walked over to Second Avenue to see what had happened to the old White Horse saloon.

The joint looked the same. The brass fittings and the mahogany bar were still there, but lord what a change prohibition had made. There were guys at the tables drinking what smelt like real beer, but the tightlipped little barkeep, in spite of me being in uniform with service stripes and all, wouldn't sell me anything but that legal brew that tasted like soap in your mouth. When I asked about Patrick O'Dwyer he pretended he'd never heard of him. I was walking out in disgust when I ran smack into the old gent.

Eileen's father had failed a good deal. His hands shook and all the blood seemed to have gone out of his face into his eyeballs, but he recognized me and hailed the conquering doughboy and dragged me into a little back office. The syndicate he'd sold the place to still let him use the office. Gave him some place to go. No life for an honest publican any more. He gave me a drink of real good whiskey out of a pint he had in his overcoat pocket.

When I asked about Eileen he wiped his bleary eyes with

A Creature That Builds

a rag of a handkerchief. He wheezed that his boys would pass in a crowd, but the girls had set themselves to break every law of God and man. Kate went around the country airing blasphemies at subversive meetings. The old gent started sniveling that he guessed he was oldfashioned but he found Eileen's verses distinctly offcolor.

His complaints came in a rush. He was lonesome in his old age. Mrs. O'Dwyer, God rest her soul, was dead. He himself had one foot in the grave and the other on a banana peel. Prohibition had taken away his livelihood. The reformers had made a ruin of dear old Tammany. Maybe the way his children behaved had been sufficient punishment to ease some of his torments in the life to come. The old gent really was pitiful.

"Francis Xavier," he said to me, "now that you are home get ahold of that girl and reason with her. As her husband it's your bounden duty to keep her on the right path."

Reason with Eileen. I couldn't help laughing at that.

He seemed proud of her all the same. He brought a wad of clippings out of his pocket and held them under my nose in his shaky hand. "Read them. They must think it's good or they wouldn't print it." They were verses of Eileen's out of the *Globe* and that Sundial column they used to have, and off the editorial page of *The New York Times*. He had a drawerful of magazines and back copies of the *Masses* and *New Republic*. He had kept every word Eileen had ever written.

"The money they pay her has clean gone to her head. It isn't that she hasn't the talent. It comes from her mother's side of the family. God rest her soul . . ." He crossed himself hurriedly. "The O'Dwyers were great talkers but none of them ever put pen to paper."

The old gent told me that the girls were in New York, but he didn't have their addresses. "They don't tell me anything." All he had was a telephone number on a scrap of paper in his vest pocket where he could leave a message for Kate in case of serious emergency. "If you can't get her there, try the Brevoort café. They tell me she's there every day sitting at a table with August Fairfield Donohue who, if you ask my opinion, is a very silly man, and the rest of the self-styled celebrities."

It was hard getting away from him. When I called the

number he'd given me a surly foreign voice answered that Comrade Levine had gone to a meeting. When I asked where I could reach her he hung up. It was already getting dark and I was tired and discouraged by the time I got down town to Eighth Street. At the Brevoort I went into the café they used to have in the basement and ordered a cup of coffee. People stared at me like I was some kind of a strange beast. Servicemen weren't popular in those quarters. What a hell of a homecoming!

Expecting to get the bums' rush any minute I sat there drinking my coffee and looking around the room. Sure enough, there sat Kate at the big round table in the far corner that all the loud talking came from queening it over a bunch of longhairs. Whatever it was they were drinking out of those coffeecups it surely wasn't coffee.

Kate had put on weight. Her bosom stuck out. She was getting to have that old battleaxe look with her shortcut red hair flung to the breezes. Eileen was sitting behind her with her face in the shadow. She looked frail and sweet and beautiful. There were some goodlooking women in the room but Eileen was by all odds the prettiest girl there. What made me mad right away was how she was carrying on with a big soft towhead in a black Russian blouse. If it came to a fight I decided he'd be the one I'd take a poke at first. I walked over to the table but they were all too busy listening to the sound of their own voices to pay any attention to a member of the hoi polloi.

From seeing their pictures in the paper I recognized Mr. Donohue's pink face under its white thatch and his handsome feminist wife Elsbeth Mills. They were the moneybags of the occasion. There I stood first on one foot, then on the other. It was Kate who recognized me.

"Here comes the cannon fodder," she said. She must have been drinking. She shook her finger across the table at me. "I don't care if you are my brotherinlaw. Every working man who wears that uniform is a scab against his class." I thought she was going to spit in my face.

The rest of them tried to shut her up. In the spring of 1919 talk like that still could land you in jail. Mr. Donohue tried to quiet her down with a Latin phrase which he right away translated "Abhor the crime but pity the criminal."

Eileen really surprised me. She pulled away from her

towheaded friend and advanced towards me with her arms stretched out. "Francis Xavier darling," she crooned with her mouth against mine, "I'd given you up for dead."

A pretty scene. I couldn't figure out whether it was plain dramatics or that she was mad at Kate that day. Maybe she was sincere. Anyway Eileen took my side when the whole tableful began to give tongue about the evils of militarism. I said they couldn't make me mad. I was damn sick of militarism.

The Donohues plied me with questions about what it was like overseas. They couldn't seem to understand that the biggest part of an army spends its time transporting supplies. They seemed to think I ought to have been skewering Huns on my bayonet every minute. No use trying to explain to a civilian what war's really like.

It was a relief when the party broke up. Eileen and I and the towhead found ourselves straggling along Eighth Street in a shower of rain. She finally got around to introducing him, some kind of Icelandic poet with a long Scandihoovian name. I was all ready to take a poke at him, but I held off. You ought to have seen the look he gave me. I was determined I'd stick to Eileen like a burr until I got a chance to talk to her alone.

She started plucking at my sleeve in that confidential way she had, asking in a whisper if I had enough dough to pay for supper. Sure, I'd been lucky in some crap games on the transport. Right away she herded us into an Italian speakeasy named Maria's.

We were the only people in the joint. Reeked of olive oil and parmesan cheese. The poet sat there silent as a fish, drumming with his fingers on the stained tablecloth. I couldn't find anything to say either. We were two glum-looking guys.

If that Icelander couldn't talk he sure could eat. Kept asking for seconds. I was too much on tenterhooks to be hungry. All I could think of to do was order up more and more dago red.

Eileen was in the pink. She sat there looking from one to the other with little sidelong looks, rattling along cheerfully about how she had joined the Lucy Stone League. She'd learned to live her own life in those months I'd been away overseas. She'd been supporting herself on the thirtyfive dollars

a week she earned writing up news of the garment trade for
Art and Apparel. She was cocky about that. Not a word did
she say about the allotment she got off my army pay. I was
too much of a gentleman, at least right then, to bring the
matter up.

She leaned over and gave my hand a little pat. Her eyes,
big and blue, looked up into mine. They had that full to the
brim look they had when she was really moved. Maybe now,
she was saying, it would be even-Stephen between us.

The Icelander jumped up like he'd been shot and made
Eileen a stiff bow and walked out on the street. He'd eaten
three orders of scalloped veal and I guess he'd had enough.
"Thank God for that," I said. "Oh Gunnar'll be back," Eileen
answered cheerily. "He always comes back."

I had the bill paid and Eileen out on the street in a
twinkling. For some reason she didn't want to take me to
her place. Sitting on a bench in Washington Square she let
me edge up towards her a little. I was courting her all over
again as if we had just met. I suggested we go to a hotel. At
a shabby old doss on University Place we had a time convincing the clerk. I slipped him five dollars and Eileen put
on her wedding ring she had found in her handbag and
finally he let us upstairs without a suitcase.

As soon as the door closed Eileen ran into my arms. "It's
just like we weren't married at all," she said. "The clerk didn't
think we were married."

Being with Eileen that night seemed more wonderful than
ever before.

I had to leave her at six in the morning to get back to my
outfit that was moving to a camp out on Long Island to be
mustered out. I never could remember the name of that camp
though it's written on the copy of my discharge they have
right here in the VA office to this day. I was too busy thinking
of Eileen to remember anything else I guess. All I can remember is being in a fidget for fear I'd break some damned
army rule and land in the jug before my discharge came.

At last they handed me a "testimonial of honest and faithful
service" and I walked out of that camp a free man with a
hundred and seventyfive dollars in my pockets and rode back
into New York on the Long Island Railroad. It never occurred
to me I'd spend the last years of my life bumming off that
discharge.

Those years in New York were one of the good times with Eileen. The slavemarkets were full of returned doughboys willing to work for a nickel, but I managed to hire out at reasonable pay on a construction job over in Perth Amboy where they were building a new cracking plant for Standard Oil.

Though I was making enough to support us both Eileen insisted on working full time at *Art and Apparel*. That made us pretty flush. To show that she really meant to give me a break she rented us an apartment up on Weehawken Heights. Big oldfashioned rooms with a view of all the shipping on the Hudson and the city across the river. She took the ferry to work and I took the train to work and we both got home in time for supper. Neither of us was drinking. We didn't need to. We had the world to ourselves.

When we had saved up a little jack I bought a secondhand Essex. That made it easier for me to get to my job. It was a touring car. We drove out to the country with it fine Sundays with the top down. The roads weren't so good but there wasn't the awful traffic there is nowadays. We ate at country inns in places like Nyack and Haverstraw. Sometimes we packed a lunch to eat outdoors in the Poconos or up Bear Mountain. A couple of Sundays we made it as far as Delaware Water Gap.

When she got that faraway look on her face and brought out her notebook and started to put words down, I'd leave her alone. When she was through we'd walk around hand in hand just looking at things like children. We both loved a clear mountain stream and firtrees and birches and airy green meadows. Just looking at each other made us happy.

I never was much of a home guard, but this time I began to get ideas of turning into a family man. A man wants kids of his own even if he is a rolling stone. I couldn't get Eileen interested. I couldn't get her even to talk about it. At the least mention of anything like that a spasm of pain would cross her face. She said that would spoil everything.

She began to develop a real fear of having a baby. I guess she thought it would end her independence and her career as a literary young lady. That fear cast a shadow between us. The precautions cramped my style. When she did accidentally get pregnant after we'd been living in Weehawken six or eight months she went to some quack sawbones, without telling me

a word about it, and had an abortion. Her story was the doctor told her she was too nervous and delicate to have children.
Delicate, hell: Eileen looked frail but she was strong as a
horse, every one of the O'Dwyers was. She came home that
evening all white and weepy and said it had been a terrible
experience. That was the first I knew of it. Nothing in my life
ever shook me up like that.

She had borrowed the money from the Harris plan, and I
had to put the car in hock to buy off those bloodsuckers before
the interest ate us out of house and home. From that time on
a tension began to grow up between us. We couldn't see eye
to eye about the least thing.

Part of it may have been my fault for giving so much time
to the cause. On the job at Perth Amboy I'd been running into
a scattering of old IWWs. Scattering is right, because whenever I asked about some oldtimer the answer was always the
same: in jail in Sacramento, in jail in Walla Walla, or Atlanta
or some other damn federal penitentiary, serving ten, fifteen,
twenty years. When we wobblies got together to try to revive
the Railroad, Canal, Tunnel and Bridge Construction Workers'
Industrial Union, we talked big about organizing the refinery
job, but we never did get off dead center. We couldn't organize the scissorbills because all our energy and all the money
we could spare went into defense. We were fighting a losing
battle.

Judge Kenesaw Mountain Landis intended to destroy us
with the terrible punishments he meted out at the Chicago
trial and he just about succeeded. Working people were intimi-
dated. What impressed Gus Rarick, the little bohunk we made
our secretary at Perth Amboy, who had sat there through most
of the trial in Chicago, was how the judge could hand out
twenty year sentences as lightheartedly as he'd fine some Joe
five bucks for speeding. It didn't seem to occur to him that he
was destroying the lives of decent men. Landis's crackerbarrel
manner had even taken in some of the defense lawyers. Underneath he was a butcher. The punishment was all out of pro-
portion.

The crime our boys committed was to take the unpopular
side in the struggle to keep America out of war. The statutes
they were convicted on all infringed the Bill of Rights. Every
good lawyer admitted that. Convictions were expected but

the sentences knocked our breath out. How could a man live with himself after doing what Kenesaw Mountain Landis did to men's lives for just saying a few illegal words? He throve on it. His recompense was to be handed $25,000 a year as czar of organized baseball. Me, just the feeling I hadn't done all I should have done to help my fellow workers made my conscience ache.

It wasn't that Eileen didn't sympathize with my defense work. She was a very romantic girl. She liked to think of me as a leader of the working stiffs waving a red flag from the barricades. I never quit trying to explain to her that in the IWW we were all leaders, but she never could get it into her pretty head. We wobblies never did fall for the hero bunk.

To show that her heart was in the right place she wrote a poem on Joe Hill for one of our defense bulletins. All her friends thought it was wonderful but I realized even then it was only a rehash of the lines Joe Hill himself wrote the night before he was executed:

> My will is easy to decide
> For there is nothing to divide.
> My kin don't need to fuss and moan
> Moss does not cling to a rolling stone. . . .

I forget the middle part. I never thought I'd forget a word of that poem. I know it ended:

> This is my last and final will.
> Good luck to all of you: Joe Hill.

All Eileen did was dress it up in fancy words but it sure did appeal to the intelligentsia.

We were appealing to the intelligentsia ourselves. Gus Rarick and I had decided to hold a meeting down in the Village to try to shake down the New York radicals for the benefit of the General Defense Committee. We ended by hiring Webster Hall and netting two thousand dollars.

We never would have pulled it off without the O'Dwyer girls. Kate lined up backers by sheer force of vituperation and Eileen by that lovely frail heartbreaking look she knew so well how to put on. You could have knocked me down with a feather when Eileen told me her employer Murray Katz, who was editor of *Art and Apparel*, had slipped her the three hundred dollars she needed to guarantee the rent of the hall. Of course it was Eileen who induced Freddie Davis to speak. Eileen and Freddie had had kind of a letch for each other since those grand old days before the war when we all bummed around with the longhairs in the Village.

Freddie was a strapping guy with bulging brown eyes and uncombed hair and a Harvard accent. We used to kid him as the college boy radical. As a journalist he'd been an eyewitness of the Russian revolution and the setting up of the soviets. When he stood up on the platform to talk he always looked like he was going to bust into tears. He had that helpless puppy expression that broke the girls all up. When I saw the way Eileen never took her eyes off him while he was speaking at that Webster Hall rally it was like a knife stuck into me. I had a feeling then my days were numbered.

It was Eileen he sought out after the big ovation he got from the crowd. He came up to me first with his hand out and that innocent just between you and me look in his eyes: I couldn't find it in me to hate him. When Freddie and Eileen picked up some conversation about poetry they had been having before, as if they'd never left off, my heart sank down into my boots. Talk between Eileen and me had never been that easy.

The Webster Hall meeting was a success for the General Defense Committee but it busted up my life for fair.

We never reached first base organizing the construction job. Still we stirred up enough commotion to get the contractors hot and bothered. Some stoolie turned in my name and Gus Rarick's and we woke up one fine morning to find we were fired. Not only fired but blacklisted. Construction was picking up in New York City. All the contractors were hiring but none of them wanted to take on a couple of hellroaring reds. It wasn't too much skin off my ass but it was ruinous for Gus. Gus had a wife and six children, and was making payments on a house. He had to go to work under an assumed name digging ditches for sewerpipe with a gang of wops.

I decided I'd move to Chicago. The office there was the center of IWW defense work. A convention was going to be held. I wanted to get back into the movement. The feeling that I'd been acting like a goddam scissorbill began to burn me up.

When I suggested to Eileen we move to Chicago you'd have thought I was trying to ask her to take up residence in Baffin Land. The sidewalks of New York, those O'Dwyers were dyed in the wool . . . If it hadn't been that it would have been something else. We had a yelling match one night and Eileen wouldn't speak to me at breakfast and when I got home from a last effort to find work in Hoboken or Jersey City I found Eileen had packed up bag and baggage and moved out. She'd set her cap for Freddie Davis was one reason, but I guess neither one of us was made for cunnubial bliss.

It was too bad because I had a meal ticket all made in South Chicago. Chuck Donovan and me we'd written each other since coming out of the army and Chuck had kept in touch with Colonel Hogan who had retired. Ed Hogan was an old-fashioned entrepreneur. He'd moved out to the Middle West and was starting one of those longhaul truck lines that were a new thing in those days with Chuck Donovan as general manager, and Chuck was collecting some of our old buddies from the traveling circus to drive for him. Chuck promised big money. If Eileen hadn't been so touchy and redheaded and so hipped on being a literary genius, we might have made a go of it, a new life in a new city, all that sort of thing. No use crying over what might have been.

Beating my way to Chicago I began to figure up how much I'd lost. I'd gotten accustomed to having a woman around. Though a man has to keep in pretty good shape physically to sling those red hot rivets the way we used to in structural steel work in those days, married life had softened me up, morally I guess you'd say. I didn't have the migratory worker's psychology any more.

The first part of the trip I made in applepie order in the old Essex. I was too blue to get into trouble. Trying to keep Eileen away from the bottle had gotten me out of the habit of drinking. While we lived in Weehawken whenever I felt a yen for a drink coming on I'd just go to a postoffice and send whatever change I had in my pocket off to the General Defense Committee. It wasn't till I got to Cleveland that I fell off the wagon.

In Cleveland I went around to one of our Marine Transportation Workers' locals looking for a free flop. I was lonesome as hell. I really went in search of human companionship.

It was October by that time. The hall was full of deck-hands pouring off the oreboats with their pockets full of back

pay. I ran into a couple of oldtimers I'd known following the
harvest as a kid out West. We started on near beer with a stick
in it holding sort of a wake over the good old days of revolutionary syndicalism. The working class was on the run, the
movement was all broken up. I was lonesome and starved for
a woman, not for any woman, just for that one woman. Why
the hell shouldn't I drink? Each of the other guys was suffering from his particular brand of desperation. We drank the
blind pigs dry that night.

Next morning I was so overhung that to keep my breakfast
down I took a couple of swigs out of a pint of rotgut I'd
stowed away in the car. In some damn little tank town west of
Cleveland I ran through a red light and slam into another car.
There was a hell of a row. Nobody was hurt but both cars
had to be towed away. A hick cop dragged me into traffic
court for drunken driving. Fifty dollars fine. Then there was
the hauling charge. I had to sell the wreck of the Essex to pay
my bills. The cops, the judge, the garage man, they were all
in cahoots. Did I get cleaned in Lakeview?

They left me just fifteen cents for the four hundred miles to
Chicago. In the days when I was still a practicing hobo it
would have been a cinch. Every railroad line in the country
converges on Chicago. Now I was thirty years old. I'd lost the
knack of jumping on a moving freightcar. I was scared of getting hurt. I'd forgotten how you had to have eyes in the back
of your head to look out for yard dicks.

I was disappointed in the company I found in the jungles.
Gone were the days of the Wabash Cannonball when a red
card was a ticket for a free ride on any freight train in the
West. The boes seemed to have degenerated. No revolutionary
spirit in them. All I met was tramps and dead beats headed
for Madison Street before the snow began to fly. After a lot of
narrow squeaks I ended riding blind baggage into South Chicago on a New York Central train. I tumbled out into the
yards one raw frosty morning with a sprained ankle and a dis-
located thumb. I was such a wreck it was laughable.

In fact Chuck Donovan almost split when he opened the
back door of his nice new home on a nice new residential
street in response to my timid knock. He told me afterwards
he thought it was a gag. Chuck was round and rosy and pros-
perouslooking and so was Mrs. Chuck and so were their three
little roundeyed brats. They were all dressed up in their best

ready to go to early mass. Chuck told me it was only by my thatch of black hair that he recognized me.

When he introduced me as Sergeant Bowman the round eyes of Mrs. Chuck and the little Chucks narrowed to slits. "Another of daddy's dead cats," the oldest girl piped up echoing like kids will something their elders had said. "Happy Hooligan," squeaked the littlest. They all giggled their heads off.

While Mrs. Chuck was squelching the small fry, Chuck led me into a downstairs bathroom and found me a razor and a clean shirt, so that I was fairly presentable by the time they got back from church.

The Donovans couldn't have been nicer. Chuck took me around to a doctor to strap up my ankle and they put me in their spare bedroom until I could work enough time to pay rent on a room in the local boardinghouse. Driving for the South Chicago Trucking Corporation was the old traveling circus all over again, except that we didn't move in convoys. Chuck had a remarkable knack for making men who worked for him feel they belonged. If you had a blowout or engine trouble Chuck had a way of turning up himself with the spare part you needed, scorching over the roads in an old red Stutz. You could get him on the telephone any time of the day or night. I'd gone to work with a little notion in the back of my head of organizing the truckdrivers into an industrial union, but you just couldn't do that to Chuck. If you worked for Chuck you just had to let him do the organizing.

So there I was acting the perfect scissorbill. Chuck wanted me to join the American Legion. Respectability was holding out its arms to me again. Mrs. Chuck had a mighty huggable looking unmarried sister. Fresh and wholesome as a loaf of new bread. If it hadn't been for my marriage to Eileen I sure would have been tempted. Mary Ellen wasn't planning to stay unmarried any longer than she could help. I had to watch my step on that score.

I blew off steam by going into Chicago and shouting my head off for the class war prisoners every Sunday night. In the defense committee's back room we organized a speakers' bureau. We covered Bughouse Square and joints like The Dill Pickle and The Green Mask where the local longhairs gathered. I got to be quite the soapboxer. I learned how to lay on the pathos. A Sunday afternoon or evening I would

drag in fifteen or twenty bucks. I'd add to that whatever I
could spare from my week's wages, which was considerable.
Since Eileen walked out I had only myself to support.

Nobody around the trucking concern knew a thing about
my radical activities until they saw my picture in the *Chicago
Tribune*. Some damn reporter had been around taking snapshots and they ran a scare article headed WILDEYED REDS IN-
CITE TO CRIME in their Sunday supplement. There I was on
my soapbox large as life.

That Monday morning instead of my usual assignment to a
run I got a message that Colonel Hogan wanted to see me. He
wasn't too stinking about it. He told me he hadn't had any
complaints as yet, but that when it got around that one of his
truckdrivers was an IWW it would hurt his business. Customers just wouldn't stand for it. If I'd give up my agitation
and let Chuck try and railroad me into the local American
Legion, I might be able to keep my job. He wasn't sure but
he'd do his best.

Me join the American Legion after what they did to Wesley
Everest? I blew up in his face. He was the puzzledest looking
man I ever saw in my life. Chuck came in and tried to argue.
I told them they were a pair of right guys even if they were
exploiters of the working class. They stared at me like they
thought I'd lost my mind; maybe I had. It was a question of
conscience, I told them. "Let's part friends," I said, and that
was that.

So there I was working full time for the defense committee.
The trouble was the defense committee didn't have any ap-
propriation for feeding its help. I had to subsist on what I
could pick up doing odd jobs round the city.

This was the winter Harding and Coolidge won the presidential campaign. The Socialists ran up pretty near a million
votes. All fall the Socialists on Bughouse Square had been trying to talk the IWWs into registering and voting. The IWW
leaders were in jail, weren't they? Well, Debs was in jail too.
A vote for Debs was a vote for all class war prisoners. The
Socialists were mostly Germans and Norwegians and Swedes.
No convincing those opinionated squareheads that the vote
was a snare and a delusion. Some of the arguments wound up
in fights.

Harding's "Normalcy" meant a certain quieting down of

wartime hysterics. One of the first things he did was hand Debs a pardon. Offers were made to some of the IWWs to commute their sentences. There was a big argument in the defense committee on whether applying for a commutation was an admission of guilt. The argument left hard feelings. Some of our brightest guys like Ralph Chambers accepted commutation and resigned from the movement forever. The diehards were so bitter they made "fellow worker" sound like an insult.

None of this made it any easier to raise money for defense. Anyway I was getting sick and tired of the sound of my own voice. I began looking around for some way of getting out of Chicago.

The IWW was breaking up into a thousand little splinters. The one place there seemed to be solidarity was Omega, California, where the lumber workers were on strike. We had a free speech fight on there. From all over the country hardbitten wobblies were converging on Omega. When I lit out for Omega my shadow went with me. The boys had been kidding me about my shadow. I'd been trying to shake him all that winter.

My shadow was a young punk everybody called Froglegs. When I'd be batting the breeze from my soapbox Sunday afternoons I'd sometimes see a sort of curlyhaired ghost staring up at me out of the crowd. He did look like a frog with those big glistening eyes and the broad face and the vacant grinning mouth. Then one night he came sidling over with his funny bowlegged walk and handed me two dollars all in pennies and nickels and dimes.

I didn't want to take his money. The poor devil looked half starved. He had on a pair of old rubber boots that didn't match and the darndest rags you ever saw. I could see under the dirty railroaders' cap that one ear was all swollen up with frost bite. He'd lost a couple of teeth. Froglegs was a wreck when I first saw him.

We argued back and forth a little about whether I'd take his money or not for the defense committee. To make things worse the guy stuttered. He said he knew he was in a bad way but at least he was out of jail. Those guys needed it more than he did.

It was a miserable March evening like they have in Chicago with a freezing wind off the lake. I asked Froglegs if he had any place to sleep. He said no, he dassent go back to any of the missions he'd worked them all so hard that winter, so I told him to come along. He could flop on the floor in the defense committee's back office. At least he could keep warm. On the way he looked so hungry I took him into a lunchroom for a hamburger and a cup of coffee. He wouldn't eat until I swore he was eating on me and not taking anything away from the class war prisoners.

After he'd eaten he began to talk. He didn't stutter so bad with some warm food in his belly.

I never knew whether his story was true or whether he made it up for the occasion. Several times while he was tagging along after me I heard him pouring it out into some sympathetic ear and it sounded different each time.

He told me his real name was Tony Gonzalez. He had some Mexican in him that was for sure. He said his mother was an educated Mexican woman who'd kept the books and worked as housekeeper on a ranch out near Marathon in the Big Bend country. His dad was the rancher. His mother couldn't marry him because she had a misplaced husband south of the border somewhere. There were a couple of younger brothers and sisters born the same way.

It was wild country in those days. The neighbors weren't too nosy about who had a marriage license. He grew up helping his old man and attending the nearest school in full expectation that some day he'd inherit the ranch and a thousand head of cattle more or less until one fine day his old man decided he'd marry sure enough.

It was the daughter of a real Texas cattle baron. She got hold of the immigration people and worked out a way of deporting Tony's mother back to Mexico. Illegal entry. Tony's mother had lived in Texas twenty years but she'd never thought to take out citizenship. What chance did a friendless Mexican have against a woman whose father owned half of the western part of the state?

What Tony's mother did was to shoot his dad dead one fine morning with his own automatic and then shoot herself. Tony heard the shots and found them both lying dead beside the kitchen stove. At least that was the tale he told.

Relatives turned up to claim the ranch. The other children were sent off to an orphanage for little Mexicans. Tony was an American. He wasn't no goddam greaser. So he hit the road and told everybody his name was Tony Merriman. That was his father's name. He'd never walked a step till he went on the bum at fourteen. So much riding had given him the cowhand's bowlegged walk. That was why they called him Froglegs.

Froglegs stuck like a leech from that day. We got him cleaned up and a doctor one of the boys knew treated his frosted ear and we installed him as office boy. One of the signs of the dissidence in our ranks had been that our office was a pigpen. Once Froglegs took charge it was neat as a pin. Right away the IWW became father and mother and brothers and sisters to poor Froglegs. If the rest of the fellow workers had shown half his devotion we'd have damn well built our new society in the shell of the old instead of just talking about it.

Froglegs was a treasure. He carried the mail to the post-office and kept our mailing lists in order. He even tried to learn to type on our cranky old typewriters when he had the office to himself after the boys had gone home. After a while we let him handle the petty cash: for the first time in history the account checked at the end of the week.

Whenever he found me alone he'd back me into a corner and ask me questions about the revolution. How soon did I think it would be? Would it come in time for him to go back to highschool and graduate? Would college be free after the revolution? Where would a young fellow like him apply for a job? Would he have a chance to get back into the cattle business? Would there be some way of finding his brothers and sisters?

Those stuttering questions were plenty embarrassing. He read all the literature in the office and he believed every word of it. Literally, like you'd believe the telephone book. What could I tell him? I couldn't stand up there and tell him it was pie in the sky. That boy had me worried.

He never would take a cent off the IWW. When he needed dough he put on his old rags and those rubber boots that didn't match and hit the stem. That popeyed grin melted a lot of hearts. I've known some pretty successful panhandlers, but Froglegs had them all lashed to the mast.

When I left for Omega Froglegs tagged along. I told him he couldn't but how could I stop him? It turned out I couldn't have done without him. When we began hopping freights it was me that tagged along after Froglegs. As a bo he was really accomplished, and I had years of soft living behind me. I didn't have what it takes any more.

We started out a fine April day, one of those sunny mornings in the Middle West that make you think that spring is coming when it isn't. At first we had luck. In the Chicago yards we managed to slip into an empty boxcar manifested for Davenport, Iowa. It was a long hungry ride but it was fast. The trouble was that when we stuck our noses out after dark we found we were on a siding on the Rock Island side of the river.

It was cold as hell and snowing. You couldn't see your hand in front of your face. Froglegs had been telling me about a Salvation Army shelter he knew about over in Davenport. He'd found a piece of meat in the soup they'd given him there and he'd never forgotten it. We tramped across all those long trestles and bridges in the driving snow. Never saw the Mississippi River look so cold. The bottoms were flooded and littered with piled up icecakes. Rows of street lights stood up out of the water.

Davenport looked dismal. We arrived at the Salvation Army dreaming of hot soup with meat in it but the shelter was full and the door locked. The snowstorm was a blizzard by that time. White deserted streets. No streetcars running. Nothing for it but to apply to the city jail.

The cop on duty smiled at us like we were visiting royalty and led us in to see the Chief of Police. The Chief of Police gave us a greasy smile. We thought we were nuts. He was a big fat man in hip boots and a slicker. He had a fireman's hat pushed back off his sweating head. He looked all tuckered out. He told us he had a job for any vag was willing to work.

The river was reaching flood stage. He needed hands to work on a levee. The whole town was clubbing together to build a levee to protect the riverside sections. He told the cop to lock us in one of the warm cells for the night and to let us have clean blankets. The horrible thing about sleeping in jail is they never turn the lights out but we slept like the dead all the same.

That Mississippi flood proved a lucky break for Froglegs and me. The next morning a deputy sheriff herded us into a lunchroom across from the courthouse for breakfast along with a bunch of riffraff they had drummed up out of the missions and flophouses. They were paying anybody who would work three dollars a day and found. They furnished us with army surplus boots and gloves and slickers. It was heavy work but they fed us well. Every restaurant in town donated food. At that most of the migrants soldiered. The guys who really worked were solid citizens with property to protect.

The wind changed to the south and the snow turned to slush during the first morning. It was the damndest mess you ever saw trying to fill floursacks with frozen earth in all that muck. I was never much of a one for soldiering so I shoveled and shoveled.

Froglegs had the situation sized up at a glance. He wangled himself a detail bringing out hot coffee and doughnuts to the work gangs. Every time he made a trip he managed to come by where I was. He almost foundered me with coffee. With his pop eyes and his froggy grin and his eager beaver manner he was the most popular boy on the levee.

We broke our backs on that damn levee for ten days. All the thanks we got was an order to leave town the day the crest began to subside, but Froglegs and me we had sixty bucks between us. We slipped away without turning in the boots and slickers. I was in a hurry to get to California so we bought tickets to Denver on the through train and managed to play hide and seek with the conductor all the way to Salt Lake City.

At least it was warm in Salt Lake City but those Mormons are death on vagrants. It was in Utah they shot Joe Hill. To keep off the road gang we looked for work right away. The stockyards were right there at the edge of the marshaling yard. It just happened they were shorthanded. They took us on at a dollar a day and a place to sleep in a shed that reeked of that sharp stink of sheepmanure. The foreman made no bones about it. We worked for him or else . . . They sure are tight-fisted tough customers out there.

Froglegs showed he knew how to handle steers, so part of his story must have been true. He took a powder one noon. I couldn't imagine what had become of him. Afterwards he told me handling cattle made him unhappy thinking of his brothers and sisters and the good times back home on the ranch. He'd heard somebody say that if you went to the Mormon Temple for instruction in their church they'd give you free meals and even lodging, so he thought he'd try his luck.

The Mormons weren't that dumb. Next morning he came

back running between the cattlepens white as a ghost. The elders had gotten wise to him and set the police on his trail. We must take it on the lam. I didn't wait to collect my pay. We jumped an empty cattlecar in the middle of a moving freight.

That was one of the coldest rides I ever had in my life. There was still snow in the mountains. The open slats of the cattlecar gave us no protection from the wind. At one tank stop Froglegs went nosing around the depot and rustled up an armful of newspapers. Then he showed me how to wrap them around your arms and legs under your clothes. He made me wrap my feet in them inside my shoes. Damned uncomfortable but even with our gloves and slickers we would have frozen to death that night without those newspapers.

When the sun began to warm us a little next morning Froglegs showed me what he had in his pocket. It was a handsome pigskin wallet with ninety dollars in it.

"Froglegs," I told him, "'Wobblies don't steal.'"

"Blackie," he answered back without a trace of a stutter, "you said expropriate the expropriators."

The wallet had a name and address in it. I told him I was going to make him send it back when we got to Omega. With tears streaming down his face he swore he'd found it in a toilet in the Mormon Temple. What could you do? I always intended to make him send it back, but by the time we got to Omega we'd spent it.

Our cattlecar ended up on a siding in Elco. In the yards Froglegs got chummy with a brakeman. The brakeman took five bucks off us to look the other way while we slipped into the front end of a passenger train that was changing locomotives. We rode blind baggage through the deep snows of the Sierra. We were about starved when we tumbled out at the passenger station at Sacramento but we'd made five hundred miles in two days. We were too stiff to run when we found we'd fallen into the arms of a couple of yard dicks. They literally had us by the collar. They shook us down for another five bucks before they would turn us loose.

In Sacramento it was warm sure enough. We were sweating in those heavy slickers. The streets were crowded with guineas, greasers, Hindus, Chinamen, every kind of migratory worker. I began to breathe easier about that wallet. Even if the cops had broadcast a description from Salt Lake City in that mob we were a needle in a haystack. We went to a chink joint and ate the biggest meal they had on the place.

While we were eating we decided what to do. Froglegs insisted I take the money and go on to Omega. If I had anything left when I got there I should donate it to the strike fund. I gave him my waterproof hat and slicker to sell and bought some sneakers instead of the heavy rubber boots. I'd ride to Omega like a goddam capitalist on a passenger train and Froglegs would sell our Davenport outfits to a secondhand dealer and beat his way up on the freights. The story in the damn lying Sacramento papers was that the sheriff had thrown a cordon of deputies round the whole town of Omega.

I told Froglegs I'd expect him when I saw him. He said please not to start a general strike until he got there. All night huddled together in that baggage car he'd been asking me questions about the general strike. I'd told him it had been tried out in Seattle. He had it all figured out that the general strike would start in Omega and spread up through the Northwest and across the harvest fields to the Eastern cities and, presto, we'd have the revolution.

His questions were getting me down. It's upsetting to have everything you say taken so damned literally. "A good riddance," I told myself when I saw him laden down with slickers and boots lurching off down the street with that bowlegged walk of his.

It wasn't until I was sitting all alone in that day coach wondering what the hell was going to happen to me in Omega that I really began to miss the lad. You can't laugh off real devotion. That kid was just like a woman doing little things for you, sewing on buttons, mending ripped pants and things like that. He'd been treating me like Jesus Christ himself, but I knew he wasn't doing it for me personally. I stood for the revolution. Any little thing he could do for me was bringing the revolution that much closer. I was scared I'd let the kid down. I was kinda hoping he never would show up in Omega.

My train pulled into Omega in the rain. So far as I can remember it never stopped raining the whole time I was there. On one side of the track shiny black mudflats stretched out into the mist. On the town side you could just see the outlines of jerrybuilt storefronts through a sheet of falling water. The air smelt of wet sawdust and saltmarsh mud.

The waiting room at the depot was tracked with mud. Glum-looking stiffs in dripping slickers sat around the benches. I ducked into the toilet to keep out of sight until I could figure out which of them were dicks.

A whiskery old fellow with a straight back was washing his hands at the sink. He had on stiff clean levis. When he turned my way I saw he was wearing a carpenter's apron.

He gave me a steely blue look out of searching eyes. It wasn't a plainclothesman's look. There wasn't that kind of suspicion in it but it was plenty sharp. While he looked he slowly dried his hands on his apron. After he stared at me a while the muscles of his face relaxed. When he was through drying his hands he held out his big knotty right and bared the uneven yellow teeth under his gray soupstrainers in a smile.

"Blackie Bowman," he said.

"What the hell?" It was my turn to stare at him.

"I'm Yohansen," he said. "I saw your picture in that goddam yellow journal the *Chicago Trib.*"

I knew that Nils Johansen was the Swedish carpenter who represented the shingleweavers on the strike committee.

His face turned to wooden again. "Come," he said gruffly. "Keep some distance." He slid out of the door that led onto the platform and hurried across the rutted puddles of the muddy street. He walked with a long stride. The deputies in the station couldn't have seen us go. It was raining so hard it was all I could do to keep Johansen in sight. Right away my sneakers were soaked. I could have kicked myself for dumping that slicker and boots in Sacramento. He stopped at a door next to a boarded up grocery, rapped and disappeared. I stood so long rapping at the same door I was soaked to the skin before it opened.

Some kind of a slanteyed broadcheeked little yellow runt in a poncho who might well have been an Indian let me in and bolted the door after me. He spun around to point up the stairs with a swing of his hand and leaned his broad back against the door. Every step creaked as I walked up those steep straight stairs that led into a long narrow hall between plank partitions that ended in a groundglass door.

I pushed through the door into a brightly lit office. Johansen with a green eyeshade over his face was already at work planing the boards on some sort of a counter he was fixing in back.

He never looked up once though he put in a grunt now and then.

Three men and a freshfaced girl with bobbed yellow hair sat on folding chairs round an oldfashioned rolltop desk under a cluster of electric light bulbs in the middle of a bare boarded room. They had a tense look about them like I'd seen in a command post in a dugout behind the front lines overseas.

Ferd Smithers jumped forward and almost wrung my hand off. We'd been shipmates on that Canadian tramp in the West Indies. In spite of all his years in Canada and the States he still talked the clipped cockney of a Liverpool slummy. Ferd was hollowchested as ever. He introduced me to a big muscle-bound giant of a fellow worker with a square jaw named Englehardt and to the redheaded young Paul Jones whom I'd heard about as a real intelligent rebel. Then he pointed to the girl: "And this is Joan Smart. She's from the wrong side of the tracks to our way of thinkin', but she's a little bit of the all right."

Joan was a sociology student from Eugene, Oregon, where her father operated a planing mill. They all fell over each other to explain that in this fight she was on the side of the working stiffs. She was a nice girl but I could see right away that she was on the side of one particular young redheaded working stiff. Something about that girl's being there made us stand around chatting and gossiping like a goddam teaparty, till Johansen, who'd been making more and more noise with his plane, finally rapped with the edge of it on the board he was working on and growled: "Fellow workers the meeting will please come to order."

Then Ferd Smithers began to fill me in on the course of events.

The strike was a hundred percent effective among lumber workers in Klamath County. It was spreading to logging camps and sawmills up through Oregon and Washington. The workers were fed up with wage cuts and rotten grub and bedbugs in the bunkhouses. During the war, when Colonel Round was organizing the industry for war production, they had gotten used to being treated like white men. What our boys were telling the working stiffs was that if they didn't put up a fight now it would be back to the wooden shoes.

The lumber kings had been showing themselves in their true colors. They'd clubbed together to hire special deputies out of American Legion halls in other parts of the state. They had the local courts in their pocket. The San Francisco railroad interests were backing them. The Northern California Better Business League was announcing that the time had come to drive the IWW out of the state if it cost a million dollars. The newspapers were lashing up a lynching spirit.

Our answer was to be general strike like in Seattle the year before. If we could tie up the railroads we would win. The Brotherhoods were dead set against it but the gandywalkers and yardworkers and maintenance men knew that if the interests got away with wagecuts in the lumber industry their pay envelopes would be the next to suffer. Too damn many hungry men walking the tracks.

"Fellow workers we have an open and shut case," shouted Paul Jones in his high tense voice. "This is our chance to educate the scissorbills through the whole Northwest."

While we talked the room was filling up. The air grew steamy with wet ponchos and mackinaws and worksweated flannel shirts. Each man's story added a new touch to the picture. The minute the sheriff started making arrests our tactics had been to fill up his jail till it burst. The charges were obstructing traffic, disturbing the peace and things like that. We turned it into a free speech fight. Already we'd had three men arrested for reading the Declaration of Independence on the courthouse steps.

The jail had eight cells built to hold four men each. They had forty men shut in there. The bosses sitting in the Lumbermen's Association across the square could hear them singing "Solidarity Forever." In spite of the yard dicks and the special deputies fellow workers rode in on every freight. The railroad men were helping them.

Joan Smart piped up to put in her fifty cents worth. "It's not only the railroad men." She never took her eyes off Paul all the time she talked. She said she happened to know that the plain people of Omega were disgusted with what the railroads and the lumber companies were doing. Not all the sawmill operators were with them by a long shot.

She had talked to her dad long distance last night and had almost talked him around. Almost but not quite. He'd promised this much. He was a great friend of Colonel Round's and he'd written a telegram asking him to come back as a private citizen and set up a mediation board.

Just on her own she thought she could talk Mayor Pritchard into getting up a committee of fairminded business men to cooperate with Colonel Round. The mayor wasn't such a bad sort as we thought. She was going over to his office right now to talk to him about calling off the deputies until mediation began.

She was sweet and pretty; the boys couldn't help giving her a hand. She slipped into a becoming-looking raincoat with a hood over her head and bustled out into the rain.

When she'd gone one lanky lumberman with a three days growth of beard spat in the corner of the floor and said, "Ain't mediation another word for sellout?"

Paul flushed red. "What's the harm in trying to educate the bourgeoisie along with the rest of the scissorbills?" he asked pleadingly.

With Joan gone the meeting got down to business. The room was jampacked with men sitting on the windowledges and leaning against the walls. Where the mud wasn't too thick they sat on the floor. Johansen had to give up his carpentry work to let men sit on the counter.

"Mediation shit," shouted a heavyset guy with his hair plastered down over his forehead. Was this class war or wasn't it? If we were fighting a war we ought to act like soldiers. A couple of sticks of dynamite in the basement under the Lumbermen's Association office would teach 'em a lesson. Direct action.

Right away it hit me that the heavyset guy might be a stooly or provocator. "Hold your horses, brother," I told him. "In this fight we're fighting for the law not against it. We are demanding our legal rights as American citizens."

He came back nastily: What had Blackie Bowman ever done for the oppressed workers except send out appeals for funds from a cushy office in Chicago? How did he know I hadn't spent the money on liquor and broads?

From his perch on top of the desk, Ferd called for order. Then he asked the heavyset man in his most withering tone what he'd done that was so wonderful. Everybody started talking at once. Were we just trying to improve temporary conditions like the labor fakers or were we revolutionary syndicalists? Guys began calling each other names. The heavyset man and me were just about ready to take a poke at each other.

The meeting would have broken up with nothing accomplished but a few bloody noses if Nils Johansen hadn't stomped out into the center of the floor pushing guys apart like the referee in a prizefight.

We were all arguing about direct action, he shouted well let's have a little action. He looked around with his blue eyes blazing out from under that eyeshade until all the wrangling groups shut up. Then he said quietly that he was ready to open up his soupkitchen in the back of the hall but he needed contributions to buy grub.

The strike had been going two weeks, but more dollar bills than anybody had imagined came out of that crowd. Johansen shoved the money into the pockets of his apron. It wasn't enough, he grumbled. He'd have to send Joan and Paul around to beg food. It was all very well to yammer about the exploiting classes but if it wasn't for the kind hearts of some of the small merchants in town we'd be damn well starving to death.

Nils was an imposing fellow with his square narrow shoulders and straight back. Nobody let out a peep. Then he turned his cold stare on me and the thickset man who were still making mean eyes at each other in the middle of the floor. If we had such a head of steam why didn't we blow some of it off in the free speech fight.

There was nothing for me to do but to say I'd be there at eight o'clock tomorrow morning, rain or shine, reading the Declaration of Independence on the courthouse steps.

The heavyset man stammered that he'd be glad enough to do it but he couldn't read so good.

That brought a laugh that relieved the strain. The boys elected a few more members to the strike committee and me among them and sang a few songs and the meeting broke up.

I couldn't read so good either that morning. Standing around in my wet clothes all day had given me an awful cold. I always was subject to colds. It had stopped raining but the air was raw and misty. "When in the course of human events . . ." I coughed and wheezed and stumbled over words. Nobody seemed to be paying a damn bit of attention. A few people passing on the street did look up as if they were wondering what the hell I was doing. I'd just gotten to "Life, Liberty and the Pursuit of Happiness" when I caught sight of Froglegs. There'd been so much doing since I hit Omega I'd forgotten about Froglegs.

There were his popeyes shining up out of the mess of faces

on the sidewalk. He was just drinking in every word. Seeing Froglegs made me feel responsible. I wanted to stop to explain to the kid that all this guff about government was just a lot of words made up to delude the working class. Then as I read on it began to sound like the Preamble . . . "That to secure these Rights governments are instituted among men . . ." I cleared my throat and really shouted when I read "Whenever any form of government becomes destructive of these ends it is the right of the People to alter or abolish it." That was good wobbly doctrine. I was looking right down at Froglegs, talking straight at him, saying to him as I read, "Now you can believe this, son."

That's as far as I got. Those two deputies must have been standing behind me for some time because they both grabbed me at once. One pinned my arms and the other caught my neck in the crotch of his elbow. They pulled me up those steps like a sack of flour.

I didn't have a cent in my pocket because I'd turned over all the change I had left to Nils Johansen for the soupkitchen like I'd promised Froglegs and I didn't have an address so they booked me for vagrancy and shoved me into the cellblock with the rest of the boys. They were in high spirits and just beginning to tune up for the day's singing with "Longhaired preachers come out every night!"

Later that day the turnkey came around leering at us through the bars to announce that we were getting a break. The town of Omega was tired of feeding us and was going to turn us loose up near Happy Camp where he knew we'd enjoy the scenery. "Happy Camp" he kept saying it over as if he found the name hellishly funny.

There must have been fifty of us by this time. We were herded out of the jail and marched between two files of deputies out into the yards. One little skinny fellow tried to run, and a deputy brought him down with a load of buckshot in the legs the way you'd bring down a jackrabbit. We learned afterwards he was three months in a hospital and walked with a limp for the rest of his life.

They loaded us on flatcars at the end of a freight and the deputies rode in the caboose with their guns sticking out of the windows. It was raining again by that time and it got cold as hell as the train chugged up through the redwood forest up into a mountain valley all streaked with mist.

I was just beginning to get my bearings when who should come wriggling his way through the guys on the flatcar but Froglegs. He was wearing a nice newlooking poncho. He squatted down beside me with a "Howdy Blackie" and pulled out another poncho he had tied around his waist.

When I asked him how come, he started to giggle. All he'd done was stand in line at a window in the alley back of the Lumbermen's Association when they were handing out ponchos and blankets to a bunch of deputies. Damned if they wouldn't have given him a gun if he'd asked for it.

It was cold up in that damn coastal range. Whenever the clouds moved aside a little you could see snow on the upper slopes.

Up at some kind of a mountain junction the deputies swarmed out of the caboose and herded all of us into a sheep corral. Anyone who tried to climb out was going to get shot they told us. The sheriff made us a speech about how we were being treated with humanity and kindness and if any of us showed his dirty face in Omega again he'd sure enough get his block knocked off and he and his deputies piled on the down train and the engine hooted and they pulled out. There we were seventyseven miles from nowhere.

The boys were starting to debate about what to do, but this was a time to go it alone, so as soon as the two trains were out of sight Froglegs and I started off down a logging road. Afterwards I thought I ought to have stayed on account of being on the strike committee but that was how we wobblies were. Froglegs and I were just about spavined when we came to a camp. This camp was so isolated they hadn't heard of the strike yet. Nobody there but the cook and a couple of stiffs who'd reported sick. When we told 'em what was being done to their fellow workers down in Omega they were burned up. The cook gave us a place to sleep and to dry our clothes and all the grub we could eat. Even the foreman seemed sympathetic. When he came in with the work crew that evening he didn't run us out.

Five days later Froglegs and I slipped off a freight a couple of miles outside of Omega and waited in a jungle Froglegs knew that was a dry cave hidden in a thicket of saplings until it was dark enough to slip into town. Nobody said boo to us. The little Indian grinned his head off when he let us by the door at strike headquarters. Up in the hall we found Nils's soupkitchen going great guns, and the boys lined up at the counter for their chow and Nils stirring the slum and Paul and Joan slicing sandwiches just like a Sundayschool picnic.

They told us the deportation hadn't gone so good in the national press. A couple of politicians from districts where lumberjacks voted had raised hell in the legislature. A delegation of ministers had waited on the governor. Colonel Rounds was in town staying at the Redwood Hotel and arranging a meeting between the Lumbermen's Association and the strike committee. "If that ain't recognition what is it?" Paul kept asking.

Joan put in that she'd called a massmeeting in the Opera House to hear the strikers' side of the story. Reporters from the national press were going to cover it. Nils was going to speak and Ferd and Paul. Kate Levine had telegraphed from Chicago she could come, the famous Kate Levine of Paterson and Passaic and Mesabi Range fame.

"Humph," I said.

I knew what kind of a hellroaring orator Kate was. I knew damn well that if we were trying for a peaceable settlement she was the last speaker in the world we wanted, but it was too late. Anyway there was nothing I could do. My cold had gone into my chest and first thing I knew I was down with pneumonia and laid away in a bed being nursed by Paul's grandmother, a nice whitehaired old lady who kept a boardinghouse down by the depot. They told me afterwards I was pretty near kicking the pail.

Anyway the fever had gone and I was sitting up in bed when who should come storming in but my blessed sisterin-law Kate. "Can't take it eh?" was the first thing she said. Then she began on the family news. Freddie Davis had been indicted for his part in setting up the Communist Workers Party USA at that meeting that got raided on the Indiana dunes and had skipped off to the Soviet Union. That had left Eileen at loose ends and she'd taken up with Murray Katz her boss at *Art and Apparel*. Probably been sleeping with him all along. "Job security," said Kate sourly. Might as well call her a kept woman and be frank about it. She hated to tell me but she thought I'd rather hear it from a member of the family than a stranger.

Kate added with a toss of her red head that she'd come to town in the nick of time to head off a sellout that Johansen and Smithers were negotiating behind the workers' backs. This

must be turned into a revolutionary strike. She was going to
tell the lumber workers that the international working class
was behind them. Discipline, solidarity. No concessions to the
exploiting class. Everywhere the workers of the world were
casting off their chains. Now was the time for every man to
stand up and be counted. I was an enthusiast in those days
but it gave me cold chills to hear her.

They had me sitting on the platform that night with the rest
of the strike committee. I was pale and shaky, wrapped in a
blanket to look like a sort of small time class war martyr. Kate
was at her best. Her speech was magnificent but it was a declaration of war. She had half the audience singing the International before she was through. After it, before the applause
had died away Paul drove her to the station in Joan's car to
catch the train. Kate was comfortably asleep in another state
in her Pullman berth by the time the consequences of what
she'd said began to take shape.

The state attorney general was in the audience. He had a
stenographer with him taking down every word. He sat up all
night at the Redwood Hotel drawing up an indictment for
criminal syndicalism of every man who sat on that platform.
His heart was in his work because, if he could make the indictment stick he could see a nomination for Lieutenant Governor on the Republican ticket in the cards.

At the same time the Lumbermen's Association jumped at
Kate's speech with glee. Reds were a real bogey in those days.
All they needed to prove it was their patriotic duty to run us
out of the lumber camps was to have the strike committee
turn out a bunch of reds. Bright and early next morning they
sent word to Colonel Round that they wouldn't negotiate until
he found them a legitimate union to negotiate with. At the
same time they got hold of the dago who owned the building
where our hall was and terrorized him into signing a notice of
eviction for nonpayment of rent. That was true enough. We
intended to pay next day.

They served that notice next morning while we were ladling
out the breakfast. They rushed the hall from two sides. The
fire department set ladders against the back windows. We
fought back as best we could but our boys didn't have any
guns. We sure busted some heads among the strong arm gang
before they overpowered us. It was as bad as Centralia except
there was nobody killed.

I was so damn weak from the pneumonia I couldn't put up much resistance. They dragged me down the stairs first thing. The last thing I saw was that poor little Indian who acted as doorman lying face up with his eyes closed, on the pavement outside. His face was pulp. I heard afterwards that the fight went on until somebody upset one of the primus stoves we used to cook with and the fire department had to go to work sure enough to save the building. The smoke did what those damn deputies couldn't do. It cleared the hall in short order.

This time there was no nonsense about singing jailbirds in the Omega jail. The attorney general had warrants all ready for us and packed us on the first train to Sacramento to be held for a special grand jury. They treated us like really important prisoners. They had Nils Johansen and me in a drawing room with a pair of plain clothes dicks. I was too sick to do anything but sit there, but Nils was absolutely unperturbed. I never admired a man more. All the way down to Sacramento, in that grumbling voice he had, he lectured me and the two flatfeet on syndicalism.

Syndicalism he said was organizing society according to types of production. Lumber workers, railroad workers, carpenters, construction workers, architects, doctors, scientists, engineers should be organized according to their craft. That's what syndicates were, craft guilds to do the world's work. There would be no room for leeches, politicians, lawyers, money lenders, labor leaders—all the bloodsuckers who lived on other men's work. A world without exploitation. Such a plan may be visionary, he said to the flatfeet, but why should you yentlemen say it is criminal?

They didn't have a word to say in reply.

I always figured it was on account of Nils Johansen's respectable manner that they treated me as well as they did while they held us for trial. They kept me in the hospital much longer than they needed to. Evidently the attorney general didn't want to present Nils to a jury because he got him deported to Sweden instead of including him in the indictment. The rest of us were held on fifteen thousand dollars bail, which we weren't able to raise. Since Big Bill Haywood had jumped bail and run off to the Soviet Union it was hard to find a bondsman for an IWW. The trial was a Roman holiday for the newspapers. That case was the beginning of Coates

Anderson's political career. I'm glad somebody got some good out of it.

Judge Marvin Squires, the judge we were tried before, must have had political aspirations too because he and Anderson worked hand in glove to railroad us. Joan's dad hired Paul Jones a good lawyer who got him off with a suspended sentence on account of his youth, but Smithers and I didn't have any money and the defense committee was on the rocks with so many cases to defend so the judge appointed a toadying little bastard named Briggs to defend us. The conclusion was foregone. The jury found Guilty. Judge Squires slapped on ten years in jail. Maybe he was hoping to emulate Kenesaw Mountain Landis.

The last time I saw Froglegs was the day the Judge delivered his verdict. Froglegs had beaten his way back to Sacramento. He didn't miss a minute of the trial. I always wondered how he ate. There he was every day staring at me from the public seats. After my conviction, before sentence was passed, they let me sit a few minutes at the lawyers' table to talk to my great friend Briggs about the chance of an appeal. That was when Froglegs came squirming past the court attendants and tapped me on the shoulder.

"Blackie," he said earnestly. "I've got something for you. You'll need it in there." He slipped something into my pocket. I didn't dare look till I got back to my cell, and then I had to give it to the turnkey to keep with my valuables. It was a handsome gold huntingcase watch. God knows who he'd lifted it off of, or what he thought I'd do with it in stir. Count off the hours of my time maybe. All those hours when I was wondering who Eileen was sleeping with now.

When I emerged into the world again a couple of years later after a civil liberties committee induced a new liberal governor to issue us pardons, I used to tell the story that Froglegs had asked to see Judge Squires in chambers and had lifted the watch right out of the judge's own vest. He could have done it if he had a mind to. That boy was a real sleight of hand artist. I like to believe that was how he got it.

I came out of jail with a horrible thirst. It wasn't long before I hocked the watch to buy liquor. I never heard of Froglegs again.

Documentary (12)

UPWARD SURGE PUTS BUSINESS ON RIGHT PATH

Sulphur Endures an Unhappy Year

His job is to set up the marketing climate a great advertising campaign needs to achieve greatness. He can and will walk with the client every step of the way, from the plant to the point-of-sale, through distribution, merchandizing dealer relations.

Shoe Advertising Becomes Casual

"Do not think of Mother's Day as a one-day or one-week event. It's a three-week business festival."

"This has been dramatically demonstrated for us by the high mortality rates of new products," Mr. Harris said. "New products today are the key factor, not only in company growth but in company survival. Yet it's estimated that seven out of ten new products fail."

BIGGEST MOTHER'S DAY EVER

More Mothers to remember. 25,650,000 in 1940 increased to an estimated 40,000,000 in 1959—nearly 60% more mothers to give gifts to in 1960.

More devoted fathers enjoying higher incomes than ever and with more money to spend. And millions more children who love to give Mother gifts especially the 'teen tycoons' earning money and eager to remember Mom. More lavish and expensive gifts to be given than ever. The whole trend in gift giving is a continuous trading up.

NO TRADES AT OPENING

Inviting sales climate

plan a strong instore display program using posters, display cards, badges for sales people, pennants, package stickers, streamers and carnations

Rover

On September 11 1884 there was born in a tall brownstone house in a fashionable section of New York,

with a silver spoon in her mouth and all the aristocracy the Empire State could afford in those great days of the high bourgeoisie,

a little girl. Eleanor was a Roosevelt, an Oyster Bay Roosevelt. Her father was T.R.'s kid brother Elliott. Her mother was Anna Hall of a rich upstate family of Halls.

Except for T.R.'s roughhousing affection for his homely little niece (she had the same buck teeth he had) her childhood was miserable.

Her father shared T.R.'s cult of the outdoors, loved dogs and horses and back country travel, but Daddy was a ne'erdowell and mostly he drank. He was a handsome man, debonair. The little girl loved him but hardly ever saw him because he was always off taking the cure in some sanitarium. Finally he retired to the Valley of Virginia where drunkenness was still considered a rather gentlemanly profession.

Her mother was a tense nagging woman with a taste for amateur theatricals. She called little Nell "Granny" the child was so glum. She suffered from headaches.

Both parents died by the time Eleanor was ten.

She was raised by a succession of German and English governesses at her Grandmother Hall's place at Tivoli up the Hudson. Mrs. Hall didn't believe in sending girls away to school. The only outings in Eleanor's life were in connection with the doing of good. The Hudson River aristocrats never forgot their duty to those less fortunate than they.

Charity was fun. The Hall girls, Eleanor's aunts, properly chaperoned and at suitable times and seasons, sang hymns in Bowery missions or dressed Christmas trees in Hell's Kitchen. As a special treat little Eleanor would be taken along to visit a children's hospital.

How the other half lived: there was a smell of sweat and grime and adventure about poor people's kids. What daydreams would be touched off by a greedy glance from a sullenfaced Jewish boy, or the grin of some ruddy little Irish mick. Their morals were deplorable. The aim of charity was to reform the morals of the poor. Their deplorable morals, said Grandmother Hall, was why they were poor.

Grandmother Hall hated Roosevelts. She wasn't too fond of shy gangling Eleanor. She discouraged her visits to her rambunctious uncle's house at Oyster Bay. Eleanor bit her nails and yearned, cooped among maids and governesses in the big old bracketed mansion at Tivoli. She read and reread her dear dead father's admonishing letters, and books with titles that seemed to apply: *Misunderstood, Sans Famille, The Man Without a Country.*

When she was fifteen there was a break in the clouds. She was sent to boarding school in England.

Allenwood, near Wimbledon Common on the outskirts of London, was, around the turn of the century, in charge of a remarkably intelligent French spinster. Mlle. Souvestre was a woman of letters, an agnostic, (atheist, hissed her enemies) of the Voltairian school now exemplified by the gentle Renan, an anticlerical Dreyfusard, a pacifist, a feminist: give women votes and they'd see about man's perfectibility or know the reason why. Just the woman to stuff the head of a yearning young girl from Tivoli up the Hudson with all the glowing nineteenth century notions of the good the beautiful and the true.

A Miss Strachey, of the literary Stracheys, taught literature. This was no ordinary school. Eleanor Roosevelt was happy for the first time in her life.

Mlle. Souvestre liked Americans. She liked Eleanor and took her along on summer tours of the artgalleries of Europe

The story goes that Eleanor was still so shy and bucktoothed and gangling that Mlle. Souvestre had no qualms about letting her run around Florence all alone (no danger of her being picked up by a gay deceiver); but in the school she was a leader. She had found her place in the world.

It was real heartbreak when at eighteen the family brought her home. She wanted to go to college but her grandmother insisted on her coming out instead.

She took refuge in the Junior League and teaching calisthenics and dancing at the Rivington Street Settlement. Uplift. She became interested in sweatshops. She never forgot her duty to those less fortunate than she.

On the train back and forth between New York and Tivoli she began occasionally to meet another Roosevelt, a cousin, who got off at Hyde Park.

If Eleanor had a formidable grandmother, her cousin Franklin, an only child, had a mother who was allconsuming. At Groton she appeared almost weekly to heckle Dr. Peabody. When Franklin went to Harvard he rented a house at the edge of the Yard. When he took up law at Columbia there she was making a home for him on Madison Avenue. Maybe it was parental tyranny that brought Franklin and Eleanor together.

When she discovered the cousins were "interested" Sara Roosevelt promptly took her boy Franklin off on a Caribbean cruise to break it up. After that she dragged him to Washington, but who should she find, when she took her boy to the White House for a cousinly visit, but Eleanor eating lunch with her Uncle Ted.

In spite of Mama they became engaged. Maybe it was Eleanor's influence that caused Franklin D, brought up as a proper gold Democrat at Hyde Park, to vote Republican for her Uncle Ted in 1904.

Their wedding on March 17th 1905 was the social event of that New York spring. The newly inaugurated President was there, bubbling with "Bully" and grinning his bucktoothed grin. Vanderbilts, Sloans, Belmonts, Riggses, Van Rensselaers, Mortimers represented the Four Hundred. A rowdy mob of T.R.'s political supporters cheered in the street outside.

Hyde Park was an anticlimax. Franklin's mother took charge of everything, hired nurses for the numerous babies that appeared promptly in order, decorated their rooms, and ordered their servants around. It wasn't much fun. Franklin D was bored to death with the law. His pleasure was sailing his schooner yacht which, like a good Hudson River man, he named *Halfmoon*. At Hyde Park he served in the vestry, joined the volunteer Hook and Ladder, was director of the bank. In the same spirit he let himself be elected to the legislature.

Eleanor Roosevelt was developing a ferocious energy equal to the energy of her Uncle T.R. No outlet for it at Hyde Park where her motherinlaw wouldn't even let her boil an egg. Her real life lay in the settlement houses; uplift, the wrongs of the working girl. Conditions: the horrible Triangle fire kindled a torch.

At Albany in 1911, though his mother tried to take over Franklin's political career as she had everything else, Eleanor had her first taste of politics. There was a smell of sweat and grime and adventure about politicians. They hadn't had the advantages. She took to them. Politics like settlement work was dealing with those less fortunate than she.

Reform was in the air. The better element was going in for public service. Wasn't Uncle Ted in the White House? Professor Woodrow Wilson, late president of Princeton, was Governor of New Jersey.

Sara Roosevelt, an old lady and behind the times, still felt it was infradig. Her boy Franklin was developing a knack for dealing with people who weren't the kind of people she would want to invite into her home. Eleanor was all for it: it was the duty of the better element to improve conditions.

In Albany Franklin D acquired a familiar. An odd uncouth individual, an oldtime newspaperman named Louis Howe decided he'd dedicate his life to building a political career for Franklin Delano Roosevelt. When Representative Roosevelt came down with typhoid while running for the state senate, Eleanor had to do the campaigning. Louis Howe coached her. Eleanor learned to make speeches. They were halting but they were sincere. People responded. She loved it.

Where Franklin D still showed, at that stage in his career, some difficulty in disguising his feeling that the plain people

existed mostly as convenient steppingstones on which young
Hudson River magnates,

could climb to high office,

his wife Eleanor just loved them. She wanted to be folks.
She'd never heard of fatigue. She poured all the capabilities
that her motherinlaw frustrated at home into doing her duty
toward those less fortunate than she,

and pushing her husband's career.

Louis Howe saw that as a team the young Roosevelts would
go far. Already he dreamed of the presidency for Franklin D.
Woodrow Wilson, the first Democrat since Grover Cleveland,
had just been elected by a good majority of electoral votes.
He was combing the better element (among Democrats) for
deserving civil servants. After considerable backing and filling
it was arranged that Josephus Daniels should offer

to Franklin D. Roosevelt of New York

the post of Assistant Secretary of the Navy. It fitted Franklin D to a T. The man was crazy about ships and the sea.
Eleanor and Louis Howe couldn't help having it in the back
of their minds that this was the post from which her Uncle
Ted had embarked on a triumphant career.

The story is told that it was the seventeen gun salute,
given her son when the warship *North Dakota* put in to East-
port, across the bay from their summer home at Campobello
Island, that finally convinced Sara Roosevelt that politics
might become a gentleman's career. She hurried off to Washington, where the young people were setting up housekeeping
in a house lent them by one of Eleanor's aunts, to boss the
household as usual.

         Young Roosevelt impressed official Washington. Tall
and slender, with a hearty laugh and a clear profile that might
have been drawn by Charles Dana Gibson, he was so handsome people called him "The Gibson Man." Already he was
developing the subtly condescending smile that was later to
sweep all hearts.

With the declaration of war against the Central Powers on
April 2 1917 Franklin D's post in the Navy Department became a cornerstone of the war effort. Eleanor's Uncle Ted
kept teasing him to resign and enlist for front line service,
but he was doing a good efficient job where he was and he

intended to stick. It broke Uncle Ted's heart when Wilson's administration, suspecting that he wanted to steal the front line limelight from the Democrats, refused to let him raise a division of new Rough Riders to lead overseas.

In the winter of 1919 Uncle Ted died a frustrated disappointed man. Eleanor and Franklin were touring prostrate Europe at the time, liquidating Navy hardware and surplus stocks. They came home with the presidential party on the *George Washington* with the glamour of victory about them.

Louis Howe was busy. Berty McCormick in the *Chicago Tribune* was already promoting Franklin D for the presidency. He was nominated for Vice-President and campaigned with a forgotten gentleman named James M. Cox who was soundly trounced by Harding in the election of 1920.

It was a discouraging campaign. The following summer Franklin D suffered a crippling attack of poliomyelitis at Campobello Island. His mother's attitude seems to have been that now at last she had her baby back, a lifetime invalid. Everybody thought he was done except his wife Eleanor and his friend Louis Howe. Never say die. Eleanor had some of her Uncle Ted's ferocious spirit. Louis Howe was a man dedicated to the point of mania. Franklin D would be President all the same.

The man's affliction transformed his public presence. Overcoming paralysis took an enormous effort of the will. Fortunatus was laid low. Misery may ennoble but it also levels. The raggedest streetcleaner out of work had not had to endure the misery Franklin D. Roosevelt endured and overcame in the four years before his return to politics. To go from room to room without his braces he had to drag himself along the floor. He ended by pretending he wasn't crippled at all. The reporters favored him. Even the hardboiled press photographers tacitly agreed not to photograph him in an embarrassing position.

No more private life for the Roosevelts. Louis Howe arranged every detail with an eye to the presidency.

Her husband's affliction put work on Eleanor Roosevelt's shoulders, speeches, meetings, decisions that affected the welfare of those less fortunate than she. She loved it. For the first time she had a cottage of her own at Hyde Park where she

could entertain her dogooder friends. As depression threatened
she fought local unemployment by starting a furniture factory
to give winter work to the Dutchess County agricultural
laborers.

The last of her brood was in college. Now she could devote
her whole day to movements, to uplift, to improving conditions. She was a force in the Women's Trade Union League.
She'd always wanted to teach. She owned an interest in the
Todhunter school in New York. She began teaching classes
there three times a week. Maybe she was still modeling herself
a little on Mlle. Souvestre.

With the Al Smith campaign Eleanor began to sense
the first intimations of New Deal politics. She and Louis Howe
convinced Franklin D that in spite of his braces he must act
as Al Smith's floor manager at the Houston convention. They
induced him to run for Governor of New York and succeeded
beyond their wildest dreams. While Al Smith lost his home
state by a hundred thousand votes, Franklin D carried it by
twentyfive thousand.

Eleanor had her own office now in the General Motors
Building, her own staff of secretaries to handle her burgeon-
ing mail. It was Eleanor who put Frances Perkins in the state
labor department. In American politics the day of the social
worker had come.

When Franklin D was nominated for the presidency in
1932 in Chicago Eleanor celebrated the occasion by performing one of her few recorded acts of domesticity. She herself
personally cooked ham and eggs for the assembled company
at the governor's mansion in Albany before flying to Chicago
with her husband for his speech of acceptance.

When Franklin D was inaugurated as 32nd President of the
United States it was his mother he gave his arm to when they
went in to their first lunch at the White House. Eleanor
trotted along behind.

But soon she was being described as "the woman who in all
American history has played the biggest part in public affairs."

The hundred days. Social workers, bright young men, youth
leaders, the brain trust. It was Eleanor who uncovered that
astute uplifter Harry Hopkins from among her social worker
friends. Figures from every movement for social betterment in
the country crisscrossed on Mrs. Roosevelt's White House

calendar: folkdancers, arts and crafters, Communist organizers, campfire girls, Negro waitresses, delinquent boys, unmarried mothers, young peoples leagues for this and that. She found time for them all. She encouraged them all. She was a pushover for the word youth.

Politics costs money. Being President is an expensive business. Like many of the congenitally rich the Roosevelts counted themselves poor if they had to dip into their principal. Franklin D was always fuming about how broke they were. Eleanor went to work to make money.

She wrote articles, she lectured, she became editor of a Bernarr McFadden magazines: *Babies, Just Babies*. Radio programs. She went on the air to advertise a facial cream. An endless stream of words poured out to secretaries, into dictaphones, was scribbled on scratchpads on planes or railroad trains or in the back seats of automobiles. In "If you ask me" she answered questions monthly for the readers of the *Ladies' Home Journal*. In "My Day" she prattled about her doings for all the world to read.

She was for uplifting everybody everywhere, right away, now: working girls, bonus marchers, sharecroppers, unemployed veterans, Negroes, delinquents . . . if only they said the right word.

(A word is a package. Packaging is the national obsession. No need to look inside if you say the right word.)

As First Lady she was the supreme right thinker of the age.

In the wartime hierarchy Mrs. R became the global VIP.

Like royalty she hurried through the daily hour, the endless inspecting, of hospitals, jails, insane asylums, nursery schools, kindergartens, training camps, housing developments. The laying of cornerstones, the commemoration of events: Mrs. Roosevelt was always so interested. Always she found a way to blurt out a few words straight from the heart. In England during the bombings she walked Mrs. Winston Churchill into a collapse. People fainted in hospital corridors trying to keep up with her. Her code name was Rover.

Twenty appointments a day. Always on the move. In the hurry of secretaries and the babble of visitors and the bustle to reach the next appointment on time there was never a moment to distinguish between a good cause and a shady one. The way some people reach blindly into the medicine cabinet. Any medicine will do. Mrs. R was for youth or labor or working women or the underprivileged, for people discriminated against, come hell or high water. Sometimes there's rat poison in the medicine cabinet. It never occurred to the right thinkers that the resentments they fanned up among the underprivileged might become the sinew of new oppressions.

At that there were moments when the old humanitarian impulse rang true. Mrs. R did her best to oppose the brutal measures against American citizens of Japanese ancestry the winter of Pearl Harbor. When President Truman appointed her, after her husband's death (of course she was off lecturing when he suffered his fatal stroke), to the delegation that went to London to set up the United Nations she gave the terrible prosecutor Vishinsky a piece of her mind when he tried to get his hands on the refugees who had fled to the West from the Soviet police.

First Lady of the United Nations; uplift became global.

A tall spare blue-eyed woman, living in a second floor apartment in a brownstone house in the East 60's in New York . . . At seven sharp she got out of bed, turned her own mattress, did calisthenics. She never smoked or drank. Her diet was spare. By eight when her secretary came in with the mail Mrs. R was ready to begin her eighteen hour day
     of dedication
to the word with the welfare label.

At seventyfive she was knocked down by a car on the street. She was on her feet in a jiffy. Before anyone could help her, she brushed herself off and went on to deliver three speeches that morning without losing her breath.

Documentary (13)

PROFIT RATES REPORTED DOWN

The Indians Are Coming

opulent Eastern atmosphere combined with Western know-how in a uniquely personal service

JUDGE TO ASK MONITOR TO LEAVE

Teamster Chief Talks with South Jersey Group in Move to Unionize Farmers

MULTIMILLION MILE PILOTS

Each human cell has about ten thousand genes, the basic units determining all hereditary characteristics. Genes act by dictating the structure of enzymes. These are protein substances that promote and control chemical actions in all living things.

A VERSATILE HAT THAT CAN BE WORN IN A VARIETY OF WAYS

As a Massager the Electric Hair Brush Relaxes Tired Muscles, Relieves Muscular Tension, Eliminates Fatigue

LONG EARTHQUAKE WAVES
now available in actual sizes

"We have been under pressure for five years," a railroad worker wrote his lawyer, "not knowing which day was the last one we would work or which knock at the door would mean an act of violence or

187

which phone call would be a threat. This duress is more than is expected of an honest man to endure. Doesn't sound like we live in America. . . ."

The Big Office (*continued*)

The whistles are blowing. Terry walks back into the plant with the words International Union ringing in his ears. Washing up to go home after his shift he finds himself next to Steve Slansky. Steve's a handsome young fellow and Steve knows it. He has the same black hair and big eyes as his brother George without the puffy white fishfaced look. After rubbing the suds off his neatly cut features he stands combing his hair in a small handmirror he keeps in his locker. The younger guys on the shift call him Clark Gable.

"Let's you and me have a talk, Steve." Terry's voice is muffled by his towel. Steve gives Terry a standoffish look as if he half expected him to make an indecent proposal. "Why not?" he says as he pulls the shirt over his brown shoulders. As they walk out the gate he adds hastily, "I got a date but it never hurt a dame to keep her waitin'."

"Is it true?" asks Terry when they are out of earshot of the groups of men streaming into the parking lot. "Is it true you got a brother in the International?"

"Sure," says Steve. "Milan. He's the oldest."

"Then Shorty was right."

"Sure," says Steve. "We got six in the family. Three boys and three girls. Where's your car?"

Terry answers in an embarrassed voice that he's sold his car. He has other things to pay for. The wife is having a baby.

"A married man don't need no car," says Steve soothingly. "Not unless he's playin' around. We'll take mine."

They climb into a flashy old Chrysler roadster. "You sure keep your car up nice," says Terry. "It goes big with the women," says Steve with a wink as he slips her in gear.

They stop at the Melody Inn on Route 1 for a beer. Steve proves an easy fellow to get along with.

He rattles on about how his brother Milan is Field Representative. He'd have sent organizers into Raritan long ago only he didn't want to embarrass George and then they only had three hundred workers. Milan had bigger fish to fry. George and Milan they didn't see eye to eye. Milan kept telling George a feller had more of a future in labor than with the goddam employers. Labor took care of its own. But George's wife she had other ideas. She saw herself the young executive's wife, joining the country club and all that. "They don't see eye to eye"; Steve shrugs over his beer, "but blood is thicker than water."

Terry says he can't see why, since they already have an organization set up across the street at Consolidated, the International can't spare a man for Raritan. He's been talking around a little on the q.t. The men are ripe for it but they need somebody of their own kind to help head it up. They know the independent union is for the birds. They respect the Slansky boys.

Terry can see Steve puffing himself up when he hears that. "The old man was in politics," Steve drawls. "He was gettin' to be a pretty big wheel before he died." Steve shows his small even teeth in a grin. "The trouble was he blew in his dough as soon as he laid his hands on it. I guess I take after him," Steve laughs. "Milan and George now, they invest their money."

Terry launches into a plan he had to teach American to the men in the plant. They'll never get a break until they can read and write the language.

Steve begins to catch fire. "That was how the old man got his start in Democratic politics. The East End Naturalization Club. He never did learn real good himself, but he'd have gone a long ways if he hadn't lived it up."

By the time Steve dropped Terry off at his home after Terry had bought him a couple more beers, Steve was seeing himself as a leader of men. He was puffed up like a toad in the spring. "Next time I see that bossy big brother of mine," he said belligerently, "I'm goin' to ask him right out why he won't help us get an International Union."

Tasha was a little miffed because Terry was late. "Those Slanskys," she said with a toss of her head when he told her who he'd been with, "I don't know how far I'd trust 'em." Since she had been out doing the shopping she had been talking with the women at the A & P. She'd heard plenty about those Slanskys. That was where you learned about people, shopping at the A & P.

Tasha wasn't any girl to hold a grudge. While they ate their supper she began to get all enthused talking about teaching those people English. Once the baby had a good start that was something she could help in. After all they were her folks. The old man came from Montenegro. She didn't remember much, but she guessed she knew enough Serbian to interpret a little. She didn't know how far she could get with the Poles.

The next thing Terry did was to ask Steve over after supper one night to meet Earl Fagan. Steve thought Earl was great. After that they talked union every noon hour.

The baby turned out to be a little girl. They named her Natalie. The delivery took hours more than Terry thought it would, but the doctor said mother and child were both healthy specimens and that everything would be all right. When Terry walked back into the hospital lobby after taking a long look through the glass at the little pink bigeyed thing the nurse said was his daughter who should be hanging on his coatsleeve but Mom.

Good old Mom had come all the way over from Ridgefield. Terry hadn't dared go to see her since he got married for fear of a run in. Now she was too excited about the baby to think of anything else. She'd had to change buses four times. "I reckoned I better come and not sit there worrying," she said.

They blarneyed the head nurse into letting Mom in to see Tasha and the baby. When Mom learned that Tasha had plenty of milk and was going to breast-feed the baby it broke her all up. Tasha and Mom were friends from then on.

The trouble began when they took Tasha and the baby home from the hospital. Tasha's mother was waiting for them at the apartment with her head tied up in a shawl, a peasant type from the old country. The two old women bristled and spat when they saw each other like two cats in an alley. Mom bundled up her things and caught the first bus home to Ridgefield.

The baby got along and Tasha got along. Tasha put on a

little extra weight but Terry said it just made more of her to love.

The English classes were fun. About ten men would crowd into the Bryants' tiny front room two nights a week. Tasha complained that they tracked in dirt and that she never could get the smell of cheap tobacco out of the window curtains, but she was the one who really did the teaching. By the time they called the classes off on account of the hot summer weather the four younger men had all applied for naturalization. The older men only held off because they were afraid they'd make fools of themselves in court.

The International sent in a hollowchested little grayfaced middle-aged guy named Fred Russell for an organizer. Fred sure didn't have the build for a rubber worker Terry thought to himself; it was all heavy work in a rubber shop and you could usually tell a rubber worker by his big hands and thick chest. When he asked him Fred said what the hell, he'd worked fifteen years as a shipping clerk in one of the Akron factories and he'd walked the picket line and slept in the plant with the rest of them during the sitdowns. If that didn't make him a rubber worker he'd like to know what would.

Fred was a little shrimp of a man but a first rate organizer. The International had sent him to take a course in labor organizing in a middle western university. Fred furnished all the papers and hired them a smart young local attorney named Wyzanski and Terry and Steve saw to it that the men on every shift got a chance to sign a petition to the NLRB for an election. The management didn't put up any opposition. Terry figured George Slansky must have talked the management into thinking it would cost them less money to roll with the punch.

The trouble was with the foremen. They were most of them foreigners. Some of them barely spoke English. They didn't come out in the open, but they went around hinting darkly about how these damn newcomers who didn't have any seniority didn't have no right to stick their noses in other people's business.

The foremen were powerful men in that plant. Some of them did a little moneylending on the side. The one they called Duke, a big swarthy hunky with a black mustache over his mouth, was supposed to hold mortgages on the homes of half the men in his department. Men hinted to Terry that

Duke took a kickback whenever he got them a raise in classification. There was favoritism in wage scales and even in piece work rates. The slogan of Terry's that went over biggest in inducing the men to sign up for the election was: "Equal pay for equal work."

The day the International won the election, Terry hurried home to tell Tasha that it was the happiest day in his life: except the day they got married, he added hastily putting his arm around her shoulders.

She grabbed hold of his ear and kissed him where his neck was ticklish right under it. "You big old labor organizer you," she whispered.

They held the first meeting of the new local at Ukrainian Hall downtown. Fred Russell and the boys from the state organizations sat on the platform. Earl Fagan was there grinning all over his ugly face. Milan Slansky as field representative was chairman. This was the first time Terry saw Milan in action.

Milan Slansky was a big square man with a spudshaped nose over a squarecut black mustache. He sure did know how to run a meeting. He talked slow and easy as if he just couldn't imagine that anybody could disagree with anything he said. If a guy spoke out of turn he just gave him a hard black stare out of his long slits of eyes from under their heavy lids.

Milan had told Terry he would have the honor of nominating Steve Slansky for president of the local. About a dozen men jumped up to second him. Steve was elected and the whole slate. Terry found himself a trustee and a member of the executive board along with some of the officers of the old independent union. The men voted everything just the way Milan said. They all went home to their wives with flushed faces and shining eyes. From now on things were going to be different at Raritan's Plant #7.

Terry was the most popular man in the plant. His department unanimously re-elected him shopsteward. He was chairman of the new safety committee set up according to the rules laid down in the booklet Fred Russell distributed to every member. Terry kept one in the back pocket of his overalls. Wherever he went he met grins and confiding nods.

The next evening Fred Russell came around to say goodbye. "Congratulations Terry," he shouted as he came up the stairs. He'd be off next morning on another assignment.

Tasha made him stay to supper with them. While she was working over the stove, Fred gave Terry the lowdown.

"Never make a move, Terry, unless you are sure you have the boys solid behind you, then make it snappy." They sat on two chairs facing each other. Fred kept edging up so that his knees touched Terry's and pushing his thin nose towards Terry's ear. Fred didn't drink or smoke; his breath smelled of some kind of mouthwash. He'd occasionally lay a crooked finger along the side of his nose. "Don't try to get everything you want all at once, see?"

"All we want is the conditions they got across the street at Consolidated," said Terry hotly. "Equal pay for equal work. That's what won the election."

"Play your cards close to your chest, Terry. You're a small local. You've got this foreign born problem. In the big office they stick with the overall picture. They have to think of per capita."

"I don't see what per capita's got to do with right and wrong."

Fred drew himself up. "You've joined the cleanest damn union in the country, don't forget that Terry. Mr. Worthington is a man of spotless integrity."

"I sure would like to meet him," said Terry.

Tasha was bustling about putting dishes on the table. Fred rose to his feet and said in a loud important voice so that Tasha would hear, "I'll see that they know how to spell your name in the big office, Terry. You been a real help. They are on the watch for clean cut young fellows to train for organizers. Keep your nose clean, Terry boy."

"All right gentlemen, come and get it," said Tasha as she brought in the last steaming dish.

"Now if that isn't the finest lookin' corned beef I ever saw," announced Fred as he dragged his chair over to the table. Right after they'd eaten he was on his feet saying he was sorry to have to eat and run but he had an important meeting over in Trenton. That was the last they saw of Fred Russell.

Terry didn't have to go out that night. After they had done the dishes and rinsed out the diapers, they sat happily side by side on the couch talking about the future that might be opening up for Terry in the labor movement. Fred made seventyfive a week and his expenses paid. The Bryants sure were going to need money. Tasha was pregnant again.

This time it was a boy. He came in jigtime while Terry was out of the hospital buying an evening paper. They named him William Terence Bryant and had him baptized by the priest.

As soon as her mother moved out to California to live with her older sister there, Tasha had applied for instruction in the doctrines of the church. What did it matter? It was the same Lord Jesus, she said with that little sharp smile she wore when she'd found some way of bypassing a problem. When the priest suggested baptizing little Natalie too for good measure she didn't tell him her mother had taken her around to an orthodox pope when she was three weeks old. "Two blessings are better than one," she said.

The Bryants had to do a lot of scrimping after Billy came along. The hospital expenses took the last of their war bonds. The rent went up. The telephone was an added expense. The cost of groceries was always on the rise. What with the diapers and the washing and ironing and the cooking and making clothes for the chlidren and trying to get them out for an airing every day, Tasha never had a spare minute.

Terry's naturalization course at the Knights of Columbus Hall and committee meetings and conferences with Milan Slansky and Attorney Wyzanski about negotiating a new contract kept him on the run every evening till bedtime. The state organization began to call on him for special jobs. He was elected a delegate to the state convention.

It was at that Atlantic City convention that Terry noticed the change that had come over Steve Slansky. They were assigned to the same double room in one of the cheaper hotels. Steve was drinking. His face was getting a jowly look. Somehow he always managed to have a bottle of whiskey in the room. He was a loud dresser; some woman or other was always giving him a new fancy tie. He'd be up all night and would sleep through the sessions. Once when Terry went back to the room to wash up he found the door bolted inside. Steve's muffled voice came through the door begging him to have a heart and come back in half an hour. Terry could have sworn he heard a woman's titter.

There was a good deal of partying up and down the hotel corridors the last night. Terry couldn't imagine where all the liquor came from. All he knew was that he couldn't afford to pay for any of it. He had hoped to get some of the boys together in his room to talk about the campaign they were putting on to organize Raritan's Plant #2 over in Perth Amboy. A fat chance. Steve had the room full of women.

"Come in," shouted drunken voices when he pushed open the door. There was Steve and Shorty and Duke, all in their shirtsleeves pouring out the liquor and mussing up the dames. "Come right in Terry," shouted Steve. "Good old Terry, the whitest man in Raritan Rubber." "Atta boy Terry," Duke's and Shorty's thick foreign accents joined in.

Big hands grabbed him and forced a tumbler of whiskey on him. He'd look too silly trying to back out now. "Here's to the new Perth Amboy local," he said taking a short swig.

He tried to get Steve's attention away from the girl he was pawing over. "Steve, where's Milan? I want to ask him why the big office is taking so long to get organizers over to Perth Amboy. We got to work fast or District 50'll get in there ahead of us."

"Milan," roared Steve, keeping a sort of half nelson on his blonde. "He's in New York City right now sittin' in the front row of the biggest musical in town. Milan don't let no grass grow under his feet and we ain't neither. The big wheel's got all the free theatre tickets, but we got the liquor and the dames. We saved one out for you."

Duke pushed a sullen short ratfaced girl at Terry from across the room. She wore her black hair in a pageboy bob. He felt the little sharp beaks of her brassière against his chest. Half the whiskey in his glass spilled down both their fronts.

"Quit it, it'll ruin my dress," she whimpered.

Terry was thinking fast. He put his arm around her and patted her gently on the shoulder. "That won't stain girlie . . . I'll help you mop it up. Maybe we better step out in the hall and talk things over."

"Ain't he the fast worker?" Shouts and wolf calls followed them as they slipped out the door.

Out in the dim hall she snuggled up against him whimpering that she wasn't used to these gorillas. She was used to going out with high class men, insurance men, bankers, real big wheels sometimes, men who knew how to treat a girl respectable. Her name was Laura. She liked to be treated respectable. George had promised it would be a nice quiet respectable little party, just for good will.

"George who?" Terry asked sharply.

"George Slansky of course. I thought I was going out with George and his brother. They treat a girl real nice."

"Steve is their blood brother." Terry tried to quiet her down.

"That creep. He thinks he looks like Clark Gable but he's a creep just the same."

They were sitting side by side on the settee in front of the elevator. Terry had moved a little away from her. "Who's paying for all this, Laura?" he asked suddenly.

"George does of course. He's a real heavy spender. It's not his money, natch. Expense account money."

She was looking up in Terry's face out of black little gimlet eyes. "I don't know what your name is. I'm goin' to call you Butch. . . . Now Butch, don't you tell a living soul I told you that."

She waited for an elevator to go past and threw back her head with her mouth fixed for him to kiss it.

"You're the quiet kind, Butch. I like the quiet kind."

Terry felt himself getting dizzy. After all he was only human. He pulled away from her and got to his feet.

"This ain't the place, I know that," said Laura. "Suppose we go around to a cocktail lounge around the corner and you buy me a drink and we get acquainted."

Terry blurted out that he was a married man with two children and he didn't have no money to spend.

Laura turned on him savagely: "What kind of a monkey does that make out of me?"

Terry just stood there. If the girl's eyes could have killed him they certainly would. "What a bunch of creeps." She spat the word out and turned her back on him and strutted huffily off with a wiggle of hips down the hotel corridor.

Terry went out on the empty boardwalk. He took a deep gulp. The surf on the beach and the wind off the sea had a lonesome sound in spite of the bright lights. From a drugstore he called Tasha long distance. Her warm sleepy voice in his ear melted the lonesomeness out of him. If only he had her in his arms. "Kids all right?" Sure. Natalie had asked where Daddy was. "Tate convention," Billy said. "What do you think of that?" Billy was beginning to talk a blue streak. Trying to keep his voice casual Terry said Steve would drive them back for their shift at the plant, he'd be home for supper. "See that he drives careful. Good night, dear." "Good night, dearest." It was a wrench to hang up.

Terry dozed in a hard leather chair in the hotel lobby until it was time to rout out the rest of them. He was the only one in any shape to drive Steve's car. He left Steve and Butch and Shorty snoring in the car in the parking lot at the plant. It was a relief to get back to the hot smudgy work on the Banbury.

The first Terry heard of the Hillsdale strike was when Earl Fagan called him on the phone. Terry hadn't seen much of Earl since he quit going over to the diner for his lunches.

"It's this here strike at Raritan's West Virginia plant." Earl's voice sounded worried. It was an AF of L union. A carload of strikers had driven all those miles from Hillsdale to picket plant #7. More on the way. Earl had been talking to the West Virginia boys over in the diner. They knew Terry's local was negotiating. They wanted plant #7 to strike too and make the negotiation companywide. They'd called up Steve Slansky but couldn't get nothing out of him.

"Tell 'em to hold their horses, Earl. We may have to call a membership meeting."

It was midmorning before Terry found Steve in the head foreman's office. Steve sat glowering behind a desk with a paper cup half full of whiskey in his hand. His business suit was all mussed up. His tie was crooked. He'd had a couple of drinks before this one. He was hot about something. He was talking Polish or some such language to a lame guy they called Charley who was one of the sweepers. They were arguing hammer and tongs. Terry had just opened his mouth to say "Good morning" when Steve got to his feet. He crunched up the paper cup and let it drop on the floor and hauled off and hit the old lame sweeper on the side of the jaw with his fist. It made a crack like a ball hitting a bat. The man gasped and staggered and hobbled away holding his jaw with his hand.

Terry felt all his muscles grow stiff. He kept his voice under control. "That's no way to do, Steve," he said. "The man's a cripple."

"Only thing they understand. Goddam donkeys. You don't know 'em like I do."

Steve made Terry bring him another paper cup from the water cooler. "How about a drink, Terry? Hair of the dog." He gave Terry a heavy wink. "Had my bachelor dinner last night. . . . After this it's the straight and narrow. I'm gettin' married. Phil Darrow the big contractor's daughter. He's buildin' us a home next to his, a thirty thousand dollar home in Mountain View."

"Congratulations," said Terry but he wouldn't take a drink on it. He forced a laugh. "I'm keeping my nose clean. After the amount my safety committee's costing the company, they'd jump on me for the slightest infraction."

Steve was staring pevishly into the whiskey in his paper cup. "Guys who won't learn what the score is," he grumbled, "they give me a pain in the ass."

Terry let that drop. "One day," a little voice deep down in his head was saying, "I'll slam that sonofabitch." He tried to be as diplomatic as he could bringing up the West Virginia strike, but at the word Hillsdale Steve blew his top.

"The goddam hillbillies," he raged. "What do they think they're doin' tryin' to foul up our contract negotiations? Membership meetin'! There ain't goin' to be no goddam membership meetin' unless Milan says so."

"Let's see what Milan has got to say," said Terry very quietly.

Steve was too jumpy to dial the number. Terry dialed Milan's office and his home and another number that sometimes reached him; no Milan.

Next morning Terry was at the plant half an hour early. Steve was sober for a change. "I got news for you," he said with a nasty sneer on his mouth. "Milan says to cross their goddam picket lines. The shopstewards are to police the plant. You can talk to him yourself."

He dialed a number and handed the phone to Terry.

"Who's this talkin'?" There was a menacing rattle to Milan Slansky's deep bass.

"Hello Mr. Slansky." Terry hated the kind of servile tremble that came into his voice. "This is Terry Bryant, one of the shopstewards."

"Hillsdale's a low wage area. They ain't got no call to come here and louse up our contract negotiations. We're goin' to cross their goddam picket line. The stewards will police the plant. You'll all get your pay just like you was workin'."

Terry stammered something about oughtn't they to call a meeting and take a vote.

"Vote hell. This is under my jurisdiction," roared Milan and hung up.

Steve was laughing at Terry's glum face. "Might as well argue with a ten ton truck as with my brother Milan. . . . Get wise, feller, get wise," he added cheerfully.

Next morning sure enough the shopstewards were out patrolling the entrance to the plant. They had been told to pick up clubs and armbands at the superintendent's office. It was a miserable February day with a low ceiling of speeding gray clouds and a sleety rain. Terry never felt worse in his life. It looked like there were more shopstewards than there were pickets. The state police kept a patrol car parked at the curb all day for good measure.

The picketers had a hungry scrawny air. Their knobby red wrists stuck out from dripping sleeves. Some of them wore old army slickers. They walked like their feet were wet. They had little signs on sticks that might have been lettered by kindergarten kids. They tried to sing "Solidarity Forever" but their voices were lost in the hiss of the sleet and the din of the heavy truck traffic on Route 1. There wasn't the least bit of trouble. Most of the workers didn't even know there was a picket line.

At noon redheaded Sam Hawkins, who'd taken George Slansky's place as personnel manager when George was transferred to the main office, called in a couple of taxicabs to take the shopstewards to lunch at the Lotus Garden, a Chinese restaurant. They were told to drink as much beer as they wanted but Terry wouldn't drink. As it was, the food stuck in his gullet. Milan was there to pick up the tab, but everybody knew the whole thing was at the company's expense.

Terry kept Tasha up half that night telling her how lousy it had all made him feel. She was a little haggard herself. Billy had been crying all afternoon because his gums hurt him and she was walking him to try to get him to go to sleep. "Those guys believed in me when I told 'em we'd get them a break if they joined the International and the only thing that's happened is they pay a few cents more dues so that the International office can get their per capita. And now they've seen me out there scabbing with the rest."

Tasha walked Billy up and down the floor saying she'd known the Slansky boys were crooked right along, but they had to live with them now, didn't they? She was just beginning to put a dollar or so away each week. For God's sake he mustn't do anything hotheaded. Remember what that organizer Fred Russell said? "Play it close to your chest." Fred knew the score. Fred had been trying to warn him.

Even after Billy quieted down and they got to bed they couldn't sleep. "We're in it together," Terry whispered, pulling her to him, "that's some consolation."

The picketers faded away after a day and a half, but Terry didn't dare go to the diner across from the plant for a cup of coffee any more for fear he'd meet some of the boys from Consolidated and they'd call him a scab and he'd get into a fight.

Downtown one Saturday night in the glare outside a movie house he saw Earl Fagan coming towards him. He fixed his face to say hello but Earl walked right by without seeing him. When the NLRB held an election at the Perth Amboy plant District 50 won hands down.

Terry did everything he could to keep from having a run-in with Steve. He stuck close to his work and when he did have to go to the chief foreman's office in connection with his duties as shopsteward he kept his eyes straight in front of him. Steve never showed at meetings of the safety committee any more. That was just as well because Sam Hawkins who represented management was a reasonable kind of an egg. When they came to an argument he and Terry would agree to disagree. Terry gave up trying to go further than strict enforcement of the state safety regulations. The safety committee ran pretty smooth with Steve out of the way. Now that Steve was married and moved into his new home, half the time he didn't put in an appearance at the plant at all. Terry marveled that the management let him go on drawing his pay.

One summer day Terry took his lunch out on the old loading platform where it was cool in the shade back of the plant. He found himself sitting next to Duke on the edge of the concrete. Duke had just been made foreman in Terry's department. When Terry sat down Duke smiled at him ingratiatingly with his thick lips under the spreading black mustache. "Attaboy, Terry," he said. Terry started munching on his sandwich. Duke rolled his eyes back and forth to make sure they were out of earshot of the rest. "Why you no more friend with Steve?" he asked in a sudden whisper.

Terry shrugged.

"Steve he goin' to be beeg man like his brudders. Marry rich girl. Maka beeg money on Valla Street. Brudders geeve him teeps. Buy dis, sell dat."

"I just have to do the best I can, Duke," said Terry.

"Terry you nice clean American boy." Duke's voice was muffled by the long roll stuffed with salami he was eating. He ate his way through it, belched and wiped the crumbs off his mustache with the back of his hand. "Why not you make money too?" he whispered. His heavy hand came down on the small of Terry's back. "Be beeg man." He threw back his head and let out a rich garlicky laugh.

Luckily the whistle blew before Terry had time to think up an answer. He ran off laughing as if he thought Duke meant it all for a joke.

Terry would have gotten along all right with Duke if Duke hadn't taken it into his head to bring a green hand into the department. Duke was always moving his pets around from one job to the other. Terry tried to argue with him that the old contract said only experienced men should be set to mixing compounds, but this was one of the days when Duke wouldn't understand English.

Terry ran down to his locker to get a copy of the contract to spell it out to him. On the way back he ran into Steve. Steve must have just been talking to Duke because he was in a towering rage. His face was red. His fists were pumping. Terry could smell the whiskey on his breath as he came close. "You goddam troublemaker," began Steve and he let fly with his fist.

Terry ducked and took it on the shoulder. Then he squared off and let Steve have it. Left, right. Left, right. By God I'll kill the bastard. Steve was down on the floor and his nose was bleeding before the other men could get between them.

Terry was breathing hard. "If you want any more you just come outside. I'll show you who's a troublemaker you crooked son of a bitch."

Every word was a pleasure. Terry's hand hurt where it had connected with Steve's jaw. He felt ferociously happy.

Steve was being helped to the washroom leaving a bloody trail from his nose. His bright blue business suit was gray from powder off the floor.

Sam Hawkins stood beside Terry shaking his head dolefully. "You boys ought to have sense enough to know this ain't no Madison Square Garden."

"He hit me first. What do you want me to do? Stand there and let him beat up on me? Every man in this department knows he hit me first."

Terry demanded to see Mr. Briggs.

Waiting outside the dusty ground glass partition of the superintendent's office all the elation ebbed out of him. He stood first on one foot and then on the other glumly rubbing his bruised knuckle.

A man came out of the office leaving the door open. Terry had just taken a step towards Mr. Briggs's long gray face dim under the eternal green eyeshade behind his brightly lit desk when Milan Slansky jostled past. Steve, all hunched up with a bloody handkerchief held up to his nose, followed half a pace behind him. Duke's broad thick figure swaggered after, like a bodyguard bringing up the rear. Terry had a glimpse of the deep lines that ran from the flanges of Milan's nose to where the mustache ended at the corners of his mouth as the door slammed in his face. He tried to push on through, but Duke had his shoulders against it.

After a few minutes Milan came out alone. Milan was sickly pale. His eyes were a slit under their thick lids. There was a nasty smile on his lips.

"No need for you to say anythin' Terry, might make it worse," he said in a quiet confidential tone. "I got the best deal I could for the both of you young damn fools. Ten days suspension and no questions asked."

There was such a fatherly tone in his voice that for a second Terry asked himself whether maybe he hadn't figured the guy out wrong after all.

Milan put his arm round his shoulders. "Go change your clothes and I'll drive you home . . . Duke'll take Steve to the doctor to see if his nose is broken . . . You sure have got a left hook boy."

"The old man taught boxing," muttered Terry.

"The gentle art of selfdefense?" said Milan with a cold laugh.

Still puzzled Terry slipped into his street clothes and out into the parking lot. Milan leaned towards him to push the door of his creamcolored Buick coupé open. "Hop in Terry," he said kindly.

He talked as he drove. Steve was sorry. Steve wanted to let bygones be bygones. He knew Steve got nasty as hell when he was drinking, Milan explained in that deep fatherly voice. He'd told him a hundred times not to drink on the job. Frank Worthington was dead set against drinking. Steve was still just a kid. Maybe his marriage would sober him down. Right now Steve wasn't mature enough to be president of the local, but what could you do when all the damn membership thought he was the second comin'. We rubber workers believed in democracy. The thing to do about this little ruckus was to forget it as if it had never happened. It was bad for Steve and it was bad for Terry. Milan wanted to see the local one big happy family. "Both you boys got a future in labor."

Terry felt the way he'd felt when he was a small boy hauled up before the principal.

"I don't hold no grudges, Mr. Slansky," he mumbled staring at his feet, "but I do feel we owe those workers a better deal than they've been getting."

"Wait till you see the new contract," said Milan. He added hastily that he hated to do it but in view of the circumstances he'd had to drop Terry from the negotiating committee. Company wouldn't stand for him. Take it easy, Milan told him as he drew up to the curb in front of Terry's walkup, a man had to live and let live, especially dealing with these foreign born workers who were so set in their ways. "Us Slanskys we talk their language. We know what makes 'em tick."

Milan's jaw set square under the square mustache. His eyes hardened to black pellets on each side of the spongy nose. "Steve's just like me," he said. "He'll string along with the guys that string along with him. And get this Terry. A labor union ain't no Young Men's Christian Association."

His heavy lids drooped over his eyes. "You keep your nose clean and learn what the score is," he added in a bantering kind of a tone, "and you won't have any more trouble. I can see a big future for a guy who's quick with his head and handy with his fists."

Tasha raised a worried face from the ironing board as Terry walked into the kitchen, Billy and Natalie came running. Terry hoisted one in each arm and hugged them to him. "Suspended for ten days." He talked over their tousled silky heads. It broke him all up to see tears spurt out of Tasha's eyes; Tasha never cried.

"It wasn't no fault of mine," he explained eagerly. "Steve tried out his strongarm tactics on me an' he got what was coming to him." Terry tried to make it sound funny. "I had to muss him up a little." Tasha smiled. "Now Milan's scared I'll report his goings on to the big office. He just about came out and told me that if I'd play along with the Slanskys they would treat me right." He laughed grimly. "He seems to like the way I use my fists . . . How would you like to have a gangster for a husband?"

"Terry you can't fight 'em singlehanded."

Tasha switched off the electric iron and carried a pile of children's clothes over to the bureau. Terry quietly folded the ironing board and set it in its place in the corner of the kitchen.

"I'm not scared of anybody," he said sullenly, "and especially rats."

"Why can't you grow up," moaned Tasha. "You're not a boy scout any more."

"Milan said the same thing," Terry snapped back bitterly.

Tasha ran over to him and kissed him. "Terry I thank God every day you are not one of those gangsters."

The kids were pricking up their ears. They had to lay off. Terry helped her clean the front room and get supper. Tasha said she'd been planning to have pork chops but she thought she'd better spread these out over the rest of the week. Tonight they would eat beans, period. Losing ten days' pay was sure going to set them back. They had just gotten the kids in bed and asleep and were beginning to discuss what Terry ought to do when the phone rang.

The voice was Shorty's. He seemed out of breath. He whispered that Terry must come right away to Ukrainian Hall. Knock three times on the back door, the one around in the alley. It wasn't open to the public tonight, there would be nobody there but the boys. They all wanted to see him. "Attaboy Terry."

Terry wasn't too sure he wasn't stepping into some frameup

of Steve Slansky's but he decided he'd better go. "It's union business," he told Tasha. "I won't be long."

Terry had to repeat his three knocks several times before the door was cautiously opened a crack. There was Shorty's eye under a bush of sandy eyebrow. His mouth was grinning. He pulled Terry in and closed the door gently after him. Terry put his back to it and kept his hand on the knob until he could find out what was what.

About thirty men were standing around in the dim back hall. Some of them had cans of beer. Others had soft drinks. It made Terry feel good to see that every man who worked in his department was there, even the guys on the other shift. He let go the doorknob and stepped into the midst of them. Another Banbury operator, Ed Banning, who'd been a paratrooper in the ETO, stepped forward, gave Terry's hand a wrench and began to make a little speech.

He just wanted Terry to know they were with him. They wanted Terry to be the next president of this goddam local. They were goin' to make a clean sweep. All they had to do was look at Steve's new home on Mountain View Avenue to know he was selling 'em out to the company. Where else could he get that kind of money? "If we had an honest leadership we'd have the same conditions they got over at Consolidated. They average twentyfive cents an hour more than we do, right across the highway. Can you beat that? We're goin' to nominate you from the floor Terry and we're goin' to stampede the next meetin'. We are goin' to tell those Slanskys to blow it out of their nose."

"Well?" asked Tasha, sitting bolt upright in bed when Terry got home. "The boys want me to run for president," drawled Terry as he pulled off his clothes.

"Terry those Slanskys are a power in this town. They are tied in with politics. They got all the money behind them the management wants to spend. I know what I'm talking about."

"The International's a clean organization. Suppose I put the whole story up to Frank Worthington. All he needs do is pull out his field representative. Steve couldn't get to first base without Milan."

"I'll start looking around for work," Tasha cried out in that little practical tone that always pleased him.

"It won't be as bad as that."

Tasha was running her hand up the back of his neck. "I

can't stop you Terry." Her eyes bulged with love. "I wouldn't have you any different."

When Terry went back to his job, things seemed pretty quiet around the plant. Steve said hello to him as if nothing had happened. Milan was nowhere to be seen. Nobody in the department said a word about the coming election, only now and then, if nobody else was looking, a man would give him a wink or a mysterious smile. Terry stewed inwardly. Weeks were going by and he was getting nothing accomplished.

At last Terry made up his mind he had to write a letter to the International president. He put in all one Sunday working over the spelling and punctuation. He made Tasha go over each fresh draft. He must have copied it out ten times. He didn't want the men in the big office to think he was a screwball. He had to make them understand exactly how the Slansky brothers were playing both ends against the middle. He addressed it to Frank Worthington and marked it "personal."

INVESTIGATOR'S NOTES III

The tall man who opens the door is certainly Mr. H. H. Hendrikson. He has white cropped hair. His eyes are blue as his starched blue denims. Lean, lanternjawed, slabsided he stands stiff as a rod in the middle of the low attic room itemizing certain deficiencies in the apartment for which he feels he must apologize. It's his daughter's . . . You know, young people . . . He has had no heart for housekeeping since his wife died. "Be seated, please."

It's no surprise to learn that Hendrikson was a sergeant in the Swedish army. When he was eleven he learned the carpenter's trade at his father's bench. When his mother died he felt his father was hard on him so he ran away from home and joined the army . . . You know, young people. He ended his enlistment as the youngest master sergeant first class in the Queen's Royal Guard.

Hendrikson squared his already square shoulders.

How had he happened to come to America?

Accidentally almost . . . An older brother served in the US Army during the first World War and was gassed on the battlefield. Hendrikson came over to see what had happened to him. After his brother died he stayed on working as a carpenter for those wartime wages. He offered his services to the US Army but was told he couldn't be spared from a Navy construction project he was working on. In off hours he worked for USO, gratis of course. He built their first information booth in the city with his own hands out of donated lumber.

In America everything went well for him. He married a girl from the old country, bought a nice home, raised a family, made investments, put money in the bank. Naturally he joined the union. He had been brought up to believe in trade unions.

Everything went well until, during the second World War, he was elected president of his union local. "I guess I stuck my neck out. . . . But how could I help it? A man feels responsible. . . ." For seventeen years the boys had been trying to pry this particular local loose from the trustees appointed by the International. At last when they were allowed what they called a partial election, they elected Hendrikson president and a majority friendly to him to the executive board.

Right away they went to work to try to get an accounting from the general representative of the International who acted as trustee of the money taken in, particularly for the past two years.

Figure it out for yourself. Before Pearl Harbor there were only eight hundred carpenters employed in the area. A few months later there were twentyfive or thirty thousand. Dues came in so fast they had to stuff the money in mail bags.

Every newcomer had to apply for a work permit. He had to plunk down $23.50 with his application. If within thirty days he didn't pay the full fee of $55 he forfeited his money.

The BA's game was to get the men laid off within thirty days so that they'd forfeit their application money. Then he just put it in his pocket. It was war work. The contractors were so afraid of a strike they did anything the BA suggested. At one time they printed up 85,000 permits. Figure out for yourself how much money that represented.

The secretary was a bonded man. When the secretary was ordered to produce the books he went home sick. He was the only one who had the combination of the vault. When they routed him out of bed a few days later he opened the vault at the bank all right but there was nothing in it. The secretary explained that the general representatives had sent the records to the International for audit. They'd asked for an accounting, hadn't they?

They sure had but not quite that way. Hendrikson and his friends would have been up against a blank wall if the general reps in their scurry to make a getaway hadn't dropped some papers on the floor. Hendrikson picked up a packet of canceled checks which matched some stubs he found in the office. There was a check for seventyfive thousand dollars made out to cash and signed by the general rep. And another for thirty thousand. Chickenfeed.

In another hideaway he found a couple of hundred thousand dollars in work permits that hadn't even been deposited.

Hendrikson and his friends went to work to make an inventory of the property of their union local. It was tough work. They were carpenters, not public accountants. It took them five or six months to get their bill of particulars. They found that every bit of property the local had was titled in the names of the general reps. Their cars had been bought out of funds of the local. And still there was around a quarter of a million dollars unaccounted for.

Hendrikson called a special membership meeting to let the carpenters know what he'd found and they appointed a committee to visit the International president and ask him for an accounting.

That International president was a fighter, Hendrikson had that to say for him. Damned if he'd talk to any committee, not unless it was filled up with his own appointees.

Nothing to do but take him to court. The International president was a powerful politician in conservative circles. So powerful in his home state that Hendrikson had trouble finding a lawyer to take his case. Finally he found a lawyer willing to bring suit to recover the records. He didn't tell him about the shortages at first, just brought that up later once the lawyer was thoroughly wrapped up in the case. The trial opened in Superior Court.

All this meant Hendrikson's livelihood was interrupted, paperwork, figuring, letterwriting, anxiety, months away from home preparing the case with the lawyers. His wife was getting fretful. She wasn't well. His life was a nightmare. He wished he could get a job carpentering and forget it. But the boys had elected him president. He felt responsible.

The International president sent his top lawyer to try to get

Hendrikson to settle out of court. How could he? It wasn't his money. He was told how well he'd be taken care of if he dropped the case. Wouldn't he like to be a general rep himself? At a salary in five figures. Nothing doing, said Hendrikson. It was his business to get that quarter of a million dollars back in the treasury of the local it belonged to.

The International had plenty lawyers. They managed to stall off a verdict. The International president threatened to suspend the local's charter. Back home Hendrikson swore out a warrant for the general rep's arrest for stealing the local's funds. But the general rep had gone to Florida for his health. Stayed in Miami until the statute of limitations ran out. Impossible to interest the Internal Revenue Department. Letters to the Attorney General had no results.

He tried to take the case to the membership. Hendrikson wrote letters to twenty eight hundred locals. If they could steal a quarter of a million from his local what were they getting away with in the others? The only thing left was to bring it up on the floor of the next convention of the whole International union. They wouldn't even let him in the door.

The president denounced Hendrikson by name from the chair in a foul and libelous speech and moved his expulsion from the union. The few members who tried to protest were threatened with the same fate. When he got back home he found a general rep in charge of the local.

Threats, threats of cutting him off from his livelihood, threats by telephone of bodily harm to his family. Hendrikson's eyes glared blue. "I fear no man, only God in Heaven." He squared his square shoulders. "I was out. My wife took sick and died. That took the starch out of me."

After this Hendrikson was a man with one idea. He dragged out his years in law offices. He sold his home and raised $24,000. He spent every cent of it in the legal battle to keep his union rights. He won that case. A judge issued an injunction, but his own local refused to reinstate him. When he sent in a check for his dues they wouldn't cash it.

He sued the International president for libel. That took two years. His lawyers made him settle out of court for thirty thousand dollars. The lawyers got most of it.

Threats and bribes hadn't shut him up. The International had influence in Washington. They tried to take his American citizenship away. He'd already used a US passport to go to

Sweden to see his wife's people after she died. Now he found himself subpoenaed by the Secretary of Labor to show cause why he shouldn't be deported for illegal entry. He produced his naturalization papers: they were found in order.

Still he couldn't work as a foreman or as a carpenter. He could work as a supervisor but he had to have a union foreman under him. It took another court order to force his own local to let him take a job as a carpenter. At that he couldn't vote or hold office pending an appeal. They had been forced to give him a working card. He was working on the Social Security Building. At sixtyfour he could do as much work as the next man, more than some of these young fellows who had never learned to hammer a nail. But what had happened to his fine life in America that had started out so happily? What would it be like for his children? He used to be proud of being an American but now sometimes he thought it might have been better, maybe, to have stayed on in Sweden where the laws protected a working man.

Documentary (14)

ATLANTIC OYSTER BLIGHT BAFFLES SCIENTISTS

engineers will develop and design circuits for inertial, astronertial, and space navigation systems

This is Chemagination:

combine rubber's elasticity with phenolic resin's hardness— and you get a long wearing shoe-sole material or an adhesive that seals the metal skin of a jet plane with a giant grip

WATER MAKES 'EM DRUNK IN BRITAIN

Their enormous intake of fluid dilutes the blood and their speech becomes slurred, their eyelids droop, they feel giddy and get the feeling of being in another world. Some of them become bad-tempered and get hangover headaches. If they have one too many, they are sick.

Take the case of Mrs. X. She was a florid, plump woman of 57 with thick red hair. She started hitting the water bottle eleven years ago in a fit of depression. Her water intake was sometimes as much as 30 pints a day.

In desperation she once drank the water out of a flower vase. Finally her craze for water got so bad she moved a mattress into the bathroom to sleep beside the water faucet.

THIS TAKES COURAGE

They are plenty rugged. Why? Because they are made of steel. Steel makes the strongest blades, frames, handles and housings. Frames and handles that won't bend and twist and work loose when you treat them rough. Blades and housings that will take hard knocks and smashing blows year after year.

Men of Enterprise

In the very early nineteen hundreds
the men who drove the carts and wagons and heavy drays
(in winter they ran on runners) that hauled goods between warehouses and stores and railroad depots and steamboat wharves in the large towns and cities
became known as teamsters.

A teamster worked six full days and mornings on Sunday. He was lucky if he made eleven or twelve dollars a week, but those were gold dollars and food and lodging were relatively cheap. Rough work. Chilblains. Dust and burning sun in summer. Outdoor work. Men went into it for the freedom of the life.

The teamster drove his team for as many hours as there were in a day. Often he loaded and unloaded. He currycombed his horses and fed and watered them and shoveled the manure out of the stalls. He greased his axles and cleaned up his harness and polished the brass.

Teamsters gloried in muscle. They were hard eggs, brawlers and barflies. They could take it; but it began to occur to them, chiefly in Chicago and Boston,

that they might get to enjoy a little more

of the life, liberty and pursuit of happiness which the spellbinders told them were democracy's boon,

if they banded together in unions.

Dan Tobin was the first Teamsters' boss.

Dan Tobin was a modest man, a thrifty man, a serious godfearing man with glasses. He came to America for the opportunity. He arrived in Boston round the age of fourteen, a greenhorn from the banks of the Shannon. Immediately he set to work to better himself. After laboring long hours in a sheet-metal plant in Cambridge, he studied at nightschool, attended lectures, read books in his room.

When a depression in the nineties closed down his sheet-metal plant he worked as a stableboy, drove a streetcar. He saved up to buy his own horse and wagon. He huckstered butter and eggs and cheese and coffee and tea. With his own team he drove for a meatmarket, hauled coal and sprinkled the streets for the politicians.

He married and raised a decent family.

He had a knack for business and did pretty well as a huckster, but it wasn't long before he discovered where his real talents lay.

As a horsecar driver he'd joined up with the Knights of Labor. In 1900 he joined the "Team Drivers International Union." His mates sent him to represent them at the convention at Niagara Falls which organized the International Brotherhood of Teamsters. The employers marked him down for an agitator.

He had trouble finding work.

Dan Tobin had a wife and six children to support. He was a steady man fond of expressing his disapproval of liquor and ragtime and loose living. His local elected him business agent. From then on his business was Labor.

By 1907 he was president of his local. In that year he induced the International to hold its convention in Boston and in spite of vociferous opposition was elected International president.

Dan Tobin watched the union treasury as carefully as if it were his own. He was leary of sympathy strikes and high-sounding handouts to struggling fellow workers. He was a downtoearth man with downtoearth ideas and he liked to expound them in print. For almost forty years he wrote every editorial in the Teamsters' monthly magazine. Often he wrote the whole issue.

Riding herd on the Teamsters was a man's work. Factions kept trying to slug their way to the top. Malcontents formed new unions and branched off. Meetings broke up in fights.

At one brotherly meeting in New York a business agent broke a chair over Dan Tobin's head. His nose and his spectacles were broken. He was carried off to a hospital with a concussion and broken ribs. Blood poisoning set in and he very nearly died.

The union's growth was slow. At first the pay for officials was small. Tobin's salary was eighteen hundred in 1909 with two dollars a day for traveling expenses when he was away from home.

The Teamsters' locals were rowdy and intractable. Transportation is a vulnerable industry. At markets and railheads where perishable goods had to be moved quickly goons kept establishing their shakedown baronies to levy toll like robber lords on the medieval traderoutes. It took endless pulling and hauling and fighting and conniving to keep the Teamster locals in line:

only in Washington, as one of the vice-presidents of the AF of L, did Dan Tobin find the status he sought. In Washington the hardworking laborleader could bask in the national sun, petted by the politicians, protected by eager lawyers from accusations of wrongdoing.

The New Deal brought in the labor leader's golden age. The Wagner Act put the law on his side. By 1940 Dan Tobin was being paid thirty thousand a year and magnanimously refusing fresh raises. The depression had scared working people by the millions into joining unions. If you didn't join you were likely to get your head bashed in. At the very least you were punished by the denial of employment.

Trucking had become the nation's key industry. Managing

the Teamsters was a man's job. Wartime organization built the
unions into the political machinery of the Democrat administration. Dan Tobin would be photographed at banquets sitting
at President Roosevelt's right hand.

The loving delegates at the 1947 convention couldn't do
enough for good old Dan Tobin. They bought him a mansion
at Miami Beach and another at respectable Marshfield on the
South Shore near Boston. They voted him vacations out of
union funds. When he retired as general president emeritus
in 1952, they made him a present of a Cadillac, all expenses
paid including the chauffeur's wages, the services of a fulltime
maid, maintenance on his two homes, and fifty thousand dollars a year for life. Why shouldn't men of enterprise be attracted to Labor?

It wasn't only in Boston and Chicago that such men
were attracted to the organizing field. The Pacific Northwest
came near to becoming the feudal domain of a gentleman
named Dave Beck.

David D. Beck was the son of an unsuccessful auctioneer
who moved West from Tennessee to seek his fortune but
found himself eking out a living cleaning carpets instead.
Dave was born in Stockton, California, but he was raised in
Seattle where his mother worked in a laundry. Dave was a
stocky little boy determined to get ahead. He sold papers and
peddled Christmas trees. He had to leave high school to help
support the family. He worked in his mother's laundry and
then drove a laundry truck. Having joined the Teamsters at
an early age, after some service in the First World War, he
made good money driving for the laundry in Seattle and became a power in the laundryworkers local of the IBT.

He was a deadly serious young man who neither drank,
smoked nor used foul language. He didn't even play pool.

Handling money was where he found his fun.

Dan Tobin noticed him at a convention of the International
held in Seattle in 1925. A young man after Dan Tobin's own
heart. Tobin got him appointed general organizer for the
Pacific Northwest.

Dave Beck threw up his job where he was already earning
a hundred a week with the prospect of being made manager
of a new string of laundries. Laundries were chicken feed. The
big money was in Labor.

As general organizer for the Pacific Northwest he organized laundryworkers, truckdrivers, delivery men, warehouse workers, chauffeurs, bakery employees, garage mechanics, filling station men, shipping room employees, platform men, people who worked in dairies and bakeries and icecream plants and freezers, and in breweries and soft drink plants, automobile salesmen and cannery workers, haulers of logs and timber, common carriers, busdrivers: anything on wheels or served by wheels.

Dave Beck knew what was best for them all.

He was proud of the Teamsters' record. In 1943 truckdrivers' wages were two hundred dollars a year less than the industrial average. By 1955 they averaged eight hundred more. Dave knew what was best. Local autonomy was all right so long as the locals did what they were told. Dave didn't like back talk.

"Unions are Big Business," he was quoted as saying. "Why should truckdrivers and bottlewashers be allowed to make big decisions affecting union policy? Would any corporation allow it?"

He thought of himself as a successful businessman. If some of his subordinates used strongarm tactics when they raided other unions, or if bombs were exploded or nonunion cabs driven off the streets or trucks overturned in a labor dispute hadn't William Randolph Hearst's gangs done the same and more in the circulation wars of the press? Big Business looked for results.

He fought rival unions as vigorously as he fought recalcitrant employers. He carried on a longtime battle with the brewery unions. When Harry Bridges started to organize warehouse men Dave Beck, as a patriotic American, fought the Communists to a showdown. He got along famously with cooperative personnel departments. He understood their problems. He invested in businesses himself. He had a good reputation for living up to his contracts.

He discouraged competition. Stabilize the industry. His great word was stabilize. If more filling stations opened than he thought were good for trade he'd put a few out of business. He successfully kept eastern beer out of the Northwest.

In the course of these activities Dave Beck became the most important man in Washington State. In 1938 he handpicked a mayor for Seattle. "Dave Beck runs this town and it's a good thing he does," said Mr. Mayor. As a public figure he loved the respectable cloak. A great joiner, he was early elected Grand Exalted Ruler of the local Elks. He pulled his weight in the American Legion and the Veterans of Foreign Wars. He served as chairman of the Civil Service Commission. He was appointed to the state Parole Board and in 1945 presided over the Board of Regents of the University of Washington.

When Dan Tobin resigned from the top office Dave Beck was unanimously elected to replace him as international president of the Teamsters' Union and became thirteenth vice-president of the AF of L.

Dave Beck in his sixties was roundfaced and ruddy. His confident cards on the table manner was offset by the little pig eyes deepset in folds of fat. A man accustomed to having his way: well tailored; ate in the best restaurants; hired suites in the best hotels; drove the most expensive cars.

Just at the moment when he would seem to have reached the pinnacle of success his career was poisoned by unfavorable publicity. Unfavorable comment greeted the publications of the terms on which he induced the union to buy from him his lavish Seattle residence and its furnishings. Whose damn business was it? Union funds appeared to have been used to finance his real estate investments. Witnesses, standing up before the Select Committee of the United States Senate over which Senator McClellan presided, testified to every conceivable malpractice in handling of union funds. The Internal Revenue hauled him into court for unpaid back taxes. Beck used the union treasury like his own bank account, complained editorials in the public press. "There ought to be a law against it."

Dave Beck was hurt. Dave Beck was indignant. He took the fifth amendment when he was questioned and was forced off the executive board of the AFL-CIO, but he retained enough control of his own union treasury to hire a stockade of lawyers to protect him. Prosecutions dragged in the courts. Convictions were appealed. Delay.

(Since the politicians of the fifties were as queasy about calling union bosses to account as the politicians of fifty years before had been in dealing with "earlier malefactors of great wealth," it seemed likely that in spite of the efforts of a few reformers to send him to jail Dave Beck would live out his years in the satisfaction of a life well lived.)

Still the uproar was such that he had to forego the honor of being re-elected president of his International union.

The brash marblefaced palace he built facing the Capitol for the Teamsters' offices in Washington fell into the hands of his successor.

The man who succeeded Dave Beck as the Teamsters' International president was James Riddle Hoffa, a sturdy young man in his forties who first saw the light on Valentine's Day 1913 at Brazil, Indiana. He was the third of four children. His father was a coal miner of Dutch extraction who died when Jimmy was seven, as a result, so the boy was told, of silicosis contracted while working as a driller. His mother, who was Irish, moved the family to Detroit and went to work in a factory. A widow supporting four children; it was a tough struggle.

Jimmy was a stocky short lighthaired boy handy with his fists. He didn't get beyond the ninth grade at school. At sixteen he held down his first fulltime job as stockboy in a department store. Then he went to work unloading boxcars for a wholesale grocery.

Jimmy was the kind of streetcorner scrapper who uses his brains. He might have gone far as a boxer, but he was more ambitious than that. His poverty filled him with a sense of outrage. He had a chip on his shoulder and the leadership knack. At seventeen he was already ganging with four friends to organize a union in his grocery warehouse.

It took guts to talk union in Detroit in 1930. He forced recognition by striking his workers just when a shipment of strawberries came in. Strawberries spoil fast. He won recognition and got his union accepted by the AF of L.

Unions were poison to the business men who ran Detroit in those days. They had the cops on their side and unemployed thousands walking the streets. Hoffa needed the support of some outfit with fight in it. He hooked up with the Teamsters and before long was merging bankrupt locals, expanding, dragging in membership.

Hoffa was a leader who was always in there swinging. In

one picket line he was arrested eighteen times in twentyfour hours. He looked on convictions for assault and battery as service stripes in the class war. He gloried in being hard as nails, but always he used his head. Labor was his life; no time for tobacco or booze. His stimulus was the organization of men.

The tide of the times was with him. Jimmy Hoffa studied trucking and transportation as another man would study mathematics or atomic structure. Transportation was the key to the industrial complex.

There were big ideas in the air. In Minneapolis a group of teamsters who read Marx were planning to use control of longhaul trucking as the first step towards the socialist revolution. The Smith Act stopped them cold. The Dunne brothers were Marxists, but heretics of Trotskyite hue . . .

(by prosecuting the Dunne brothers the Roosevelt administration managed to please such disparate forces as the Communists who temporarily were in a position to tip the political scales in New York City, and conservative old Dan Tobin beloved of the Irish Catholic workers of New England)

. . . the Dunne brothers went to jail.

Socialism, Communism, the Cooperative Commonwealth— that was all hogwash to young Hoffa. But nationwide organization of longhaul trucking: there was food for thought for an enterprising young man who had thrown his lot in with Labor.

The tide of the times was with him. Young Hoffa slugged his way to the top in the Teamsters organization. "What we want we try to get. What we get we keep," was his motto.

He couldn't do without help. If a man helped Hoffa, Hoffa stuck by him.

In 1953 he was elected a vice-president of the IBT. Dan Tobin, mellow with prospects of retirement, greeted him as "the biggest small man in Detroit . . . when you go to Detroit," he added, "you hear about Hoffa but you don't hear a word about Henry Ford . . . He's pretty nearly civilized now," Dan Tobin added with a smirk. "I knew him when he wasn't."

Under Hoffa's generalship the Teamsters spread mightily through the Middle West and even into the open shop South. Transportation is a vulnerable industry. A few

enterprising organizers could accomplish wonders in the
trucking business.

Hoffa's first large scale nationwide contract was signed
with Montgomery Ward.

(The story should prove diverting to social historians. The
president of the great mail order house was the same Sewell
Avery who during World War II defied the Roosevelt
Administration by refusing to bow to the ukase of the NLRB
that he allow his employees to organize. Under some totalitarian wartime enactment Franklin Roosevelt seized the enterprise for the government. Mr. Avery claimed constitutional
rights and refused to leave his office. In the end he was
carried out bodily.)

The tide of the times ran strong. The Teamsters put on
their organizational drive just when Sewell Avery, older and
tireder by a decade, was locked in battle with a young upstart
named Louis E. Wolfson who'd come to the verge of buying
control of Montgomery Ward stock. Hoffa threatened a strike
just at the time the crucial stockholders' meeting was coming
up. He'd taken the precaution to buy, through two Teamster
organizations he controlled, a quarter of a million dollars
worth of Montgomery Ward stock, just enough to tip the
scales if need be between Mr. Wolfson and Mr. Avery. A
mere coincidence, explained Dave Beck. The Teamsters considered Montgomery Ward a good investment.

No outsider knew in just what terms the deal was made,
but Montgomery Ward signed with the Teamsters. The employees willynilly went along and when the Teamster stock
was voted it was voted for Sewell Avery. Mr. Wolfson,
foiled, sought greener pastures and the Teamsters, to show
their approval of management policies, invested large blocks
of their welfare funds in Montgomery Ward.

The climb to empire didn't always run smooth for
enterprising young men in the labor movement. Personalities
clashed. At home in Detroit Hoffa's rise involved a lifetime
duel with Walter Reuther. The idealistic Reuther was cozy
with the press. He appealed to the better element. Hoffa
called spades spades and took little trouble to conceal the
fact that his attitude was: "The public be damned." When
Congressional Committees or courts of law tried to press the

public interest through investigations and indictments Hoffa
hired the best goddam lawyers in town.

He had a shrewd eye for angles. When he was indicted
in the District of Columbia for an alleged attempt to bribe
an employee of a Congressional Committee, his lawyers
managed to have some Negroes in the jury. Hoffa's good friend
Joe Louis just happened to turn up in the courtroom. What
selfrespecting Negro juror would vote to convict a friend
of good old Joe Louis? Acquitted.

        Hoffa was closemouthed about his own affairs. Only
through the probing of an investigating committee did the
public learn that through his wife and the wife of an
associate he was in the trucking business. Who had a better
right? A longhaul enterprise called Test Fleet was so admirably
managed that out of a four thousand dollar investment the
ladies were said to have received dividends amounting to
sixtytwo thousand in four years. Tales were told of realestate
developments and a loan syndicate and trotting horses and
a girls' camp.

Witnesses criticized his style of life. "Just because I'm in
Labor do they expect me to wear baggy pants and drive a
three dollar car and live in a four dollar house?"

        About the time when Dave Beck, like Insull in the
old days, was enjoying the cultural advantages of European
travel while he gave the scandals stirred up by the McClellan
Committee a chance to blow over, a group of associates
decided to present Jimmy Hoffa as a properly whitewashed
public figure. Already he'd lectured at Harvard.

A dinner in Detroit to celebrate the culmination of twentyfive years in the labor movement turned out to be the biggest
thing ever. Leaders of management and labor poured in to
serve as sponsors. The head of the AFL-CIO Ethical Practices
Committee took the chair.

Two thousand six hundred and fifty persons paid a hundred dollars a head. The profits were sent to Israel to found
a children's home near Jerusalem to be named as a memorial
to James R. Hoffa.

        In the old days rough and ready characters became
teamsters for the freedom of the life. Teamsters' organizers

moved among the rank and file slugging it out with those who opposed them. In midcentury they took shortcuts. Men of enterprise among the organizers went to an employer and told him to sign up his employees or else. In California at least they were backed up by the courts.

The tide of the times ran strong.

The Big Office (*continued*)

Mighty few letters went through the big office without coming under Frank Worthington's eye. He was particularly careful about giving attention to beefs from the rank and file. Keeping in touch with the grass roots was how he put it to Grant Graham to justify his spending so much time on this particular type of correspondence. He read Terry Bryant's long carefully typewritten letter through twice. Then, he turned it face down on his desk and called Grant Graham over the interoffice communications system.

"Grant tell me more about the field rep who handles all those small locals in Jersey, Milan Slansky."

"My God, Frank, you ought to remember Milan. He's the man put your name in nomination at the 1949 convention . . . a good conservative union man."

"Read this letter," said Frank Worthington when Grant appeared at his desk in person.

Frank waited tapping with his pencil while Grant read the letter. "Well?" he said when Grant had finished.

Grant breathed heavily. "Frank, the situation in that local is that you have a majority of foreign born workers. Slansky and his kid brother can talk to 'em in their own language. That's how they brought 'em into the union. Naturally they've got the inside track in union affairs. There's probably a minority of guys who don't like it, like this Bryant. Wild Irish probably. A lot of these fellows are just trouble-makers."

"But he says he helped found the local. He's been elected shopsteward and trustee and executive committee and all that. . . . That takes votes. . . . A lot of the boys must be for him."

"Frank, we can't take sides in these local rows now can we?" Grant rolled his eyes towards the ceiling. "You wouldn't have the International discriminating against the foreign born?"

Grant reached for Terry Bryant's letter. "Lemme handle it Frank. I'll call up Milan long distance tonight."

"All right Grant, don't forget to give me a report on it."

Grant walked off with the letter.

Already Frank Worthington's eye was on another letter. This was from a man who felt he'd not been getting enough encouragement in his effort to organize a chemical plant in Kankakee.

Terry waited four weeks for an answer. Then he wrote again. Then he called up long distance at his own expense.

It was a person-to-person call. A woman's voice said that Mr. Worthington was in conference, but would Mr. Graham the organizational director do as well? Terry said go ahead.

Mr. Graham's voice sounded very tired. Mr. Bryant's letters had been received and the contents noted. Mr. Bryant must understand that Mr. Worthington's time was taken up with contract negotiations with the big companies that set the pattern for the industry. His letter would be answered in due time. Why couldn't Mr. Bryant make his complaint to the field representative? "But that's the man I'm complaining about," Terry shouted into the receiver.

In that case, answered Mr. Graham's voice severely, instead of taking up Mr. Worthington's valuable time with personal letters, the thing to do was to file formal charges. A formal charge accompanied by substantial proof, such as affidavits or sworn statements by union members, would be thoroughly investigated. Mr. Graham added that he understood the local was negotiating a new contract with the Raritan Company . . .

"That's one of my charges," Terry broke in. "The field representative is infringing on the autonomy of our local. Negotiations been dragging on for months and they won't tell the membership a goddam thing."

Mr. Graham's voice said the big office disapproved of the use of foul language over the phone. Personally as a loyal union member he felt that during negotiations was no time to wash dirty linen in public.

Terry said he would wait until after the contract was

signed. "Spoken like a loyal union man," said Mr. Graham's voice. The call cost Terry three dollars and seventyfive cents.

It was about that time that strange women started calling up Tasha. "Did you ever know a girl named Laura?" Tasha asked Terry when he came home from work one night. Her voice was not exactly suspicious, but puzzled. "Laura, I don't know any Laura." Then he remembered Atlantic City, the hotel room, the girl on the settee in front of the elevator. He told Tasha everything he could remember. He'd had so many things on his mind when he got home from that damn convention he had clean forgotten about Laura.

It was a relief to see Tasha break into a laugh.

"Well for about fifteen minutes I was getting ready to put the children on the bus and join my mother in California and then I began to smell the Slansky boys at the bottom of it. I told you those brothers would stop at nothing. . . . It wasn't this Laura," Tasha went on. "It was a woman said she was a friend of hers. My she was a dirty talking girl. She tried to tell me you'd been with this Laura and had given her a filthy disease and she felt I ought to know on account of protecting the children."

Terry stood looking at her with his mouth open.

"She had me about crazy until I suddenly thought: 'But Terry hasn't got any disease. Who should know better than me?' "

The telephone started ringing. Tasha listened with an incredulous look on her face and then hung up. "That's another one." Tasha gave him a teasing nudge with her elbow. "I guess where there's so much smoke there must be some fire."

Those weren't the only stories that were being circulated. One day in the washroom Ed Banning got Terry off in a corner and asked him if it was true he'd gone off his rocker on Okinawa and served time in an army mental hospital. Ed said he didn't believe it but that was the story somebody had started. "After I came home," said Terry, "I was detailed to a rehabilitation center. I knew what battle fatigue was from my own experience. They made me a staff sergeant to help take care of the other guys."

Ed Banning was staring in Terry's face with narrowed eyes. He didn't look any too convinced when he walked away.

Then came the business of the pressure gauge. The minute Terry saw it he showed Duke how the gauge was flooded. Duke just shrugged and turned his back.

Terry thought afterwards he might have been a little jumpier than need be but something about Duke's manner made him blow his top. Terry ran all over the plant till he found Sam Hawkins. He demanded a meeting of the safety committee. He was going to write up a grievance. "But why can't your foreman report it and get a maintenance man to fix it?" said Sam in astonishment. "No need to bleed and die over a pressure gauge."

By the time Terry got back to his machine the gauge wasn't working at all. He went off looking for Duke. Why wouldn't he report it to Mr. Briggs? "Crazy son of a beech alla time make trouble" was all he could get out of Duke.

Terry answered in kind. In the end he had to get Mr. Briggs out of his office to take a look. Mr. Briggs promptly shut down the whole department. Maintenance and repair took over and production was stalled for five hours.

Next day after the department was running smooth again, one of the sweepers came by with a message that Mr. Briggs wanted to see Terry. Terry was all smiles as he barged into the superintendent's office. He thought Mr. Briggs was going to thank him for reporting the breakdown before it caused a serious accident.

Not a bit of it. Mr. Briggs was writing up the foreman's report accusing Terry of using foul and abusive language and being unduly absent from his department.

"But you know yourself Mr. Briggs that it was only in performing my duties as shopsteward according to the contract."

Mr. Briggs didn't answer. He kept his eyes on the papers in front of him. He never looked up once. Terry stared down at the long gray mournful face under the green eyeshade. These were serious charges and he thought Terry ought to know about them, Mr. Briggs mumbled. Terry stood there shuffling his feet. No way of getting the man to look him in the eye. He walked out of the office.

There was a good turnout at the membership meeting that night at Ukrainian Hall. The meeting was scheduled to hear a report on contract negotiations. As the men shuffled in every eye was on an importantlooking bluebound document that Lawyer Wyzanski had on his lap. Milan and the men from the field representative's office were late. After a while Steve took the chair and called the meeting to order.

Terry was on his feet and managed to get the floor before Steve recognized who it was. Steve tried to call him out of order but from all over the hall voices shouted "Let him talk." Steve slumped back in his chair looking sick enough to throw up. Lawyer Wyzanski started importantly whispering in his ear.

Terry knew he had to make it fast.

He had a motion, he shouted, to discharge the negotiating committee before listening to their contract. The committee had been kept in the dark. The field rep had done all the negotiating. The field rep and the local president were in cahoots with their brother who was on the company payroll. All kinds of intimidation was going on. The proof was that Terry himself was being framed because he'd tried to stand up for the men's rights as shopsteward. His safety committee was costing the company money. Milan Slansky had as much as told him that.

Terry felt he was getting what he had to say across. Faces were turning towards him. The hall was so quiet you could hear Lawyer Wyzanski's shoes creak when he got up with an important frown on his face and walked heavily off the stage.

Terry reached the part of the speech he'd jotted down on a pad while he was choking down his supper under Tasha's anxious eyes.

"It doesn't matter too much what happens to me personally, but if you let the company frame me for doing my duty as a shopsteward and if you let your elected officials help and participate because I know they are selling you out for favors and cases of whiskey and boxes of cigars and tips on the stockmarket, no union member's going to be safe. The rubber workers is the cleanest union in this great country of ours. No international union is cleaner than its smallest local. It's up to the rank and file to keep it clean. The labor movement is the heart's blood of American democracy. If we are going to keep American democracy we've got to act on it at the grass roots. If you let one man be framed, every man in this room is in danger. The way to keep union democracy

perfect is to clean out leeches and bloodsuckers the moment
they appear. A man who betrays his union is betraying his
country and his flag."

Terry ended by moving that they take the negotiations out
of the hands of the field rep and appoint a new negotiating
committee according to the terms of the union constitution.
Would anyone second the motion?

Some men clapped. Some cheered. Some booed.

"Terry Bry-ant for our next pres-ident," a few younger
men started chanting.

Before anyone had a chance to second Terry's motion
Milan Slansky walked with heavy tread across the stage,
snatched the gavel out of Steve's hand and rapped for order.
Men in business suits filled up the chairs at the speakers'
table. A few still shouted "Good old Terry," but most of the
men sat staring up at Milan with frightened faces.

"Anybody want to second that motion?" Milan roared. He
stood square and black with his legs apart in front of the
stage scowling up and down the rows of faces. "Any more
disrupters present? If there are they had better speak up."

Not a voice was raised. The men shrank into their seats.
Steve and Lawyer Wyzanski were whispering noisily with
their heads together. Milan rapped with his gavel. "Quiet,"
he shouted back at them. Then he turned toward the hall
again.

"If no more graduates from a Veterans' Hospital for the
Insane want to louse up the proceedings," he said with a deep
rumbling easy laugh, "we'll continue with the agenda."

Silence broke into laughs, boos, catcalls. Milan looked back
and forth over the hall smiling that sneering smile of his.

"Mr. Bryant, with your kind permission, I shall ask Lawyer
Wyzanski to read a summary of the new contract which the
company has expressed its willingness to sign without delay.
Then they'll know what we are talkin' about. Improved rates
of pay and fringe benefits will average up to the equivalent
of twelve and a half cents on every dollar you find in your
pay envelope next Friday. Listen carefully please. If any
young Johnny come lately has any objections to making a little
more money he can speak up after he's heard the terms."

Lawyer Wyzanski cleared his throat. He opened up the
document in the blue cover. His importantsounding voice
droned out a long rigmarole. Nobody understood a word of

it. A motion to accept the terms was passed unanimously. The Slansky boys' friends had taken over the hall. Terry was on his feet shouting that he wanted to be heard but Milan would never look at him. A motion to adjourn passed by acclamation.

As Terry walked out of the hall no eyes met his. All he saw of Shorty was his back. Men who'd said they would nominate him for president were busy looking the other way as he passed. Only the old lame sweeper said "Good night Terry."

When Terry went to work next day he found a notice on his locker. Report to the pay window. He was fired.

INVESTIGATOR'S NOTES IV

April. The sun shines after rain. The wet streets of the modest little residential section of the modest little mid-American town are fragrant with lilacs. It is Saturday afternoon. Lawn mowers putter on every block. Their exhaust mingles with the warm smell of grasscuttings. The man comes to the door immediately. "I'd ask you to sit on the porch this fine afternoon," he says, "but I've been advised not to. If word got around I'd been seen talking to an investigator I might lose my job."

It is surprising when he says he works in the local food-processing plant as a laborer. He looks a notch above that. He is a thoughtful man with rimmed glasses and a low confidential voice. His crewcut light hair already has a little gray in it.

He routs his freshfaced twelve year old daughter out of the living room. She makes a face and carries the radio off somewhere else. The thump of Rock 'n Roll comes faintly through the partition as they sit in the small livingroom behind halfclosed venetian blinds.

"We still don't know what happened," the man is saying. "We thought we had a perfectly good union. Maybe I'm a stickinthemud but I thought it was all right. I've always been for unions, belonged to the brotherhood when I worked for the Pennsylvania Railroad. Our independent union was all right. For one thing it was cheap. Dues were $1.75 for three months and that included death benefits. The officers weren't paid much. The president and the committee members got twentyfive a month and the shopstewards got ten. The officers all worked in the plant. The plant employs about a thousand people. No need for such a hell of a lot of union."

He lets his voice drag in a nostalgic sort of way. "The main thing about it was it was ours. We had monthly meetings and a man could talk his head off if he wanted to. I guess some of us talked too much but after all it was our privilege. We had a grievance committee meeting with management every Friday to take up any little complaints. We had about eight thousand dollars in the union treasury. And then these Teamsters' (every time he says Teamsters he lets his voice drop) organizers came around to tell us our contract wasn't no good, it was yellow dog, and what we had was a company union without knowing it. They just tore that old contract up."

Although the two are alone in the room, the man starts to whisper: "The Teamsters must have put pressure on the company too because management acted odd. At first they seemed against a change and then suddenly they were for it. It's hard to put your finger on how but management makes its influence felt. I have no way of proving it but my way of figuring it is that the Teamsters have the company's other plants organized and could put pressure on them that way." He yawns and goes on. "There was so little excitement about the election a third of the men didn't take the trouble to vote. They won by fifty votes. The boys were carried away with promises. Most of them wish they hadn't. Right away there comes in a BA nobody's ever seen working in the plant. Things sure are different at meetings. If a fellow gets up to talk they roar him down. Won't recognize you if you raise your arm. A group of men goes to the office to complain that the votes weren't counted right and they are threatened with being fired. The first thing they put in is the checkoff. Before we paid our dues direct. They handle the people just like the Russians do. That's what we call 'em—'the Communists.' If two or three fellows get to chewing the rag together in the plant somebody'll say 'The Communists are watching us. We'd better split up.' We don't even know how much we're paying our officers. All we know is the dues are three dollars a month and we had to sign slips to authorize the management to take out another three dollars for welfare and the BA sits right next to the Personnel Director on payday glaring at us till we've signed our John Henry. That's what I call a Communist deal."

He pauses. An Elvis Presley voice comes crooning off key through the partition. The man gulps and goes on.

"A lot of the guys were all hot and bothered about what happened to the old union treasury and we appointed a delegation to go ask the new president for an accounting. The union has an office now right in the plant and there were all these toughlooking customers we'd never seen before. They told us to get the hell out if we didn't want our necks broken. And that was it.

"I went over to the state capitol at my own expense to see if there was any way of petitioning the NLRB for another election. They said we'd made our bed and would have to lie on it. A man who went over with me talked too much and he got suspended for a year. How the hell is he going to support his family? There aren't too many opportunities in this town."

The investigator finishes jotting his notes down and rises slowly to his feet.

The man shuffles after him to the street door. "It's nice having it all written up," he says earnestly, "but don't forget you're not mentioning names and places."

He clears his throat.

"What struck me most was how quick it all happened: One minute we were free men and now I don't know what we are. If the Communists took over the country do you suppose that's how it would happen, just quick and before you know it's happened, like that?"

Documentary (15)

DEFEATED VICTORIES

What better way to celebrate the signing of the historic document than by depriving men of one of their basic rights, namely the right to work?

The Widow's Millions

Just as engineers discovered what had caused the com-

munity's entire 61-million-dollar watersupply to vanish overnight—a tremor-born fissure in the reservoir—the heavens
opened and torrential rains flooded the whole town preventing repairs. There was water water everywhere but not a drop
to drink.

MEETING TODAY'S DETECTION PROBLEMS

*faced with extravagant claims and "price cut" ad-
vertising which promises "big discounts" it is difficult to judge values*

SHORT CUTS TO EXECUTIVE SKILLS

But the cause of many of the more distant noises
still remains a mystery, although some scientists believe they may be due to previously formed galaxies
colliding at enormous distances from the earth.

Applied Research and Development on an Interdisciplinary Basis

"A pool," he said, "would be able to invest a reasonable portion of its funds quite soundly in the
highest quality "blue chip" industrial bonds and
most of the balance in the highest yield long term
governments. . . . The pool would have a continuous
inflow from maturing investments and from new
investments and, therefore, would have to keep on
hand only a relatively small amount of short term
low yield governments. This fact alone would ap-
preciably increase the return."

Improved Infrared Lensing

"Is it going to be possible for any individual to recover any
of that loot from Beck?" a California truckdriver wrote the
Congressional Committee. "I have paid dues every month
since April 1931. I have derived no benefits whatsoever as
I have explained at meeting after meeting of the members . . .
All that happens is that I have paid my hard-earned money,
it has been stolen and I am in the same position as if I'd

thrown all that money down the drain. . . . Is there any provision in the law in favor of the individual?"

Blackie Bowman Speaking

(Scene: a bed in a Veterans' Hospital)

They've brought in a new doctor. The trouble they go to to keep this old cracked carcass alive. Sometimes they give me a whiff of oxygen. I get a sort of a jag out of it. I haven't the heart to tell them what's the use? It don't mean that much to me any more. What's the use of being alive if you can't act like a living man? But then I keep thinking, when I die for sure will all that life I keep remembering die too? Somehow it seems to be still living in my head. It was years ago and it's still living, so much vivider than the ward and the nurse and the sick guys gasping at night and the doctor's treatments that don't do any good. It seems to go on existing outside of this paining carcass that has nothing left for lungs but an old pair of leather bellows.

Take the day I ran away from home.

Maybe it's because I've thought about it so often and told the tale drunk or sober in a hundred different shapes to fellows I was exchanging confidences with or girls I was making up to that it all seems so clear. You don't suppose I made it up do you? You would think I'd have talked it away by this time but it is still one of the vividest things in my life. I can even remember thoughts I had about things that were happening to me. I know, a fifteenyearold kid all steaming inside, with two fresh eyes and strong anxious muscles and blood at the boil, is a very different creature than a sixtysevenyearold wreck trussed up and helpless on a hospital cot like the sea turtles I've seen trussed up in rows on the decks of fishing smacks off Honduras, but that kid is me just as much as this old wreck is me.

I was the youngest of the boys but I was the first to leave home. All through grammar school and the first year high I did all right. I was the pet of the family on account of being a pretty fair pitcher on a ball team we had that played kids

from other neighborhoods in Patterson Park. Sundays Dad
brought his cronies to watch me pitch.

Dad was a stubby shortnecked man with curly red hair all
over him. It was very thick on his chest. His tread was heavy
on the stairs. It was a relief to us kids when he left the house
early to go to work. He was a foreman at a Sparrows Point
shipyard. He kept us all scared with his temper and the un-
reasonable way he'd act after even a bottle of beer, but I
worshiped him from a distance when I was little, because he
seemed so strong and tough, and had such a joshing confident
way of making friends with other men. Nobody ever seemed
to be able to put over anything on Dad.

We lived in a narrow new brick row house that everybody
said was very well built, in East Baltimore, with white marble
steps that my mother used to scrub every morning and a bead
curtain that made a picture of Niagara Falls across the entrance hall. Outside it looked like all the other houses on the
block, but we thought it had something special about it.
Everything about the Bowmans was special.

Mother brought us up to think that the Bowmans and her
people the McMahons were the grandest people in the world.
The fact that we weren't as rich as some people didn't count;
it was what we were inside that counted. Though the girls
were younger than me I was younger than my two brothers.
I didn't remember the times when we lived in a tenement
downtown and were what Mother called dirt poor.

During the years I remember Dad was always coming
home all puffed up from getting a raise or from being elected
to something in the local Democratic club or the Masonic
lodge or one of the societies he belonged to. He always
seemed to have something to be puffed up about. Maybe
that was why I began to hate him.

Or maybe it was on account of the split in our family that
I didn't really understand till years after I'd left home. It
never came out in the open but it was there just the same.
Mother was a Catholic but Dad wasn't. Mother did needlework so that the girls could go to parochial school but us
boys went to public school, except for my oldest brother Joe
who had a scholarship at Notre Dame and was planning to
study for the priesthood. He was Mother's favorite. She was
all wrapped up in him and us younger kids felt it.

I must have grown five or six inches the year I was fourteen. That was the year the whole world changed on me. All of a sudden everything I did was wrong. The house began to feel like a jail. Dad became a mean old tyrant with a beery breath. My brothers were dumb clucks. They didn't understand me. All my little sisters were good for was to snitch on me.

Sure I loved my mother but she threw me off by always telling me to be a good boy like Joe. I hated the sanctimonious bastard. Ed was the worst. For as long as I could remember I'd slept in the same room with Ed, but now we were always stepping on each others' toes. Ed was two years older than me but he wasn't growing so fast. The minute I was big enough I socked him in the jaw. Ed never forgave me for that. He just wouldn't speak to me. That was where all the trouble began.

Up to the time I had that fight with Ed I'd been near the top of my class at school. The teachers used to write nice little messages on my report cards. All Dad cared about was getting his own way but Mother was ambitious for her children. She used to tell me that because I liked to study and was good at science and arithmetic and stuff like that I ought to go to college and learn to be a civil engineer. It was an awful shock to her when the truant officer came around to ask where Francis Xavier was.

I know I didn't exactly plan to stay away from school so many days, but I was mad at the folks and other things seemed so much more important, particularly loafing around with a bunch of kids my own age who used to gather to smoke cigarettes and cuss and tell dirty stories behind the piles of teakwood and mahogany logs in Higgins' Lumber Yard down on the harbor. The good opinion of my folks and the schoolteachers and of Father Carroll, Joe's friend whom Mother made a great fuss over when he came to dinner on Sundays, suddenly didn't mean a damn thing to me any more. What I wanted was the good opinion of Bug Evans, a gawky towheaded guy with a mean pair of fists who talked big about getting drunk Saturday nights and going down to the Block to pick up a hooker. Even when I did go to school I couldn't think about anything but girls.

There was a family that had come to Baltimore out of some West Virginia mining town to work at the shipyards that lived in a shack on the alley back of our house. My mother and sisters had their noses in the air about them. Mother said they lived more like niggers than white people.

There was a gang of children, all barefoot. Two of the girls, Lou and Dovie, were about my age. I don't know that I really liked them. They were damp smelly little girls with stringy hair but they were mighty curious to learn all about what it was little boys had behind the front of their pants.

We used to sneak up into the loft of a stable down at the end of the street. Right now I can smell the sweated harness and the horse manure and sweet hay. Hosea, the old colored man who took care of the two white delivery horses they kept there, thought it was a great joke. He used to give me pointers about how to handle the girls.

Hosea was proud of his big white mustaches. He had seen better days as a coachman with a family that lived on Mt. Vernon Place. Drink had been his undoing. He never tired of telling me about the patent leather hat and the livery and his wives and children and the high yallers he'd had when he was a young buck. He never did tell on us. Hosea and me were real friends. Now and then when I could snake a bottle of Dad's beer out of the pantry back of the kitchen, I'd run down the street with it under my shirt for Hosea.

Now when Bug Evans carried on about how hot the floosies were down on Baltimore Street I could come back big about how I had all the girls I wanted without paying them a cent.

Bug said I was a goddam liar and that led to a fight. I didn't exactly lick him but I held my end up pretty good. We each had a bloody nose and a black eye when Bug suddenly said "Let's shake." A couple of the other guys who were standing around watching the fight grumbled that we were a pair of sissies and ought to fight to a finish; then Bug and me, we joined forces and ran 'em out of the lumber yard. Then we went to the nearest pump and washed our faces. The two of us were friends after that.

It was trying to tap a keg of beer Dad had keeping cool in the basement one Saturday afternoon to give Bug a drink that I had my run in with the old man. Of course I did it all wrong and the beer spurted out all over the place and Dad, who was shaving in the kitchen before going out to some kind of political oyster roast, heard us giggling and came running down the steps with his chin full of lather.

When he saw the beer foaming on the basement floor his

face got red as a beet and he grabbed me by the shoulder and started to beat me with the razor strop he had in his hand. I couldn't stand there and let Dad give me a licking right in front of Bug so I ducked and slid out from under his hand and Dad tripped over the beer keg trying to catch me and measured his length in all that foam on the floor. Bug and I didn't stop running till we slid through a hole in the fence into Higgins' Lumber Yard.

I said honest I dassent go home. Bug said he'd be damned if he'd go home either. His dad was an awful religious man. He had taken to beating him with a blacksnake whip, not to hurt Bug, so he said, but to beat the devil inside him. Bug showed me the great red welts he had on his back. "I'll tell you what let's do," Bug said, "let's run away to sea."

There wasn't all this business about work permits and union hiring halls in those days. Bug and I just went around to every old freighter we saw tied up to a dock and asked if they were signing on hands. Most of 'em ran us out when they saw how young we were, but at last we caught up with a Captain Connor in a saloon on East Pratt Street who was in trouble because he had to sail Monday for New Orleans with a cargo of steel plates and would be clearing short-handed. Three of his crew had gotten into a fight in a joint on the Block and landed in jail for thirty days. He signed us on as boys at fifteen dollars a month which sounded like a fortune to Bug and me. No he wouldn't advance us a cent. He was afraid we'd give him the slip.

It was Saturday night and suppertime and our pockets were inside out. Bug's old man made a practice of taking charge of all the money he brought home but I had twelve dollars saved up from a paper route I'd been running. It was in a castiron bank shaped like a windmill I had in my room. The hardest thing I ever did was go back to the house to tell Mother what we'd done.

Afterwards I was glad because it was the last time I ever saw her in my life. Her eyes were red from crying. Dad had stormed out of the house in a pet. When I told her I was going to sea she didn't protest a bit. Making my own living was the best thing I could do. She packed up my clothes in an old suitcase and put in a prayer book and hung a scapular round my neck and made me swear I'd wear it always.

My brothers and sisters had eaten and gone out. Mother

fried up a steak specially for Bug and me. It sure smelt good sizzling in the pan but when I got it on my plate I just couldn't eat. Bug ate his share and mine too and then we went to hunt up Hosea to see if he'd let us sleep in his loft. He was a good old thing. He cooked us up our breakfast next morning. There were tears in his bulging old bloodshot white eyes when he said goodbye.

I had to share my twelve dollars with Bug to get him outfitted a little in the jewstores. They were open Sundays on the waterfront in those days. He was going to pay me back when we got paid but as it turned out we never did get paid.

The SS *Ossining* was quite a ship. Bedbugs in the bunks. Cockroaches everywhere. Weevils in the bread. Coffee that tasted of bilge. We hadn't cleared the harbor before a surly Scot everybody called Mr. Mack put us to work chipping rust. It wasn't so bad going down the Bay, sprinkled with the white sails of oyster boats, but the minute we poked our nose out of the Capes the wind turned cold and the sea got rough. Nobody would lend us any oilskins and we crawled around the deck drenched and shivering chipping and scrubbing at the wet rail. We were seasick and the stuff they gave us to scrub the paint with burned our hands, and every man on the ship seemed to go out of his way to kick us around.

Off Hatteras we shipped so much green water the captain sent us below to keep us from being washed overboard. We neither of us had anything left on our stomachs to puke up, but the stench of stale pipes and wet oilskins and of the stuff the cook spread around under the bunks to kill bedbugs made us start retching all over again. Back home we'd thought we were a pair of pretty tough kids but we didn't feel tough then. I don't know about Bug but I just lay there listening to the seas slamming against the bow and hoping I'd die. In the end I cried myself to sleep like a baby.

Off the Florida coast the weather moderated. The sun came out and the wind smelt of spring. It was March. The days were only twelve hours long, but that Mr. Mack had us chipping and scrubbing from the first dawn till after dark, and the Swede who followed after us with the red lead kept bawling us out for not working fast enough. They kept us at it sixteen hours a day. When they ran out of paint in the locker we thought they'd let us rest, but there was the deck to scrub, and the portholes to clean and the brass to polish.

We'd hardly finished that job when they hung us over the side to chip the plates. We had a smooth sea by that time and were steaming with a balmy following breeze up the Gulf of Mexico. We'd been chipping rust when we got our last sight of Fort McHenry and we still were chipping rust when we passed between McKees Jetties into the smooth earthsmelling swirling Mississippi water.

Our hands were all raw around the nails and our arms felt like they'd fall out of their sockets, but when we smelt the land and saw the palegreen canefields sliding by behind the levees, and plantation houses with columns and the steamboats with iron lace around their twin stacks set way aft over the sternwheel, we were crazy with excitement again. When one of us got close enough to another to nudge him while we worked, we'd give each other sly winks and whisper "New Orleans."

We had dreams of a day off and creole girls in the French quarter and minstrel shows and I don't know what all but the minute we tied up to the dock we had to work harder than ever handling the heavy tackle on hoists and lugging up sacks of coal for the old donkey engine forward that seemed to be Mr. Mack's particular pet. Unloading those steel plates with the equipment we had was slow as cold molasses.

That night we couldn't sleep. The warm air smelt of sugar. The arclights behind the levee glared into the portholes. At last when everything was quiet Bug shook me by the shoulder. He had that wild look in his eyes. "Let's go," he whispered with his mouth close to my ear.

In the fo'castle everybody was snoring. We went tiptoeing around the decks trying to find some way of getting off the damn boat. The skipper and mate had had the gangplank hauled up before they left for the night. The watchman must have strayed away for a drink because nobody saw us when we let ourselves down by a loose end of a hawser. Bug even remembered to bring my suitcase and his little seabag.

Once we had our feet on dry land we ducked into a dark alley behind a warehouse. We knew the cops were tough on seamen jumping ship.

The trouble with New Orleans was everything cost money and money was what we hadn't got. We didn't dare show our faces in any kind of a joint for fear Captain Connor would have us arrested and hauled back on board. We were dead tired. We were hungry and sick of hauling our duffle around the streets. We had only a dollar between us. We just roamed around back alleys between the foreignlooking houses. Every cop we saw threw us into a sweat.

At last Bug got into conversation with a hooker. We caught up with her coming out of the Absinthe House. She'd had a few drinks or maybe she wouldn't have been so kind. Still Bug had quite a way with the women. We walked one on each side of her and told our sad tale. She sized up our situation and said times were bad and she was through for the night and if we gave her our dollar she'd let us sleep at her place. Only no monkey business. She looked us each in the eye one after another just like a schoolteacher. The cop on the beat was her friend and she slept with a police whistle under her pillow. "Savvy?"

Her room was up some iron corkscrew stairs on one of those upper galleries they have in the French quarter. A big meanlooking white cat was waiting outside the door. The cat was mewing his head off. She was crazy about that cat. She had to get him his saucer of food before she'd pay any attention to us.

Her room was neat as a pin. An embroidered cover on the bed. Clean lace curtains in the windows. She laughed at how surprised we were to see things so shipshape. "Ain't you boys ever heard the saying: 'Disorderly life, orderly house'?"

She began to loosen up after she'd fed the cat. Her name was Myrna. She was from Missouri and that went all around the clock. Myrna was a thin skinny palefaced woman with a bony jaw. She looked awful old to us but she sure had a kind heart. She spread out everything to eat she had in the house and a growler half full of stale beer.

Bug began to perk up and get a little fresh when he'd eaten. He was used to getting away with murder with the women on account of his baby blue eyes, but Myrna slapped his face and said she wasn't robbing no cradle. There was only one man living could have her ass for nothing. My that woman had a raucous laugh.

She got out some blankets for us to sleep on and bedded us down in an old closet in the back of the house. She locked the door on us from the outside. She wasn't taking no chances, Myrna said.

Next day round noon she let us out and made us clean up

real good at the washstand. She even made us wash our ears.
Myrna was a stickler for cleanliness. Then she cooked us up
the best breakfast you ever saw and told us twentythree skid-
doo, she had her customers to think of. I was hoping she'd
give us back our dollar but she never did.

She told us there were no jobs to be had for young punks
like us in New Orleans, we'd find a line of buck niggers a mile
long at any place they had work. Jump a freight and get out,
was her advice. She stood there as we scrambled down the
corkscrew stairs, leaning over the rail of the gallery and yelling directions at us about how to reach the yards where they
made up the westernbound freights. That cat was arching his
back and rubbing against her bare legs that showed through
the frilly pink wrapper that kept coming open in front. "You
kids head for Texas," she screeched. She was a hardlooking
woman but all my life I've remembered how kind she was.

Bug and me we didn't know a damn thing about freights.
We sure would have landed in some chaingang if it hadn't
been for Earl Gates. We ran into Earl in some little tank town
south of Texarkana. We were hipped on getting to Texas but
all the trains seemed to be going the other way.

That day we were standing under the drip from the water
tank crouched to make a run for a string of flatcars just gathering speed when a heavy hand came down on each of our
shoulders. "Take it easy boys," came a deep voice behind us.
We were scared out of our wits. We thought it was a yard
dick.

When we turned around we both burst out laughing. It
was a runty little guy with a rusty goatee and red hair that
stuck straight up in the middle of his head like a rooster's
comb. He was small but he was wiry and God he had a grip.
He had the pleasantest sounding deep voice you ever heard:
"Don't get killed before your time, boys," he was saying.

Earl Gates was one of the really great guys I met up with
in my life. It was Earl who first called me Blackie. Right away
he started to call me Blackie and Bug Evans Whitie. He made
out we were so green that it was the only way he could tell
us apart.

Earl must have been twentyfour or twentyfive. He'd been
on the bum for five years. The way he liked to put it was
that he was carrying on a private scientific investigation of the
lower strata of society. Earl sure did love big words. Earl told

us his old man had a nice little farm in southern Illinois, but he had left home because he wanted an education. His old man said no amount of booklearning would raise a crop of corn and was dead set against it. He must have been as pigheaded in his way as Earl was in his.

Earl had been beating his way back and forth across the country trying to get a college degree. He'd tried the Cooper Union and nightschool at Northwestern and a whole raft of state colleges, but he never could get credit for his courses because he talked back to his profs. I guess he really wanted to be teaching the courses himself. I never knew a man so crazy about reading. He'd read Marx and Henry George and listened to lectures by Daniel De Leon. When I first met up with him he was a Socialist. Eugene V. Debs was his god. Right away he told Bugs and me he was going to educate us if it killed him.

Texas was no place to go, we'd starve to death in Texas. Earl was headed for the harvest fields. It was only April so we had more than a month to make it out to southern Missouri for the barley and oats. Meanwhile he'd learn us the lore of the road. First lesson: never ride flatcars. A hobo on a flatcar was a sitting duck. Second lesson: never jump a freight on an empty stomach. A man needed all his strength not to make a false step and get killed.

Right away Earl led the two of us down through a gulley back of the water tank to a jungle under some cottonwood trees. Three old tramps were sitting around a little fire. They had a gunny sack full of turnips and beets and cabbage and spuds some farmer had given them because they'd been damaged by frost in his root cellar. The tramps treated Earl with respect. They gave us kids some sidelong looks but they didn't try to molest us.

Bug had been standoffish with Earl at first but those spuds roasted in the ashes convinced him Earl was on the up and up. After that he listened to everything Earl said meek as a lamb. Bug wasn't any reader He sure was the puzzledest kid in the world when he heard Earl and me, after we'd wrapped ourselves in old newspapers to go to sleep by the fire because the night was cold, go at it hammer and tongs about unearned increment and the labor theory of value.

Somehow I'd just eaten that stuff up since I'd read a copy of *The Appeal to Reason* one of Dad's friends left lying around the house one day, but Earl was the first man who laid socialism on the line so's I could understand it. I was just a highschool kid but I'd heard and seen enough around home to know that, in Baltimore at least, money ruled the roost. The interests did what they pleased and the working man got the short end of the stick.

Dad seemed to go along with that system. He always sided with the strong. He'd tell about the streetcar company buying some city councilman, or the raw deal some poor ignorant bohunk got at the shipyard as if he liked it that way. That was one of the things made me maddest at him. After all poor Mother had tried to bring us up Christians.

Earl was a natural born teacher. Talking to Earl, Christianity and socialism all fell into place. Earl left you thinking that Jesus Christ the carpenter, the first apostle of the working class, and Eugene V. Debs, the railroad leader, had really been out for the same cause. Capitalism was the moneychangers Christ had driven out of the temple. Democracy would be a grand thing if the vested interests weren't in a position to buy all the politicians. Abolish the power of money. All we needed to set things right was for the guys who did the work to take over the running of the industrial system. It wasn't our fault we was starving to death as bums instead of being in school studying, it was the fault of the system.

What convinced Bug and me was that Earl was such a warmhearted guy. That first day we saw him give away his extra shirt to an old stumblebum who'd lost his trying to wash it in the Red River.

Earl watched over Bug and me like a father. When we met Earl we didn't have a plan in the world but Earl always had plans. If we came along with him we'd follow the wheat harvest up from Missouri through Kansas and Nebraska up to the Dakotas. We could go clear to Winnipeg if we wanted to go that far north but this summer he had a notion to beat his way into one of the Colorado mining camps.

He was planning to save himself up a little stake and try mining. Miners were striking it rich. We might try placer mining for gold. He wanted to make enough money quick to go to a first rate college and really get himself an education. I figured I'd try to get me an education too. Plans sounded so easy talking to Earl. I began to see myself walking in on Mother and Dad with a college diploma in my hand. That would show 'em who the smart boy was in the Bowman family.

We had our share of trouble before we got to the wheat-fields. We weren't the only ones who had this idea of follow-ing the harvest that summer. Business wasn't so good and the freights were crowded. The railroads were putting up No Trespassing signs and hiring fresh dicks to keep migrants off the trains.

Trouble comes up so fast when you are on the bum, always when you don't expect it. The three of us were riding in an empty gondola with a couple of Mexicans we'd met up with, sitting there in the warm sun looking out at the pretty rolling springtime country while Earl talked up socialism and the brotherhood of man in his low even voice that you could hear pretty well under the slambanging of the wheels and the couplings.

The train was slowing down and we were all settling back to listen to Earl talk when we heard yelling and shooting up the line. As the train slowed to a stop a bunch of armed deputies were pulling the boes off the cars and beating them up with their clubs. We jumped and ran for it into a little patch of woods beside the tracks.

At the edge of the wood I turned. Bug wasn't with us. He'd slipped and twisted his ankle maybe jumping. I saw him sprawling on the track. As he struggled to his feet a big plug-ugly came down on his head with a baseball bat held with both hands. Earl said afterwards he could hear Bug's skull crack right from where he stood. There was nothing we could do because right then a couple of deputies started shooting. They must have been drunk. Their guns were loaded with rock salt. I got a piece in my shoulder and it stung.

On the far side of the wood was an open field and beyond that a dirt road that had a look of leading into a town. Earl and I slackened our pace.

"We got to do something," Earl said as soon as he caught his breath.

The Mexicans never did stop running, but Earl and me, we waited to think what to do. Then we started walking into town. "Our only hope," Earl was saying, "is that the local doctor is an honest man." Already we could see houses through the trees ahead.

We stopped and cleaned ourselves up at a horsetrough on

the edge of the village. Earl always carried soap and a razor and a little round mirror in his pocket. He insisted we both of us shave. A mockingbird sang like crazy all the while in the oaktree overhead. It seemed to me desperately long before Earl was satisfied we looked respectable enough. Then Earl asked our way to the local doctor's.

The doctor was a shortnecked grayhaired man with a trimmed beard. He was sitting in his shirtsleeves in his office with his stethoscope hanging over the stiff starched front. Earl talked mighty sweet about how a young boy he knew had been beaten up by the railroad police and he knew he was hurt bad, maybe killed and wouldn't the doctor go with us to try to find him.

The doctor kept saying this was his office hours and he had nobody to leave in charge, but Earl came back about how the boy would die without medical assistance and quoted the Hippocratic oath—now who but Earl would have been able to quote the Hippocratic oath?

The doctor sighed and got to his feet and slipped on his vest and his black coat and made us hitch up his horse and buggy for him and drove us by a crossroad over to the railroad tracks.

We found the place all right on account of the little wood. The train had pulled out. There were dropped bundles and bits of torn shirt and broken bats and other signs of a pitched battle, but not a hobo or a deputy in sight.

In the ditch we found Bug. His head was caked with blood. At first I thought he was dead but there was a bubbling sound from his mouth. His eyes were open but they seemed to have lost all their color. They didn't have any focus. We couldn't tell whether Bug could see us or not.

The doctor wouldn't let us touch him. That sawbones was troubled with shortness of breath but he knew his business all right. He told us he had been a field surgeon in the Philippines. He wouldn't let us move Bug till he drove back to town to get a colored man with a spring wagon and a stretcher. Back at his office he worked over Bug half the night.

We sat on the front porch steps and worried. When the doctor came back he looked haggard. He asked if we knew the address of Bug's parents. For a wonder I did. He said he'd telegraph them, that the boy must stay here but he added that we'd better move on out of town. The sheriff here was mighty tough on vagrants.

"Will he get well?"

The doctor was breathing hard. He shook his head. How did he know? Compound fracture of the skull. It would be months before he could tell how badly the brain was affected.

"This is going to put me to a lot of expense," the doctor complained peevishly after another fit of panting.

We said we didn't have a cent in the world but Earl announced in his deep confident voice that when we made our stake we'd surely pay him for his trouble. Earl made a great show of writing down the sawbones' name and address. He'd convinced the both of us by that time we'd get rich in the goldfields.

We walked out into a drizzly night. We were wretched. We were hungry. We didn't know where we were going but we walked and walked. As we walked we swore to each other that no matter how rich we got in the goldfields we'd never forget Bug. Everything we made, everything we learned we'd dedicate to creating a country where things like that couldn't happen. To tell the truth the world never did seem the same to me after that night.

A day or two later we were so busy we didn't have time to grieve for Bug Evans. We hit a farm where they were harvesting a hundred acres of barley. They needed hands. Right away instead of being kicked around we found ourselves honored guests. The farmer's wife found us clean straw to sleep on in the hayloft over the cowbarn. At meals at a long table set on trestles outside the kitchen door she couldn't feed us enough. Evenings we sat around with the family on the back stoop. One of the young sons had a ukulele and we sang all the songs we knew.

It was hard work but it was cheerful. They had me feeding the shocks off the wagons into the big old steam threshing machine set up behind the barn. On account of his strong hands they had Earl tying the bags. It was heavy work and dusty work and the dust was full of the sharp beards of the barley that got up your sleeves and down your neck and you were soaked with sweat and the chaff stuck to you and you itched, but Earl said you felt what you were doing was of use to the world. He'd been raised on a farm and the work came easy to him.

When we were through at one farm we moved to another. Often we went along with the threshing machine and the reapers and binders or rode in a wagon some farmer who needed hands would send over for us. It was a grand summer.

Earl wouldn't let me spend any money, so I had sixty dollars saved when Earl and I piled off the train in Trinidad, Colorado.

The first thing we saw was a deputy with a gun standing guard at the depot.

I don't know what I'd been expecting but listening to Earl I had gotten to thinking of a mining camp as some wonderful thing. Trinidad was nothing but a mess of rock piles and mineheads and unpainted shacks in a wilderness of bare gray mountains. It was an oriental despotism besides. The coal company owned everything. They paid good wages but they got back every cent through the company stores and the crib-houses and the bars. Half the miners coudn't speak English. Poor dumb oxen right out of Ellis Island, they didn't know how they were being exploited.

Earl and I, we'd been bitter ever since we saw that happen to Bug but now we found ourselves on the firing lines of the class war. There was terror in the air. A man would look behind him before he came out with what he had on his mind. Wherever a few men who talked English could get together out of earshot of the stoolpigeons they talked organization. Bill Haywood, a handsome lion of a man with a fighter look from only having one eye, had been shuttling back and forth through the mining country, always one jump ahead of the bulls, preaching the Western Federation of Miners. The miners had guns, they knew how to use dynamite. Big Bill told them the day would soon come when they would take over the mines for themselves.

Earl Gates ate it up. He had a natural yen to sacrifice himself for a cause. In the WFM he saw the beginning of the revolution that would inaugurate the promised land. Earl forgot all about his plans for college and for making his pile. Before I knew what had happened he was secretary of the miners' secret lodge. Earl's was the spirit that brought forth the Industrial Workers of the World a few years later.

I forgot about my plans too, but the trouble with me was I was just turned sixteen and thought I knew it all. I had money in my pocket and wanted to show those Trinidad floosies how I knew all there was to know about liquor and women. Earl hated drink and loose living. When he found me drunk in a crib one night with a little girl named Suzy Ann he gave me a tonguelashing I'll never forget.

If I hadn't thought so much of the guy I'd have punched him one. I flared right up in his face and asked him who the hell he thought he was, my old man? That was why I'd left home, to do what I goddam pleased. Earl stood there patiently listening with a hurt look on his face. Then he saw it was hopeless and left.

Suzy Ann almost split a gut laughing. She was a dark little rolypoly girl with shoebutton eyes. She claimed to be just my age. She certainly couldn't have been much older. The tale she was telling me was that she'd been kidnaped over the mountains out of a respectable home in Santa Fe. She begged me to take her back. It sounded like something out of Dick Deadeye. Maybe that was where she read it. Anyway I believed every word of it.

The same night I had my run in with Earl, Suzy Ann and I climbed on a couple of saddled horses we found hitched to a rail back of one of the boardinghouses and rode up over Raton Pass in a flurry of snow. Suzy Ann knew the trail. It was a hundred and fifty miles but we made it to Santa Fe. We would never have gotten away with it if the mining camps hadn't been in an uproar. In Trinidad the sheriff and his deputies were too busy trying to round up labor agitators to worry about a stolen cayuse.

Maybe it was being scared to death on account of the ponies —they were still hanging horsethieves in the mountains—or maybe it was just the damn magnificence of the scenery, but I can still see it, like a photograph inside my brain, the way the mountains looked with the dawn at our backs lighting the high snowy peaks and the purple upland country and the broad spread of the pines and the tremblingasps yellow with fall in the valleys. Why we didn't starve to death or freeze to death I'll never know, but somehow we managed to drag those spavined ponies as far as Taos.

There was nothing to Taos but the Indian pueblo in those days. Our mounts were worn out. Mine had gone lame. We sold them for five silver dollars to an old halfbreed sitting on his haunches outside the trading post, and the saddles for another five. That redskin knew what was what. Before we could turn around the ponies had vanished into an arroyo. We rode down to Santa Fe with the mailman on his wagon. Suzy Ann told him she was my sister.

The laugh was on me when we got to Santa Fe. Suzy Ann's folks she talked so big about turned out to be a fat Mexican woman with a mustache who was madam of the local bordello. The old lady greeted me in style and put on the longlost daughter act with Suzy Ann but when she found I'd spent all my money, that is all that Suzy Ann hadn't stowed away in the chamois skin bag she carried inside her corset, she began to talk about how it was time I was moving along. Suzy Ann said be sure and write.

One of their clients was a kind of a padrone who was up there hiring Mexicans for a construction job in LA. Labor was scarce on the Coast that year. I signed his cutthroat contract and he took me down to the railroad station with the rest of his deluded slaves. All I had to remember Suzy Ann by was a dose of clap that developed while I was working as waterboy on that job in LA.

By the time a Mexican doctor had dried me up at the cost of most of my pay I was a sadder and a wiser boy. I decided the seabreezes would do me good and signed on at San Pedro as deckhand on a tramp bound for Panama with a cargo of steers. Teddy Roosevelt was busy digging his canal through the Isthmus and the merchant marine seemed a fine career for a young fellow to go into. It would have been a fine career for me if I hadn't gotten into the habit of blowing in my pay on liquor and broads every time I hit port. It's not my fault, it's the system, I said to myself. After five years all I had to show for it was a few cuts and bruises and my papers as an ablebodied seaman.

The fall I decided to take a spell on the beach in San Pedro while I looked for better paying work was the fall they blew up the *Los Angeles Times*. To tell the truth I got my first job in structural iron because the cops rounded up so many bridgemen that work was at a standstill on a new downtown hotel. At least in the merchant marine I'd learned how to balance on a scaffolding and paint. The day they arrested the McNamaras, just to prove I wasn't a scab I went around and joined the International Association of Bridgemen and Structural Iron Workers, not that I approved of killing innocent people—that was no way to fight the class war—but I honestly believed the McNamara brothers were being framed.

When McManigel squealed and the McNamaras changed their plea to guilty I felt like I'd had a hodful of bricks dumped down on my head. I wasn't the only one. I understand that Sam Gompers never recovered from the blow. I still think they ought to have kept their mouths shut and taken their medicine like men.

I was never an officer in the union so I didn't get indicted when they railroaded that bunch out of the Indianapolis office. They pinned every dynamiting on those boys that had happened since the Molly McGuires. Still I did enough talking to get my name on the Erectors' Association's blacklist, but particularly as girder construction was on the increase nationwide and qualified men were hard to come by, the bosses found it convenient to have short memories. I don't think I ever lost out on a construction job by being a red, not in those early days. It was later they gave us the works. A bridgeman was the best paid worker in the country.

New York was where the pay was. For a while the Flatiron Building had been a nine days wonder, but now they couldn't build skyscrapers fast enough. It took a lot of structural iron workers to put up that famous skyline. In 1912 I headed for New York. New York's no good without plenty of kale. Soon I was making enough to like it fine.

On my way east I attended an IWW convention in Chicago. It was on Earl Gates's invitation. We kept in touch all those years through a postal card or a letter now and then. He was head over heels in the labor movement. He had a lot to do with getting the miners off who'd been accused of murdering the Governor of Idaho. He'd become Big Bill's right hand man.

At the convention he was so busy I didn't get much chance to talk to him alone. At IWW conventions there used to be as many ideas as there were working stiffs in the hall. Earl had to talk fast to keep even half the boys headed in the same direction.

It was the same old Earl only gaunt and pale. He'd shaved his goatee. His hair wasn't so red as it used to be and was getting thin at the temples. He had a look of strain under the eyes. He was the same smooth talker, but now he was always laying down the law. He never stopped to listen.

The boys had been reading Sorel and were all agog over

sabotage. I raised questions about it. I was convinced before I came that solidarity and the one big union and the general strike were the roads to freedom for the working class, but I didn't want any more McNamara cases to set labor back for fifteen years. I never could quite swallow sabotage. I couldn't get Earl to see it my way. We were fighting a class war weren't we, was how he put it to the crowd, well all was fair in love and war. That brought down the house, but I came away uneasy. Too much like the *Los Angeles Times* business to suit me.

I've carried my red card from that day to this, though now it's more of a souvenir than anything else. But those were fiery years just before the first world war.

It was coming back from Mother's funeral on the B & O Railroad I first read in the paper of the Paterson strike. I hadn't been home when Dad died, I was off at sea somewhere and never got the letter, but now I had the price of the trip and dressed good and all that: I figured it was time to make my peace with the family.

It was heartbreaking how empty the old house was with Mother and Dad gone and just Ed and his frizzlyhaired wife living there. It looked so dark and narrow and small. I had remembered it an enormous place. Joe was a priest all in black with a sleek round face teaching in a Catholic college. Ed worked in a bank and the girls both had prosperous middle-class husbands. Our grief brought us together. I will say this much for the Bowmans; we never thought of quarreling over the will. Mother left nothing but the house, and Joe and I we said leave us out, let Ed and the girls take it on shares and we all shook hands. It made me feel good for Mother's sake. Except for one black sheep they had all come out the way she wanted them. I kept my face buttoned up on the subject of politics and we got along fine.

Now sitting with my necktie loose and my coat off in the daycoach after having gone into the diner for a couple of drinks I could really let myself go reading about that strike. I got so excited with the mass demonstrations and the singing girls I went over to Paterson next time there was a day's layoff to see the fun.

What I saw was a redheaded girl on the picket line. We were marching with red flags and placards on sticks past one of the big silk mills. We were singing the "Marseillaise." I sure forgot my duty as a classconscious worker that day. I couldn't keep my eyes off that girl's face. When the interests staged their daily atrocity trying to break up the demonstration I pulled her out from under a police officer's club and through a back alley out of harm's way.

She fought me as hard as she fought the cops. No use getting unnecessarily arrested I told her. "But I wanted to get arrested," she kept saying with tears of vexation in her eyes. "They are holding my sister in the bastille right now . . . my sister Kate O'Dwyer."

She said it like she expected me to be impressed and of course I was. Kate O'Dwyer's speeches were in all the papers. After Big Bill Haywood and Quinlan and Tresca she was one of the top leaders of the strike. That was great I told her, but she was too young and too pretty to go to jail.

My that made her mad. I had to take her to a lunchroom and feed her a chicken sandwich and a cup of coffee to quiet her down. She wasn't really pacified till I showed her my red card. Then she admitted her name was Eileen and that she was only a junior in highschool. I couldn't stop looking at her as she sat up on that stool nibbling at the sandwich with her even little teeth.

Eileen always did have a good figure, but at seventeen she was the prettiest slenderest creature you ever saw in your life. You could measure her waist with your two hands. She had skin like a lily and eyes that you could never tell whether they were green or blue, and her hair was the color of new copper wire. She moved like a leaf blown by the wind.

Eileen and I we just hit it off from that first minute. We got so busy telling each other about ourselves we forgot all about the strike. We had started squabbling like old friends before we even knew each other's names. When she told me her folks didn't know where she had gone I made her take the first train home to New York.

The O'Dwyers lived in a brick house on Tompkins Square though the saloon Patrick O'Dwyer kept was further uptown on Second Avenue. "The holy saints be praised," cried Mrs. O'Dwyer when she saw me ushering Eileen in through the front door. Mrs. O'Dwyer was a cheerful dumpy dark woman from Enniscorthy with her hair parted in the middle and a brogue you could cut with a knife. The O'Dwyers were all mad she told me but by all that was blessed she thought Eileen was the maddest of the lot. For bringing home strange men she was even worse than her sister Kate. "At least she brings them home Mrs. O'Dwyer," I said.

She looked me up and down and with a sharp kind of a smile that seemed to mean "You'll do young man." Right away she asked me to stay and eat with them. She was just about to put a bit of supper on the table.

The O'Dwyers became a second family to me from the moment I brought Eileen home safe that night. Mrs. O'Dwyer sat us down at the oval table set at the end of the oldfashioned kitchen that occupied the whole back of the house. While she was piling our plates with stewed steak and potatoes, the rest of the family came straggling in. The older boys Pat and Jim were redheaded with big opinionated mouths. Little Benedict was quiet and darkhaired and looked like his mother. They called me Blackie and seemed to take me for granted as Eileen's young man right from the first.

The O'Dwyers ate and drank and slept politics. It was all freedom for Ireland and stand up for the poor Boers. England was the root of all evil.

They went at it hammer and tongs about which was more on the side of the common people, William Jennings Bryan or T.R.'s Bull Moose. A proof that T.R. was an honest man was that the capitalist press was trying to frame him on a charge of drunkenness. They thought Debs was a great orator but they said Gompers as a practical man was doing more for the working people. They were all for woman's suffrage and the referendum and recall and the popular election of senators and the eight hour day. They wouldn't even listen when I said politics was a stageplay arranged to delude the working stiffs.

At that they favored the Paterson strikers against the mill-owners though Mrs. O'Dwyer cried out to the saints to blast the godless anarchists who were leading her daughter Kate astray. That was hitting me where I lived. I didn't tell the O'Dwyers I carried a red card but I did pipe up to say that there wasn't any conflict between syndicalism and Christianity. We argued and shouted at each other till we must have been heard halfway around the block. I sure felt at home in that house.

In the middle of it, Patrick O'Dwyer, the old man himself, came in. He had a red face and a blue eye and shaggy sandy eyebrows and roared everybody down. His family all called him the Boss. He reminded me a little of my own father except for the glib Irish wit. The difference was that O'Dwyer was a laughing man.

In Paterson he said both sides were wrong. No leadership with a heart. Nothing like that could happen in this great city of New York—he pounded on the table to make us listen—with a great organization like Tammany fostering kindness between rich and poor.

Just about that point Kate O'Dwyer burst into the kitchen. "Tammany," she cried. "That is the rottenest example there is of class collaboration." Kate was a big rawboned girl. Her hair was red but it didn't have the lovely color Eileen's had. She was the eldest and the only one who dared talk back to the Boss. The old man just sat there swallowing air while she went on: "It's collaboration all right. Collaboration to pick the public's pockets."

"And why aren't you in jail with the other agitators?" asked her mother sarcastically.

"Bailed out, my dear, bailed out by a capitalist who believes in fair play."

The Boss shouted that she was an ungrateful hussy, she'd be rotting in a cell right now if he hadn't pulled a few strings over at Tammany Hall. "Tammany watches over even the black sheep that stray from the flock."

Kate didn't listen. She was never one to pay much attention to what other people were saying. She had launched into a speech about how we must all dig into our pockets to support a pageant the strikers were putting on in Madison Square Garden. She'd just come home to change her clothes before going to the house of a wealthy woman who was going to bear part of the cost. A famous young journalist was waiting for her in a car outside. We all must have heard of Freddie Davis.

"Madison Square Garden, that's rich." The Boss laughed with a roar like a bull. "Let the agitators and the millowners step out into the ring. Let 'em put on the gloves and I'll put up a purse to see them fight. Nothing illegal, but a friendly athletic contest. Or make it a battle royal over in Hoboken but leave the poor working people in peace."

Kate went on without paying the slightest attention: the pageant would show the people of this city that it was real flesh and blood struggling and suffering in Paterson and not just foreign names you read about in the newspapers. I could see that the Boss's bark was worse than his bite. He pulled a tenspot off his roll of bills and Kate was gone out the door without so much as a thank you.

That night I went back to my furnished room with my head reeling. I lay down on the bed and smoked a cigarette trying to straighten out my ideas after all that argument, but all I could think of was how crazy I was about Eileen. I could see her every time I closed my eyes.

To tell the truth I'd had my fill of the sailor ashore kind of life, raising hell Saturday nights and getting drunk and whores and waking up with hell in your heart after you've been rolled by some floosy's pimp. No man ever did get much satisfaction out of prostitutes. I was telling myself that that was all over for me now. I was taking a pledge to lay off the liquor. No girl would do any more except Eileen.

One Saturday night in June I took Eileen to the Paterson strikers' pageant. Luckily we arrived at the Garden early because the cops were already trying to keep people out of the hall pretending the place was too full. It was the most exciting meeting either of us had ever been to in our lives. In the gallery people were standing in the aisles. I never saw so many young faces. All the girls wore something red. People waved straw hats and handkerchiefs and cheered and clapped at the slightest thing. That was one show where the audience really did take part.

When we first came in a banner reading No God No Master was stretched across the hall right under the ceiling. I was just telling Eileen that those were my sentiments exactly when some men started climbing up the girders back of the galleries to take it down. It was Big Bill himself who shouted through a megaphone that sentiments like that had nothing to do with the Paterson strike. There were cheers when the crowd recognized him. I guess he knew what he was doing but it left me disappointed.

The band was playing and Eileen and I were standing up on our seats singing the "Marseillaise." A huge stage filled the end of the hall. When the lights went on they lit the backdrop that showed the great square buildings of the Paterson mills and their tiers of windows. Searchlights picked out the action that was all in pantomime. To the music of the band and the singing of strike songs working men and women who had come over from Paterson on a special train acted out the story.

The big moment was the funeral of a worker killed by the deputies. When they took the lid off the coffin and the strikers filed by each dropping in a red carnation they showed such grief on their faces that the enormous audience was silent as the dead. Eileen grabbed my hand and held it tight. Not a sound in Madison Square Garden except now and then a woman's sob.

From where we were sitting—or standing rather—all the people around us were so excited they stood on their seats instead of sitting in them—we couldn't hear too well the speeches the leaders made over the coffin. Only when Big Bill bellowed "We'll fight the strike till hell freezes over and after that we'll fight on the ice" it brought a roar from the crowd. He ended up reminding us that the working class produced all the food people ate and the clothes they wore and the buildings they were housed in and yet it was the working class that suffered hunger and cold and had no place to lay its head. Eileen and I had our arms around each other's shoulders. We looked into each other's faces with wet eyes.

Kate's voice carried well. She looked handsome and dramatic all in black talking about the suffering of the housewives and the mothers with little children. Let the bosses and their wives and daughters go into the silk mills and work and see how they liked the pay and conditions. If the rich wanted to wear silk let them weave it themselves.

The people gave Kate an ovation. Eileen actually hugged me she was so excited at her sister's triumph.

Eight men with bowed heads and dragging steps carried the coffin off to a rolling of drums and the sound of a slow funeral march. There was a touching scene of the mothers waving their children goodbye when they were being sent off to a place of safety and the pageant ended with a victory march across the stage by all those working people singing the "Marseillaise" in all the different languages the strikers used.

Afterwards, Eileen and I, we were walking on air. The streets outside the Garden were full of people humming the "Marseillaise" and waving bits of red bunting. The cops had roped off Madison Square for fear of an outdoor meeting. Mounted police, cossacks we called them, kept the crowds moving. We walked in step, moving slowly with the slow-moving crowd.

Eileen with her arm in mine was steering us down Fifth Avenue. Kate had said to meet her at the Hotel Brevoort. All the strike leaders would be there. Eileen rubbed her face against my arm in that little catlike way she had. "Blackie take me to the Brevoort."

I told her I'd take her any damn place in New York she wanted to go. I'd like to see any goddam copper try to stop us. That pageant had left me full of beans. I felt I could take on any police force in the world singlehanded. The words "No God No Master" kept running through my head.

I tried to explain to Eileen how it made me feel, the general strike rolling up the storefronts and freeing the people imprisoned in the sweatshops in the city slums, the wind of freedom blowing away all the shams and hypocrisies and exploitations of the world. I ended by singing "Solidarity Forever" at the top of my lungs. If I'd brayed like a jackass I couldn't have been further from explaining exactly what I meant.

But that night Eileen and I we understood each other without words. She'd nod blinking and smiling at everything I said before I half got it out. By the time we reached Eighth Street she was tired. She said her shoes hurt her. She had a funny little way of lifting up her feet and shaking them, the way a kitten might do.

The Brevoort café was so crowded there was no way of even looking inside. The entrances were packed tight with people trying to get in. When a broadshouldered young man turned to look at Eileen I didn't think much of it, because there was something about Eileen that stopped all sorts of men dead in their tracks. He said "Excuse me, aren't you Kate O'Dwyer's sister?" Eileen nodded excitedly.

He looked me straight in the face out of schoolboyish brown eyes. "My name's Freddie Davis." We shook hands.

"No use trying to get in here. Let's go see if she's at Mabel's," he said. "Kate said to bring you along if I found you." I couldn't help liking the guy but something about the way Eileen looked at him gave me a twinge. I felt better when, rattling along as if he'd known us all our lives, he started to tell us about a beautiful girl he was in love with and how he wanted to spend his life writing poetry about her; but that in spite of that he was leaving for Mexico in the morning to report the revolution for the *Metropolitan Magazine*. Freddie

was an attractive young fellow but it sure put me off the way
he kept sharing his private life with strangers.

He ushered us into a big fine room in a big fine house, full
of the damndest congregation of people you ever saw in your
life. There were people in evening dress and Orientals in
turbans and working girls from Paterson, strike leaders, and
writers and poets, longhaired men and shorthaired women in
smocks. This was my first view of Greenwich Village. I wish it
had been my last.

It made me feel good that all these different kinds of people
were so worked up over the plight of those strikers in Paterson. Made me feel the solidarity of the human race, I said,
when Freddie introduced me to a dumpy little woman with
cold violet eyes in a white dress with a lot of jewelry hung on
it who was the hostess.

What I said pleased her so much she kept repeating it to
everybody who came in. She seemed all set up at having a
real working man at her party. She kept pointing me out as a
structural iron worker to her guests. Looked like some of them
had never seen a working stiff before.

We never did find Kate. It wasn't too long before we
wearied of the yammer of voices. I'd already worked a ten
hour day before I went by to take out Eileen and man I was
tired. Evenings seem long when you aren't drinking.

Eileen wasn't half ready to go but I took her on the cross-
town car and we sat spooning a few minutes on a bench in the
square in front of her house while I tried to bring up the subject of getting married. She kept beating around the bush and
never would let me pop the question. She did let me kiss her
though and that left my head whirling so I could hardly find
my way home to my lodging house after I'd left her at her
door. All night that drab old room seemed full of the smell of
her hair.

Next time the O'Dwyers asked me to eat at their house I
got the Boss in a corner and asked him if he'd have any objection. Why should he have any objection? He clapped me on
the shoulder. Didn't I come from a Catholic home and wasn't
I in the way of making a good honest living? I stammered
something about being a bit of a red but he roared me down.
Any boy worth his salt . . . He himself had been the hellroar-
ingest Fenian you ever saw till he was twentyfive. Then he
laid down the law. We could be engaged and I could take her

out but he didn't want to hear a word about matrimony until the girl had finished school.

Looking forward to it a year seemed a century; but as it turned out I had no choice because that spring Mrs. O'Dwyer noticed I wasn't getting over a cough that had come on with a cold early in the winter. The Boss sent me to their doctor who found I was running a temperature and sent me to another doctor who said I had a spot on my lung. Tuberculosis. The Boss got into a great fright for fear I'd given it to Eileen and arranged overnight for me to go to the state sanatorium at Saranac. To tell the truth I always thought it was me caught it from Eileen because she came down with it soon after.

That was in early July. In those days they made you lie in bed in big open porches for TB. The mania was fresh air. I'd been lying there worrying myself sick over what Eileen might be up to, because I knew she had started to write poetry and had been corresponding with Freddie Davis about it. Then I got this letter from her that made me feel better and worse at the same time. The O'Dwyers' doctor had been checking her over and decided that she had a touch of the white plague too and shipped her to the woman's department of that same huge Saranac hospital. I was scared for her but relieved in my mind in another way. At least it would keep her away from Freddie Davis. It was us both having the same sickness that finally tied the knot on us.

Afterwards Eileen and I used to say that Saranac was where we'd gone to college. We read a lot of the same books and wrote each other notes two or three times a day. I thought Eileen's little poems were the wonderfulest things I'd ever read. She read mostly fiction and plays and verse and I read history and economics. It was the nearest I ever got to an education. We were so busy with our funny little cooped up private lives we hardly noticed the outbreak of the world war in Europe.

Of course it was Earl Gates who directed my reading. We'd kept in touch but now for the first time in my life I got a chance to become a real letter writer. We started up the old argument about sabotage, only this time by mail. Earl was knocking himself out trying to set up a bureau for migratory workers for the IWW. He sent me lists of books on socialism and syndicalism and anarchy he hadn't found time to read himself. I thought Kropotkin was great. I stuffed my head with long words like a regular sea lawyer.

Eileen's health was improving but slower than mine was. I'm ashamed to say how relieved I was to have her in the sanatorium. Under wraps. She'd be safe there until the time came for us to get married was how I looked at it. My belief in free love didn't stand up when it came to Eileen. I wanted her all to myself.

For months there was no seeing her, but in the spring we were both on the ambulatory list. They turned us loose on the grounds one day a week. Putting our arms around each other again made us almost crazy with delight.

I'd discovered a hidden nook by the lake in a grove of young balsams. If the crushed sweetfern was any indication, we weren't the only couple who found it. Before I'd been the eager one but now she threw herself against me as if she'd tear me to pieces. She was so passionate I was scared. "Love me, Blackie, love me," she'd whisper in a new deep throaty voice. Her hands would be all over me. When the time came to report back to our various wards we'd tear ourselves apart and hurry off in our separate directions shaking and trembly from the violence of it, without looking back. We were under each other's skins all right.

Earl and I had been making plans to repeat that jaunt we'd made through the harvest fields years ago as soon as I got out of the hospital. The doctors recommended outdoor work for me and Earl wanted to see the harvest stiffs organized at first hand.

I met him at the IWW hall in Kansas City. Earl looked pale and thin from slaving in the office all winter and he had a kind of a wild glitter in his eye. The fellow workers looked up to him like a god. The place was full of young kids who expected the revolution to be tomorrow. They just drank up everything he said. Earl always had the gift of gab, but this summer his deep voice seemed richer and his choice of words better than ever before. Those kids made me feel right ashamed of myself. All I'd been thinking about, riding out in a daycoach like a regular scissorbill because I still had a little dough saved up from flush times in New York, was how I could go to work to earn enough to give Eileen a comfortable life once we got married.

That was one of the years when wheat was king of the

world. The war in Europe was kicking prices up. The farmers were daffy with the idea of two dollar wheat. They were more worried about hail and thunderheads than they were about chiseling on the wages of the harvest stiffs. Every farmer wanted to beat the other guy to the elevator no matter what it cost.

We wobblies were hitting our peak. It looked to us that the world wide war would do more than all the strikes we could stage to dislodge the capitalist system. With the weight of parasites and moneybags off our shoulders we working people would enjoy the entire product of our labor. When Eileen and I had children they would grow up into a society based on mutual aid.

Earl took charge of me when we joined the harvest crews. I was weak as a kitten after a year lying flat on my bed just reading books and laying up fat, but he managed to steer me into light jobs at first. Earl always was the most considerate fellow in the world. It was several weeks before I really hit my stride. By that time I was lean and sunburned and tough as I'd ever been.

On the very first job we signed up the whole crew. We taught them all the songs out of the little Wobbly songbook. Word had gotten around that a red card was a protection. Fifty cents wasn't much to pay. Brakemen and yard dicks were going easy with boes who waved a red card under their noses. The grain wouldn't get harvested without the harvest stiffs. The railroads weren't worrying about hauling a few free passengers that summer, what they wanted was the profit from hauling the grain.

Once I got my strength back it was a real pleasure, in spite of the heat and the dust, to handle the warm dry grain pouring out into the bags from the threshing machines. It was happy work. Meadow larks rose piping out of the fields of wheat rolling in waves like the ocean under that huge prairie sky scattered full with white blobs of clouds. Locusts and all the little bugs that live in the wheat thudded against your sweaty skin as you toiled to tie the full bags, stripped to the waist under the baking sun. Quail went whirring up from under the horses' feet. There was pleasure in doing it well. In spite of his class war notions Earl worked like ten men. There was still a lot of the farm boy under the skin of the revolutionary agitator. "Wheat is bread," he'd say kind of apologizing for himself. "Bread is the life of mankind."

The first tractors were appearing on the larger farms, big ugly contraptions that looked like the Toonerville trolley. Motor trucks backed up to haul the grain to the elevators. Evenings, sitting around on bales of straw in the cool of the barns, Earl would talk about how once we had production for use instead of a gamble for profit mechanical inventions would take the load of work off working men's shoulders. The eight hour day was all right as far as it went but maybe the day would come when an eight hour week would accomplish all the work that was needed in the world.

We worked our way clear to Moorehead City on the Red River of the North. There Earl was able to announce to a meeting we held at the stands at the fairgrounds, because there wasn't a hall in town big enough to hold all the working stiffs who wanted to attend, that the number of migratory workers who had signed up with the One Big Union had passed the ten thousand mark.

Wages were going up, working conditions were improving. The day was at hand when the working people of America would take the country over from the moneymasters who lived off other men's sweat and the blood of the poor slaves herded to their deaths on the battlefields of Europe. How those harvest stiffs cheered. Earl Gates was a happy man that day.

At General Delivery at the Fargo post office I found the letter I'd been expecting from Eileen. The doctors had told her she'd be discharged from the hospital September 15. I must come.

Earl gave me a disappointed look when we shook hands at the marshaling yard where they were making up an eastbound freight. "Joining the homeguard, eh Blackie," he said trying to keep the sarcasm out of his voice. "Every man has to live his own life. . . . For me," he added bitterly, "it's back to the mines."

It seemed awful slow beating my way East. I was so afraid I'd be late for the day Eileen was to get out of the hospital I paid my fare on the passenger trains to Saranac Lake from Chicago. For the two days I had to wait there I put up at the cheapest flophouse I could find. At that I still had more than a hundred dollars in my jeans when I carried Eileen's wicker suitcase out past the desk in that hospital lobby.

On the way to the train we stopped off at City Hall to get married. All that summer I'd carried the marriage license in my wallet.

Eileen's folks had sent her a money order so we rode to New York in a lower berth on a Pullman. That was the happiest trainride I ever had in my life.

We sat around in the waiting room of the beautiful new Grand Central Station trying to decide whether to go get ourselves lodgings or to go straight to the O'Dwyers' to face the music. We knew there would be a row on account of our not being married in church. While Eileen went to the ladies' room to comb out her hair I sat looking at the morning paper.

IWW RIOT AT MONTANA MINE

Killed and wounded. Agitator dies in jail.

One of those police lineup snapshots that went with the article showed Earl Gates. Staring straight at me off the page. The name was spelled wrong but there was no mistaking the comb of hair and the defiant look about the eyes. I didn't have time to read the damn lying reporter's prejudiced story before I saw Eileen coming back. When her eyes met mine she smiled. I dropped the newspaper in the trashcan at the end of the bench I was sitting on. I didn't want anything to upset our happiness that day.

Documentary (16)

TRAPPED BY AN ELEVATOR

it will be a profitable experience, one that will give you a new perspective on your own research and development program. Send your key technical people, the men directly responsible for product engineering

Air Express Gives Sleepgun Fast Kid Glove Handling

DON'T LET THE LOW PRICE FOOL YOU

A New Look at Venus

Dr. Jacobson told of isolating from the abdominal segment of the female gypsy moth an oily substance that was highly attractive to males. It fluoresces a brilliant blue in ultraviolet light and absorbs infrared light the same way that a certain synthetic compound does.

KEEPS A MAN SO ODORFREE A BLOODHOUND COULDN'T FIND HIM

no upkeep no investment

"Please help us before our union is so full of corruption we'll never be able to clear it up," a sheetmetal worker wrote the Senator. "How can you call this a free country when a man has to pay for the privilege of working to a bunch of gangsters. A free American Ha ha! and the pursuit of the working man so that the Big Shot can live in clover."

TOP MEN FOR SALE

Man's Best Fourwheeled Friend

One "pfft" from his airrifle sends Jackie quickly off Dreamland and to the veterinarian. The magic bullet is a harmless tranquilizing syringe.

INVESTIGATOR'S NOTES V

Mr. Ryan lives in a small wellkept brick apartment house behind a mowed lawn and shrubbery on a welltodo street in a conservative suburb not too far out of town. Few signs of children, pet dogs on the leash. Flowered curtains in the windows.

Mr. Ryan opens his door himself, a wellpreserved man with closecropped silvery hair in a wellfitting wellpressed suit of a light gray smallchecked material. He offers his visitor an overstuffed chair in the sunny livingroom.

Mr. Ryan is a wine salesman. He talks easily in a modest tone with an occasional crack of humor. He starts by explaining himself a little. He's a lifetime Republican, a real Republican. He hates Tom Dewey and admires Bill Knowland. He's a Catholic War Veteran, belongs to organizations to promote respect for the constitution. A typical conservative he says, showing wellkept dentures when he laughs.

The children are grown, the only living thing left home besides Mrs. Ryan is a wirehaired terrier. What's a man like him doing messing with unions? Not by his own choice certainly.

Before enlisting in the armed services, Mr. Ryan was a wholesale wine salesman for many years with the same concern marketing a famous California brand. Before that he had been salesmanager for a corporation dealing in packaged foods. In spite of being somewhat over age he decided he ought to put in his two cents worth when World War II came around. He handled some supply problems for the navy and came out a Lieutenant Commander. Well when he went to get his old job back in '46 his boss told him he'd have to join the Wine Salesman's Union.

He was green about unions, thought maybe it might be a good thing. His first shock was when he went around to the union local. The dump was full of tobacco smoke and guys in their shirtsleeves playing cards. They let him wait an hour before the Executive Business Manager would take the trouble to talk to him. This was a beefy guy who looked as if he'd never done a lick of work in his life. He huffed and puffed about how getting admitted to the union would take time. Mr. Ryan's application would have to go up before the executive board. He would see what he could do. It would cost two hundred and fifty dollars.

Mr. Ryan's boss had made it clear that it was join the union or else. Trying for another job would mean sacrificing a lifetime's work establishing friendly contacts with dealers in this particular metropolitan region. When the man said two hundred and fifty dollars Mr. Ryan jumped up out of his chair like he'd been shot. He smelled a shakedown right then. The man was pretty smooth, said no need to fork up that money right today, but that Mr. Ryan might as well know he'd have a hard time convincing the executive board that the local needed any more salesmen. Too much competition as it was.

Mr. Ryan went out and walked round the block to think it over. Then he gave the man a ring on the phone. Nothing doing. The man made it clear he was waiting for the old green stuff.

Mr. Ryan began to take cross bearings. He found a name he knew on the executive board. His friend put him in touch with the president of the local. The president said sure they would take his application and told him to send in a check for twentyfive bucks to him direct. The initiation fee was twenty-five dollars, not two hundred and fifty. Well they managed to get rid of that official but the trouble with the union was, every time you got rid of one crook two more sprang up in his place.

Now the investigator mustn't get him wrong, there were things the union had done. Before the union the individual salesman was completely behind the eightball; now he had a weekly minimum draw and an increased commission on sales. The old president of their local was an honest man. He tried to get in free elections and financial reports, but the trouble was higher up.

The salesmen were subsidiary to another union that was a nest of racketeers, big time racketeers. These gentlemen had moved into the union at the same time as they moved into the distributors' organization. In the old days Mr. Ryan used to deal with the brand name direct. Now he had to deal through the distributor that had a monopoly on this whole area.

The outfit he worked for used to pay a commission on the list price but the union bosses put over a deal that the sales-men were to take their commission on the net price. Even they couldn't get away with that. That was too raw. Mr. Ryan and his friends went up to see the new Executive Business Manager. This was a big rough guy. "Go ahead and write up a complaint," he said, "I'll throw it in the wastebasket."

The union bosses were buddy buddy with the distributors and the same racketeers controlled both of 'em.

There was a valiant little guy on the executive board and he raised such hell they rescinded that regulation, but for how long? Without a secret ballot and honest financial ac-counting there was no way of telling where you stood. The working salesmen were no more than puppets. Mr. Ryan had written this whole situation up in a report to the membership.

Had it typed and distributed anonymously. He didn't dare sign his name to it. If he had he'd have been brought up on charges.

Nobody knew where the report came from. The distributors were wild and so were the union bosses. A lot of them were the same men, could you beat that? They shake down the salesmen through the union and shake down the wineries through their monopoly on distribution. Some of them are paid as high as fifteen thousand dollars a year by the wine people to push a certain product.

Mr. Ryan leaned back in his chair and put his hands on his knees and stared glumly out of the window. "At my age I begin to worry about welfare payments, medical insurance, things like that. It's all in the contract but if a man talks out of turn they cut him off. . . . I find myself in a situation that verges on involuntary servitude."

Mrs. Ryan, a rosyfaced busty woman, came bustling into the room carrying a tray with glasses and followed by their bouncy little wirehaired terrier.

Mr. Ryan stopped talking and pursed his lips. "Could we offer you a drink?" he said. "It's a very peculiar situation."

Backcountry Lawyer

When the United States Senate, goaded to action by some commotion in the public press, finally got around to solving a jurisdictional conflict between standing committees which had been impeding the investigation of alleged malpractices in the labor unions, by creating a Select Committee on Improper Activities in the Labor and Management Field,

the chairmanship devolved on the senior senator from Arkansas. John McClellan was an honest man and a sober man,

but,

went the pressgallery gossip,

he just hadn't had the advantages. He came from a reactionary semiliterate Southern state, was born on a farm, had his schooling at a hayseed high school, never went to college, or

to lawschool even, just studied law in his father's office in rural
Sheridan, right in the center of backward old stickinthemud
Arkansas. Boned up for the state bar examination by the
superannuated apprentice system like in the old old days of
Clay and Webster and Calhoun. How could he have had a
proper legal education when he was admitted to the bar at
seventeen and his father (who superintended his training) had
only been in practice five years himself. The man had hardly
been out of his home state, except for a short term in the Army
Signal Corps during the first world war, when he came to
Washington to serve as a dyedinthewool Democrat in the
House of Representatives during Franklin D. Roosevelt's first
administration.

John McClellan was known to his associates as a taciturn
man. Neither in the House nor later in the Senate did he pretend to glib pronouncements in the fashionable socioeconomic
terms of the times. He attended quietly to the interests of his
constituents, even though he went along with many of the
New Deal measures, he seemed disposed to question items
which he felt tended to inefficiency and waste.

        As chairman of the Select Committee he proved a
good listener,
    sitting quiet at the hearings, dragging through day after
day and month after month, grim with pursed mouth, a back-
country Dante
    whom dour young Robert Kennedy, the Committee's chief
counsel, ciceroned like a congressional Virgil
        through circle after circle
        of the industrial hell.
    Could this be America?

        Denial of the working man's most elementary rights,
the underworld's encroachment on the world of daily bread,
sluggings, shootings, embezzlement, thievery, gangups between employers and business agents, the shakedown, the
syndicate, oppression, sabotage, terror.

"Instead of serving the members of the unions, you are serving a national dictatorship," Senator McClellan told a restaurant workers' organizer. "Captive members have no control,
no authority, no contract, no entry to the union's affairs. They

are virtually captives. They have to do what they are told if they want to work."

The Senator from back country Arkansas showed every sign of having retained, in spite of twenty or more years on Capitol Hill, a certain reverence for the Ten Commandments and some resultant prejudices engrained in his upbringing

in favor of justice and the right of American citizens to be protected against violence and oppression.

He made no attempt to grab the center of the TV screen. He sat listening, his face a mask of patient incredulity, to the scared revelations of unwilling witnesses paraded before him,

the selfserving declarations of union organizers,

the proofs of the rascality of bosses and business agents and plain goons who were encouraged by eager bands of lawyers to stand on their constitutional right (the only thing about the Constitution that seemed to appeal to them) to refuse testimony which might

incriminate or degrade. Some of them wouldn't even tell their names.

Occasionally Senator McClellan's sense of outrage (can this be America?) would express itself

in a sarcastic outburst,

as in his vignette of a certain Mr. S. which appears in the hearings as reported for the Government Printing Office:

The man has served two penitentiary sentences for robbery and burglary; yet he was made the business agent of a local in Paducah, Kentucky. While there, he was convicted of assault and battery and indicted twice for malicious destruction of personal property, cases which have not yet been resolved. This apparently qualified him for advancement. He goes to Chattanooga, Tennessee where he becomes Secretary-Treasurer of a larger local. There he is indicted on a conspiracy charge including the slashing of truck tires, dynamitings, assault and arson. With these admirable qualifications the international sends him back to Paducah and puts him in charge of his old local which has by then been put in trusteeship.

He is unwillingly extradited back to Tennessee where the conspiracy charge against him is dismissed by the judge shortly after a fellow defendant has boasted that the case has been fixed by a payoff of $18,500. This matter neatly disposed of, the man is sent to Florida as an institutional organizer; where, according to testimony before this committee, he is involved in a dynamiting and arson case. This seems to qualify him for even higher trust and he returns to Chattanooga as president of the local.

These expressions of character qualified the man for the top job in the State of Tennessee, the presidency of the joint council, the position he holds today.

Can this be America? they asked.

Working people wrote from Maine and California, from Alaska and Texas and New Mexico, from industrial Indiana and rural Iowa . . . Plumbers, railroadmen, sheetmetal workers, dressmakers, bakers, bellboys, pastrycooks, steelworkers, carpenters, bricklayers, machinery movers and filling station operators . . . By the hundreds of thousands they wrote in to the committee. Puffing mailmen dragged the daily bagfuls of letters to the offices in the basement of the Senate Office Building.

Dear Senator, My Dear Senator McClellan:

They told him his committee had filled them with hope. "*It is really wonderful to find somebody going to bat for the forgotten man.*"

They begged him for his help: "*We pray to God that we will some day find a man in our government that will help us poor working people rid ourselves of these dictators and let us govern ourselves.*"

"*Myself and other oldtimers,*" wrote a crane operator, "*here and no doubt in other areas who did the ground work and made their local something to be proud of, and not ashamed of like we are today, beg your help. We cannot do anything ourselves now with this setup.*"

Many offered to risk everything if need be to push his investigation through: *You are our last hope . . . I don't like to testify before your committee unless there is a dire necessity that I do so,*" explained a man who worked sheetmetal. A carpenter showed fight: "*The goons have got ninetenths of the Rank and File scared that's the reason they don't come to meetings afraid of the goons. I will face any of them for you Senator. I've lived 63 years now. How much more can I live?*

but for God's sake give these young men a chance to raise their families like I did."

They implored him to be diligent: *"Look into all unions, clean up the mess and make it so a man has a right to work and not have to bow down to them damn Hitlers."* They went down on their knees to him. *"Please in God's name for the sake of millions of Laboring working men who are Human Beings and deserve the same right to live and raise families as any union official"* . . .

"So Mr. Senator, this is my story," a motion picture machine operator summed up his career. *"After being a member for 27 years the union suspended me. All the money I put into the pension fund is lost. I said I wanted my pension. Instead I was thrown out of the union." "We have no protection from graft. We have no vote on who get to be officers. If we don't like one shop we can't quit and go to another. The union won't let us. An open shop would take care of some our difficulties,"* wrote a woman from a shirtwaist factory in the middlewest.

They tried to explain their predicament in the fewest possible words: *"A fellow comes along and pushes you in a machine. You are gone. You are coming to work alone walking on the sidewalk. Union workers in a car run over you and you're gone. 85 percent of those in unions want to get out and be free. You're an American and they know you dislike their tactics, they maneuver a layoff. A party over here a few months they can milk him. The American is squeezed out." "It's the labor racket,"* wrote an Ohio toolmaker. *"We ordinary rank and file have little or nothing to say about administration or our officers, there is no such thing as democracy even attempted, and the general idea is just keep your mouth shut and go along if you want to keep out of trouble,"* wrote an operating engineer. *"If this union corruption continues it will spread like a cancer and eventually with the use of rigged elections it can jeopardize our free and democratic system of government,"* prophesied a retired railroad worker.

They asked sharp questions: *"Did you ever go hungry, Mr. Senator, on account of the wrath of the labor leaders?" "Why doesn't the recent civil rights legislation do something to protect the voting and civil rights and liberties of union members and all other citizens, Negro and White, comprising 98 percent of the population, against racketeers representing 2 percent?"* asked a brakeman. *"Isn't it enough that we have to*

pay federal taxes, state taxes, county taxes, school taxes, water
bills? Why do we have to pay the crooks $60 a year?" asked a
telegraph operator.

Anonymously yours many of them signed. *"If this letter gets*
into the wrong hands I shall be finished and also my wife and
family." "I am signing my name. I will be very thankful,
Senator, if you will withhold my name as if they will find out
they will send gangsters after me and as I am 67 years old I
am in no condition to put up any fight against them, therefore
I should not stand any chance at all." "Just to be sure I stay
alive a little longer you will have to forgive me for not signing
my name to this letter. However this omission should help to
point up the rotten conditions existing here, because I know
that I would be placing my job and my future in extreme
jeopardy if my identity were known to the union officials."
"I'm sorry I cannot sign my name as it may mean my life or
my livelihood."

The senators on the Select Committee had heard
enough. For two years they had listened to the voices of un-
fortunates chained to the circles of the industrial hell, seen
the insolence of the goons, heard the snickering of Labor lawyers urging their clients to take the Fifth, listened to the selfrighteous tirades of idealist organizers

so convinced of the probity of their own intentions they
never could believe in the probity of people who had other
ideas.

"You officers take the position that you own the union and
can run it and do whatever you please with it," Senator
McClellan lashed out at one of them.

The senators had heard enough. Not even the most
varnished politician can escape an occasional twinge of the
public good. The Senators were aging men. Feelings deep
down had been outraged, prejudices (obsolete you'll say)
absorbed in rural churches, out of old school readers, from
backward old stickinthemud country lawyers familiar with
Blackstone and Coke:

that man, rich or poor, you and me and every other man,
however roughly fashioned out of old Adam's clay—

has God's image in him,

and the right

to stand up by himself against bullying institutions;

to choose how he'll work for his living;

to choose, so long as he doesn't overjostle his neighbor, whatever opportunities offer to push his way in the world;

that he has the right to help set the rules and pick the men who handle public affairs:

selfgovernment. Freedom. The same passions that drove the institutionbuilders to victory entered long ago into the makeup of the word American.

The senior senator from Arkansas was not much given to oratory, but somehow he transmitted his sense of outrage to enough members of Congress.

so that, in spite of the shoving and hauling of pressure groups and lobbies

and the dire fulminations of laborleaders threatening defeat at the polls,

—the letterwriters had thought of that: "*Pay no attention to the cry that your committee is out to break up unions. The rank and file know better.*" "*Don't let the leaders fool you that you will lose the labor vote—we don't vote the way they would like to have us.*"

certain legislation was passed,

but its enforcement

remained in the hands of officeholders and aspirants to high office whose ears were perpetually cocked towards the lobbyists,

and who never heard

the testimony,

nor read the letters

that outraged the senior senator from Arkansas.

Blackie Bowman Speaking
(Scene: a bed in a Veterans' Hospital)

Don't tire yourself, the nurse keeps saying. She's going to take that pencil away. It's against the rules. You know me nurse. Everything I've done all my life has been against the rules. It's against the rules for me to be alive at all.

It won't be long now. I know what this nice white screen is for. I've seen it too often.

You are quite right I can't hold that pencil no more. Nobody can make out what I try to write, not even me. Just let me talk to you. You don't even have to listen. You just sit there. First I breathe then I talk a little. I'll bet I'm the gabbiest patient you ever had. Now I breathe. Here I go again.

You see it's summer and I'm just a little guy playing with my brothers and sisters out in the yard at our house in East Baltimore. There's that summer smell of trodden grass. Joe and Ed and Allie and Lou and I are playing Spanish War. Joe's the leader. We all have sticks for Moro krisses. We only let the girls play because without them there wouldn't be enough. There we go solemnly marching around the edge of the yard singing

> Damn damn damn the Filipinos,
> Pockmarked kakhiac ladrone
> Underneath the starry flag
> Civilize him with a krag
> And return us to our own beloved home.

Funny I can remember that when I can't remember the Pater Noster. You recite it for me nurse in a minute. Now I got to talk while I got the breath.

We kick our feet out in a special way because we've got an audience. Dad's grinning. "All right kids wipe them insur-rectos off the map."

Dad sits in his red suspenders drinking beer at the deal table under the kitchen stoop beside a fat whitehaired man with a pink face all crinkled like a toy balloon that's losing gas.

The fat man is our neighbor, Mr. Angelico. His face is all crinkled like he was going to cry. Mr. Angelico is a conductor on the B & O Railroad. "Don't sing that," says Mr. Angelico.

It's Mr. Angelico who leaves a newspaper around the house that Mother hurries into the kitchen stove like it smelled bad whenever she lays her hands on it. *Appeal to Reason*. It must be smut the way Mother handles it but it ain't like any smut I ever seen. Kids are funny. I've taken to snaking off copies of *The Appeal to Reason* whenever Mr. Angelico lays them down. I keep them in an old rubber boot in the closet of my room.

I don't remember a word I read in them, but it was reading that paper set the courses for my life, just like the skipper reads up in the pilot book to set the courses into a port. What was it? Pie in the sky? The Promised Land? Early Christians singing their Pater Noster down in the catacombs. Some deep unbreakable feeling that men are brothers and ought to help each other out instead of climbing to the top on each other's shoulders. I've tried to live that way nurse but I haven't done a very good job of it.

"Filipinos are people," says Mr. Angelico.

Dad's no Socialist but Dad sits up and listens to what Mr. Angelico has to say. Dad thinks the world of Mr. Angelico.

Dad had a real choke in his throat when he told us once how Mr. Angelico had climbed up on the platform at a railroad union meeting in Indianapolis and shaken the hand of Eugene V. Debs. We were sitting in the kitchen waiting for supper. "That limb of Satan," my mother muttered giving the pans on the stove an awful rattle. Made me think maybe he had cloven hoofs instead of hands. Kids are funny I tell you.

Well there we go all hot and sweaty marching around the edges of the yard stomping our feet in time to the song and singing "Damn, damn, damn the Filipinos." Mr. Angelico holds up a spread hand as if to flag a train. It isn't a cloven hoof, it is the large pink hand that shook the hand of Eugene V. Debs. "People are brothers," says Mr. Angelico. "Filipinos have mothers and fathers and brothers and sisters just like you kids."

"Even if they are black as the ace of spades?" roars Dad.

"That's no song for little children to be singing." The hand that shook the hand of Eugene V. Debs raises the frothy beermug to his lips. "Never forget," he spouts across the beer mug, "that the working people in the world are brothers."

The words send a cold scare through every vein like once after catechism class when I thought I'd committed the Sin Against the Holy Ghost.

Dad grumbles that it's a toast for a Socialist picnic. Dad and Mr. Angelico go on arguing each other's heads off over their beer. Talk talk talk. How ever can grown people think up so many things to talk so long about?

"Damn, damn, damn the Filipinos," Joe and Ed start bawling and marching again. I'm scared to sing on account of Mr. Angelico and scared not to sing for fear the others will call me a sissy. "Damn damn damn," the girls pipe up.

Mother pushes out through the screen door of the kitchen wringing a wet dishtowel in her hands. "I'll wash your mouths out with soap every one of you if you don't quit that."

"Grown men," Mother lashes out at Dad, "loafing over their beer and encouraging little children to curse and swear."

The screen door bangs behind her.

We sneak off into the alley to play San Juan Hill out of sight. And just to show how big I am I chase the girls off shrieking by yelling out all the dirty words I know at the top of my lungs. But that night lying with my eyes closed pretending to be asleep on my cot between Joe's and Ed's cots in the hot airless upstairs room we boys sleep in I'm stealing looks at my brothers kicking and tossing in their nightgowns because the night's so hot, wondering if they are really truly pockmarked Filipinos like Mr. Angelico said when he raised the hand that shook the hand of Eugene V. Debs.

Brotherhood of man. Me and my brothers fought like hell, but it was my religion just the same.

All men are brothers when they're asleep, ever thought of that nurse? Asleep or dead. I seen plenty dead men. They have a family resemblance.

You say not to talk about dying but why not talk about dying?

Dying don't embarrass me.

No don't bother to pick up that pencil. Why try to hold a pencil when I can't . . .

. . . or talk either now that it's so hard to breathe. . . .

Here I go again. Just breathing would be enough . . .

but I can't. . . .

3.
Systems of Enterprise

What man can contemplate the aardvark without astonishment?

Who, should he be happy enough to have the zoo attendant hand him the little creature, can feel in his hands the odd ambiguous body,
    between fur and feathers,
    of the duckbilled platypus
    without a catch of the breath and awful wonder (suppose you were me and I were you): what impulses,
    wakened by the intake of the soft fluvial eyes,
    trigger the cells of that small brain.

Or the spiny anteater?
    what dreams, when he curls in the dark of his box, luminesce inside the wedgeshaped skull? The variousness of life
    as if in whimsy
    constantly cracks the dogmatic mold
    which man the classifier laboriously constructs to ease the pain of sorting out diversities.

In man himself there are more variants
    than in the animal kingdom or the vegetable
    or the crystalline realm of minerals; sometimes, when man the classifier slackens under the endless drudgery of arguing away complexities; man, the curious viewer; the other man, the naïve,
    the astonished child
    looks at himself in a mirror or lets his fingers explore the dissymmetries of his uneven carcass or maybe, taking a peep through a fluoroscope,
    discovers enough aberrant factors to outdo the bestiaries from aardvark to zebra.

277

"Did you know,"
asked Dr. Roger J. Williams the biochemist from Texas,
of a tableful of punditry at a symposium at the Princeton Inn,
*"that the size of the human stomach has a sixfold
variation
or that the small intestines of men and women have measured out anywhere between eleven feet and twentyfive feet
nine?"*
Eleven different patterns have been plotted for the muscle
that controls the index finger. The blood's path through
vessels and arteries flows in courses as various
as the earth's great river systems. Cell chemistries and
the matching electrical impulses vary from individual to
individual. We none of us smell alike. (That's how the bloodhound earns his kennel ration; the bloodhound can tell.)
And when you try to chart the convolutions of the brain,
each one's a universe where the layered cells multiply a tril-
lion interactions into infinity.
"Can it be,"
Egghead enquires of Doubledome,
*"that variety instead of uniformity
is nature's law?"*

Documentary (17)

How about the label on your whiskey bottle? A telltale document if there ever was one.

PURE WHITE: PURE JET: PURE LUXURY

Hour by hour and minute by minute a clock is ticking out the economic future of America.

A COMPACT WITHOUT A COMPROMISE

chemically inert it does not rust, rot, corrode, deform or disintegrate . . . safely handles detergents, ground garbage, chemicals, acids, hot liquids, anything that normally empties into a sewer

HOW TO HEAR A FLOWER BLOOM

creates the smart exteriors . . . designed in crisp, clean, important-looking lines with exclusive concealed locks

STYLED FOR AN ERA JUST BEGINNING

"How will we use it?" scientists ask as they strive to meet the challenge of an unusual molecule with extraordinary properties.

EARNINGS TO DOUBLE THIS YEAR

one of these days you may shop by twoway TV . . . have an appliance that takes food from the freezer to the range, then cooks and serves it, all

electrically, and a scrubber that cleans the kitchen
floor automatically and then scurries back to its own
wall cupboard

NO OTHER LEADING LOWPRICED CAR CODDLES YOU WITH FULL COIL SPRINGS ON ALL FOUR WHEELS

Paper Does So Much for People

RR

In the eighteen nineties there flourished in Canadian,
a tank town in the Texas Panhandle, a family of Youngs.

They were stockmen and business men. The grandfather
came over from Scotland. The father founded the first bank
in Canadian. The Youngs grew up with the country.

The third generation was represented by a small spunky
boy named Robert R. He was short. He had a thatch of
strawcolored hair and blue eyes in a face that peeled but
wouldn't tan, scorched red by the Panhandle sun. The kids
called him Punkinhead or sometimes Railroad for his initials.

RR was short and slim and shy with the grownups but he
generaled his gang of smalltown kids. Out of history it was
the pint-sized corporal, Bonaparte, who came to be his lifetime admiration. The bunch hunted rabbit and prairie chicken
and ran wild among the fallingdown shacks of an old shantytown across the Canadian River, abandoned when the work-
gangs pushed the tracks of the Chicago, Rock Island and
Pacific westward across the plains.

The place rejoiced in the name of Desperado City.

His mother, who had raised him on tales of the early
days on the range and raiding Mexicans, and the gallop of
Apache hoofs,
died when he was ten.

He took to writing verse, a habit he never could quite
shake off. He was sharp as a tack but wild. The local Baptist
Academy couldn't hold him. His father decided on military
school.

At Culver he headed his class in English and Math, but his behavior was marked down as "devilish." At the University of Virginia he showed enthusiasm mostly for liquor and poker and craps. Sophomore year he failed to turn up for the final exams.

Instead he ran off with a girl he met at a party and married her in Baltimore without benefit of parents. Her name was Anita. Her older sister, who taught at the Normal School in Amarillo, was soon to be known to the artgalleries of the nation

as Georgia O'Keefe, the painter of lilies and skulls and bleached barns

and of the skeletal New Mexico hills.

RR loved solitude too, he never lost his taste for wild country.

        At nineteen RR had his living to make and a wife to support. The war in Europe was on. Powderfactories were hiring all comers. It was dangerous work but well paid. He got a job with the Du Ponts at Carney's Point. When they discovered his knack for figures he was promoted from powdermonkey to the treasury department in Wilmington.

The year he came of age a daughter Eleanor, his only child, was born in a Wilmington bungalow.

When he got his hands on the small inheritance his mother left he threw up his job and moved to New York. There he lost five grand in a project to market dehydrated foods; the rest he put into Mexican oil stocks that went down the drain. The apprentice financier took his lesson. By 1921 he was broke; only one suit to his name, a wife and child to support. He went to work for the Allied Chemical Corporation.

The following year, John J. Raskob who had noticed the unassuming little punkinhead with the deadpan manner at the Du Pont offices in Wilmington offered him a job in the finance department of General Motors.

By the time RR was thirty his salary was thirtyfive thousand a year.

He made investments, speculated hard; the market was his hobby. He read everything he could find that bore on finance. He took nothing for granted. When in 1928 Raskob resigned as chairman of the Finance Committee of General Motors to

head up an investment house, he carried RR along with him
as his personal assistant.

The year was 1928: the New Era of margins and
mortgages. Stocks soared into the blue blue sky. The bulls
ruled The Street. A man who whispered a bearish word risked
lynching. Confidence was the shibboleth.

To suggest that what went up came down was, to say the
least, unAmerican. There was a blowup in the Raskob office.
RR broke with his boss on his bearish views and set up as
investment counselor on his own.

"Sell," he told his clients in the summer of 1929, "sell while
you can."

All that fall he played the short interest. Out of the avalanche of falling prices that swept the New Era into perdi-
tion he made his first important money. With his partner
Frank Kolbe he became the scavenger of ruined corporations.
"Sharpshooter," sneered the old Wall Street hands.

In 1932 he bought a seat on the Stock Exchange at a record
bargain price.

Railroad had been his nickname as a boy. RR began to take
an interest in railroad stocks.

Among the more spectacular casualties of the Great
Depression was the farflung complex of holding companies
and dummy directorates through which the Van Sweringen
brothers had managed to hold in their hands,
    over seven railroads,
        twentythree thousand miles of track,
            marshaling yards, steamboat companies
                officebuildings,
                    docks
                        and warehouses, real estate developments
and coalmines, an armored car service, a department store,
a dairy farm,
    and a number of peach orchards. The capstone of this
disparate structure was a holding company, a paper edifice
most ingeniously contrived out of assorted debentures, which
was principally in hock, for seven or so millions of dollars, to
a Morgan bank.

The Morgan partners had lost pride in their creature: (the
very name "holding company" was in rare disrepute. Frank-

lin Roosevelt was excoriating the moneychangers from his
fireside mike in the White House; Burton K. Wheeler roasted
railroad financiers over a slow fire every afternoon in the
Senate Office Building for the edification of the press. Bankers
—if you called a man a banker you were supposed to say it
with a smile—were nervous as witches).

"Any man who buys into Alleghany," a Morgan partner was
heard to declare, "ought to have his head examined."

RR bought Alleghany whenever he could, at anything under ten dollars a share.

The Morgan partners never wanted to hear that
name again. They placed their foreclosed shares of Alleghany
in the hands of a discreet auctioneer on lower Broadway,
where,

amid choice lots of superannuated office furnishings, discarded law libraries, obsolete oil paintings, dusty busts and
front hall bronzes

. . . going, going . . .

bang goes the hammer

. . . sold to an elderly gentleman named Ball from the Middle West who had gotten much too rich manufacturing mason
jars (the demand for mason jars had been terrific during the
prohibition years. From what else would a man drink corn
liquor?)

Mr. Ball rushed in where bankers feared to tread and
draped Alleghany in the new plush of something he called the
Midamerica Corporation which he placed tenderly for management in the hands of the last Van Sweringen.

RR who had been enthusiastically accumulating
shares in Alleghany for some General Motors executives who
were his clients, and on his own behalf besides, watched
spiderlike from the corner of his web. Not to show his face
he asked his partner to keep an eye on the auction. When
the last Van Sweringen died a few months later leaving the
railroad empire even more inextricably hobbled with receiver-
ships and foreclosing obligations than it had been before,
RR was ready. Mr. Ball wanted out

but the General Motors magnates who were to put up the
money felt a chill in their shoes. They had sent their lawyer
to inquire of Senator Wheeler what his attitude would be

towards their reorganizing Alleghany. The senator answered
that he was ready to broil and publicly barbecue any automobile man who messed in railroad finance.

"Buy it yourself if you think it's so hot," his General Motors customers told RR.

He did.

With the help of a sleeping partner, the heir to a Five and
Ten fortune who wanted to play some part in the world, and
laid out three million on the barrelhead;

with two hundred and fortyfive thousand, two hundred and
ninetyfive dollars of his own cold cash,

and a hazardous note in the hands of the same Mr. Ball,

RR took charge,

forced his election as chairman of the board,

and sat looking out over the drizzly lake from amid the
splendors of the office at the top of the skyscraper railroad
station the Van Sweringens had built in Cleveland to command their empire from;

a solitary, Napoleonhearted, introspective, pintsized man
with graying hair,

scheming to consolidate his gains.

        "Shoestring finance," sneered the old Wall Street
hands. "Who is this young upstart?" the Morgan partners
asked each other. Tom Lamont invited him to lunch. RR
had the gall to refuse. It would be politically embarrassing, he
explained, to be seen at lunch with a banker.

Instead he invited the press up to his Park Avenue apartment, poured the reporters cocktails and announced that he
favored open competitive bidding in railroad finance. He introduced his partner, Mr. Allan Kirby, tall, bashful and bald.
"We are obligated to no one. We are completely independent." Allan Kirby nodded and smiled.

It was a five years battle: Alleghany was full of mantraps
and springes, a skeleton in every closet, files stuffed with past
due obligations; the Morgans had retained a subtle stranglehold through a trusteeship of the Chesapeake and Ohio Railroad by the Guaranty Trust. The railroads ran; some were
well managed and made money, but the sick corporations
drained off the health of the well.

        Burton K. Wheeler called RR to Washington and was

amazed to find him as voluble a reformer as the Senator himself. RR talked public service and the interest of the small investor, but he had to steer a careful course between the devil of the congressional investigation and the deep blue sea of the Morgan banks. He talked reform to the senator but in the end he had to go hat in hand to the Morgans: "I humbled myself for the good of the cause."

The stockmarket break in the fall of '37 almost wrecked his plans. His health collapsed. He fell into a depression and retired to his bed in Palm Beach to think and write verses.

When he came back into the fray it was as the palladin of the small investor. A great reader of Dumas he liked to think of himself as the subtle swordsman d'Artagnan. He dragged railroad finance out of the bankers' inner offices into the arena of public discussion. He circularized the stockholders and solicited proxies. He tormented the bankers with lawsuits, obtained an injunction against the Guaranty Trust. When Mr. Ball, the mason jar manufacturer, tried to foreclose on his note, RR took him to court and charged him with violating the Securities Exchange Act. Mr. Ball settled.

RR wrote his own advertising copy. He pleaded the cause of honest management, streamlining, modernization, service. He appealed to the potential passenger.

"A hog can cross the country without changing trains but you can't."

He formed the Federation for Railroad Progress, inaugurated the auto-ferry system, showed motion pictures in renovated coaches, introduced credit arrangements. Patiently he was putting together the broken pieces of the Van Sweringen system.

When he finally took his seat as Chairman of the Board of the C & O his hair had turned completely white but he was accepted as the railroads' young Lochinvar. In Richmond management wined him and dined him. When he paid off the indebtedness of the Alleghany Corporation it was the Morgan banks that lent him the money. The occasion was celebrated by a banquet at the Union League Club.

In the forties war infused temporary prosperity into the senile structure of American railroading.

Robert R. Young had arrived. He owned The Towers at Palm Beach for winter; for a summer home bought a forty-

room misconception of the Tudor style that had been built
for a Drexel on the seacliffs at Newport. There he enshrined
his favorite masterpiece, a portrait by David of Napoleon. He
and his wife entertained ostentatiously: five hundred guests
for his daughter's comingout.

He was a solitary brooding man, stayed away from his
office, loved to walk alone with his dog along the clifftop
trails. His daughter married a naval officer, was divorced
the same year. At twenty-three she was killed in the crash of
a private plane.

The Youngs lived high. Dinners, luncheons, cocktail parties.
They played café society. The Duke and Duchess of Windsor
were their guests for a week.

RR was a Democrat, he made large contributions to the
party funds. The liberal financier, and literate: he explained
his plans for revitalizing the railroads in articles (which he
wrote himself) for the liberal magazines.

RR was no writer. He teemed with salty opinions, but he
lacked the gift of logical progression. As a poet he was
boyish:

> No dank churchyard for me.
> I would toss in the sparkling sea,
> Torn flesh to go still sweet
> Into gull dung and crab meat,
> Polished bones to pulse that night
> At the surf's edge in the starlight.

He failed in his dream of reorganizing the railroads.

        He died many times a millionaire. Money meant
power, but not power enough. He was a skillful financial
manipulator but not skillful enough
   to bring a successful reorganization of the railroads out
from under the dead weight of the bankers' interests and the
insurance companies' interests and the brotherhoods' interests
   and the seventy year old senile strangling hand of the
bureaucracy of the Interstate Commerce Commission.

Restrictions, procedures, prerogatives hampered his every
move. Although the two roads were logically complementary,
in order to take the chairmanship of the New York Central
he had to resign from the Chesapeake and Ohio. RR lost his
zest. In the apathetic fifties the railroads sank back into the

doldrums. Passengers took to airplanes and buses or to driving themselves. Trucks hauled the freight. Featherbedding, bureaucratic routine, overcapitalization, too many taxes, too much regulation from Washington. Decaying maintenance. Lack of initiative. Arteriosclerosis: the railroads were dying.

Towards the end of January, 1958, RR presided on a blue Monday over a meeting of the board of directors of the New York Central held at his stupidlooking palace at Palm Beach which had been built for Atwater Kent in the early bad taste of the first Florida boom. The report for the past year was dreary. The board voted to pass the dividend. RR himself had been suffering reverses in the stockmarket. He had been forced to sell big hunks of his darling Alleghany to raise cash. It was a bad week. All his life he had been subject to fits of depression.

Saturday morning his breakfast was served to him as usual at eight. Unobserved by the servants he carried a 10 gauge double-barreled shotgun into the billiard room, sat down in a chair and shot himself with both barrels through the head.

It was remarked on the Stock Exchange that it was most considerate of Mr. Young to wait till Saturday to shoot himself.

The suicide of the chairman of the board of the New York Central Railroad might well have precipitated a panic

if it had happened during office hours.

INVESTIGATOR'S NOTES VI

The place was to hell and gone out a long avenue encumbered with truck traffic. It was so dimly lit it looked at first as if there were nobody there. Behind the grimy store window marked H. J. Pfaff and Son in flaked gilt lettering that glittered in the glare off the street, a glow came from the back of an officelike room. The investigator knocked. After a while a stocky man unlocked the glass door from the inside. "Are you the feller who called up? Come in," he said.

His manner was dismally jocose. He led the way through another glass door back into a livingroom behind the office.

"Is it the woes of small business or the woes of the working man?" he asked with an elaborate wink. "Mine qualify either way."

Henry Pfaff settled his guest in one of a group of Morris chairs set in a half circle around a TV set, found him an ashtray, meanwhile chatting briskly about the weather and the baseball scores. Mrs. Pfaff a small shrill woman with apple cheeks interrupted to ask if they wanted icecream. "Me too Mom," intoned in a cracked foghorn voice a boy of about fifteen who was doing his homework half hidden by a screen at a table in the corner.

When Mrs. Pfaff brought Henry Pfaff his plate of icecream he spooned it rapidly into his mouth without looking at it and started to talk.

He started work as an apprentice plumber at about Jimmy's age. He flicked his thumb over his shoulder towards the boy in the back of the room. They wouldn't take him in the union. The Plumber's Union was mighty exclusive in those days. It didn't matter too much because he was working for his dad. Still he'd always been a union man and his dad before him so about ten years ago when Dad passed away and the children were little he'd managed to join up. He was already doing his own contracting. He paid his hundred and seventy-five dollar initiation fee and the twentyfive dollar building assessment and ten dollars a month dues.

The trouble was that in this city the union was all tied up with City Hall through the building inspector racket. Money poured in during the war when they charged fifty dollars for work permits and still the union was broke. Well once he'd joined he was interested in making it a crackerjack organization. He wasn't the only one who wanted to know where the money went. At one of the first meetings he ever attended he helped put through a vote for an audit by a CPA. It turned out that twenty thousand dollars had disappeared from the treasury. That wasn't big money in those days. "But hell"— Henry Pfaff flashed a stare and a wink at the investigator—"I don't know about you, but when I join an organization I want to know where my money goes."

He'd had nothing but harassment ever since he'd stood up and been counted. Out of eight hundred members only twelve had the nerve to vote for the resignation of the finance committee. The members of the finance committee were all plumbing inspectors, paid with the taxpayers' money. That was where City Hall came in. Five big contractors handled all the important plumbing work in the city and they played footsie with the politicians to keep outside plumbers out. The BA was in between. All he cared about was not doing a lick of work in his life and of course his little private take. He controlled the hiring of the union plumbers.

Once Henry Pfaff was in wrong with the BA he got all the drunks and loafers put on his jobs. Once he had a shopsteward to every five men. One of 'em was a truckdriver at that. The business of the shopsteward was to see that the men didn't work too fast. As soon as they saw a man doing honest work they'd pull him off the job. Pfaff had a big contract to do the plumbing for a new modern shopping center. They made his life a hell at that shopping center. There were endless delays in getting the work inspected. Then the inspector quibbled about every little thing.

As if Pfaff wasn't in bad enough anyway the architect had specified Kohler fixtures. He ran up against the boycott. The BA's son was a salesman for a local plumbing manufacturer. The union wanted him to buy his fixtures there. Maybe, said Pfaff, he'd been too stubborn. Somebody poured creosote over his fixtures as fast as his men unpacked them. They dumped cement in his bathtubs. When Mrs. Pfaff went to clean them they threatened her. The sabotage was so obvious Pfaff wanted to bring suit against the union. Would you believe it? He couldn't get a lawyer to take his case. Couldn't get a judgment, not in this county they all said. He tried to appeal to the state labor board but no way there for an individual to get a hearing against a union. He finished the job six months late. He lost thirty thousand dollars on that contract.

Sure he brought it before the executive board. They kept him waiting two hours. "Pfaff," they told him, "you're just trying to make trouble. You just go back and keep your nose clean."

Since then Henry Pfaff was reduced to little jobs he could handle with his boys or with one elderly man for a helper. His wife kept the books. Before he'd tried to tangle with that finance committee he employed fiftyfour men. A few arrogant men settling personal grudges had ruined him. Thank God his older boy had already graduated from architecture school. Now he was in debt and had spent all the money he had put away with a Savings and Loan concern to put Jimmy through college. Jimmy wanted to study medicine. What was he going to do about Jimmy?

Henry Pfaff shook his head. His red eyes looked as if he were about ready to cry. "Twelve out of eight hundred," he said as the investigator rose to his feet. "I don't know what's come over the people in this country. They just don't seem to care."

Prime Mover

Jasper Milliron sat staring at the combination electric clock and calendar in a brass frame made specially to fit on the back of his desk which the office force had presented to him the afternoon before. Snow on the roofs and streets below threw a reflection of blue twilight up through the broad windows to the ceiling over his head. The room was filling with dusk but still he had made no move to switch on the fluorescent lighting. He didn't need a light; he wasn't doing anything anyway. Staring at the clock, what a hell of a way to pass the afternoon.

The calendar read January 31, 1950: the clock read 4:29.

Though he had always considered himself one of the busiest of men at that moment Jasper Milliron had nothing to do. His desk was empty. There was nothing in the wire baskets for incoming and outgoing mail. Not a spot had appeared on the hennacolored blotter that came with the set. Nothing to look at but the initials JM entwined everywhere on the brasswork round the clock and the calendar and on the ornate brass corners of the blotter.

Thirty mortal years.

Blue twilight seeped in through the row of windows in front of him the way the bluing used to tinge the water in his mother's washtub. The memory startled him. What the devil made him think of his mother's washtub?

He couldn't have been more than fourteen, because he was fourteen when he left home. Like the glimpse of an old snapshot seen turning the pages of a family album there appeared in the corner of his mind the shadow of a young frecklefaced

Jasper standing in the warmth of the range in his mother's kitchen and watching the bluing slowly tinge the steamy water of the washtub. That was the Jasper before the hunting trip with Mr. Allardyce, before the summer in the East and the forestfires on the lake and Lulie Harrington and Georgie Warner, before the Marines and overseas and Château Thierry, a Jasper standing in his mother's kitchen in the middle of an unexplored world with Granite Peak just outside and the Big Horn Mountains in the distance and canyons and woodlands full of game, and plains and rivers and seas stretching out east and west and north and south in every direction without limit.

Thirty mortal years.

On a marble stand in the corner of the office stood a green globe speckled with red dots that marked the cities where they sold Abington Products. An eighteen inch globe. My God how small the world looked to him today.

Jasper sat up with a jerk when Miss Lockett switched on the light. "Colonel Milliron," she exclaimed, "what on earth are you doing sitting here in the dark?"

Jasper got guiltily out of his chair as if Miss Lockett had caught him doing something he shouldn't. "Just staring at the calendar," he croaked in a phlegmy voice.

"Isn't it beautiful!" chanted Miss Lockett clasping her hands.

"But you didn't need to stay so late." He tried to turn the tables on her. "On a Saturday afternoon."

"Didn't I? And all that correspondence to catch up. Office parties have to be paid for."

Jasper cleared the phlegm out of his throat. "I wish the boys held their liquor better."

"Colonel Milliron," she interrupted in the tone she saved for portentous events. "I have a message for you from Mr. Allardyce. Parker delivered it himself."

She laid it before him on the desk. "Jasper; waiting for you at home. ABA" was scrawled at random on a slip of brown paper.

Miss Lockett started to murmur that it broke her heart how the dear man had aged these last months.

"Miss Lockett, as soon as I've gone," Jasper said in a voice that brooked no further confidences, "please call Mrs. Milliron and tell her I'll be a little late."

Miss Lockett smote her forehead with the flat of her hand. "Of course. That dinner. I should have reminded you earlier."

"You go home young woman and get a nice rest over the weekend."

"You're the one that needs the rest Colonel Milliron." Miss Lockett always had to have the last word.

Driving his new Buick out onto the street from the parking garage in the basement, in spite of his heavy overcoat and the closed car and the heater he felt the sudden grip of the zero cold. It was bracing: it made him feel the warmth of the blood in his veins. A snowy Saturday evening. The night was crackling clear. The traffic was light on the fresh-swept downtown streets. Signs and streetlights sparkled like jewelry.

Out on the suburban avenues near the lake a little fresh snow crunched crisply under the tires. Jasper drove with a speck of extra caution between the high banks the snowplows had left. Turning the car off the lakeside drive to bring it to a halt under the arched carport of the Allardyce mansion he caught sight of muffled figures and fires and the fishermen's shelters out on the ice. Fishing through the ice with a stove in the hut and a bottle of bourbon, he said to himself: Gosh I like winter.

Parker must have been on the lookout because the front door was thrown open before Jasper reached it.

"Evening Parker, how's the boss?"

Parker furrowed his black brows under the gray fuzz that grew low on his forehead.

"Poorly, Colonel," he drawled. "I wisht I had him at Palm Beach. The missus has went weeks ago."

"How's your arthritis Parker?"

"Fierce, Colonel, fierce. Cold weather ain't helped. You'll find the boss sittin' in the conservatory under the night-bloomin' cereus . . . what's left of him after that last pneumonia."

Jasper strode through high dim rooms stacked with French gilt furniture and painted cabinets and marble mantels. Mirrors in intricate gold frames reflected chandeliers muffled in gauze. The house smelt of moth crystals.

As he went he kept seeing himself in the mirrors, from one angle then from another. He was no longer the broadshouldered young ranchhand or the lightfooted field officer he still pictured in his mind's eye. Jasper had become a heavy redfaced trudging man. Thank God he'd kept his paunch down. The closecropped hair on his bullet head, almost as close and crinkly as Parker's, still had a reddish tinge among the gray.

What could the Allardyces possibly do with so many rooms? He threaded his way through the walnutpaneled diningroom gloomily ranked with highbacked Spanish chairs. Next was the library with its tiers of books bound in calf and morocco. Already he could see Mr. Allardyce's lean white head tilted into the pillows of a wicker reclining chair beneath an explosion of tropical foliage.

Jasper stood at attention beside the reclining chair, and gave a snappy salute. "What is it boss?"

He grinned. It was an old joke between them but not quite a joke. Jasper hardly remembered his father; ever since he'd been that fourteenyearold dreaming over the bluing in his mother's washtub Mr. Allardyce had been to Jasper something between a father and a CO. Mr. Allardyce had an iron hand he had to admit. Right now Jasper felt that same eagerness to prove himself he'd felt on those early hunting trips back on the range. He could see by his face now that Mr. Allardyce was planning to give him a rough time.

"Jap I don't see why you couldn't have gotten here a little earlier," the old man started in a low peevish whine without looking up. "You know I have to have my supper at six." It was a habit of Mr. Allardyce's to begin with the complaints. "Nobody thinks of consulting my convenience any more. . . . The madam has gone off to Florida and left me alone in this . . . this mausoleum. . . . It's largely on your account I've held on. They forced my retirement but I won my last fight."

"Atlanta?" Jasper shouted in case Mr. Allardyce didn't have his hearing aid turned on.

"All sewed up. Vice-president in charge of the Southeastern Division," Mr. Allardyce shouted back as if it were Jasper who was deaf. "Announcement on Monday." He sat bolt upright and started to wriggle out from under the blanket. "Help me with this damn thing, Jap."

It caught at Jasper's heart to see how frail and shrunken the old man was. He seemed half transparent like the feebly moving larva of some insect.

"No need to tell you I'm grateful sir," he shouted.

"I didn't do it for you. I did it for the company."

Mr. Allardyce sat up coughing on the edge of the reclining chair. When he got his breath again a certain tenderness crept into his voice. "Don't you ever go and let yourself get old, Jap, it don't pay. . . . How are the girls?"

"Fine," said Jasper. With the years so much common ground had developed between them. Jasper had no father: Mr. Allardyce had no son. They had each produced two daughters of whom they were inordinately fond. Mr. Allardyce had one advantage, Jasper was thinking: five grandchildren.

"Well Jap," the old man's inflection was taunting again, "I presume this anniversary has given rise to reflections . . . or maybe you didn't notice it."

"They've been rubbing it in all week. The thirty year club." It was Jasper's turn to air his grouch. "Thirty wasted years, I was thinking driving out. Those guys fishing on the lake made me think of all the things I'd missed all my life."

Talking with Mr. Allardyce, Jasper tended to think out loud. Half the time the old man didn't hear. This time he heard every word.

"Maybe you're right, Jap"—one of the pleasures of Mr. Allardyce's company was his way of suddenly getting interested in a fresh train of thought—"maybe you could have led a happy life just hunting and fishing and grazing cattle. I know I couldn't. . . . But look what we've built up out of the old Abington Milling Company. Sometimes I wish Dad had lived to see it. He used to think I'd grow up a waster. Well you've done your part Jap. It was more like forty years ago that I had my first hunch about you. Remember that night we baited the bears with the old dead mule back of the Bar T Ranch and they were too slick for us? You weren't dry behind the ears and I picked you for a comer. That was before the war and you getting yourself a commission and getting educated."

"A gentleman by act of Congress," snorted Jasper. "To tell the truth I wanted to make good because of a particular girl I wanted to marry. Then she married somebody else."

Mr. Allardyce laughed a rusty laugh. There was a blue flash in his bleary old eyes.

"But Jap you made an excellent marriage."

"That don't mean that I didn't want something different."

Jasper couldn't tell whether Mr. Allardyce heard him or not. He was off on another tangent. "My purpose in holding on as chairman of the board . . ." Mr. Allardyce began. His voice trailed off. The library clock was striking six. He rose quaking to his feet. Jasper held out his hand to help him but he pushed it away. "Walk me to the dining room."

Parker in a white jacket was fussing over a place set for one at the end of the carved walnut table.

As he let himself drop into the highbacked armchair Mr. Allardyce started complaining again: "No wonder I'm just a bag of bones. Damn doctors won't let me eat anything." He glared bitterly down into the plate of clear soup Parker was ladling out of a silver tureen. "Parker why haven't you brought the Colonel a drink of bourbon? What's the matter? Have you drunk it all up you old devil?"

"No sah, no sah," said Parker grinning and bobbing his gray head. "The boss knows, Colonel, I ain't tetched a drop in forty years," Parker chattered as he collected a decanter and a glass and a pitcher of icewater from the sideboard.

"Take an extra splash for me Jap. God knows I'd like a drink." Mr. Allardyce grimaced over a spoonful of soup as if it were medicine and went on in his old firm sensible voice. "It was to settle your proposition, Jap, that I held on as chairman of the board. For the last five years I've been the fifth wheel to the coach. You know that. They won't listen to my hunches any more, that bunch of stuckup stuffedshirt bastards!" The old man spat out the words. Then he poked Jasper in the ribs with a trembling hand. "I've always played my hunches eh? They've gone big, haven't they? You know that Jap. Remember that time you called me up from Detroit about that trainload of beetpulp? Buy it, I said. What the devil was a flourmill to do with a trainload of beetpulp?" His laugh ended in a wheezy cough.

Jasper laughed too. "You sure wanted to wring my neck Mr. Allardyce."

"That beetpulp was the foundation of our animal feeds business. . . . Remember when people were always bringing suit against us for dumping our offal in the Mississippi River?"

Jasper nodded happily.

"Now our offal is one of our most profitable items."

Jasper noticed that Parker was listening with a happy grin on his face. Parker had heard it all before. It was a recitation that always left the boss feeling more cheerful.

"And wheat germ, Jap. Remember how you dredged up some damn little veterinary who said wheat germ overcame sterility in minks? That got us into vitamins." Mr. Allardyce fell into another fit of coughing. "Jasper," he added in a weak wheezy voice when he could speak again, "This was my last fight."

Jasper and Parker started to mumble something in unison about how Mr. Allardyce had many happy years ahead of him.

"Shut up Jap," the old man snarled. "I know when I'm a goner. . . . High time I got you out of the St. Paul office before you get to be a mushmouth like the rest of the palace guard. . . . Bloomer, Parkinson, Griswold; we've got some good men, but they go by the book."

"Do I really have the seven state area?"

"Vice-president in charge of the Southeastern Division, that's how it reads." Mr. Allardyce was himself again. His voice was firm and amused. "Griswold's damn glad to get you out of town. He's giving you enough rope to hang yourself."

"We'll see who hangs himself."

"Not me . . . I won't see it. I don't care too much, Jap. I've outstayed my welcome already. They have put me out to grass. How old are you, Jap?"

"The same age as the century, plus two."

"A mere boy. You've got another thirteen years of active life."

Mr. Allardyce was sourly inspecting a lamb chop with a paper frill on the bone which Parker had uncovered in front of him.

"Will they let me pick my own personnel?" Jasper shouted.

"That's up to you, Jap. I won't be there to fight for you." Mr. Allardyce seemed completely absorbed in trimming every speck of fat off his lamp chop. "That's all I had to say."

Jasper swallowed the last of his bourbon and rose to his feet.

Mr. Allardyce looked up at him with a scrap of lamb poised on his fork. "I wish we were out in Montana again and you smelling the elk on the breeze and asking about the great world," he mumbled as he chewed. "I used to love to instruct the young."

"Good night, sir."

"Good night, Jap." The old man's voice rose: "Show fight, God damn you."

Back in the car Jasper admitted to himself he felt shaken. "Old age," he was muttering. "I don't know if I want to face it."

Just as he feared his wife's guests were already arriving as he came in the door. Dave Griswold was pulling off his overshoes in the front hall. Dave lifted his moonface and gave Jasper an expressionless gray stare. "Congratulations, old man," he said puffing from the effort of bending over, "but I can't see why you wanted Atlanta when you could have had New York or Chicago."

"Independence, Dave. Opportunity. Did you ever hear those old copybook maxims?"

"Well don't come running to me if it don't turn out what you hoped. You could have played it safe."

The doorbell rang. More guests. Dave closed his upper lip down tight across his yellow teeth. Jasper could feel the inquisitive gray eyes following him up the stairs.

Two tours of duty in the Marines had taught him to be a quick dresser. Harriet had his clothes laid out on a chair. Tails for God's sake. What a goddam bore. In seven minutes flat he was down in the livingroom again. Harriet looked imposing, almost threatening, in a pink dress with sequins. "Why did it have to be Atlanta?" she hissed in his ear as he gave her a glancing kiss on the cheek. "What do you expect me to find to do in Atlanta?"

"The seven state area . . . our great coming market," he whispered. "Have a heart, Harriet."

She masked that savage henpecking look with her prettiest hostess smile. Right away they were a team attending to their guests: the hospitable Millirons. Jasper knew it was an act and he knew Harriet knew it was an act, but while it was going on it made them feel less estranged.

It seemed to Jasper that Harriet had collected everybody he most disliked in St. Paul that night. Of course they had to have the Griswolds and the Parkinsons and the Boomers, but why Courtney Cooper from the Red River Savings Bank?

By the time the last of them had gone he was worn out acting the good old grizzly from Granite Peak, a rough diamond in a white tie, what shit.

He kept away from Harriet for fear of a run-in, but now and then he got a glimpse of her across the room. All keyed up: she'd taken to drinking too much at these parties. Maybe they could get together a little when the folks had gone. In the old days helping Harriet pick up after a party was the pleasantest time. He used to look forward to the two of them sitting down to have a quiet nightcap together and taking a last look at the girls so sweetly asleep in their little white cots before they went off to bed themselves. Tonight he did his best to get a smile out of her but all he got for his pains was Harriet sticking her face into his with a breath full of martinis and spitting out: "Why do you have to be such a stinker, Jap?"

Red in the face Jasper strode off into the pantry and poured himself half a glass of bourbon whiskey. He could get as drunk as the next man. Then he picked up a tray and started circling around the rooms collecting empty glasses and ashtrays full of cigarette butts. About half of the butts were cork tips with lipstick on them. He almost bumped into Harriet coming into the livingroom with a full tray from the library. He meant to say something disarming but what he said was "You women smoke too much."

Harriet put her tray down on the kitchen table with a bang and walked straight upstairs without looking at him. He heard her bedroom door slam. "Oh hell I oughtn't to have said that."

He was just starting to follow her upstairs to say something nice and apologize when the phone rang. It was a collect call. Evie was saying "Congratulations." He heard Harriet's voice droning "Good night darling" from the upstairs extension. Jasper held the receiver without listening to what she was saying. "Dad," Evie asked when Harriet had hung up, "what's the matter with Mom?"

Jasper tried to seem unconcerned. "She's just tired, Evie. We're both tired. Imagine a dogfood salesman in tails. This highlife wears me down."

"But Dad, you're not just a dogfood salesman."

"We do market a few other items," he said laughing, "but Evie where are you calling from?"

"It's a New York night club. I'm spending the weekend with Mrs. Vansant. All very antiseptic. You know Vassar. Then Fred suddenly plays the big bad wolf and takes me to El Morocco."

"Don't sound like Fred. Maybe a rich uncle died. Give him my best. He's a nice quiet sensible boy."

Evie giggled. "Daddy he's not as bad as that. Daddy, I'm just crazy about going to Atlanta. I've been rereading *Gone with the Wind.*"

"Miss Lockett has too. I wish you could talk your mother into a better frame of mind about it."

"Wait till Christmas vacation, Dad, Maddie and I will converge on her. Well good night Dad. Fred'll be wondering whatever became of me."

"Good night dear."

Jasper hung up reluctantly. It was having Eve and Madeleine both gone to college that made the house seem so horribly large and lonesome and bare. Before it had been so full of beaux and girlfriends and youthful shrieks and giggles that he and Harriet hardly had time to get on each other's nerves. He turned off the lights and leaving half the downstairs rooms still not picked up walked upstairs. What a blessing those girls were. He was all in a glow. Maybe talking about the girls a little would put Harriet in a good mood. They could go happily to sleep, after talking about what sweet daughters they had, in each other's arms maybe. He'd fought separate beds. Separate rooms were a curse. Smiling in anticipation he put his hand on Harriet's doorknob and tapped gently with his fingers.

No answer. The door was locked.

"Harriet," he called.

No answer.

He felt a rush of angry blood to the head. "God damn it to hell," he roared and went stamping off to his own room.

Thank God he was dead tired. He was drunker than he had intended to be. He tore off his clothes, tumbled into bed and switched off the light.

It seemed as if his head had hardly hit the pillow before he was asleep and dreaming.

He was out in a little hut on a lake in winter fishing through a hole in the ice. His levis were too tight. Somehow he'd

gotten into a pair of levis he must have had as a boy. He had
that small boy playing hooky from school feeling, scared he'd
be caught but excited. The fish were biting but they were all
catfish. How come there were so many catfish in this lake? The
fish piled up in the bucket wriggling, squirming, swimming
around with little wiggling motions like the girls when they
first learned to swim in the pool. But the catfish didn't have
any water to swim in. There was something horrible about the
whiskery squirming catfish swimming in no water. They had
little faces like the people at Harriet's dinner. There was a
Dave Griswold fish and an Ed Boomer fish and Mr. and Mrs.
Courtney Cooper fishes, little faces, little faces he knew but
couldn't remember the names of. He was getting scareder by
the minute. It was absolutely horrible. He had to throw them
away. When he lifted the bucket the bottom dropped out.
Up to his waist in squirming swimming catfish with horrid
human faces he let out a strangled scream.

It was six o'clock sharp when he woke up. He had a real
headache. All that wine and brandy with whiskey before and
after you damn fool. It was Sunday morning and he had a
hangover and Harriet was mad at him and what the hell was
he going to do with himself all day?

Just his luck to have it Sunday, he told himself while he
shaved. He had plenty hangover but he knew exactly how he
wanted to go about setting up a central sales office for the
seven state area. Right away he had to check with the files.
There were faces he knew but couldn't put names to like the
horrible catfish he'd been catching in his dream. Some kind of
frustration had turned something that ought to have seemed
funny into a nightmare. Freud. The old wolf sex rising up to
snap at his heels. He had to get to work fast. Forget everything
in work. When he walked downstairs all showered and shaved
and dressed it was still only six thirtyfive by the kitchen clock.

To pass the time he squeezed himself orange juice and
cooked himself a breakfast of bacon and eggs and coffee and
toast. When he went out on the front stoop to fetch the Sunday
paper he stood there in his shirtsleeves eagerly breathing in
the dry cold. Better than bromoseltzer for what ails you, he
told himself. Coming back through the pantry with his skin
tingling from the cold he caught himself with his hand on the
phone. Five minutes of seven. "Christ you can't wake a guy
up that early Sunday morning," he said aloud. "Not even to

give him good news." He killed another hour eating his breakfast without tasting it and reading through the newspaper
without retaining a word he read.

Five minutes to eight. He couldn't wait another minute. He
dialed the number.

A sleepy Mrs. Dale answered; then Larry. The phone must
be beside their bed. "Larry old man . . . I wouldn't wake you
if it weren't good news"—Jasper marveled at the amount of
molasses he heard in his own voice—"The Atlanta proposition
has gone through. . . . We're putting the show on the road. I'm
taking you down to set up personnel . . . of course it will mean
a raise. But we've got to work fast . . . before . . . oh before
you know what. It'll mean skipping church just once but the
missus will forgive you when she knows what's cooking. You
meet me down in the parking garage at eight thirty?"

"OK Jap," said Larry.

When Jasper turned his car off the cold crackling street to
dive down the ramp under the bluegrass tiers of the Abington
Building into the parking garage below, he found Larry Dale's
Pontiac there ahead of him. Six feet four, Larry was cautiously
jackknifing his great length out of the car. He looked down
into Jasper's face with a suspicious bucktoothed grin.

"Jap," he drawled, "if this is one of your practical jokes, I
swear . . ."

"No. Honestly, Larry. Mr. Allardyce told me last night.
Then I found everybody knew about it but me. . . . What do
you bet we do a million dollar business the first year?"

"Betcher a dollar we don't." The small selfservice elevator
was taking them up to the personnel department. "But no
kidding Jap, this is the greatest thing that ever happened to
Larry Dale. . . . What do you want to know?" He led the
way through white silent corridors with his long stride.

"I just want the ten best salesmen," Jasper was saying. "I
can develop the rest from what I find down there. My those
boys'll be surprised when I walk in on them. They've been
Saturday's child long enough. Here's the fastest growing consumer demand in the country and we've been letting Pillsbury
and General Mills walk away from us. . . . Now by God we'll
give them a run for their money."

Larry was stooping over his file and picking out cards and
setting them in a pile on his desk.

"There'll be some screaming in the front office, I suppose you know that, Jap."

"That's why we better move fast before they get the lead out of their tails."

"I wish I could see Dave Griswold's face."

"I've seen it," said Jasper fixing his own face in a mulish stare.

"It will mean dislocations." . . . Larry let his long jaw drop. "Kids changing school, jollying the missus."

"You just explain to Alice how much more fifteen thousand is than ten."

"When do we make the move?"

"Jan. 1. I'm taking the Chicago train at 12:45. That'll give me a chance to talk to Jim Swazey tonight."

"The heir apparent."

"I dunno, now that Mr. Allardyce has resigned as chairman of the board . . . But Jim's all right and Sylvia, Sylvia's a peach. Sylvia is all Allardyce."

Jasper sat smoking his pipe and furrowing his brow over the cards . . . The names brought up faces, voices, attitudes. His mind was full of nudging wriggling faces. "I got to talk to each one of these guys slowly and carefully . . . You know the South ain't the Middle West. I'm picking the Southern background every time."

"Where did you find out so much about the South Jap?"

"Ever heard of the United States Marines?" Jasper glanced down at his wrist watch: already eleven o'clock. "By the way Larry would you mind calling Harriet? She's so mad at me I don't dare to. Ask her to pack me a bag for four or five days and bring it down to the Chicago and Northwestern. She'll do it if she knows it's in line of duty."

"General Tazewell's daughter."

Jasper nodded with pursed lips.

At twelve fortyfive, all reservations made, telegrams sent, long distance calls completed, Jasper Milliron sat eating his lunch in the diner of the Chicago train. The sharp pain he'd felt from the sight of Harriet's closed face turning bitterly away in the gray of the trainshed was beginning to fade. He sat looking out at warehouses, freightyards, snowshrouded grain elevators sliding into a gray horizon and vast acreages of snowcovered stubble and frozen lakes fringed with birch and fir. The cornbeef hash tasted delicious. He was ferociously happy.

Next morning he climbed out of the plane into the misty-mild autumnal sunshine of the Atlanta airport.

While Jasper was waiting for his suitcase a sallow short waddling man wrung his hand.

"Abe Merman, Mr. Milliron," the man said in a selfdeprecating tone. "We met at a sales department meeting in New York in 1946. I wouldn't expect you to remember." The man spoke with just a trace of a foreign accent. He looked up in Jasper's face out of uneasy little blackbutton eyes bedded in gray sacks.

He didn't sleep a wink last night, was Jasper's first thought.

"A pleasure, an unexpected pleasure." The man was rubbing pudgy hands together. "I was telling Mrs. Merman not two days ago: the man we need to head up the seven state area is Jap Milliron." He smiled hard up into Jasper's face. There was an abject surrender about that smile, like a beaten dog rolling bellyup, that made Jasper want to kick him.

Abe Merman would carry Jasper's suitcase. Puffing and wheezing he bowed him into the wellkept old Cadillac sedan. Jasper sat with his knees tight together, sweating under the heavy overcoat. As he drove Abe Merman was whispering that he would be glad to put Mr. Milliron up, but he thought it would be more practical for him at the hotel. Mrs. Merman, however, she just insisted on giving Mr. Milliron his breakfast.

Jasper growled that time was short, he wanted to take in Memphis and Chattanooga on this same trip.

"Of course, of course," murmured Abe Merman.

It was a modern brick apartment house. The Mermans' apartment was handsome but cluttered. Everything you sat on was plush. The air smelt of food and houseplants and shaving lotion as if the windows had never been opened. Mrs. Merman looked just like Abe, the same waddle, the same sallow skin, the same frightened groundhog glance out of blackbutton eyes. They might have been brother and sister. It was evident that the couple had no children.

The breakfast was wonderful: Persian melon and scrambled eggs and Danish pastry and Vienna coffee with whipped cream. Mrs. Merman really had put herself out. They both waited on him with breathless attention. They couldn't have been kinder. It made Jasper feel like a damn sadist to keep

them on tenterhooks. He enjoyed it. How could he tell at this
stage of the game whether he could use the guy or not? All
he'd say was he was taking a Cook's tour.

Right after breakfast Jasper started his tour by making a
round of the customers with a salesman who said he had
worked eighteen years for Abington. This was a darkhaired
fellow with closecropped hair who certainly looked younger
than he was. He was youngtalking too. As he drove him
through treeshaded residential streets he talked to Jasper
just like he would to anybody.

Atlanta was his hometown but he was only now beginning
to appreciate it, he drawled. His name was Rollins, Ed Rollins.
Folks were real Georgia crackers, he guessed you might even
call them poa' white. He'd grown up in the back lots, wanted
to be a ballplayer, but he'd had to leave school and go to
work. Old people to take care of. He pointed to the green
lawns, the magnolias, the whitecolumned houses. When he
was a kid a street like this would have scared the daylights out
of him. But working for Abington was like a college education,
now he could look anybody in the eye.

Jasper didn't say anything but he sure warmed to Ed
Rollins. That was the kind of guy he needed. Going the
rounds with him brought back his own early days.

Ed brought his car to a stop in front of a corner grocery
store. "Residential," he said. "Charge accounts. Place ain't too
good. No inventory . . . Still he keeps his winder clean."

Jasper helped Ed fish an armful of posters out of the boot
of the car.

"Hello Jimmy boy," Ed hailed a stubby clerk in a smeary
apron, "where's the boss?"

"Out." The clerk made the shape of the word with his
mouth. There was a trace of malice in his eye.

"Gone for the day is he? Well Ah can't hardly blame him,
a perty fall day like this," drawled Ed Rollins. "Ah wouldn't
mind goin' fishin' maself."

"Have a heart," said the clerk when he saw the posters. "If
we put up a sign for everybody had a contest we'd have a
window like a billboard."

"This is a special contest, Jimmy boy," said Ed as he arranged his posters, "and Abington Mills ain't everybody."

Already Jasper was entering the name Ed Rollins in his
little notebook.

The next place was in a shabbier neighborhood. A hound dog dozed on the dusty pavement outside. The window was scrawled over with priced items in white chalk. Selfservice. Inside the swinging doors a housewife with a head full of bobbypins was pushing a towhead child in a wire cart between ramparts of packaged groceries.

This grocer's name was George, a swarthy blackeyed man somewhere out of eastern Europe. Ed kept him entertained talking about the football scores while he moved along the shelves inching packages of Abington Products forward so that the lettering would catch the light. While the grocer was distracted by a little boy buying a nickel cupcake, Ed hurriedly knelt on the floor to bend the cutout he'd brought in under his arm along the dotted lines. The cutout represented a pilgrim couple coming home to their cabin. He had a blunderbuss and a wild turkey slung over his shoulder. She carried a package of Suzy Standish's Special Thanksgiving Cake Mix.

Ed set it up on a breakfastfood box. "Now ain't that sumpen?"

"Eye appeal, eh," said George, who had come shuffling up behind them. He stared at it without a smile. "How about that football helmet you promised? My boy, he's hollerin for it."

"A helmet comes with every fifteen cases, George. You ain't got far to go," said Ed.

While George was attending to the woman with the child at the cash register, Jasper pitched in to help Ed build a pyramid of cakemix packages in the middle of the store.

George came back frowning. "I can't handle too many. Just makes cats and dogs."

"If you sell this lot by the end of the week," Ed's voice was wheedling, "suppose Ah finagle you two seats to the football game?"

A corner of a smile started on George's fleshy face. "Gimme that cakemix. Wanna see me make a sale?" He snatched up two packages.

A middleaged woman was standing beside the cash register with a glider full of groceries.

"Mornin' Mrs. Delano." George's face was a bouquet of smiles. While he punched out the items on the cash register he talked in a singsong voice: "Suppose I add two packages of Abington's new cakemix, Mrs. Delano . . . introductory offer

. . . two packages for the price of one, plus a teeny little dime."

He balanced the two packages on the palm of one hand.

"But I wasn't intending to bake a cake this week. My husband's on a diet." The woman was staring at the pilgrim couple on the brightcolored package. Her eyelashes fluttered. "Only a dime more, I guess I can afford that."

"Can't afford not to," said George jovially.

"Ed," said Jasper chuckling as they came out of the store, "that was all right . . . Couldn't have done better myself."

He was remembering his first sale. It was a hot summer day in Minneapolis. He had been sent down to sell the owner of a downtown restaurant, a hard nut that nobody else had been able to crack. He had taken one look through the glass at the glumlooking old man with walrus mustaches. He had to walk clean around the block before he could get up his nerve to go in. He could swear the old man was wearing a frock coat. The old man bared his teeth like a cornered rat and ran him out of that restaurant before he could say Jack Robinson. It had taken five separate visits and taking a girl in there and buying a big meal Jasper could ill afford before he nailed down that account.

"Ah guess George wants to see that football game," Ed drawled as they drove off. "Ah let him off easy-like this time. . . . Don't pay to highpressure people."

"Next time Ed," Jasper broke in, "you hit him on the head with a big order."

They stopped at a few more neighborhood stores and a redfront and a couple of supermarkets. Then Jasper looked at his watch. "I could do this all day Ed," he said, "but I'm expected at the Confederate Mill."

While Ed drove him out towards the railroad yards at the edge of the city, Jasper thought out loud: "The way I figure it Ed, our market in this whole seven state area is the folks who used to buy a barrel of flour or even take their own corn and wheat to the mill. Now tell me if I'm wrong. Ain't these folks just getting prosperous enough to go for packaged goods, laborsavings, timesaving packages and mixes? White and colored, that's a market that's been neglected, Ed. Am I right?"

"Ah'll say Amen to that Colonel Milliron," Ed announced in

a solemn tone. As they shook hands Jasper felt this was one guy who believed in him all the way.

The plant superintendent was waiting in the cramped up office of the Confederate Mill. Frank Gherkin was a rosy blue-eyed man with brown curly hair and a kind of oldfashioned yeoman expression. "Looking us over, eh, Colonel Milliron, well God bless you come along." He bounced his words out like tennisballs as he helped Jasper into a white duster and handed him a cheesecloth cap. "But don't forget that what we got here's an oldtime mill hitched on to a modern cereal plant."

Jasper could see there were reservations about the super-intendent's welcome. "Thank you Frank," he said with a laugh, "I guess I'm as popular here as a case of bubonic plague."

"The boys are worried," exploded Frank, "about who's going to get the axe and that's the truth."

"Sales is my business, Frank." Jasper let out a laugh he hoped was infectious. "I'm taking a Cook's tour to get the feel of things . . . been sitting too damn long in that office in St. Paul."

Frank sized him up with a long blue-eyed stare. "Honest? Well at least you are not coming flanked by the high brass." He slapped his thigh and started laughing himself.

Jasper grinned: "Jim Swazey's only going to meet me in Memphis. That chemical plant. That's the real problem."

The miller, a lugubrious stocky man with short cut light hair and a skin white as flour, stood in the office door. "All right let's go Frank," Jasper began. "How much do you know about these pneumatic mills where everything is worked by blowers?"

Frank's answer was lost in the whir of machinery. They were standing beside the sleekly cased motors that furnished the power for the farflung complication of belts and shafts that stretched up seven stories over their heads. "These are the prime movers, Colonel," intoned the miller with a voice full of awe.

The three men talked in snatches as they went up and down in elevators, climbed stairways, soared in one man lifts. They went up and down so many lifts that Jasper wondered if they were trying to tire him out. For a man of his weight it was a little tricky jumping on and off. Everywhere they went, beside them, underfoot, over their heads, the stream of grain hurried up conveyors, flowed down chutes, danced on belts, poured through rollers. Everywhere, like rain on a roof, their ears were filled with the rattle of moving grain. The miller kept peeking through glass lids, opening little traps, rolling samples through his fingers. Frank Gherkin gave Jasper a nudge. "The miller's thumb, see? In the end we come down to the rule of thumb."

"The Swiss do it with dials," grumbled Jasper.

"But does it pay?" shouted the miller in an exasperated voice. "No need to tell you Colonel, that there's been no real practical advance in the art of milling in seventyfive years."

"This is an example," Frank Gherkin roared cheerfully, when he next could get his voice heard, "of a real modern mill in Grover Cleveland's day."

They were walking along a row of machines that looked a little like small upright pianos. "You know these gradually reduce the grain," the miller was saying. "We've already taken off the bran. Here's where we knock off the germ."

He opened a trap and took out a handful of soft meal that gave off a rich wheaty smell and held it under Jasper's nose.

"Old Lew Sykes," the miller said in his mournful voice; "he was a wonderful old rule of thumb miller. . . . I took his place when he retired. He like to had a fit when we told him we'd have to amend the process so's to save out the wheat germ."

"I understand," shouted Frank with a roar of laughter, "that was one of Colonel Milliron's innovations."

He caught Jasper's arm as he hopped breathless off the lift onto the slippery floor. The miller went on with his story. "Now it's been through the breakrolls and the beeswings have been blown off. These are the sifters." He pointed through a forest of oscillating machines masked in canvas that jiggled like African dancers. "Sifting and bolting," he shouted. "This is where the flour comes out of the middlins. Right now we're running high grade patent flour."

They ended coming down a narrow winding stairway into the corridor outside of the superintendent's office. "After this," said the miller in a lackluster voice as if it hurt him to kiss it goodbye, "the flour goes over into the packaging department across the tracks."

"How long have you worked here, Si?" Jasper asked as he shook the miller's floury hand.

"Thirtyseven years . . . When you learn this business a feller tends to stick. Started as a sweeper when I was fourteen."

"So did I, Si, so did I . . . in the old Minneapolis mill," shouted Jasper jumping up and down with laughter. "Mr. Allardyce sent me there with a letter telling 'em I wanted to learn the business from the ground up. The trouble was I stayed on the ground."

The superintendent and the miller were laughing with him now.

"Then the war came, the first one. When I came back they had to find me a job. They couldn't very well set a Marine Corps captain to sweeping floors, so they found me a job in sales . . . How about a bite to eat?"

The miller shook his head, but he was still smiling. He darted like a squirrel back up the corkscrew stair.

"He's got to check on his grading," Frank explained. "People don't realize," he added accusingly, "that we sometimes run as many as sixteen different grades in a day."

Frank Gherkin had to skip to keep up with Jasper's stride as they followed the cindered roadway across the tracks to the new concrete building of the cereal plant. "Sometimes I think the men in the front office . . . you know what I mean," he sputtered. "They forget that milling's a personal business . . . We depend on the feel of Si's thumb."

"That's one reason I'm setting up my office in Atlanta. This thing's all too big, Frank. We've got to decentralize."

"You were asking about that Swiss mill, Colonel. Sure I read about it in the *Abingtonian*."

They were standing in line in the gaycolored cafeteria.

"Give me your private opinion, Frank. It won't go any further than me," Jasper asked in a low voice.

"The man didn't tell us how long it took 'em to get the bugs out, you know that, Colonel Milliron. Five years, that's my bet. I'm telling you the same thing I told Mr. Swazey and Mr. Griswold when they were here. The Confederate Mill may be antique but at least we know how to run it."

"That don't mean we don't want to keep our minds open for improvements, now does it Frank?"

"But is it an improvement? Every goddam thing that's new we have to think it's an improvement. I doubt it sometimes."

They had their trays. Frank Gherkin was leading Jasper over to a table, introducing him to a row of faces, experienced faces, tired faces, sharp young faces. Jasper repeated each name to himself so that he could match it with the face in his memory.

"Colonel Milliron," Frank Gherkin announced in formal tones, "is taking over the Atlanta office after the first of the year."

"Don't mind me boys, I'm just on a Cook's tour," said Jasper.

Immediately Frank broke out into his volleying laugh. "Now who's going to pay for my icecream . . . No the colonel can't . . . He's our guest."

The men had nickels out and started matching. Everybody shouted and protested. "The beauty of this game," roared Frank Gherkin into Jasper's ear, "is that the feller who loses not only has to pay for our icecream but he has to fetch it."

The Products Control man lost. "Serve him right," they all shouted. "He's the man's always on our tails in this plant."

After they had eaten their icecream Frank Gherkin ushered Jasper into the cereal plant. The place was as full of sideshows as the midway at a county fair. There were boilers for softening the grain, hot rollers for roasting and crushing it, big conical steamers that traveled on an overhead trolley for cooking the paste before it was pressed through metal dies, a shooting gallery where the puffed cereals were exploded in guns. In a reek of steam and chocolate and burnt sugar and roasting flour, mountain ranges of biscuit flour and cakemixes traveled through on conveyor belts to vanish into stainless steel hoppers.

"We may be stickinthemuds over in the mill," Frank whispered into Jasper's ear, "but here we've got all the new developments." They were walking downstairs in the packaging department. "See what I mean?" Frank exploded.

The first thing they saw was a stalled machine. Breakfastfood boxes waited on a motionless conveyer like people lined up in a queue. A young man in blue jeans with a streak of oil on his nose had his face poked into a tangle of levers and rods. He had the tip of his tongue between his teeth. With a screwdriver he was trying to pry loose a scrap of torn printed stock from under a roller.

A colored man was collecting the bashed and damaged packages on a hand truck.

"Thank God for the dogfood man," said Jasper.

"We use girl inspectors on the day shift." Frank changed the subject abruptly.

"What about the night shift?" Jasper asked nudging him.

"Disabled veterans." Frank ignored the joke. "They do fine."

Jasper fell to talking with one of the inspectors. She was a quiet spinster with clear gray eyes. She used to be a schoolteacher, she told him, making her voice heard above the rhythmic thump and clatter of the packaging machinery and the creaking of conveyor belts overhead.

Jasper was interested. He drew her out. She'd gone to college in the North and majored in Latin, natural enough because her people were Scotch. She laughed. She had been at that work seven years. Better money than teaching school. They had elected her shopsteward. Her only complaint was that there was no way for a woman to earn over $1.26 an hour.

"Some day," said Jasper soothingly, "we might have supervisory positions open to women. Maybe it won't be too long. . . . Fine woman that," he confided to Frank Gherkin.

As he walked out the door he made an entry in his notebook.

Abe Merman's Cadillac was already waiting outside the superintendent's office to take him to a meeting of the consumer research team downtown. As Jasper shook hands with Frank Gherkin he entered his name and face into a classification labeled "honest men" he carried in his head.

"Well?" Abe turned a face towards him that looked worried as a monkey's as Jasper slid into the front seat. "It's an antique, Colonel Milliron, but it is a valuable antique."

"I'm just a tourist taking a look-see, Abe," Jasper yawned. "That damn place. I didn't get any sleep last night."

"This meeting won't keep you long. Then I'll drive you straight to the hotel . . . Now what do you want to arrange for tomorrow?"

"Tomorrow I got to meet the Swazeys in Memphis."

"The fatty acids plant." Abe rolled up his eyes.

"Our big moneymaker," murmured Jasper still yawning. He was letting himself doze off. The sunny city afternoon came to him as a red blur through halfclosed eyes. The hum of traffic made him drowsy. Going up in the elevator he would have fallen asleep on his feet if Abe hadn't nudged him.

Abe was introducing him to a woman: "Mrs. Lorna Hubbard. You've seen her a thousand times. The Suzy Standish hour." Jasper was startled. All these years he had thought of her as a figure on the screen. But here she was a woman in the flesh. She wore green. She had a firm handshake, a pleasant firm smile, grayish blond hair firmly coiled against her head. There was a lovely freshness about her matte white skin. Jasper just liked her looks from that first moment he saw her. It wasn't that she wasn't nicelooking on TV but her real looks were different.

Jasper was wide awake again as he followed Mrs. Hubbard into the conference room with its long table and its rows of windows masked by venetian blinds. On the long wall opposite two young men in their shirtsleeves were tacking up colored charts. Abe opened the meeting with a regretful little speech. Then there was a college professor who had been hired to make a survey. Comments by sales personnel, jobbers, the buyer for a chain of grocery stores.

The few times Mrs. Hubbard spoke it was just to ask a question. She had a trace of a Southern accent but no more. Her questions were all about how this and that would appeal to the housewife. She seemed to have really thought about the needs of millhands and tenant farmers' wives. He liked her tone of voice. He liked the things she said.

Jasper didn't have to listen to the rest of them. He'd made up his mind long since about all these things so he didn't have to listen. He just sat there looking at Mrs. Hubbard and trying not to show how interested he was.

The minute the meeting was over she vanished somewhere out a side door. There wasn't any way of asking for her. There wasn't time. When he was finally alone in the hotel room, lying on the bed with his shoes off trying to pull together his impressions of the day, he kept remembering the warm intonations of her voice, the gardenia fragrance that seemed to come from her white leather handbag.

He jumped to his feet and started walking up and down the room. Act your age. Damn lucky you're leaving in the morning. He shook himself and went into the bathroom to slosh off his face with cold water.

Late next morning after a bumpy flight across the mountains he went barging into Jim Swazey's suite at the Delta Hotel in Memphis. The Swazeys were still eating breakfast. Jim was in bed, propped in pillows, his freckled face all puckered with discomfort under the scanty russet fringe of hair. "Why do I do these things? I don't know why Sylvia lets me do them," he started talking through a damp handkerchief as soon as Jasper came in the room. His nose was stopped up. He could barely make himself heard. "You both ought to know that every time I step into an airplane it sets my sinus off on a rampage."

The room smelt of coffee and some kind of vapor rub and benzoin inhalant.

"Fatty acids," Jim Swazey went on grumbling, "just imagine what the fumes of that chemical plant will do to my sinus."

"They might cure it Jim," said Sylvia as she came forward to press Jasper's hand. Sylvia was the one of Mr. Allardyce's daughters he always had a special understanding with. She'd grown into a tall slender silverhaired woman but they still thought of each other as kids on one of Mr. Allardyce's camping trips. "Jap tell him its antiseptic."

Jasper grinned. It was always a pleasure being with Jim and Sylvia. They didn't take each other too seriously so they never had a falling out. The three of them understood each other.

Every time he saw them Jasper couldn't help the flicker of a wish that he'd married Sylvia instead of letting Jim carry her off. He bet he could have given her a happier life even with her being so much older. Then he'd remember the gawky young guy he was then. At that stage of his career he just plain hadn't had the nerve. All those millions.

Somehow whenever Jasper and Sylvia met they telegraphed the whole story back and forth without a word. Too late now to do anything about it. She really was a sister to him. Then he had grown fond of Jim, that big old piece of suffering malarkey. Right away the two of them fell into their old role of seeing to it that Jim put his best foot forward.

"Why the hell does a milling company have to produce fatty

acids?" Jim was complaining from the bed. Jasper opened
his mouth to answer. "Shut up, you old rascal," rasped Jim.
"I know the answer but it still don't make sense."

"Jim, it's twelve o'clock," said Sylvia severely. "You and
Jap have got to be out there at one."

Jasper announced that he was going by his room to pick
up some literature. He'd be waiting for Jim in the lobby in
half an hour. When Jasper stepped out of the elevator he was
astonished to find Jim suddenly healthy and full of beans
rapt in conversation with a very young man with a very long
neck and very large ears. The young man's shirt was frazzled.
He looked like a bellhop out of work.

"Here's Colonel Milliron." Jim's head had cleared. He was
using his resonant executive's voice. "Jap meet Dr. Lorillard. . . ."

"The monosodium glutamate man?" asked Jasper.

The young man cast down his eyes under their long lashes.
He was blushing. "That's all set up," he said modestly. "It's
fatty acids now . . . You gentlemen must remember," he
went on as he ushered them into a long Lincoln driven by a
young fellow in overalls, "that the better designed a plant is
the more sensitive it is. The more sensitive it is the more it
depends on the training of personnel."

"You've been running it six months Dr. Lorillard," said
Jim making a glum face. "We combed the country for trained
personnel, you know that."

"Sure, the supervisors have all had excellent experience;
but it's like setting a pianist to playing a very complicated
organ." There was something like a sob in his voice. "A
chemical still is not something you can put into production
overnight."

Jim started tapping with his finger on his knee. He had
stopped listening.

They had a glimpse of red tiled buildings wreathed in a
tangle of aluminum piping as they drove in the plant gate.
Then they were being ushered into an airconditioned lobby
tinted in deep blue and tan. "Looks more like the Museum
of Modern Art than an industrial plant," grumbled Jim.

"Exactly," exclaimed a stocky young man looking like a
football quarterback in his sweatshirt who rushed forward to
greet them.

He was as brash as Lorillard was bashful. "Mr. Swazey,

Colonel Milliron, I'm Jack Yates of Simonson, Yates and Ibarra. Phil Lorillard and I collaborated to produce this little industrial nightmare." He paused for a laugh. "Suppose we eat some lunch."

He led them to a table set with a tablecloth in an alcove in the plant cafeteria. The whole wall was glass. The cafeteria had the quiet feeling of a college classroom during a final examination. A sprinkling of pallid young men, some in overalls and some in tan dusters, sat talking in low voices over their food.

While a waitress in uniform brought them their meal, Jack Yates was pointing through the tinted glass at the silvery bottle shapes ringed with catwalks of the great stills. "It's a pipefitter's dream," he said. "Miles and miles of different sorts and sizes of pipe."

"Every one of them ready to stop and burst when you least expect it," said Jasper.

"Phil finds that farm boys accustomed to patching up machinery with haywire do the best," Jack Yates said slapping his thigh.

"I tell you, it takes it out of you," interrupted Lorillard in a sorryforhimself tone. "Everybody's lost weight since we started operations. Some of these runs we have to sit up all night with."

"They have trouble explaining to their wives why they are always home so late," cried Yates.

Jasper had been studying a mimeographed sheet of figures on the table beside his plate. "Overtime." He cleared his throat.

Lorillard nodded blushing.

After lunch they walked through corridor after corridor of strangesmelling laboratories and ended up in the brilliantly lit drafting room.

"Well gentlemen here is the pneumatic mill," said Jack Yates with a flourish.

The four men stood staring at a row of blueprints clamped down on a set of tables that looked like pingpong tables. Using a ruler for a pointer Jack Yates indicated the outlines.

"Is this a flour mill?" asked Jim Swazey. "Looks like the same goddam thing we've just been walking through."

"Except that here we are dealing with fluids and gases." Jack Yates set him right. "In the new mills we'll be dealing

with grain and its byproducts delivered to each operation
through ducts activated by compressed air."

"The Swiss process?" asked Jasper.

"The Swiss process," insisted Jack Yates, "with the bugs
left out."

Jim Swazey stared at the blueprints a long time. He followed the ducts with a stubby finger.

"Well I'll be goddamned," he finally exclaimed.

Jack Yates tapped on the table with his ruler: "What we've
done is turn the oldfashioned flour mill inside out. We have
found the answer to infestation and to the dust hazard. Everything except the control rooms will be out of doors." He
waved his ruler over the blueprint like an orchestra leader.
"These are the great aspirators that suck the flour from process to process." You could hear the compressed air in his
voice when he said "aspirator." "The whole operation is pneumatic. Air is used as the classifier of the flour and its by-
products."

"Jim," said Jasper trying to keep the emotion out of his
voice, "this is the first radical change in milling in seventyfive years."

"It replaces the rule of thumb by the rule of the dial."
Jack Yates emphasized each word in his portentous bass.

Dr. Lorillard stood at the edge of the table silently nodding like one of those toy birds that bobble perpetually at
the edge of a glass of water.

"I may be crazy Jap," cried Jim Swazey when at last they
found themselves alone in the hotel elevator, "but if we can
get some assurance the damn thing will work I'm for it."

"How much assurance do you want?"

Sylvia, cool and slender and gray, opened the door of the
Swazey's suite for them while Jim was fussing with his key.
"I have the setups," she said brightly, "but the bourbon seems
locked in Jim's bag. I knew you boys would need a drink."

"I'm higher than a kite as it is," said Jasper throwing himself into an easy chair.

"The fatty acids have gone to his head." Jim slipped back
into the old kidding routine when he came back from the
bedroom with a bottle of Jack Daniels.

"Jim," said Jasper soberly, "suppose we put it this way. We
wait till this Memphis plant is operational, until it really can

custom-produce fatty acids for the detergent plants and the soapmakers and the paint and varnish industry. We know the demand is there. The minute we can deliver the product at a profit we'll have a fair assurance that this plant will work . . . We'll build a pilot mill."

"What will it do to job classification?" groaned Jim. "I just see years of headaches ahead, a century of headaches."

"The headaches will be mine," said Jasper gruffly, "if we build it in Chattanooga. If Abington won't build it by God I'd be almost tempted to go out and raise the money myself."

"What about the board?" asked Sylvia.

Jim poured himself another drink.

He looked from one to the other with big round eyes: "I'll ram it down their throats."

When he said good night after a pleasant cozy dinner with Jim and Sylvia, Jasper carried off a copy of Jim Yates's blueprints of the pilot mill to study before he went to bed. He always liked working in a hotel room. He called down to the switchboard that he'd accept no calls and pulled off his coat and necktie and spread the sheets out on the writing desk and weighted them down by the telephone book at one end and the Gideon Bible on the other. With a pencil in his hand he tried to follow the process as he'd followed it up and down those athletic one man lifts with Frank Gherkin yesterday in Atlanta. On the telephone pad he jotted down points to take up with Yates and Lorillard in the morning. The more he studied the plans the better he liked what he saw.

After an hour or so, for a breather, he turned on the TV.

While he was fiddling with the dials to get a stationary image something familiar struck him about the announcer's voice. He looked at his watch. Of course it was the Suzy Standish hour. He walked up and down waiting for the Western to subside. Then suddenly he was looking Lorna Hubbard full in the face. She was demonstrating an electric iron the Mechanical Division was putting out. This time he was thinking of her as a woman instead of a program. Her voice came over remarkably well. Her voice filled the room. He stood with his hands in his pockets staring breathless into the ground-glass screen.

She was taking one of the shining new irons out of its box

decorated with polkadots. He noticed that she had a polkadot scarf around her neck.

Now why the hell, he was asking himself as he watched her setting up the steam attachment to press a pair of pants, does that woman affect me that way? There was a twinkle in her eyes, an offhand way of doing things. She wasn't shoving the electric iron down people's throats. At the same time she was showing people how the thing worked just the way she might to somebody in her own house. For an instant he had a dizzy feeling that she was in the room with him, he could feel the remembered gardenia fragrance in his nostrils. He couldn't stand it.

He switched the damn thing off.

It was then he noticed how desperately alone he was in that hotel room between those four walls with the airconditioner in the window, so exactly like a thousand other hotel rooms. When he sat down to his blueprints again they swam before his eyes. He buried his face in the palms of his hands. I need somebody he told himself. Oh God how I need somebody.

Documentary (18)

WHO OWNS AMERICA?

Hairless Seagoing Apes Called Ancestors of Man

There are sometimes two kinds of youngsters playing around a farm cabin, the "yard chile" so-called bore unmistakable resemblance to both parents, the "woods colt" to only one or sometimes neither.

Two Hundred Pounds of Soundhushing Silencers Bring a New Dimension in Comfort

the brilliant irons have a wider hitting area, with a rounded leading edge designed to dig out the ball crisply and cleanly. Of course the shafts are reverse-threaded into the heads so that there is no pin to work loose, ever

"Many apes," he said, "were driven to hunt in the sea by fierce competition for food in the forests. Over a period of several hundred thousand years the species lost its hair as it carried on its marine life. The only hair left was on the very top of its head to help protect the creature from the sun. The sea ape learned to stand upright because the water helped support the body. It developed longer legs than its landbased brother ape for swimming."

SWEET SUCCESS FROM SQUEEZING LEMONS

"Its hands became sensitively shaped to allow it to feel along the seabed for shellfish and open crabs. It learned to use tools by picking up stones to open sea urchins. I estimate that apes were driven into shallow sea waters a million years ago. They emerged as men five hundred thousand years ago."

No Flaw Found

Things are going fine and then, suddenly, everything goes to pieces. An accident, fire, robbery, disabling illness, autocrash, lawsuit.

THEY'VE WORKED THEIR WAY INTO THE LANGUAGE

Asia's Songs Found Set to Liberty's Key

The Uncertainty Principle

In the entrance of the office of the Director of the Institute for Advanced Studies at Princeton, housed away from the town and the university, in plain brick buildings out among the fields, for many years there hung a hat.

Round, brown, with a tuckedin crown, it was a Harvard

man's hat, but with dust of the West on it, a hat that had been worn for mountain walks, gnawed by friendly dogs, sat upon by children in stationwagons. It was not exactly a proud man's hat: a mendicant friar might have worn it during the Middle Ages, yet its possession indicated some disregard of public opinion. It was a hat with a history; in the days when there was an atomic secret that battered felt had sheltered for a while the magic formulae that blew up Hiroshima.

A knowledgeable visitor coming to call would glance at the hatrack. If the hat was there he knew that Dr. Oppenheimer was in his office.

The man who appeared at the half open door would be tall with very large gray eyes set in a slender closecropped skull and a lean face with a long inquisitive nose and unquiet features more like the faces Italian engravers of the Renaissance liked to engrave on their medallions than the jowly countenances of his American contemporaries.

There was a monastic quiet about the office into which, walking with irregular steps with a certain courtesy of gesture, he would lead his visitor. The attitudes of the taffy-colored chairs set about the conference table would still seem to bear the imprint of the deliberations of those who had recently sat in them. Behind the Director's ample desk a band of windows opened on a green lawn screened with willows. The opposite walls were set with blackboards chalked over with lines of symbols. Little printed signs hanging from hooks read on the one side ERASE and on the other DO NOT ERASE.

Dr. Oppenheimer's sentences were rather long. There was a wistfulness about his tone. His English was clear and fastidious, with very little trace of Harvard or Cambridge or of New York where he grew up. The initial constraint of his manner would turn to eager grace if what the visitor had to say aroused his interest or his curiosity. His eyes would become extraordinarily luminous. To students he was irresistibly stimulating. Both men and women found him handsome.

Julius Robert Oppenheimer was born in New York of ancient Rhineland Jewish stock. His mother, a Baltimorean, had been an art teacher before her marriage. His father had emigrated from Germany at seventeen and made money in business. Fond of music, sensible of his duty to his fellow man, he had raised his boys in the easy humanitarianism of the affluent world of the nineteenth century afterglow, a world of ocean liners and European watering places and chamber music and civilized sympathies where ethical culture displaced the superstitions of the Hebraic or Teutonic past.

Robert Oppenheimer was a bright student at the Ethical Culture School, which was full of bright students. The west side New York he was brought up in was a beachhead of European culture on the crass continent of baseballplaying torchlightparading Bibletrained, moneymad, raucous America.

He was ten when the traditions of his European civilization received their first shattering blow with the outbreak of a general war in 1914.

At eighteen he entered Harvard, where he earned his B.A. in three years. Then he went abroad to Cambridge and Göttingen for his Master's and his Ph.D.

Einstein's great prediction: $e = mc^2$ had enlarged the already scintillating possibilities of investigation of the atomic microcosm in a hundred directions. The uncertainty principle, the hide and seek of the electrons, the now you see it now you don't of wavelengths and particles became the playground of Oppenheimer's subtle and energetic mind. He was of the generation of which one physicist was able to say without too much hyperbole: "Ninety percent of all the scientists who ever were are alive today."

Coming young physicists were hardly without honor in the world. Oppenheimer when he returned to the United States at the age of twentyfive had already made himself such a reputation that he could choose between invitations to teach from ten universities, not counting a couple he'd turned down in Europe. He went all the way west and accepted an assistant professorship at the University of California.

Later he spoke of being homesick in those years overseas for the United States.

Like many young Americans of European upbringing it may well have been abroad that he got his first inkling that there was something a little special about the hinterland west of the Hudson. Sophisticated Europeans in the nineteen twenties were full of naïve enthusiasm for American jazz and skyscrapers and transatlantic literature.

In California he oscillated between Berkeley and the Cali-

fornia Institute of Technology. His students followed him
from one faculty to the other. Ever fresh insights into the
nature of matter or the nature of energy (the concepts were
becoming interchangeable) opened dizzy perspectives. He
was excited by the idea that the new physics should be American. "When we first met in 1929 American physics was not
really much, certainly not consonant with the great size and
wealth of the country," Isadore Rabi said in 1954. "We were
very much concerned with raising the level of American
physics. We were sick and tired of going to Europe as learn-
ers. We wanted to be independent. I must say I think our
generation, Dr. Oppenheimer's and my other friends' I could
mention, did that job and that ten years later we were at the
top of the heap."

A great teacher, a natural leader of inquisitive young minds.
There was still a streak of the melancholy Dane in Oppenheimer. The further he went into the inner world of the in-
terplay of energies the more he was impressed by the limitations of his own mind. "Any form of knowledge really pre-
cludes other forms," he said during a lecture at Caltech in
the plaintively ruminative tone he had a way of falling into.
"Any serious study of one thing cuts off some other part of
your life."

Though a learned professor he was still a young man.
He suffered from his separation from the run of the mill boys
and girls he saw jostling and tussling and hugging on campus.
He was a gregarious man. There was something priestly about
the office of physicist that cut him off from the world of
action.

So many Americans felt that their neighbor had no right
to know more than they did. A college professor, whose days
and nights were taken up with exploring, through symbols
and equations, a universe which wasn't the universe of every-
day, couldn't help getting to feel a certain guilt as if he were
a practitioner of black magic. Lucifer's guilt becomes Lucifer's pride. In another context Oppenheimer said somewhat
vaingloriously, "We physicists have known sin."

When he appeared years later before his inquisitors in
Washington he tried to describe this state of mind:

"My friends, both in Pasadena and in Berkeley, were

mostly faculty people, scientists, classicists and artists. I studied and read Sanscrit. . . . I read very widely, but mostly classics, novels, plays, and poetry; and I read something of other parts of science. I was not interested in and did not read about economics or politics. I was almost wholly divorced from the contemporary scene in this country. I never read a newspaper or a current magazine like TIME or HARPERS; I had no radio, no telephone; I learned of the stockmarket crash in the fall of 1929 only long after the event; the first time I ever voted was in the presidential election of 1936. . . . I was interested in man and his experience; I was deeply interested in my science but I had no understanding of the relations of man to his society."

It was through a love affair—possibly he was a late bloomer in that direction too—that he was introduced to the Party.

Particularly in California (home of Jack London and Aimee Semple McPherson, Sinclair socialism and the Townsend plan) the Communist party and its flock of dogooder fronts had taken over the utopian ardors that spring eternally from the soil of that land of golden whales.

The girl was a college professor's daughter who seems to have been full of unassuaged emotions that drove her to break out from the faculty teas into the Real World. She took her handsome physicist to meetings where young people bubbled with enthusiasm for the downtrodden. As Einstein's relativity had knocked Newtonian physics slabsided so Marx's certainties furnished the formula that would right all wrongs by turning the social order upside down. There was material at hand for the Party to work on. The dynamics of the downtrodden was part of the heritage of American democracy.

Dr. Oppenheimer was not a bit downtrodden. He was a magnetic and popular professor with a mind extraordinarily well adapted to the promotion of the fastest growing science of the day. Physics was not enough. He needed a creed. He wanted to take part in the drama of history. Perhaps he felt the need to expiate the crime of individuality (as much of a crime to the solid citizens of the American Legion posts as to party functionaries Moscowtrained in revolution). He was rich. He owned a ranch in New Mexico. His father's

death left him so wealthy he could afford the generous gesture of willing his fortune to the university. Perhaps he was
made to feel these sins could be atoned for by a patient following of the Party line, and the shelling out of several hundred dollars a month

for good causes. Outsider would become insider; and the
cultivated dilettante who had never missed a meal in his life

would find mystical transformation

into a triumphant proletarian.

"I liked the new sense of companionship, and at the time
felt I was coming to be part of the life of my time and my
country," Dr. Oppenheimer was to tell his inquisitors.

The meetings were a revelation to a young man who
had led a sheltered life. There was an air of fashion and right
thinking about the parties in welltodo people's drawingrooms.
Causes are attractive to young women without mates. The
raising of money

for Spanish refugees

or for the sharecroppers or the migrant stoopworkers from
Mexico

or the longshoremen of Harry Bridges' red brigades

gave an air of high righteousness to the social whirl. (Dr.
Oppenheimer had a younger brother, Frank, who followed
in his footsteps. Frank followed him into physics and into the
movement.) The magnetic Oppenheimer was a pied piper
to all sorts of impressionable young scientists. While the fit
lasted he was a bonanza to the Party regulars. "I probably
belonged to every Communist front organization on the west
coast," he said in a jocose moment of reminiscence.

The Communism of the affluent Californians was
mostly socialfaddish like a taste for nonobjective art, but
with the rise of Hitler real passion fired the United Front.

European relatives of the Oppenheimers, who probably
hadn't thought of themselves as Jewish since the Dreyfus
case, were harried and despoiled. People had to be helped out
of Germany to save their lives.

(How the anti-Nazis in the American colleges squared
their horror of Hitler with Communist affiliation after the
Hitler-Stalin pact has never been explained. Maybe it just
was they didn't read the newspapers.)

No real conflict was allowed to rise in a fellow traveler's mind when Pearl Harbor bludgeoned the American people into the anti-Fascist war. Ipso facto the United States was allied to the Soviet Union. What a happy solution. The myopic enthusiasms of the parlor revolutionist crying for revenge against Hitler slipped into gear with the accumulated skills and the theoryweaving mind of the physicist. Everything that had ever happened in Oppenheimer's life had been a preparation for his extraordinary functioning as organizer, inventor, orchestrator of diverse personalities, catalyst, in creation of the Manhattan Engineer Project.

"To live through the life of that community at Los Alamos," he said once, "was an extraordinary experience . . . We were physicists, chemists, mathematicians, engineers . . . There was a community of aim and effort . . . The work went on in an atmosphere of intellectual cordiality. People took pleasure in fitting their minds into other people's minds. That's what made it a community. Of course there was the wartime pressure and perhaps the setting had something to do with it. There was the aloofness, the rare beauty of the desert."

Los Alamos
in the dry New Mexico hills,
daybreak of the hazardous glory
of the age of fusion and fission.

The Manhattan Project kept its dread work completely secret (from the American people at least). Its two fission bombs that ended the war came as a sharp surprise. A big bang, the biggest bang ever. The home team won. America demobilized with the lightheartedness of a crowd going home from a football game. Among the war heroes was Dr. Oppenheimer, deferred to on the boards of a dozen federal agencies. President Truman handed him a Medal of Merit.

It was only gradually that people in America discovered that the war had been won, not by their kind of democracy (where everybody tells everybody else what to do)
but by "people's democracy" where everybody does as

he's told under the rule of a worldwide superstate . . . can
that be what the dogooding college professors wanted?
"Strange, strange," sang Sophocles, "is the mind of man" . . .
        managed with an iron rod
        by the secretary of the Russian Communist Party
        who sat in the Kremlin planning the murder of his oppo-
nents,
        whose agents were everywhere, even in Washington in the
next office but one down the corridor.

        "Security" was a wartime invention: a state of affairs
that was supposed to keep our enemies (and sometimes our
friends) from knowing about troop movements, the development of new inventions, new weapons and the like.
        Security was to be our protection from the machinations
of the Kremlin.
        Security
        (after the horses had been stolen from all the stables, the
documents decoded and transmitted to Moscow, the sacred
formulae carried off in the heads of prominent scientists who
turned out to have been partymembers all along)
        became an obsession with the federal government.

        It was a good seven years after the winning of the
war and the loss of the peace that securityminded bureau-
crats began asking Dr. Oppenheimer what in the world he'd
been doing back in the thirties and right up to the inaugura-
tion of the Manhattan Project
        going to bed with Communist girls
        and shelling out good American dollars
        to all those Communist fronts.
        The Atomic Energy Commission
        set up a Personnel Security Board to sift out the evidence
presented by all sorts of agencies that Dr. Oppenheimer had
been too close to the Communists to be allowed access to the
deliberations and processes he'd played such a large part into
bringing into being.
        Everybody was determined to be scrupulously fair. For the
better part of a month the hearings (no no not a trial, not
an inquisition, oh no) continued. The good gentlemen of the
board heard forty witnesses and took three thousand pages of
testimony. Of course they listened to Dr. Oppenheimer.

One day the chairman was heard to ask if Dr. Oppenheimer was present. "That's one thing I'm sure of," he answered. Not too many onlookers were sure even of that.

Evidence was presented that he'd been a Communist and maybe still was but no evidence was presented that he leaked a word to anybody. Evidence was presented that he had many Communist friends but no evidence that any of them had been actively spies. Evidence was presented that he'd told a security officer a "tissue of lies" to protect a party-member friend (who actually would have been better protected by his telling the truth). Three thousand pages of scrupulously truthful evidence ended by obscuring the facts almost completely.

In the end though cleared of "disloyalty" Dr. Oppenheimer was declared a "security risk."

Dr. Smythe wrote a minority dissenting opinion:

> such a finding extends the concept of security risk and sets a dangerous precedent.
>
> In these times failure to employ a man of great talents may impair the strength and power of this country. Yet I would accept this loss if I doubted the loyalty of Dr. Oppenheimer or his ability to hold his tongue. I have no such doubts.

Doubts remained. The uncertainty principle: you can tell a particle's speed but not its location. The difficulty of discovering where the cleavage lies (not outside but inside civilization)

between the powers that would destroy and the powers that would save

the spirit of man:

a question for philosophers? Oppenheimer himself spoke of "the dread dead bird: 'How can you be sure?' which has stunted philosophy."

It certainly was not a problem which

with the best will in the world,

the Personnel Security Board of the Atomic Energy Commission,

sitting in room 2022 Building T3 through some hot May days in Washington, D.C.,

was able to resolve.

Dr. Isadore Rabi, chemist and physicist and a long-term friend and colleague of Oppenheimer's, who's a Brooklyn boy, blew up at the hearing:

"I never hid my opinion that this whole proceeding is a most unfortunate one. . . . In other words there he was; he is a consultant. If you don't want to consult the guy, don't consult him, period.

"It didn't seem to me the sort of thing that called for this sort of proceeding at all against a man who has accomplished what Dr. Oppenheimer accomplished . . . This is just a tremendous achievement and if at the end of that road is this kind of hearing that can't help but be humiliating. I thought it was a pretty bad show . . .

". . . We have an A bomb, a whole series of it . . . and what more do you want, mermaids?"

Documentary (19)

STRESSES IN SPACE HELD FORMIDABLE

intellectual hazards may include a tendency to drift off into highly personal and emotionally charged fantasies. The crewmen may develop doubts as to their ability to tell facts from fiction and become malleable and suggestible almost "to the point of confabulation"

BECAUSE WE SERVE SO MANY WE CAN SERVE ALL BETTER

"*A man, for example, may be angrily against racial equality, public housing, the TVA, financial and technical aid to backward countries, organized labor, and the preaching of social rather than salvational religion . . . Such people may appear 'normal' in the sense that they are able to hold a job and otherwise maintain their status as members of society; but they are, we now recognize, well along the road toward mental illness.*"

Expert Says Total Strains May Be Too Great for
Most Persons to Face

HOW TO KEEP RACE TENSIONS FROM EXPLODING

the object of such experiments is to produce a
predictable set of community attitudes, stimulated
by "key" agents who have been placed in the community according to sociometric principles of influence and leadership

MORE GRIP MORE GO IN SNOW

Not all schoolhouses are infested by the amazing
snoopers, but in schools dominated by highly experimental practices, "cum" files, when opened unex-
pectedly to prevent file-stripping, reveal to parents
an amazing sight. In a goulash of data are found
transcripts of statements uttered by parents, students' autobiographies written as classroom assign-
ments, and innocent remarks of children collected in
notebook "logs" by teachers who are thorough agents
of observation.

The Big Office (*concluded*)

For Terry Bryant the worst thing about being out of a job
was having Tasha go off to work in the morning. She had to
leave the apartment at a quarter past six not to be late at the
Rumston Tool and Dye Works. And there Terry would be,
all alone, padding about the cold room in his underwear with
the breakfast dishes to wash and the bed to make, moving on
tiptoe over the creaky floors so as not to wake the kids asleep
in their little cribs in the alcove. Nobody could have loved
his kids better than Terry did, but, as he fiddled about, doing
first one thing then the other, dawdling over the dishes, taking
his time shaving in the bathroom, he'd be hoping to God they
would put off waking up.

He had to have time to think, to plan, to decide how he'd

fight this thing: strategy, tactics; he had to think fast. Instead of plans gray gloom throbbed inside his head.

From the minute the kids woke up and came scampering out in their bunnysuits he didn't have a thought to call his own. Billy was four and chubby and blond, Natalie was skinny at five with black eyes like her mother's. They wanted this and they wanted that. He had to get them their milk and their cereal and to see to their baths and that Billy got on the potty in time, and then if it was a decent day he had to carry the express wagon and their toys down the steep steps and shepherd them over to the tots' playground four blocks away.

It was embarrassing being the only man with a lot of women tending their kids. They're turning me into a goddam nursemaid, Terry would be grumbling inside. But he had to admit to himself that it was only the continuous attention he had to give Billy and Natalie that kept him from going off his rocker for fair.

When he could get away for a moment from their piercing little demands he'd try to cudgel his brains into thinking what to do, but the same old stupid words went round and round in his head. It's the damned injustice of the thing.

He felt sleepy and dimwitted all day, but he seemed to have lost the knack of going to sleep at night. He'd try to hug and cuddle Tasha after they had gone to bed, but she would fall into a stupor as soon as her head touched the pillow. That inspection job sure took it out of her. Terry would lie beside her staring hoteyed at the ceiling, trying not to toss around for fear of waking her, going over again and again in his mind everything that had happened at the plant: the things he'd said to Steve and Duke and the things Steve and Duke had said to him, the fight, the business about the gauge, the talk in Mr. Briggs's office. It was like some damned picture puzzle. Always the same pieces. Only one way to fit them together.

At last he'd fall asleep and wake up with a start to find himself alone in the bed and Tasha, with no smile for him on her face, hurrying into her clothes in the light from the bathroom door. It couldn't be he was losing Tasha. He'd turn his face to the wall and pretend to be asleep until she poked him up to eat breakfast.

Some days Terry would talk big about having to go to see his lawyer and Mrs. Abramovich, the kind bigbreasted woman who lived on the ground floor, would take over Billy and Natalie. She had five, all ages from seven down including a pair of twins in a perambulator, and had developed a system of getting them to take care of each other. "Two more, what's that?" she would say.

The minute Terry was out of sight of the kids he'd fall into his gloom again. He wasn't a man, he was a nursemaid. He could imagine himself wearing skirts. He'd never get a man's job again. How could Tasha keep on loving a goddam nursemaid?

He had fits of jealousy. There were mighty few women employed at Rumston Tool and Dye. He knew how factory hands were. Before she knew what had happened Tasha would find herself with some guy behind a stack of cartons in some stockroom and he'd be sticking it into her and she'd be loving it because she didn't have a man at home only a damned unemployed nursemaid. He'd stride along the street with his fists clenched muttering "I'll kill the bastard" until he was scared people would notice or some cop would run him in for an escaped lunatic.

The only lawyer who would take his case without a retainer was a little man with a face like an elderly baby named Stanley Norris. Lawyer Norris talked with a lisp. "Now Terry let's not go off the deep end," he would say when he'd catch sight of Terry standing first on one foot then on the other in the skimpy reception room of the office he shared on the third floor of a crummy old building on Main Street with a flock of other attorneys.

"You think I'm crazy to fight this thing." Terry would stand over the little man's desk flailing around with his arms as if he planned to hit him. "It's the goddam injustice."

And then he'd be off explaining for the hundredth time that if he thought only of himself he'd shut up and take it and go get himself another job, but if they could do this to him what couldn't they do to some poor devil of a DP who couldn't even speak English?

It was his bounden duty. Wasn't he responsible for organizing the local over at Raritan Hard and a shopsteward and a union trustee and chairman of the safety committee, elected time and again as a delegate to union conventions; if he couldn't get justice who could? He was responsible for getting all those poor guys to join up and pay their dues: if this was the kind of deal you got they'd been better off without a union.

"No need to shout Terry," Lawyer Norris would remark with a mild smirk, "you can't blame me, at least not till after I lose the case for you."

Then they'd both get to laughing and Terry would feel almost human again. He'd have gone nuts without that lawyer to tell him what to do.

On his second visit the lawyer made him sit down at a typewriter and write out exactly what had happened. By that time Terry had told the story so often it was beginning to get hazy in his head.

"Steve Slansky was drunk and he came at me calling me dirty names while I was performing my duty as shopsteward and chairman of the safety committee and I hit him back."

Lawyer Norris was standing behind him looking down at what he wrote. "To an uninformed auditor that might sound as if you had hit him first."

"How often do I have to tell you he hit me first? My dad brought me up to be handy with my dukes, see? . . . I saw his fist coming and ducked and took a glancing blow on the shoulder."

"Which of you had to go to the doctor?"

"He did." Terry couldn't help grinning. "Say whose lawyer are you, Mr. Norris, mine or Steve Slansky's?"

"I'm just trying to imagine how it will sound in court if we sue him for assault and battery. The impression I get is that he called you a dirty name and you beat hell out of him."

"I sure did," said Terry puffing out his chest.

"With a jury it's usually the guy who gets beaten up gets the damages."

Terry felt all the fight go out of him. His knees went weak. He let himself drop into a chair.

"I don't want damages. I want my job back. I want to be reinstated by the union."

"Well the Slansky brothers run the union so far as I can see. You'll be lucky if somebody doesn't stick a knife in your back."

"I ain't scared of rats."

"Quiet down Terry. I wouldn't be wasting all this time if I didn't think you got a raw deal. The question is what tribunal to appeal to. If you would just sit down and advise with me reasonably without blowing your top . . . I'm merely thinking out loud."

Terry sat on one side of the desk with his hands dangling between his knees. The little lawyer sat on the other, his brow furrowed under his neatly parted black hair. His manicured fingers played with a yellow pencil.

Finally Lawyer Norris came out with a pronouncement. "So far as your job goes even a favorable verdict in court would not be much help and I don't think we could get one; so that's out. I've had the nearest office of the National Labor Relations Board on the phone. They doubt very much whether the case comes under their jurisdiction but they won't say yes or no until it's been written up and submitted and then their docket is in such a state they say it might be two or three years before they even gave it consideration."

"My God my kids can't wait two years to eat."

"The state labor arbitration board is about the only thing left. Your union is supposed to represent you there."

"Wyzanski, the union attorney, he's hand in glove with the Slansky boys."

"Wyzanski's not so bad," said Lawyer Norris in a wheedling singsing, "I see him now and then in a group of lawyers who meet once a week for lunch. Maybe I can suggest the choice of an arbitrator." He puffed himself up like a bird ruffling its feathers. "We are all officers of the court you know."

Terry felt his head whirl. "He associates with rats," he shouted into the little man's face, "and it looks like you did too." He stamped out of the office.

He stopped in his tracks outside the corner drugstore. Have some sense, he told himself. He called the lawyer on the phone to apologize. "Please skip it," he said. "I ought to have told you I had witnesses."

"Names and addresses please," Lawyer Norris answered dryly. "I'll jot them down."

Terry found himself stammering. Well there was Duke the foreman, Bogdan Radisch his real name was, no Terry didn't know his address, and he was the one who had brought the complaint; and then there was little Tony the green hand, Terry didn't know his address either. Didn't even know his last name.

"Those two will testify against you, that is a safe inference now isn't it?" The lawyer's voice cut like a knife.

"Well, I got Keith Jones and Ferdy Hopkins; they are both good guys and honest union men."

"You get a written statement from each of them, see?" the lawyer said severely, "or it's useless to go into arbitration."

Terry walked along the street fuming. If Lawyer Norris was so against him what the hell did he want to take the case for?

All the same by the time Terry reached home he was in a better frame of mind. As he got things ready for supper he kept rolling the word arbitration over on his tongue. He had the kids' faces washed and a potroast almost cooked on the stove and the potatoes boiling by the time Tasha came puffing up the stairs. Her face had a gray tired look but she smiled when he kissed her. "Arbitration," he said. "Lawyer Norris and I are going to ask for arbitration."

"So long as it don't drag out," said Tasha. "It's the dragging out that's getting me down." Her voice was so weak it dwindled to a whine. "I'm whipped," she whispered.

She said she liked the potroast but she wouldn't eat much of it. After they put the kids in their cribs she lay down all dressed on the bed and closed her eyes. He'd never seen her look so tired. He sat down on the edge of the bed and tried to love her up a little but she pushed his hands away. "I'm just tired," she said in a whimpering little childish voice.

Terry was standing glumly over the sink wondering where to begin on the dishes when the bell rang. Tasha sat up with a start and began to straighten her hair.

When Terry opened the door Ed Banning walked in. There was a look of embarrassment on Ed's jowly face blue from the dark beard that had just been shaved clean. He smelled of soap. Without even saying How do you do? Ed blurted out that he was sorry he'd asked Terry about that story the Slanskys were spreading about Terry having been in a mental hospital. He ought to have known better. It had been on his mind all week. Well hell he just wanted to say that the boys in the plant were still all hot and bothered about the raw deal Terry got. They'd even planned a wildcat strike in his department.

"I know," said Terry. "I told 'em to skip it."

Well; Ed Banning cleared his throat and went on. They'd all been mad as hell. Some said it ought to come up before the NLRB or maybe he could sue the company in court.

Terry heard himself announcing in a toplofty voice that

he'd decided to put it up to the state arbitration board according to the terms of the contract.

That was great. Ed jumped at that. He'd been searching for something to cheer up about. With a selfsatisfied grin he brought an envelope out of his inside pocket. The boys had passed the hat. They'd collected fortyeight dollars and seventyfive cents to help Terry hire a lawyer.

Terry didn't know what the hell to say. He found himself blushing for some reason. He pointed with his thumb to Tasha:

"Give it to her, she's the breadwinner now."

Ed stood around shuffling his feet. Ed and Tasha tried to make a little conversation while Terry stared at them stonyfaced.

The minute Ed Banning had gone Terry started to cry. He stood there with tears running down his face while Billy and Natalie, who'd crept out of their cribs to find out who the caller was, circled around looking up at him with big round eyes.

"Bad man hurt Daddy?" asked Natalie.

"Daddy 'tub his toe and fa' down," said Billy.

They both seemed pleased as if Daddy's crying made him one of them. He picked them up and hugged them both to him as he carried them back into the alcove. "Daddy you mustn't," Natalie said as he tucked in the covers around her, "grownups don't cry."

Next morning Terry was at Lawyer Norris's desk bright and early. He had Keith Jones's and Ferdy Hopkins's addresses neatly written out on a piece of paper. The little lawyer looked bleak until he saw the fortyeight dollars and seventyfive cents. Then he smiled up at Terry. A chirpy note came into his lisp. It was gratifying, he said, not the money but the expression of confidence by Terry's shopmates. Of course he'd kissed his fee goodbye when he said he'd take the case.

All the same he didn't lose any time scooping up the bills and stowing them away in his wallet. Then he got to his feet and found Terry a chair.

Now Terry mustn't misunderstand him. He hadn't waited for the money to look after his client's interests. He cleared his throat importantly as he seated himself again. He had secured a statement on Terry's discharge from the personnel department. Under the circumstances he regretted that right at the beginning Terry had not informed him completely of the scope of the charges. It made it hard for a lawyer if his client didn't keep him fully informed. He cleared his throat again and started to read off a sheet of paper in a courtroom voice.

The company was prepared to present a series of charges accumulated over a term of years, fomenting of a wildcat strike, unwarranted absences from his machine during working hours, fighting on company property, the use of foul and abusive language to his foreman etcetera, etcetera.

"Damn lies!" Terry began to blow his top. Then he got hold of himself. "Sounds like I was a bad egg all right," he added with a broad grin. "It's surprising that I can find an attorney to take my case."

Lawyer Norris looked a little pained at that. Terry felt he had him there. His voice was firm now. Wouldn't two witnesses do? he asked as he got to his feet. If they wouldn't the lawyer better give that money back and Terry would see that it was returned to the men who had contributed it.

That idea didn't seem to appeal to Lawyer Norris. "My dear fellow," he exclaimed, "life would be insupportable if we didn't believe that truth will prevail."

"Don't forget," said Terry, "that I was fired for reporting a dangerous breakdown in a pressure gauge."

"Sure, sure," said Lawyer Norris without looking up.

He was busy typing out a list of questions for Terry to ask his witnesses to fill out.

Every evening of that week after Tasha got home to hold the fort with the kids Terry tramped around town looking for his witnesses with the typed questions in his pocket. He tracked down Keith Jones in a bar where he was watching television over a beer. Keith was a tall shaggy man with a prominent adamsapple. When he first saw Terry, Keith couldn't make enough fuss over him. By God if he'd had his way he would have struck the whole goddam plant. Let 'em stay out till Terry was rehired, then by God they'd elect him president and clean that union up for fair. Anybody who tried any dirty work would get his ears pinned back.

He insisted on buying Terry a beer and talked about the wonderful speech Terry had made the last time he spoke up at the local, how Terry had said this was a great country of ours and theirs was the damndest cleanest union in all American industry and it was up to the rank and file to keep the locals clean. No union was cleaner than its smallest local. Keith knew that speech by heart and he wasn't the only one.

Terry felt he ought to buy Keith a beer.

He felt responsible, Terry tried to explain. He'd put five years of his life into organizing that damn local. He'd set up classes to teach the foreign born English and sponsored them for citizenship just so they'd understand Americanism. It wasn't all for himself. He felt it would be wrong to let those guys down.

"Fuckin' donkeys and look how they treated you." Keith rolled his eyes to heaven. He'd order a boilermaker, he added plaintively, but his change was running low. How about a shot of rye? Terry paid no attention.

"If I ever saw a man get a raw deal who didn't deserve it, Terry Bryant is that man," Keith roared out for the whole ginmill to hear.

Terry lowered his voice. "Keith," he whispered, "you saw that pressure gauge . . . I need a witness to testify." And he brought out his list of typed questions.

After one glance at the paper Keith's eyes looked everywhere except in Terry's face. He put his arm round Terry's shoulder and talked fast into his ear.

"Terry old man I dassent. As a workin' man I dassent."

He was surprised and shocked, Keith spluttered into Terry's ear, that Terry had even suggested it. Didn't he understand? A working man dassent stick his neck out. When he brought pressure it must be mass pressure, like a picket line, or a walkout or a strike . . . a feller like him standing up and testifying in court, it just wasn't good labor tactics. He was speaking as a devoted union man.

"Arbitration isn't a court. You'd appear in behalf of the union."

Keith spluttered and flustered. He ordered one last beer. He slammed Terry on the back. He wished him all the luck in the world but he could no more testify in court standing up all by himself like that with all those smart attorneys twisting up everything he said than he could fly to the moon.

Terry got to his feet. "Well good night Keith, thanks all the same," he said.

Ferdy Hopkins begged off too. Ferdy was a small rattoothed middleaged man. Terry found him at the filling station where he worked evenings.

"Don't ask me to do it, don't ask me to do it," he said right away without looking up.

He talked fast and low with his eyes on the ground explaining that his wife was sick and he had five kids to keep in shoes and payments to keep up on the car and the refrigerator and the washing machine and the new set of livingroom furniture they had just bought. That was why he had to work two jobs.

As he talked he gave an occasional worried glance around to see if anyone was looking.

His voice sank to a whisper. It wasn't that he didn't think Terry was right. Terry had been just doing his duty to report that pressure gauge. He'd seen Steve try to slug him. Hadn't he forked up a dollar when Ed Banning passed the hat? Every dollar hurt the way he was situated. That dollar was all he could do so help him God it was.

Ferdy had been keeping eager watch on the passing cars. A look of relief crossed his face when a car drew up to the gas pump. He was off like a shot to get on with his servicing.

"Well good night, Ferdy, thanks just the same."

So when the day came to appear before the arbitrator Terry didn't have any witnesses at all. Lawyer Norris drove him over to the office of the state arbitration board. Shouting to make his weak voice heard over the roaring trucktraffic of the highway he tried to keep Terry's spirits up by telling him that the company wasn't bringing any witnesses either. Just standing on the record.

Maybe Slansky had tipped them off that this arbitrator was famous for worming the truth out of witnesses. Lawyer Norris had to admit he was congratulating himself for having picked the straightest arbitrator on the panel. Put something over Wyzanski that time. Lawyer Norris's titter jarred on Terry's raw nerves like the screech of chalk on a blackboard.

As he wove in and out through the traffic, Lawyer Norris went on and on about how Henderson P. Barker was an expert in management-labor relations, how he had held a position in the Department of Labor in Washington during the New Deal, how he was thoroughly versed in the workings of the National Labor Relations Board, a man who understood the human side of things. To put it in a nutshell Henderson P. Barker was one of God's gentlemen.

Terry wasn't listening. Sitting there in the front seat of the rickety old Ford, looking out of eyes redrimmed with sleeplessness at the sunny day and the trucks slambanging by and the factory buildings and the telephone poles and the fillingstations he was wishing with his whole soul for a blowout or that some trailer would sideswipe them, or that Lawyer Norris, who wasn't too good a driver anyway, would run into some car, anything to keep them away from that damned arbitration.

Terry had fallen into a sour daydream. It was all a put up job. Arbitration was for the birds. The lawyer had been just kidding him along. Terry had already been framed and convicted. The lawyer was just talking arbitration to keep him quiet until he could turn him over to the sheriff. Terry couldn't help furtively feeling his wrists to make sure he had no handcuffs on them. Of course it was just a daydream, he kept telling himself, but that was how he felt.

Nothing happened in the arbitration proceedings the way Terry expected it to happen. Henderson P. Barker was waiting for them in a nice sunny room with a long green oak table down the middle of it. He was a smiling ruddy rolypoly man in tweeds that matched his silvery gray hair. He stood in the streak of sunlight at the end of the table, playing the genial host and rubbing his hands as if before an imaginary fire. Just as Lawyer Norris said, he was the nicest man you ever saw. The first thing he did was send an office boy out to the corner drugstore for coffee and doughnuts all around.

When Milan Slansky and Lawyer Wyzanski came in they greeted Terry as if there weren't any trouble between them at all. "Attaboy Terry," Milan growled, and Wyzanski made quite a speech about how every man deserved his day in court. Steve wasn't with them and neither was Duke, only Mr. Goldberg from the personnel department, a neat little rabbitfaced man who wore an oldfashioned stickpin in the shape of a golfclub in his fourinhand cravat, and Mr. Goldberg's secretary, quite a beauty with shining black hair and a pretty yellow dress, whom he introduced as Miss Di Maris.

Miss Di Maris flicked open her book and sat with pencil poised ready to take notes with her shapely legs crossed in the prettiest way under her tight dress.

There was a short silence. Henderson P. Barker gave each man in turn a cordial just between you and me smile, and then he lit his pipe and the proceedings began. It was such a friendly group, and everybody seemed to be getting along so nicely with everybody else that Terry felt like a heel when he had to raise his voice to ask if anybody was keeping a record of his side of the case.

"We didn't feel it was necessary," said Lawyers Norris and Wyzanski in unison, "to go to that expense." They gave Terry pained looks as if his ignorance cut them to the quick.

Everybody wore a bright attentive look and listened with interest to what everybody else had to say except Milan. Milan never said a word. He just sipped his coffee and smoked his cigar with a sleepy crocodile expression on his face, and kept his little slits of eyes under their heavy lids fixed on Miss Di Maris's legs.

Lawyer Norris seemed thoroughly pleased with himself for being in such company. He and Mr. Goldberg made twittering comments back and forth like two sparrows on a telephone wire.

Terry sat bolt upright in his chair. He had to listen carefully even if he had to pinch himself. Henderson P. Barker was talking. Henderson P. Barker was giving a short history of arbitration procedure in labor cases. If no one had any objection he was going to suggest that the Raritan Hard Rubber Company present its case first. Then it would be the turn of the grievant.

"Who the hell's that?" asked a voice in Terry's head. "The grievant's me, you poor son of a bitch," came the answer.

Mr. Henderson P. Barker concluded his remarks by pointing out in tones that would have drawn tears from a rock that since the discharge penalty had such serious consequences for the employee, he was sure that management's representative agreed with him that it should be imposed only for proven offenses of very serious nature. Then he leaned forward with a look of pleased anticipation on his face like a man waiting for the curtain to go up at a show.

Mr. Goldberg read a paper. He read it in such a smooth even voice and it all sounded so logical and convincing that Terry found himself almost going along with what Mr. Goldberg said. It was only when he remembered that Mr. Goldberg hadn't said a word about the pressure gauge that he caught himself up sharp. To make sure that his own lawyer didn't forget about the pressure gauge he scrawled the words on an envelope and laid it on top of the papers under Lawyer Norris's nose, but Lawyer Norris was so busy nodding and

smiling at every question Mr. Henderson P. Barker asked Mr.
Goldberg that he just didn't seem to find time to look down at
the envelope.

When Mr. Goldberg was through Lawyer Wyzanski talked
a long time about mistaken zeal in the enforcement of safety
regulations and added a few remarks about how perhaps the
arbitrator might find extenuating circumstances in the grievant's psychopathic history.

Lawyer Norris flared up at that and said that the grievant's
past history had nothing to do with the case. He had given
four years of his life to his country's cause in the Pacific and
come home a master sergeant and if that was a sign of mental
weakness what about all our great soldiers and sailors? Then
Lawyers Wyzanski and Norris got into a friendly wrangle
about which of them could say most in favor of the grievant's
patriotism, and Doolittle and General MacArthur, until Henderson P. Barker stopped them and suggested, grinning amiably into the faces of each of them in turn, that perhaps they
ought to hear what the grievant had to say in his own behalf.

Terry used to fancy himself a pretty fair speaker but now
he got all balled up trying to explain how a Banbury mixer
worked and what might have happened if he had not reported
the failure of that pressure gauge. After he'd been talking five
minutes he realized that none of them was paying the slightest
attention. They were all watching the cute way Miss Di Maris
had of sticking just the tip of a pink tongue out between her
even pearly teeth when she took notes.

Finally Henderson P. Barker raised the palms of his two
hands. Terry stopped talking abruptly. "Of course, of course,"
he said. "I think that we all understand that the grievant's
attitude in this matter was thoroughly conscientious. . . . Now
perhaps Mr. Bryant would relate his version of the . . . er . . .
fisticuffs with the other young man who happened, by a
strange coincidence, to be his competitor for the office of
president of the local, I believe."

The beam of Henderson P. Barker's confident smile swung
from face to face like the revolving beam of a lighthouse.

"Steve had been drinking," Terry heard himself say. "He
came up to me calling me dirty names the way I'd seen him
attack other employees before and I let him have it."

"But Mr. Bryant," Lawyer Norris cried out in an anguished

tone, "~y understanding was that he slugged you with his right fist."

Terry felt his face turning red.

"Of course I wouldn't have hit him if he hadn't hit me first."

"Sit down," Lawyer Norris hissed at him. Terry sat down.

Meanwhile Milan Slansky was rising heavily to his feet. He laid a sheet of paper on the table under Henderson P. Barker's nose. "Mr. Barker," he said in his deep rumbling voice. "I have to admit that Steve is my kid brother. . . . To keep family feelings out of it I asked Dr. Walters to describe, in the form of an affidavit, Steve's condition when he was taken into his office that afternoon."

While Henderson P. Barker puffed on his pipe and read the affidavit, the rest of them, except for Milan Slansky who had gone back to puffing on his cigar and staring at Miss Di Maris's shapely legs, all got to talking at once. Selfdefense was this. Selfdefense was that. Everybody had a different idea. Henderson P. Barker stowed the affidavit away in his briefcase and let his eye run down his penciled notes. Then he rapped on the table with his pipe.

"Gentlemen," he interrupted. A note of impatience crept into his agreeably modulated voice. "I don't think that there is any question that the grievant fought under extreme provocation."

Lawyer Norris gave Terry's ribs a poke under the table. "What did I tell you?" he whispered.

"Selfdefense," exclaimed Wyzanski. "As a lawyer I suppose I've had my share of assault and battery cases but I must admit Mr. Barker that I've never yet found a satisfactory definition."

That was Mr. Goldberg's clue to bring out of his briefcase a large green paperbound volume. He had run into an interesting discussion of that very problem in a case that had been adjudicated by the National Labor Relations Board a couple of years before. Of course knowing Mr. Barker's familiarity with these proceedings it was hardly worthwhile bringing it to his attention. But just in case Mr. Barker was not familiar with it he asked his indulgence while he read a few lines. Henderson P. Barker nodded. Mr. Goldberg read: "Approaching the instant grievance on its merits and eliminating the unmaterial details hereinbelow discussed the grievant's testimony that after another employee had struck him he stepped back and struck that employee in the face clearly establishes that the grievant was engaged in fighting on company property, a proper cause for discipline and an offense for which he was properly discharged."

Mr. Goldberg looked sharply about the table and pulled back his shoulders so violently that his starched cuffs shot out from his coatsleeves.

Henderson P. Barker listened with his pipe poised in the air.

"Now listen to this, gentlemen," continued Mr. Goldberg. "The following is if I may say so the nubbin of the decision:

"Grievant's act cannot be justified as selfdefense, since at the time grievant struck the blow the other employee's blow was completed and grievant was no longer in danger from that blow. Although provocation may have existed provocation alone does not constitute justifiable selfdefense."

Lawyer Norris was on his feet. "This decision," he cried out, "has nothing to do with the present case. The grievant was discharged for abusive language to his foreman."

Henderson P. Barker's round face was getting a sorrowful look. "We can hardly deny," he said, "that the grievant's discharge was the result of a cumulative series of incidents." He started laboriously cleaning his pipe out into an ashtray.

"In the case to which I referred," Mr. Goldberg went on relentlessly reading: "'the company's determination as to the degree of discipline to be imposed (i.e., its decision to discharge the employee) was found not subject to review by the board.'"

He handed the open book over to Henderson P. Barker with a flourish.

"Thank you, thank you," said Henderson P. Barker and stuffed the book into his briefcase. "We must all keep an open mind."

He filled his pipe and lit it again. Amid clouds of smoke he flashed his brightest smile round the table. "It's well past lunch time," he said. "Unless the grievant desires to comment I think I have all the materials in hand on which to base a decision by which the parties to this arbitration have already bound themselves to abide."

"Yes sir," said Terry in a tense voice grabbing hold of the tabletop with both hands to keep from threshing around with his arms. "I have a comment to make. . . . Let me ask each one of you men this question. What would you have done in my place? Let the man beat you up? The man hit me and I hit him back, if that ain't selfdefense what is it?"

Terry was talking to an empty room. Lawyer Norris pulled him away from the table and out the door. The rest of them had already disappeared into the hall through the other end of the room.

Going down in the elevator Lawyer Norris tried to keep a stiff upper lip. "Terry that just proves," he said, "how wrong you were to suggest an appeal to the NLRB."

Terry hated to spend the money but he had already promised Lawyer Norris to set him up to lunch. As they went through the lobby of the big hotel across the street in search of the coffee shop they caught sight of Milan's broad back. He was happily shoving Wyzanski and Mr. Goldberg before him into the crowded bar. They were laughing and chatting as they went with all the air of having had a very successful morning.

Terry couldn't eat.

"Well that's that," he said as he paid for Lawyer Norris's porkchops. Lawyer Norris shook hands with him amiably. "Sorry Terry, but thank you for everything," he chirped. "You must admit it was a most interesting discussion. I learned a lot."

"So did I," said Terry.

Terry went home alone on the bus.

Tasha was back from work and had already started supper when he reached home. "Well?" she asked. Her mouth dropped open with amazement when she saw him unwrap a bottle of whiskey and set it with a thump in the middle of the table. "Terry, you won?"

"Hell no . . . you can't win at this game . . . I been reading ads in the paper. Taximen make good money. I'm cured that's all. They are advertising for hackdrivers in Duquesne."

Tasha in her apron stood staring at him with round eyes from in front of the stove. Billy and Natalie holding on to her skirts made big round eyes from either side of her.

"Don't worry," said Terry as he worked the cork out of the bottle. "Daddy ain't crazy . . . Daddy's cured. Daddy's going to make money driving a hack."

He brought out of his pocket a little Japanese doll for

Natalie and a clockwork pig he'd bought for Billy at the Five and Ten. Right away the kids were absorbed in their toys.

"While I was feeding lunch to that lawyer who didn't do a goddam thing except kid me along," he told Tasha, "I decided I'd spend the rest of my ten dollars in a way that would give us pleasure."

Terry grabbed Tasha and kissed her hard on the mouth. Then he poured a drink for each of them. "No more inspecting tools for you young woman. Coming home on the bus I kept thinking of all the things I could do if I just quit serving my fellow man. What a thing to call a man, a goddam grievant." He banged his fist down on the corner of the kitchen table, so that the tumblers rang and a little liquor spilled out on the oilcloth. "A man's folks come first, now don't they Tasha? I'm going to make us some real folding money. . . . Driving a hack a man's on his own."

Documentary (20)

. . . Create a stream of electrons, focus them into a sharp pencil, and write or draw with it. Great Zeus. There is an idea worth noting in the history of man's climb upward from the slime. Whither it will lead tomorrow can only be guessed at. Today there are contracts to be fulfilled (and possibly money to be made) by finding a lens to image some smart writing from a cathode ray tube . . .

A lens? It so happens you have come to the right place you there with the black boxes. . . .

ELECTRICAL POWER FOR A YEAR IN SPACE

ECONOMY SHOWS FEW SIGNS OF WEAKNESS

Significantly these deviations involve the organism's response to stress and they show up most in the diverse aspects of that response. In a standard behavioral test, for example, the animal is placed in the unfamiliar but otherwise neutral surroundings of a transparent plastic box. The nonmanipulated animals crouch in the corner of the box. Animals that have

been handled and subjected to stress in early infancy freely
explore the space.

BAR HARBOR INTRODUCES THE FIFTH FREEDOM

*electronic devices useful for computer memory storage are
being developed exceedingly small. So small several million
will fit within a square centimeter. Computers are rivalling
the human brain in action, rivalling the bird brain in size*

Questmanship

if you are a seeker or a solver write the Director of
Scientific and Professional Employment

Casualty

One February day in 1953 Robert Marion La Follette Jr. walked into the study of his Washington home and
shot himself through the head. Though people still spoke of
him as young Bob he was fiftyeight years old.

It was a great and famous name. *Life* carried pictures of
his funeral in Madison, matched with photographs of his
father's funeral a quarter of a century before.

His friends spoke of illhealth, six weeks in hospital with
an ailing heart (his father died of heart failure), acute physical suffering, depression. No one could understand why this
man, able, industrious, highly regarded, should take his own
life.

The opinionmakers soon forgot him. They were too busy
pumping up their monstrous image of his successor to pay
much attention to the disappearance of a faithful servant of
the republic.

When young La Follette was elected to complete his
dead father's term in 1925 he was the youngest man to sit in
the Senate since Henry Clay. Justice Brandeis was heard to
remark that since the days of the Roman republic no boys
had enjoyed the training in statesmanship of old Fighting
Bob's sons.

Young Bob had been his father's daily companion from the time he was a blue-eyed toddler with golden curls. He was only six when his father was elected governor and the family moved into the executive mansion at Madison, Wisconsin.

From that day on the lives of the La Follette family either in town or at their farm across the lake

were an open book

for the farmers and artisans and small business men and the lawyers and teachers training at the state university

to read daily.

Born in a sure enough log house, of pioneer bible-reading stock, the elder La Follette had given up the plow and the harrow and woodchopping and milking and the lamp-lit farm chores

to study law. As a politician he had dedicated his life to the proposition that the voice of the people,

the still small voice of everyman's conscience that needed only awakening,

was the voice of God. In religion he was like Roger Williams, a Seeker. Politics and the polls were sacred rites, self-government his sacrament. *Vox populi vox dei.*

In the early days Fighting Bob would campaign from a spring wagon urging the people who did the work and produced the goods to take government

out of the lightfingered and itching palms

of agents of the vested interests.

Young Bob went along when he drove through sandbeds and muddy wallows in his first automobile from town to town to barnstorm the state for a second term. The mother, who was the first woman graduate of the University of Wisconsin Law School, made speeches, answered letters, prepared articles. Politics for the La Follettes was a family affair.

When young Bob was ten the family moved again, to Washington this time. Dad was in the United States Senate. After this the beloved farm on Lake Mendota where the boys raised ponies was merely a summer home. The elder La Follette had to spend most of the months when the Senate was in recess on the Chautauqua circuit telling the home folks about sorry deals put through on Capitol Hill.

He was the insurgent, out to remake the Republican party
into a party of the plain people.

The children went through the Washington public schools.
When young Bob was thirteen the Wisconsin delegation
adopted La Follette as their favorite son at the Chicago convention. Young Bob was carried around the hall on a tall man's
back. Out of school hours he was often found in the Senate
gallery. Once he went running to call his father on the phone
when Senator Aldrich (a malefactor of great wealth) suddenly sprang a Wall Street amendment to strike out a favorite
provision of his father's in a currency bill. Old Bob's war with
entrenched riches had almost reached the stage of personal
combat. He was an armored knight standing watch on the
floor of the Senate over the interests of the plain people.

Young Bob grew into a darkbrowed seriousfaced
youth with black hair parted in the middle and a great gift
of mimicry; he could make a group of people laugh till their
sides hurt. The state university was the elder Bob's pride and
joy; as a freshman young Bob found himself elected president
of his class.

"You have inherent strength and will not lose your head in
victory," his father wrote him exultantly about that time, "nor
be weak of heart if you are defeated. A game man is a good
winner and a good loser."

Young Bob's college years were hard years for the
La Follettes. Their insurgent friends were defeated in the
state elections. *La Follette's Magazine* which his father and
mother edited together was in financial straits. The family
farm and orchards had to be mortgaged to keep the magazine
going as a monthly. Young Bob wasn't doing too well with
his courses at the university. Too much easy living, perhaps.
His father who had worked his way through, sawing his own
wood and milking his own cow, kept writing to buck him up:
"I am bound you shall be a winner on your own mettle" . . .
"You will start life as a man, Bobbie, standing on my
shoulders."

The summer after young Bob's sophomore year his father
was taken ill. He was a game man who lived on his nerve,
always overworked, overdriven, lashing himself to always

greater effort. Since the mother and older sister were off on lecture tours, spreading the gospel of child labor laws, the eight hour day, workman's compensation, votes for women, it fell to young Bob to spend the summer in their house out Sixteenth Street nursing his father.

A year later the tables were turned. Young Bob suffered an illness resulting from a streptococcic throat infection that nearly killed him and terminated his college career. His father nursed him and, so one doctor said, by sheer willpower kept him alive. He was well enough to alternate with his younger brother Phil in driving his father's car during the campaign for reelection in 1916. The following year he became his father's secretary.

Young Bob La Follette came out of his many months of illness a mature coolheaded young man, a careful reader, a meticulous dresser. There was still a pokerfaced trace of the old drollery. He was a small man with his father's build. He had his father's gift for hard work and an ability to array facts and documents and statistics which was quite his own. Like his father he saw with his own eyes, listened with his own ears, spoke with his own voice.

During the years of struggle against Woodrow Wilson's wartime policies father and son became an inseparable team. Old Bob was a passionate man. Once he was convinced of the righteousness of his views there was no limit to his violence. During his fight against the Armed Ship Bill young Bob kept sending his father little notes telling him not to belabor his colleagues too hard, not to look so cross, to smile now and then.

By the time war was declared the feeling was so violent against Senator La Follette that hardly a senator would speak to him. His name was a scorn and a hissing in the press. There were threats of lifting his senatorial immunity so that he could be arrested for sedition. A vote of censure was attempted. There was talk of expelling him from the Senate, impeaching him for treason. He was the most hated man in America.

Woodrow Wilson spoke with fury of "a little group of willful men representing no opinion but their own."

He was expelled from clubs. Efforts were made to ruin him

financially. He had trouble renewing the mortgage on his farm.

Even the state university turned against the La Follettes. Young Bob took sick. The streptococcic infection returned. He went to bed with a high fever that no medical attention seemed to alleviate. His father was a game man. He dropped everything to nurse young Bob, borrowed money to send him to Hot Springs and then out to the Pacific Coast.

Young Bob was on his feet again in time for the 1920 campaign. Disillusionment had quieted the passions of wartime. The revulsion against Senator La Follette turned to a reluctant admiration. He scored a large vote in the presidential primary in Wisconsin.

The Wisconsin Idea was on the march again. Fighting Bob was a game man. His heart was set on a final fling for the presidency. In 1924 young Bob handled his father's campaign for nomination at the convention which selected Calvin Coolidge. Again he represented his father at the Cleveland Conference which nominated him as Progressive Republican candidate for the presidency.

Fighting Bob was seventy years old. His doctor didn't like the way his heart sounded, told him a presidential campaign would probably kill him. He was a game man. With very little money to back him against Coolidge and John W. Davis he barnstormed the country with the old insurgent rallying cries. Young Bob was always at his side. He scored more than four million votes but by the next summer he was dead.

It was inevitable that young Bob should step into his father's shoes. Where his father had been violent and oratorical (he'd wanted to be an actor in his youth) young Bob was quiet and methodical. As much as any man in Congress he was responsible for the legislative achievement for which Franklin Roosevelt's New Deal took the credit.

He was a worker. His colleagues respected the accuracy of his documentation. He had a cool knack for the bird's eye view that made him a master of committee work. It wasn't only seniority that made him a moving spirit in the Committees on Foreign Relations, Finance, Manufactures, Education and Labor.

Early in 1928 he tried to induce the Congress to put the

brakes on the runaway stockmarket which he could see was headed for a smash. In 1930 he urged the need for legislation to help the farmers and the unemployed. He was foremost in the struggle for freedom of speech and action for labor unions in industrial disputes. He predicted the 1937 recession; and as stoutly though less vehemently than his father in 1917 opposed the Roosevelt administration's sideways skid into the second worldwide war, which restored prosperity

but at a price.

When secret agreements at Teheran, Yalta, Potsdam portended the loss of the peace young Bob tried to remind the Senate

and the American people of the tragic results of the Peace of Versailles twentyfive years before.

He told the Senate in the early summer of 1945

". . . We have not mastered the lessons of the past. Thus far we have been traveling along a road which, step by step, parallels the tragic road we took after the First World War. . . . Virtually every compromise that has been made on behalf of the American government has been made at the expense of the very principles to which we have committed ourselves before the world. . . ."

He was one of the first to recognize the new alignments which had taken hold of American politics:

"It has become virtually impossible to criticize the activities of at least one of our allies—Soviet Russia—however constructively, without bringing down about one's head a storm of smearing vilification and misrepresentation by a tightly organized minority in the United States."

He was one of the first to recognize the new language of totalitarian propaganda:

"The way in which the Communists twist the meaning of words from their common usage in truly democratic countries . . . makes it very difficult to reach an under-

standing with them . . . and gives their propaganda a
tremendous advantage. . . ."

He tried to make men understand
that he wanted international peace as much as anybody:

"I am offering constructive criticisms of the proposed
world organization because I do not believe that it is in
its present form sufficiently practical. All that I am asking, Mr. President, is that it be made practical enough
to work. . . ."

—but that he feared the United Nations as it was being set
up at San Francisco would, like the League of Nations before
it, encourage aggressions against "the kind of freedom we
have here" rather than forbid them.

"Let us join with the other nations to preserve peace
but let us never give our consent or support to any extension of slavery, great power domination, or imperialism."

Young Bob spoke to deaf ears.

    The La Follettes had seemed surely a Wisconsin
dynasty. Bob's younger brother Phil had served three terms
as governor. His scheme in 1934 to revive the old insurgents
as a Progressive party hardly left the drafting board. All the
words had changed their meanings.

His brother's failures weren't much help. Young Bob's re-
election to the Senate in 1940 had hard sledding against the
charismatic pull of Roosevelt democracy.

In 1946 he was defeated in the Republican primaries by
loudmouthed young Joe McCarthy who was helped at the
polls by Communist-influenced labor union men who weren't
going to vote for any old reactionary
    who impugned the motives
of the Union of Socialist Soviet Republics. (If Young Bob
had lived a few years longer he would have seen his successor—a simple minded demagogue who thought all you needed
to go big in politics was to uncover the enemy within and to
make the eagle scream—
    hounded to his grave by the same strange alliance, the
same "storm of smearing vilification and misrepresentation"

that had caused the last La Follette to lose his seat in the Senate.)

Young Bob was game. He took his defeat well, with a public statement that no man had a vested interest in any office.

None of the La Follettes had ever been moneymakers. Bob had children to educate, a family to support. An accomplished student of the national economy, he went into business as an economic consultant. A hasbeen in any profession can always make a living as a consultant. He did well by himself. Among his clients were huge concerns like United Fruit and Sears, Roebuck (Franklin Roosevelt used to say he would make a monkey of Communist propaganda

by sending the Russians a Sears, Roebuck catalogue, but it didn't work out that way). Sears, Roebuck made Bob La Follette vice-president in charge of labor relations. Until his illness he worked with Herbert Hoover's foresighted commission which was preparing plans to make a little more rational the crazy illcoordinated conflicting mechanisms of the federal government. It was not money worry or lack of employment that drove him to his death.

In the Senate he used to admonish his colleagues that we lived in times of brutal change. Industrial society was developing in ways unsuspected by the Founding Fathers. Selfgovernment could only be saved by continual foresight, readjustments.

Foresight. Readjustments. It was a time when the American people hadn't the slightest desire to see beyond the ends of their own noses. So long as a man got his handout, who cared? Young Bob had been brought up in statesmanship from a child. He had been raised on heady hopes. Progressivism. Reform. He pined for Capitol Hill. When a man's function in society is gone he sometimes just plain wants to die.

The Senate after his death,
    at the suggestion of Robert Alonso Taft, another man raised up to statesmanship from the cradle who talked honest talk when all the people wanted to hear was guff
    and died frustrate for his pains,
    held a memorial session for young Bob La Follette,

the first the Senate ever held for any man who did not die
a senator. Perhaps
the senators sensed that with him died
something they might wish they had some day.

Documentary (21)

"As soon as any of the members are discovered to be
anti-sympathetic to the regime they are squeezed out of
the profession by way of blacklisting, intimidation, or
other means of preventing them from working."

BEAUTY LIFT WILL BUOY WEARY EGO

*the study of vibrations in crystalline substances has shown
that objects like marble statues contain thermal sound in
hyper-harmonic patterns; the lower tones are determined by
the shape of the statue. There are similar dynamic forms in
atoms, so that all of nature and art basically share a common
morphology of consonant form and a common pattern of
communication*

MEMORY PROCESS YIELDING SECRETS

Woman Fights for Life with Child's Kidney

Royally beautiful former Queen Soraya of Iran
arrived in Genoa tonight en route to the United
States saying she feels "that life starts anew for me
today." Soraya talked between bites from a salami
sandwich, which she washed down with synthetic
orange juice from a bottle.

AVAILABLE OFF SHELF

Elements Described As Born in Nuclear Caldrons of Stars

There are splendid assortments of herring in
sauces such as Madeira, Port or vinegar and spices.

There are anchovy sprats, fish balls, fish dumplings, fish puddings and jellied eel.

The cheese division is filled with Danish blue, Norwegian nokkelost, Swedish and French varieties. The bread section offers Westphalian pumpernickel in plastic, and the famed crisp breads in assorted weights.

Don't Be a Dishwasher, Buy One

VOTE FOR QUALITY

The 33-year-old English professor told Congressional investigators he had deceived his family, his lawyer and the friends he had made through television by concealing his deep involvement in a fixed nationally televised quiz show.

He told of coming to the conclusion only recently that "the truth is the only thing with which a man can live."

He recited in detail how he had been given questions and answers in advance and coached on how to act in his fourteen appearances on the defunct quiz program "Twenty-one."

He testified he had been guaranteed specific amounts of money, starting at $1,000, and how an arrangement had been made for him to lose in a "dramatic manner" after he had won $129,000.

SHORT CUTS TO EXECUTIVE SKILLS

"I read your article in the paper," a railroad worker wrote Senator McClellan, "in which you state that the members can do a lot to clean up a union if they stand up for their rights. Now there are about fifty men in our town who did just that and now we are walking the streets looking for jobs."

Sample "Memory Trainer" Kit Only 10¢

LEARN BY DOING

Mr. Derounian—I am happy that you made the statement, but I cannot agree with most of my colleagues who have commended you for telling the truth, because I don't think an adult of your intelligence ought to be commended for telling the truth. . . . Do you recall a statement: "I have not in fact been avoiding any subpoena. In fact, I would not know how to either serve or avoid a subpoena. I just wouldn't know how to go about it"? Do you recall that statement?

A.—Yes, I do.

Q.—Do you know now how to avoid a subpoena?

A.—Not really, sir.

Q.—You did not know that you were sought after?

A.—I didn't know that I was subpoenaed, sir.

Q.—I quote again: "It was not until Monday night that I learned of the committee's desire to hear me. By prearrangement between the committee and my counsel I have made myself available to a representative of the committee and within the hour accepted a subpoena for Nov. 2." Do you recall that statement? A.—Yes, sir.

Q.—Was that a true statement? A.—I meant by it that I didn't know that the committee issued a subpoena.

Q.—You said it was not until Monday night that you learned of the committee's desire to hear you. But you received Mr. Harris' telegram? A.—Yes, sir.

Q.—So that is not a correct statement? A.—Yes, sir, that is correct.

Q.—You deceived the press of the country on the 14th of October when you made that statement? A.—All right; yes, sir.

Effect on Children

Q.—At the time you were considering going on this program in order to "do a great service to the intellectual life, to teachers and to education" in general, were you thinking at all about the effect of your appearance on the children of this country? A.—Yes, sir, I was.

Q.—Did you think that your performances, as they have come out now, would be a good thing for the children of the country to know about in their respect for education? A.—No, sir, I did not.

Q.—You knew at that time?

A.—No, I didn't. Excuse me, I'm sorry. I misunderstood you.

Q.—You did not realize at that time the bad effect this would have on the children of the country? A.—Unfortunately I did not.

Q.—Boiled down to the essentials, your statement to me indicates that what you did you did for money. Do you agree? A.—I am sorry, but that was not the only reason. Of course, that was the reason.

Where in the world are there alligators in the sewers?

Prime Mover (*concluded*)

The raw April day of Mr. Allardyce's funeral Jasper drove out alone in Harriet's Buick to All Souls' Episcopal Church. He had arrived from Atlanta with a suitcase and a change of clothes only an hour before. It was eight months since he'd seen Harriet. She hadn't suggested he go up to his old room to change but instead made him use the guests' washroom off the front hall.

Though Harriet came down all dressed for the occasion at the last minute she decided not to go.

"Jap I'd feel like a hypocrite," she said, "if we went out there together."

Jasper didn't try to argue. He just asked her humbly whether she minded if he drove her car; it would look kind of funny for him to turn up in a taxi. "Why Jap of course, take it. Keep it all day if you like."

The twodoor coupé upholstered in pale blue had an intimate smell that filled him with recollections of Harriet, a flavor of Melachrinos and benzedrine inhalers and of that Chanel perfume she used. The recollections hurt. Her cigarettes and a crumpledup handkerchief with a torn lace edging reproached him dumbly from the dashboard. It was almost as if she were sitting there beside him.

Driving out the familiar street of ample stone and stucco residences set in lawns pockmarked with rotting snow, he kept up a conversation with Harriet in his mind: Tell me why did it have to frazzle out like that? Do you know? Honest I don't. Maybe we never were in love, I mean crazy, like kid love, like I had been that once before that made you so mad when I told you about it. But we had good times together when the girls were little, Christmas and Halloween, camping trips in summer, the hospitable Millirons entertaining at home. We had fun in bed, you know we did. We turned out a pair of daughters who are perfect dandies. What more could you want?

What could have gone on in that woman's head? They were so thoroughly estranged, Jasper was telling himself, they didn't even row any more. She had cleaned him out of the house. There wasn't much trace left of the girls either. Maybe she liked it that way, empty and lifeless. It left him feeling like a homeless dog. If it had been his funeral instead of Mr. Allardyce's Harriet would have gone quick as a shot, said a sarcastic voice inside his ear. A good riddance. Jasper came so near saying the words aloud he felt a sour grin appearing on his face. Come on now.

The streets around the church were obstructed for blocks with wellpolished latemodel cars. He felt so depressed he had half a mind to drive right on by and not go to the funeral at all. After circling about for some time an undertaker's man in earpads beckoned him into an area reserved for the pall-bearers behind the church.

Jasper stepped out into a pile of slush. Coming home out of springtime in Atlanta he'd forgotten about rubbers. The snow water sloshing in his shoes made him feel more hangdog than ever as he slunk through a side door into the vestry where the pallbearers were assembling.

Jim Swazey and Dave Griswold were there ahead of him, looking like undertakers' men themselves in their black morning coats. Jasper had expected Dave's greeting to be somewhat less than cordial, but it surprised him when Jim didn't meet his eye.

Jim's face had a puffy look. The freckles stood out startlingly against the lardy white skin. Jasper grabbed his hand and squeezed it. "Hello feller," he said. Jim's hand dropped limp from his.

Jim started muttering something about why couldn't they have buried the boss up on the rimrock at the head of some canyon out West in the country he loved. The words somehow didn't hit Jasper right. Sounded like Jim had read them in a book. It was a relief when Dave Griswold shushed the two of them down with one of his disapproving looks.

The other pallbearers were filing in. Rhodora's husband, Bert Hiner, a sourfaced two hundredpounder, looked as if he had just stepped in something that smelt bad. Abe Merman, with that excuse me expression that always got on Jasper's nerves, seemed to be apologizing for something he hadn't done.

The trouble was Parker. Jasper hadn't listened at first to what Abe was whispering to him but as soon as he saw Parker's black face over a gray stock set in an oldfashioned frock coat, undoubtedly a cast-off of Mr. Allardyce's years ago, he caught on. Mr. Allardyce had left instructions that Parker, his "best friend for thirty years," was to be one of his pallbearers.

Parker was in his element. Never for an instant did he overstep the bounds. He greeted each of them with a respectful little speech that made Jasper think that Parker must have been a preacher in his spare time all along. "It's the proudest day of ma life Colonel, an' the saddest," Parker said when he came around to Jasper. "You an' me, Colonel we always knowed that under that roughtalkin' faultfindin' man there was Jesus Christ hisself."

Shaking hands with old Parker somehow made Jasper feel more himself again. It was hard to keep from grinning. Even dead Mr. Allardyce had some tricks left in him, the old scoundrel. Jasper began to look forward to the reading of the will.

Morton P. Perkins of the Associated Morticians was lifting a blackgloved hand. Silverhaired, pinkfaced, in bankers' broadcloth, he was melodiously instructing the pallbearers on their positions during the ceremony.

The ceremony reeled off at top speed. Jasper couldn't get himself to pay attention. The minister intoned the funeral service so liturgically that Jasper couldn't make out the words. It was all a droning in his ears. There was something sickening about the smell of the flowers. He kept his eyes down and the muscles of his face locked stiff. He did just what Mr.

Perkins had said to do. He sat down and got to his feet and bowed his head in imitation prayer in time with the others. Everything alive in him was scrunched up inside this tailor's dummy in a morning coat. Maybe he was getting a heart attack. "Funny if I dropped dead."

After the burial, walking away from the grave along the path cut through the thawing snowbanks of the cemetery, he found himself next to Sylvia.

"It was like him to name Parker," he whispered, grinning.

She nodded into his face with a quick appreciative batting of the eyelashes. They fell into step. For a moment they were enough out of earshot of the others so that he could hazard a rapid question. "What's wrong with Jim?"

Sylvia was just parting her lips to answer when Jim himself came bustling up grumbling about how he must hurry if he wasn't to catch his death of cold. Without looking at Jasper he put his arm through Sylvia's and hustled her away. In a sudden fit of anger Jasper jostled out of the crowd of mourners and strode off across lots towards the ranked cars with his chin buried in his overcoat. The slush packed into his low shoes as he walked.

When he reached the parking lot he found he'd forgotten what Harriet's car looked like. That showed how long he'd been away. He was searching along the row of gleaming hoods when he almost ran head on into a woman in a Persian lamb coat. She had light hair and blue eyes. She was crying like a child. It was that Mrs. Hubbard, Lorna Hubbard of the Suzy Standish hour. At the same moment he caught sight of Harriet's handkerchief and Melachrinos on the dashboard of a blue Buick.

"Suppose I give you a lift," he said to Mrs. Hubbard.

"Thanks." She turned her tearstained face up to his. "I drove out with the Bartletts but I can't let them see me blubbering like this."

Before the first straggle of people coming back from the grave reached the edge of the parking lot, Jasper was turning Harriet's smoothrunning Buick into the winding cemetery road.

"You're acting just the way I feel," Jasper said. "Go ahead and bawl. It's a relief. I loved the old man."

She was sniffling now. "He was a very wonderful person." She blew her nose. "I hardly knew him."

"I knew him very well. He did everything in the world for me . . . ever since I was kneehigh to a grasshopper. . . . God it's a relief to talk to somebody who is acting human."

Where the road from the cemetery turned past a mess of fillingstations into the fourlane highway there was a kind of a roadhouse called Robinson Crusoe's Jasper had known in the old days. He acted on a sudden impulse. Just sitting next to this woman made him feel better. "Mrs. Hubbard," he said suddenly giving her a popeyed boyish look he used to know so well how to put on, "would you think it absolutely amiss if we stopped off for a drink? It's been a horrible day."

She answered with her straight from the shoulder smile. "I could go to the ladies' room and get this teary smeary effect off my face."

"And besides my feet are wet," he said as he opened the car door for her.

"Doctor's prescription," she sang out cheerfully. Jasper watched her as she walked off down the pine corridor. He liked the way she moved her hips.

The place was absolutely empty. He picked a table with a checked tablecloth next to a radiator where he could toast his feet. He had to fetch a solitary waiter from the back of the room to order double bourbons and a couple of club sandwiches.

"That's my wife's car I'm driving," he told Lorna Hubbard flatfootedly as soon as she came back. "One of the pleasant features of this visit to my old home in the Twin Cities is to get our lawyer to arrange to turn a separation into a divorce . . . We'd have done it before if it hadn't been for the girls. Now even they admit there's nothing else to do."

The way she looked at him showed that she understood. "You too," was all she said.

"Any children?" he asked.

"No, but lots of dependents." She smiled brightly when she said that. "You know, sisters and cousins whom they reckon by the dozens. . . . Wait till you meet Stan, the demon nephew."

They were both laughing now. When the waiter brought the sandwiches Jasper ordered two more bourbons. That woman's faint gardenia fragrance filled him with warmth.

"Eat something," he said. "I'm going to. Mind if I call you Lorna?"

"Your friends call you Jap?"

"Right."

Lorna didn't pull her hand away when Jasper leaned across the checked tablecloth to give it a pat. "Mind if I talk, Lorna?" She shook her head and opened her eyes wide.

The worst thing about this estrangement with his wife, he began, was not having a woman to talk to. The girls did their best, they sympathized with their old man though they loved their mother too, but that wasn't the same. He needed somebody nearer his own age. He'd always had a woman to talk to, ever since he'd tried to do a man's work as a kid after Dad walked out on them.

He and his mother had talked about every damn thing. His mother had been a schoolteacher and had been very ambitious for him. She was an outdoor woman too. They'd wrangled cattle together and in summer and hunting season they had tried to make both ends meet by wrangling dudes. That was how he first met Mr. Allardyce when he came out to hunt elk. Did Lorna know the Big Horn Mountains?

He knew he was slipping into a talking jag, but she would damn well have to put up with it. He talked on and on about his mother's ranch and the price of cattle going down and down and interest payments and amortization of the mortgage. The bank ended by taking over.

He reckoned he would have remained a cowhand to this day if it hadn't been for Mr. Allardyce and going East with Georgie Warner and meeting that Julie Harrington. That was one time he lost the gift of gab. He never could open his mouth when she was around, she just had everything, looks, attractiveness, brains. Her old man was a scholar.

All at once Jasper found he couldn't talk any more. It was like slipping down some deep well inside him into the azure of that summer by the lake: the way she laughed, the way she turned everything into a game. He was remembering the smell of wild strawberries. For a flash of a second he could see her face, the greenblue eyes under the tossing reddish hair, her throat and slenderness and then his head was full of swirling darkness again.

". . . Say what you like," he heard himself insisting to Lorna in a rasping voice, "war is a great educator."

He caught a puzzled look on Lorna's face.

"If I'd only taken advantage of my opportunities . . . Believe it or not"—he smiled at her—"I was a likely lad in those days."

"But you can't sit up there and tell me, Mr. Vice-President of Abington Products for the Southeastern Division"—Lorna was kidding him—"that your life has been exactly a failure."

"If I can make a go of Lorillard's new flour mill then maybe I can say I've done something."

Lorna's eyes started twinkling. "Why right now"—her voice rose—"if I was your mother sitting up there in heaven I'd be proud as hell of my boy Jasper."

They got to laughing some more. Their knees touched now and then under the table. They were warm with the bourbon.

Jasper felt happy at having somebody to laugh with. He was clicking with Lorna. By God it made him happy. He felt he had his muscle tone again. He was ready to get on with his business.

He thrust his wrist out of his coatsleeve. Three fifteen.

"Miss Lorna," he said, "talking to you sure does make time fly."

As he got her into her coat he breathed in that gardenia fragrance again. There were lovely little blond wavy hairs at the nape of her neck. He explained gruffly that he had to be at that lawyer's office at four; reading of the will, the embattled family assembled. That was the Allardyces' lawyer. Then he had to see his own lawyer. Then he'd be free.

As he drove her back into town he talked fast and feverishly about how they had to snatch some time alone together, a good long time: why couldn't they give everybody the slip and just happen to be on the same train to Chicago? It was going to be bad weather for flying. He'd make the reservations.

She looked serious. She frowned a little. Her only answer was a nod of the head. "The John Bunyan Hotel," she whispered, "room 1604 . . . I'll wait till you call."

They spotted an empty cab. He drew up to the curb and watched her step briskly in and drive away. As he put the car in gear again he noticed her narrow black leather pocketbook on the seat beside him. She'd forgotten her pocketbook. A good luck sign, he told himself as he slipped it happily into his inside pocket.

When he stopped by his old home to leave Harriet her car and pick up his suitcase, Harriet gave him a sharp appraising look and asked him what had happened at the funeral to make him feel so good, he didn't have the face of a man coming from the funeral of his best friend. "Oh I know," she said cattily before he could answer. "It's being an executor of the Allardyce estate."

"How come?"

"Little birds tell me all sorts of things," said Harriet with a toss of her head. "You'll sure know how to take advantage of that job."

It was worse than cattiness, there was real disgust in her voice. She thinks money's all I think about, he told himself. Well she's goddam wrong.

From his hotel he called the John Bunyan to leave word that Mrs. Hubbard's lost pocketbook had been found and that he would bring it over himself presently. He changed clothes like winking. Having charge of Lorna Hubbard's pocketbook made him feel strong enough to meet the devil himself.

Going up in the elevator to Thurmond Anderson's office in the Legal Aid Building he could feel its slender shape right against his heart in his inside pocket. He knew he was in for a tough session. He was looking forward to it. As he walked into the conference room, he locked his face into the funeral expression.

The heirs and assigns looked as full of confusion as a hen-yard when there's a hawk in the sky. Mrs. Allardyce in black, swathed in her antique crape veil, was dabbing at red eyes with a wadded handkerchief. Rhodora's plump face was all wrinkled up. Even Sylvia looked flustered. Their husbands were just this side of a fit. Bert Hiner kept wiping the sweat off his face. Jim Swazey was biting his nails like a schoolboy.

There were cousins and nephews Jasper had never seen, accompanied by a sprinkling of outoftown attorneys. Abington was represented by longnecked Eric Rasmussen, with the intense black eyes and the shiny black curl over his forehead, who had just moved up to vice-president in charge of legal affairs. Rustyhaired Thurmond Anderson, looking hooknosed and lofty as if he already had the federal judgeship he was angling for, presided at the head of the conference table.

Dave Griswold occupied the other end of the long expanse of mahogany. He sat square and silent as a roadblock. His colorless hair was plastered smooth to his head. His round face was blank. Maybe the large upperlip was clamped a little tighter than usual over the straight mouth. He recognized Jasper's presence by a slight tightening of the lids over the bland gray eyes. One hand was busy doodling with a pencil on the sheet of paper before him.

A slender underling was distributing copies of the will. When the rustling of papers subsided Thurmond Anderson started reading in an easy conversational tone. His voice seemed to dwell with some pleasure on an occasional phrase he had made up himself. Now and then he paused and took off his tortoiseshell glasses to glance around the ring of tense faces, and remarked that Mr. Allardyce had insisted on retaining his own words in such and such a sentence.

Jasper, letting himself slump a little in his chair to keep out of the line of sight, watched Dave Griswold's face from behind Rasmussen's massive adamsapple. Dave looked relaxed as a cat on the hearth while the lawyer's voice dwelt pleasantly on the five and ten thousand dollar bequests: to Parker and the cook and the laundress and the Italian gardener at Palm Beach and to the skipper of the motor sailer the Allardyces kept at Bar Harbor; to various churches; to a mission to the Seminoles in Dade County, Florida; to a couple of colleges and the Audubon Society and the Save the Redwoods Foundation and the Wildlife Conservation League and the American Indian Fund.

The real estate in Florida and Minnesota and a list of blue-ribbon stocks and bonds that added up to a couple of millions went to Mrs. Allardyce in lifetime tenure and then was to be divided in equal parts among the grandchildren. The Bar Harbor estate went to the Hiners, the Wyoming ranch and a quailhunting farm in southern Georgia to the Swazeys.

So far so good. Dave Griswold's face neither approved nor disapproved.

It wasn't until Anderson reached the words Riverside Corporation that Dave's jaws tightened and his eyes narrowed. If Jasper hadn't known him for twenty years, he wouldn't have noticed. Jasper couldn't help a catch of his own breath.

All his life the words Riverside Corporation had had an awesome sound to him. This was the holding company through which the Abington family had controlled the old milling business, and with it a large part of the State of Minnesota, until Mr. Allardyce bought it out from under them at a bargain during the panicky days of the Great Depression. Nobody sitting around that table needed to be told that the Riverside Corporation owned a controlling interest in every Abington company.

Dave Griswold was a doodler but he wasn't doodling now. He was grasping the end of the table with his short fingers. Bert Hiner was breathing heavily. Jim Swazey was jiggling in his chair like a small boy who wanted to go to the bathroom.

Don't give a damn, Jasper was telling himself. The way to lick 'em is not to give a damn. He was remembering that eighteen hundred and fifty dollars was reputed to be the over-the-counter price of a single share.

"My stock in the Riverside Corporation to the number of 8500 shares . . ."

Glancing around the room Jasper noted an abstracted look on every face. Every man and woman there was busy multiplying eighteen hundred and fifty by eightyfive. Bert Hiner was holding his breath now. Jim Swazey was staring up as if he were trying to read the answer off the ceiling. One of the cousins, a mousefaced little man in brown tweeds, was working it out with pad and pencil to the satisfaction of his redfaced fat wife. Fifteen million dollars, thought Jasper as he watched the tense set of Dave's rounded jaw, and more.

". . . I do devise and bequeath to the Allardyce Foundation, a charitable educational nonprofit corporation to be set up under the laws of the State of Minnesota with particular reference to exemption from Federal income tax as prescribed in section 501 the Internal Revenue Code."

Dave was doodling with quiet deliberation. Must have known it all along.

Thurmond Anderson had pulled off his eyeglasses and was looking around the room with the sickish smile of a man who has just set off the fuse on a charge of dynamite and doesn't know how big the explosion will be.

"I'll be goddamned," Jim Swazey began. Sylvia grabbed his arm and that was all he said.

"Since the language of paragraph 2 under heading 19 is extremely technical a few explanations may be in order"— Thurmond Anderson addressed his audience in a voice full of healing balm. "Mr. Allardyce's aim, of course, was to preserve the bulk of his fortune intact in the form of a Rockefeller-type foundation which would be dedicated to scientific research in the processing, production and use—the terms of the bequest are very broad—of the food grains and their by-products; this would include the training of students, scientists, farmers, researchers, millers; the investigation of new products, new processes, experimentation with new techniques etc. etc." Thurmond Anderson's voice thrilled with modest pride. "The wording of these paragraphs, the result of a meeting of minds between Mr. Allardyce and myself and two or three of the most eminent taxlawyers in the country, is as foolproof as human ingenuity can make it."

The room was full of rustle of papers as people turned to heading 19. Feet shuffled. The nephews and cousins from out of town let out a faint hissing as they whispered to their attorneys. Anderson's voice droned on.

Jasper listened to the long involved paragraphs without paying attention. He was waiting to hear what Dave had to say. Dave Griswold went on doodling.

Thurmond Anderson was reading a longwinded paragraph from which Jasper gathered that the board of trustees for the foundation was to be appointed by the executors of the will, according to the provisions hereinbefore set down in paragraph 4 under heading 19 "new members annually . . . for five years . . . rotating tenure . . . board self-perpetuating . . ."

Jasper snapped open the hunting case of his grandfather's big gold watch, which had been the only thing in the world his mother had to leave him when she died: 6:45. He snapped the case to. Why won't the executors run the works? he asked himself.

The big bang came with the reading of their names, alphabetically, Thurmond Anderson explained with downcast eyes as he read his own name first. He followed with the names of H. Courtney Cooper, Abraham Emil Merman, Jasper Milliron, James Jenkins Swazey. That was the lot.

Sparks flew from eye to eye. A hum went around the table. Dave Griswold's face had that balky mule expression Jasper liked to mimic.

"Thurmond," he asked in a voice that was almost too unconcerned, "just to refresh my memory when were those final provisions drawn up?"

"The final draft was okayed about two weeks before Mr. Allardyce's death. It was signed the afternoon of the same day. You were one of the witnesses to his signature, Dave. You remember Parker drove us all out in the old Rolls. Coming back you remarked on how well the boss had retained his faculties . . . 'clear as a bell' was the phrase you used."

"Of course. Of course."

Everybody was on his feet. The nephews and cousins and their attorneys were emitting various sounds of dismay. Sylvia and Rhodora each had an arm around their mother's waist as they escorted her towards the door. Mrs. Allardyce was explaining to anybody that would listen that she'd known all the time it was going to be a foundation. She thought it was wonderful of him to devote his fortune to the public good. The daughters chimed in that they were perfectly satisfied.

"But how the hell," Bert Hiner was asking Jim Swazey, "am I going to support that place at Bar Harbor with my salary from the Bankers Trust?"

As soon as Jasper had arranged with Thurmond for a meeting of executors the following morning, he slipped out the door and across the street to the Hiawatha Building where he found his own lawyer, Theo Murcheson, a lanky sallow man with untidy hair, impatiently pacing up and down in front of the receptionist's desk in the lobby of the empty offices of his firm. "What the hell took so long, Jap? It's almost seven o'clock."

Jasper burst out laughing. "I wish I'd taken you over there Theo, only I didn't want to seem that interested. . . . The boss sure fixed the palace guard. The cream of the jest was he had Dave go out and witness the will and then he left him off the list of executors. . . . I felt right sorry for him."

He handed the bluejacketed bundle of sheets over to Theo. "Read title nineteen."

Theo's brown eyes ran hurriedly through the bulky wad of papers.

"Jap," he said, "you ain't been to probate yet. Thurmond Anderson is a pompous ass. . . . I believe we've got a lawyer's paradise here. You know as well as I do Dave Griswold can line up all the big money in this town behind him."

"But man alive Riverside controls the voting stock." Jasper threw his shoulders back and took a deep breath and slapped his ribs. "Hell all I want Theo is a free hand in my seven state area for five more years and maybe a little foundation money to experiment with."

"And a divorce and a couple of million dollars in Abington stock," said Theo putting his arm around Jasper's shoulder. Then he started rubbing his hands together teasingly: "Any way you look at it, Jap, this Allardyce will is going to put the young Murchesons through college. . . . Let's go eat."

At twelve fortyfive next day Jasper and Lorna Hubbard sat side by side in a drawingroom on the Chicago train as it pulled out of the shabby St. Paul station into a day of rain and sleet. They sat without touching each other looking out the window reading the names off strings of wet freightcars in the marshaling yards. They couldn't seem to find a thing in the world to say to each other.

"A penny for your thoughts," said Lorna after a while.

"My thoughts are let's order up some drinks and some lunch before we get too goddam depressed," Jasper blurted out. "There are times when a feller wishes he'd drop dead and save himself all the trouble." He rang the bell.

"From a professional charmer," Lorna burst out laughing, "that's the worst opening gambit I ever heard."

"I'm a frustrated family man, Lorna. . . ."

"Well maybe I'm a frustrated family woman," she interrupted, looking up at him out of clear blue eyes.

He was just about to throw his arms around her when the waiter came with the bill of fare. They ordered lunch hurriedly without paying too much attention. The main thing was the bourbon.

"You see," said Jasper as soon as the waiter had gone. "I told you we'd need time. My private life has been snarled up in a knot during the last few years. You know call girls and all that. Embarrassing at my age. When I was a young fellow it was so simple . . . no it wasn't. I raised plenty of hell but I never got what I really wanted. Oh hell let's just enjoy ourselves."

The waiter came back with the bourbons and the lunch.

"Here's to good appetite," Lorna said looking at him over the rim of her glass.

"That's something I never lacked," he answered.

He started talking in bunches. She wasn't to get to thinking he wasn't interested in his present job. Abington had been his life. Streamlining the southeastern division, tapping this wonderful new market, setting up new production methods was going to take everything he had in him and more. He had a fight on his hands. He'd never messed in the financial end. Now he had to put his ideas across. Modernize. Decentralize. He'd be bucking the palace guard.

As they sat there eating and drinking on the smoothly swaying train Jasper launched into an account of the Lorillard mill. He tried to make her see what it would look like. "It's the first real innovation in the art of milling," he shouted, "since steel rollers took the place of millstones."

The conductor interrupted to take their tickets. He was a dignified grayhaired man with a clipped gray mustache. "How do you do Mr. Milliron?" he said immediately. "I recognized you from your picture in the morning paper . . . the pallbearers at the Allardyce funeral . . . Too bad, too bad . . . He was one of the great men of the Middle West. . . . And there if I'm not mistaken is the little lady who appears in the Suzy Standish hour."

"It certainly is," said Jasper.

The conductor pumped Lorna's hand. "Wait till I tell my wife I've shaken hands with Suzy Standish. That's one program she never misses. . . . Bet you're busy going over plans for next week's show right now. Don't let me disturb you. . . . If there is anything I can do to make your ride more comfortable please let me know. Proud to have you aboard." He bowed himself out of the compartment.

"There goes our interstate hideaway," said Jasper. "Lorna we're in a goldfish bowl."

They got to laughing about it. "That's why we can't be complicated inside," said Lorna, putting her hand on his, "because, at least until you get your divorce, our lives are going to be so hellishly complicated on the outside. . . . Get what I mean?"

"Am I to take it that you are counting me in?"

"For better or for worse," she said in that downright way she had.

She had opened her handbag and was peering into the little mirror of her vanity to powder her face. The light gardenia fragrance filled his nostrils, ran through his blood, melted all the little hurdles that had sprung up inside him. He pulled her to him. He felt ageless. Her lips were meeting his. Her breasts were soft against his chest. He didn't dare say a word.

By the time they reached Chicago it was as if they had known each other all their lives. They held hands all the way over in the cab from one station to the other.

They had never seen Chicago look so gay they told each other. Electric signs, neon lights, billboards, lettering, faces, eyes had a tinsel sparkle in the chill spring wind. The city was putting on a carnival just for them.

While Jasper was getting their bags checked they agreed that they'd eaten so much lunch they didn't need dinner. "Let's go dancing," suggested Jasper. Lorna jumped up and down like a schoolgirl. Jasper gave the taximan the name of a beer hall. "It's a joint used to be run by an old sergeant of mine in World War One, named Steve something, came from one of those little Balkan countries, mountaineer type. He was on the road to making a million dollars when one of Capone's boys filled him full of lead. I guess he had it coming. A rough diamond I guess you would have called him but he was a great fighting man, one of those guys who was always there when you needed him."

Lorna sat bolt upright beside Jasper in the cab, making big eyes as she listened. She was understanding what he was saying, Jasper was telling himself jubilantly. She knew what he meant before he said it.

He let himself talk: "If I didn't feel so goddam good I wouldn't have wanted to go. Ain't been back for thirty years. It was the hangout of quite a gang of fellers and girls I used to go with . . . the Tribe we used to call ourselves. Most of 'em have been out in the great world really going places and doing things all the time I was sitting in St. Paul selling dogfood and cakemixes."

The cab had stopped in front of a big fake Munich style entrance under an enormous sign BOHEMIAN BEERHALL. "I'll tell you about 'em one of these days," Jasper muttered hurriedly as he handed Lorna out of the cab.

The joint sure had changed. There were white tablecloths and cavernous halls and two bands and dim lights and entertainers moaning into the microphone instead of the accordion and the singing waiters. The beer took a long time to come. It was supposed to be Munich export but it tasted like soap. Jasper sat there feeling crestfallen until Lorna began to talk.

She knew how it used to be, she said, holding his hand firmly from across the table. Men and women weren't as different as all that. It was the way she felt when she first went up to New York from Atlanta to study singing. Stage-struck, the old story. Every night, every time you went out it was going to lead to some marvelous adventure, something comicaler and marvelouser than had ever happened in the world before. Only what she'd done was to marry a heel, a nice guy but a heel. Just because a man could tell the "Rhapsody in Blue" from a Beethoven symphony didn't mean he'd make a good husband.

That made him laugh. She laughed too but her eyes were wet. "Let's dance Jap," she cried.

Her dancing just suited him.

"That's better," she whispered up into his ear after they'd spun around the floor a couple of times, "better than sobbing out your life story. Don't let me get maudlin."

When they sat down at their table again Jasper sent away the beer and ordered bourbon and water. She looked at him over her glass with shining eyes: "Jap under the crowsfeet and the wrinkles we are still those crazy kids . . . under the skin, under the old stale wornout skin. Here's to us, Jap."

He led her out onto the floor again.

They were so busy dancing they almost missed their twelve thirty train. They had to run for it. A couple of porters just managed to pile their bags into the last sleeper while the conductor was calling his final "All aboard." They had a long out of breath tramp up the moving train to find their drawingroom.

After the porter had brought the last bag Jasper locked the door and pulled her to him. Swaying with the slamming and jiggling of the train, they took off each other's clothes. They were still laughing. They hadn't caught their breath yet. Their bodies clung to each other. They tumbled into the lower berth together as if they'd been doing it all their lives.

"I've been called difficult," she whispered. He whispered back with his mouth against her ear. "You know what the Marines used to say . . . the impossible takes a little longer."

When they woke up their sleeper was trundling through the Kentucky hills all green and misted with springtime. Jasper couldn't help whistling while he shaved. "How are you feeling Lorna?" he asked back over his shoulder when he noticed her beginning to stir. "Like a twoyearold," she said, stretching and yawning. "A sleepy twoyearold."

"Lorna I feel like a fighting cock," he spluttered as he

washed the rest of the lather off his face. "That little difference between the sexes . . . Oh God what a difference it makes."

He sat on the edge of the berth and drew her to him and kissed her. "I wish we could have kids."

"It's kinda late for that Jap."

The train had stopped. Her voice sounded lonesome in the sudden silence.

"Honey we'll have a whale of a good time." He kissed her. "I bet we're late."

"Won't make me mad"—Lorna yawned—"if we never get in."

Jasper let himself out into the corridor and followed a draft of wind to the platform. The door was open. Breathing deep of the moist morning air he let himself down onto the cinders. He was standing in a rattletrap station. Behind it was a red rutted road full of puddles from the recent rains. A sprinkling of grimed cabins scattered up the hillside beyond. There was a flavor of coaloil in the blue smoke that drifted down from them. Two hound dogs were picking their way across the road. Somewhere a mockingbird was singing.

Jasper was pulling back his shoulders to take a deep breath when he found himself shaking hands with Abe Merman of all people. Abe's little eyes sparkled. His face was a bouquet of smiles. "Two hours late," Abe announced. "On the train I am happy as a child."

"What's the trouble?"

Abe shrugged his stooped shoulders with a deprecating smile. "Spring fever, perhaps. I shall enjoy the day's vacation."

"I got enough work along," Jasper heard himself saying in a stuffysounding tone, "to keep me busy for a week."

(Now that's a damn lie, said a little voice inside his head.)

Abe was explaining elaborately with that meticulous foreign accent his speech sometimes took on that he wished he could have brought Mrs. Merman along, but Berta had had a touch of pneumonia that winter and he was afraid of the sudden change of climate for her. Jasper winced. (He knows I've got Lorna in that drawingroom.) Abe was rambling on about what a delightful thing it was to go north into winter and then double back into spring. That feeling of spring repeated made him feel he had gained something on time. "Time at our age, Mr. Milliron, is the great enemy." He sighed and then looked up with a sudden smile. "How about breakfast, the pleasantest meal in America?"

Jasper answered brusquely that he'd already ordered breakfast in his room. See him in the club car later. The guards were calling. The train was moving. "Please," said Abe Merman bowing to let Jasper climb aboard first.

When Jasper slid back into the drawingroom he found Lorna dressed and smiling in a fresh crisp pearlcolored suit with a ruffled blouse. "Well," said Jasper, "it's complications, just like you said. Here I step out to breathe God's green April and who do I meet but Abe Merman?"

"I like the Mermans," said Lorna.

"Well I don't," Jasper snapped. "That guy's got eyes all over his head. . . . I don't give a damn what anybody says but right now I'm for playing it close to our chests. . . . Until I have my decree in my hand I don't want everybody and his brother talking about how I'm sleeping with Suzy Standish."

"I'll lay low," said Lorna laughing. "I'll be the invisible woman."

"Might have known there'd be spies on the train," Jasper went on peevishly. . . . "I have the girls to think of. I want them to hear it from me and not some damn gossip column."

"That they've got a stepmother elect," cried Lorna. "Jap you order up a good breakfast and stop fretting."

He popped his eyes at her with a schoolboy grin. "Bossing me already eh?"

With the breakfast tray the porter brought the news that a washout up the line had derailed a couple of gondolas off a freight. They'd proceed on the other track as soon as the northbound local went through. The train had stopped again on a siding in a cut in the hills.

"Well I'm glad they know where it is," said Jasper. "They run hit or miss on this darned road."

There was a distant whistle up the line.

"Even yesterday," whispered Lorna, stroking the back of his hand, "I wouldn't have cared."

The northbound train went clattering past.

"I'll tell you what I'll do," Jasper said as soon as he could make himself heard. "I'll drop off at Chattanooga and check on Lorillard. They are pouring concrete. . . . If I told you how many cubic yards of concrete you wouldn't believe me. . . . Then you can say hello to Abe Merman as if nothing had happened. There's nothing off color about our happening to be on the same train, now is there?" I need to see Lorillard.

They are redesigning the classifying machinery for the flour. Then in the morning I hop over to Atlanta in time to be in my office first thing. Have you got an apartment or something, Lorna?"

She let out a little shriek. "But Jap you don't think I sleep on a bench in the park?"

"I don't care where it is so long as I sleep there too."

"My phone number's in the book. Don't come without phoning, on account of the dependents. And after all we can communicate at the office."

"That's what I want to avoid."

The train started with a jerk that spilled the coffee out of their cups, rumbled along for a while and then stopped again. They finished their breakfast looking out at the turbid red eddies of a swollen creek that was pouring over the dip in the swinging footbridge that led to a little cabin. A yellow cur dog was curled up asleep on the porch. A rifle leaned against the doorjamb next to an old blue crock. Beside the cabin a peachtree was in bloom. Only two black hens were stirring. It was so quiet with the train stalled on a siding they could hear the clamor of the creek as it poured over the little footbridge.

"If we lived there, you and me—" the frown melted off Jasper's face—"we'd be happy as hell. I was raised for that kind of life."

"You'd shoot me a buck in the fall and I'd make apple butter in a big iron kettle in the yard and we'd fish for crappies in the creek."

"No kidding," said Jasper.

"Who said I was kidding?"

After a while he got restless and wandered back into the club car to smoke. Abe was waiting for him. Abe had evidently been planning all morning on what he was going to say because he started right in about how Mr. Milliron must have wondered how an odd fish like him got into Abington in the first place. Now that he and Mr. Milliron were to be associated as executors Mr. Milliron might like to know. There were things in their backgrounds they had in common.

"Most people call me Jap or Colonel or some goddam thing," Jap interrupted in an illtempered tone.

"Please." Abe Merman raised a patient pudgy hand. He had to explain. He was choosing his words. His German accent became more pronounced. Like the colonel he was the victim of Mr. Allardyce's benefactions. Not only Abe but his whole family. He smiled that soft smile. Mr. Allardyce, he said with a trace of pride in his voice, had driven half across Europe in person with his car to save their lives.

Often, Abe went on, when he attended a sales conference or some get together of Abington employees he looked around into the men's and women's faces and wondered how many of them had come into the business in the same way. The benevolent despot. Never let his left hand know what his right hand did.

It had all started years ago when the Allardyce girls were tiny. The Allardyces had spent a winter month in the Austrian mountains. Abe's father, the colonel must understand, was a tailor in an insignificant mountain town, Schrunz in the Vorarlberg . . . a great place for snow. . . .

The train had started again. Jasper had trouble catching Abe's low hurried explanations. He had to lean into Abe's face to hear. . . . Those were the early days of skiing. First it was the Norwegians, then the Swiss and the Austrians and the Bavarians: then everybody in the world took to skiing. The first time they went to Schrunz the Allardyces didn't have any skiing clothes so they went into Abe's father's shop for their outfits. Abe's father was not only an excellent tailor but he was a wellread man, an oldfashioned philosophical Jew.

"I was not there at the time," Abe continued with that little smile. "I was a student at the University of Vienna." (Of course that accounts for the accent, thought Jasper. He learned English in school.)

His father and Mr. Allardyce, Abe was longwindedly explaining, hit it off right away. His father had all sorts of interests outside of his tailorshop; he collected arts and crafts, he dipped into anthropology, folklore, mountain climbing; he was quite a naturalist. They became great cronies. Every time Mr. Allardyce went to Europe winter or summer he would go up to Schrunz to see Abe's father. He not only had him make all his clothes but he took his advice in business matters. When Hitler's stormtroopers came Mr. Allardyce turned up a few hours ahead with his car to drive the Mermans over into Switzerland. Abe's wife—she was only his fiancée then—fled with them. His father had to leave everything behind, his collections, his books, his prints of eighteenth century costumes.

When they came to America, at Mr. Allardyce's expense of course, he set the old man up in business in Sun Valley. Business was good and the old man paid back every dollar Mr. Allardyce had advanced him, but not even the interesting wildlife and the alpine flora could reconcile him to the strange American ways. The old people were perfectly comfortable in Idaho but they pined away and died.

"Berta and I achieved adaptation." There was a hint of hidden arrogance in the way Abe said it. "We became acclimatized. I went to work in the Atlanta office of Abington Mills and I don't think Mr. Allardyce ever had cause to regret it, but it's never been quite the work I wanted to do."

The engineer was trying to make up time. The car lurched and jounced as the train clattered along the uneven roadbed. Jasper could only catch snatches of what Abe was saying.

He kept on studying for his doctorate in his spare time. Extension courses. Now at fortyseven he had his Ph.D., the chemistry of grain. Byproducts of the milling process. He was on the edge of some, perhaps merely trifling discoveries.

"But man," shouted Jasper, "you've been doing an outstanding job in sales and promotion."

Abe shrugged. Of course it would mean a salary cut. Mrs. Merman was quite reconciled to the idea. They had had some little success on the stockmarket. He wanted the laboratory at the new mill, a chance to show what he could do. If he failed well and good.

Jasper wished Abe would stop shrugging his shoulders. All the same he found himself looking at the little man with a different eye. Lorna had said she liked him.

"My lord man, that was the last thing I expected from you."

He burst out laughing and got to his feet. Abe clutched him by the sleeve.

"You see Colonel Jasper, it was really my father, the little Jew tailor from Schrunz, whom Mr. Allardyce trusted to see his wishes would be carried out in the execution of his will." He squared his shoulders. There was something brassy in his voice. "I stand in his place."

Jasper strode off through the swaying slambanging corridors of the train.

"Your friend Abe," he exploded to Lorna when he got back

to the drawing room, "wants to be put in charge of the laboratory at the new mill."

Jasper stamped up and down in the narrow drawingroom. He was talking his head off. God damn it that was the trouble with American business. Nobody wanted to be what they were. Everybody wanted to be a writer or an artist or a scientist or some goddam thing. "Look at me: I've just got the business opportunity of my life and what I want to do is hunt and fish and live in a cabin in the mountains with a woman named Lorna Hubbard."

It was dusk before the train pulled maddeningly slow into the Chattanooga depot. By the time he reached the construction site in a taxicab it was dark.

Phil Lorillard stood waiting for him under a glaring light bulb at the door of the tarpaper shack where the engineers had their office. Beyond rose the dim shapes of cranes and girders and great oblong forms for concrete.

Phil's ears stuck out more than ever. The corners of his mouth drooped. He had the face of a small boy trying to hold back the tears after a licking. In a shaking hand he held a slip of yellow flimsy. Without returning Jasper's greeting he stuck the slip under his eyes.

It was a telegram signed Howard C. Boomer, Chief of Engineering and Construction: "Suspending operation," it read. "Reducing crew to maintenance needs. Explanation follows."

Silently, batting his eyelashes as if he were just about to burst into tears, Phil led Jasper into the brilliantly lit drafting room where Jack Yates, in his T shirt as usual, sat scowling at the end of a long table piled with blueprints. "Perhaps you can explain, Colonel Milliron," Jack growled, "what the hell is going on around here."

Without taking off his hat or coat Jasper strode to the phone and put in a call to Jim Swazey at Lake Geneva . . . "Person to person . . . if Mr. Swazey is out I'll talk to Mrs."

After a while the operator reported that Mr. and Mrs. Swazey were out to dinner. The maid didn't expect them back till eleven. He told her to try Mr. David T. Griswold 1342 Lacustrian Road in St. Paul Minnesota. As he sat crouched over the phone he could feel the eyes of the architect and the engineer boring venomously into his back. If looks could kill. With the receiver to his ear he turned in his chair and gave them a wave of the hand. "Take it easy you guys," he said. "I'm fighting this thing as hard as you are."

Mr. Griswold was at dinner and couldn't be disturbed the maid reported. "Look here Ella this is Colonel Milliron," shouted Jasper. "You tell Mr. Griswold it's a very urgent matter. I don't care if he's entertaining the Pope at Rome I'll keep ringing till he comes."

"Where on earth have you been Jap?" Dave asked in his most offhand voice when he reached the phone. "We tried to find you everywhere for the board meeting this morning."

"I'm calling from the Chattanooga mill. . . . Dave this construction is set up in the budget for the Southeastern Division, you know that as well as I do."

"It was decided to retrench a little in view of the drop in retail sales, end of Korean war, all that sort of thing."

"It seems to me it's up to us down here to carry out the provisions in our budget once they are duly set up and approved."

"That was the decision," said Dave flatly.

Beads of sweat were running down Jasper's forehead from under the band of his hat. He could tell that Dave was getting ready to hang up. He pumped his words into Dave's ear at the end of the line: if the board had reversed itself once it could damn well reverse itself twice. No goddam board sitting in St. Paul could make decisions affecting the Southeastern Division once the program had been budgeted and approved. If Abington didn't build this modernized mill their competitors would. It would mean millions in savings in milling costs. If the board knifed this project after spending three million dollars in preparation he'd see to it that every goddam stockholder was informed that his best interests had been jeopardized. He'd take the floor in open meeting. He'd start a press campaign. "Dave I'm telling Gates and Lorillard we're still in business. I'm catching a plane back north tomorrow night."

He hung up.

"Give me that telegram." He snatched the sheet of flimsy out of Phil Lorillard's hand. "You never received it, see." He crumpled it up and shoved it in his pocket. "Now boys, how about the new design for that classifier?"

It was midnight before he reached his hotel room. As soon as he could get rid of the officious bellhop, who would putter around showing him where the light switches were and how the shower worked and the knobs on the TV, and the latch on the door, he called the long distance operator. It took him a half hour to dredge up the Swazeys. Jim sounded half drunk. "Just battening down hatches, Jap," he kept saying. "Dave Griswold's in a blue funk about the end of the Korean war and the coming depression, and a presidential election coming up. . . . Pull in your ears Jap we're going through a tunnel."

"Canceling those contracts will cost us around ten million dollars." Jasper could feel his neck swelling with anger.

"Those aren't the figures Dave gave me." Jim sounded cornered. He was beginning to show fight. "Dave says a small loss will be useful taxwise."

Jasper got his voice under control. "Suppose we argue some more about it in the morning, Jim," he answered mildly. "Lemme say good night to Sylvia."

Jim must have wandered off to bed because when Sylvia spoke it was just between the two of them. It was all Jasper's fault, she insisted, for not sticking around. What on earth had he been up to?

"Sylvia, even I have got to have a little private life."

"I don't blame you, Jap." It was Sylvia's old friendly voice. "I don't know what's come over Harriet. Harriet's absolutely hipped on this art museum."

"She didn't tell me anything about it."

"You'll hear about it," said Sylvia.

"But Sylvia I thought I had Jim all convinced."

"He didn't stay convinced, Jap."

"What's Jim so sore about?"

"Jap"—Sylvia's voice hesitated—"Jim's worried, and so am I to tell the truth, about your dabbling in finance . . . all that stock you bought in Central Grain. We're afraid you'll come a cropper."

"Can't a man collect a little nest egg for his old age?"

"Jap, I'm older than you and you've always listened to my advice."

"Not always, Sylvia." He laughed. "But I can remember times when you turned out goddam right."

Her answering giggle came back over the long distance.

"But Jap," Sylvia talked all in a rush: "I'm all for you when it comes to modernizing, streamlining administration . . . you know . . . Now that Dad's gone you're the only executive Abington's got who's thinking about ten years from now—" Her voice trailed off.

"But you don't want me butting into the top echelons where the money talks, is that it?"

"Jap I wouldn't just put it that way."

"Haven't too many people been telling Jim he's the heir apparent? I'd follow him to the death if he'd show some leadership. You know that, Sylvia. But this way he's just letting the palace guard take over by default."

"You talk to Jim tomorrow," Sylvia yawned: "Jap, I'm awful sleepy."

"Damn tootin' I'll talk to Jim . . . Meanwhile Sylvia, take him down to Chattanooga and look things over. Be sure to get Lorillard to show you around. Yates is just a windbag."

"I'll do my best."

"Well good night, Sylvia."

"Good night, Jap."

Next Jasper routed Theo Murcheson out of bed to ask him whether the executors could start right now to exercise their voting rights on the Riverside stock or did they have to wait till the will was probated? Theo answered that that was one hell of a question to wake a man up with in the middle of the night. But he had to move fast, Jasper shouted back. Jap would damn well have to wait until Theo got to his office in the morning. "Check," said Jasper. "I'll call you at nine thirty."

Jasper was too keyed up to sleep. He lay on the bed with his head full of stock prices staring at the ceiling with red-rimmed eyes until daybreak. At 7 A.M. he was out at the construction site greeting Guy Vecter as he backed his large frame out of his taffycolored Chrysler. "Guy did you get a telegram?"

The construction boss for the Lockport Building and Canal Company was a youngish sixfooter with a long narrow head tightly plastered with curly red hair. He wasn't quite awake yet. Doubtfully he produced a Western Union form. Jasper snatched it out of his hand. "Guy," said Jasper, "you never saw that telegram. It was just an organizational snafu. An office boy's error."

Guy was drawling that some folks around here would be right glad of a chance to sidestep the contract. Worried about the penalty clauses. Too damn favorable to Abington. Time was running out. He no sooner had a piece of equipment installed than Lorillard redesigned it on him.

Jasper jumped down his throat. Nobody was going to sidestep any goddam contract. Abington had never welched on a contract in seventyfive years of corporate life and we weren't going to start now. What he needed was a final breakdown on costs to take to St. Paul that night. The organization was backing this project to the limit.

By noon, with an envelope full of photostats of the latest cost sheets in his suitcase, Jasper was catching the plane to Atlanta. Miss Lockett was dumfounded to see him walk into his office. He spent three hours catching up on correspondence. Not a moment to call Lorna.

Miss Lockett kept poking a memo: *Call Mr. Merman* under his nose, but it was so late before he got around to the call that Abe had already left the office. Mrs. Merman said he was on his way home.

On the spur of the moment Jasper jumped into his car and drove around to the Mermans' apartment. He found Abe just stepping into the vestibule with a package under his arm which he whispered with an apologetic smile contained two Cornish hens for supper. Right away he invited Jasper to share them. While they were cooking they could talk. He seemed unusually selfpossessed.

"Please," he motioned Jasper into the selfservice elevator. They were alone in the tiny shiny box but still he went on whispering. Colonel Jasper must be wondering who held the other fifteen hundred shares of Riverside.

He smiled.

"Please."

He bowed Jasper out into the hall.

Eleven hundred and thirteen of them could be accounted for, he added hurriedly under his breath as he stood fumbling in his pockets for his latchkey. They were in Mrs. Merman's name.

"*Schätzlein*," he called as he ushered Jasper into the living room, "Colonel Jasper has consented to stay to supper."

When Abe came back from the kitchenette after having delivered his package, he explained with that half deprecating, half arrogant smile that like his father he was something of a collector. Riverside Corporation could be described as a collector's item. It had intrigued him to ferret out a few shares now and then. Jasper found himself slapping the little man on the back and shouting "Good for you, Abe."

"Ouch." Abe hunched up his shoulders and smiled up into his face. "Now if you promise not to hit me again, Jap"—he used the nickname cautiously—"I have some further suggestions to make . . . My nightmare, ever since the reading of Mr. Allardyce's very sardonic will, has been suits, lawsuits to cripple or break the foundation, injunctions that may paralyze the executors in the exercise of their rights to vote the Riverside stock. Do you follow me?"

"It's been keeping my lawyer awake nights," said Jasper.

Abe laid his hand gently on Jasper's lapel: "If you pardon my saying so, assistance at this juncture from high financial circles . . . would be providential."

"You're telling me," said Jasper.

Abe's voice was so low Jasper had to lean over to hear what he was saying. "There is a cousin of Berta's, of Mrs. Merman's, a favorite first cousin who by a curious coincidence has also shown a connoisseur's interest in Abington stocks. Perhap you have met Judge Lewin? He happens to be staying at the Palmer House in Chicago."

"Alphonse Lewin? No, I haven't, but . . ."

Abe put his finger to his lips. Mrs. Merman's colored maid was pulling open the red damask draperies that had masked a candlelit table set for three.

"It was my father," Abe interrupted with a rasp of pride in his voice, "who first interested Mr. Allardyce in the pneumatic mill." Abe made one of his stiff German bows and waved a hand in the direction of the dining table. "Please . . . In union there is strength," he whispered as he showed Jasper to his seat.

Supper was cozy. Mrs. Merman's Cornish hens were delicious. They drank a bottle of Moselle. Mrs. Merman talked with shining eyes about the pleasures of walking in the Austrian mountains and Jasper told tall tales of the Rockies. When they moved into the livingroom for their coffee Jasper suggested they had better make reservations on a Chicago plane.

Abe smiled as he stirred his small cup with its pink and blue flowered pattern.

"Anticipating your consent, I have made reservations on the eleven thirty," he said.

While Mrs. Merman was packing his bag for him Abe played Mozart on the high fidelity record player. As Jasper listened he found himself dreaming of the day when he'd have Lorna all tied up and married so that he too would have a woman to pack his bag for him again. He felt envious of the affectionate intimacy of the Mermans' little household. He hadn't unpacked since the train. His bag was still in his car with the clothes he'd taken up for the Allardyce funeral. What a dog's life, he grumbled to himself.

When they reached the Palmer House next morning they were ushered into a large corner sittingroom. They sat thumbing over a pile of New York, Chicago and foreign newspapers in the eight o'clock sunlight while the waiter set the breakfast dishes out under their white metal covers at a round table in an alcove.

Apologizing for his lateness Judge Lewin came in with a springing step. He was a tall hawknosed asceticlooking man. His skin was a dark olive and his hair and eyebrows and closeclipped mustache were a gunmetal gray. The wide arched nostrils and the exercised leanness of his tall frame under the baggy English tweeds gave him the look of a running horse.

The judge had a gusty intermittent way of talking. He started by commiserating with Jasper and Abe on the discomforts of trying to sleep on a plane, then he switched to the disappointments and frustrations incidental to the introduction of a new mechanical process. He disclaimed any technical knowledge of milling, but the more he talked the more it became obvious that he'd managed somehow to keep posted on even the latest complications in Phil Lorillard's plans for a pneumatic mill. "Blood heating, my friends," he cried out.

Judge Lewin stopped talking as suddenly as he had begun. He started to gobble up a bowl of oatmeal in big spoonfuls. Jasper, redeyed from lack of sleep, sat eating his bacon and eggs, drinking cup after cup of coffee to wake him up without finding a word to say, while Abe told his cousin Alphonse about his dear cousin Berta's health and expatiated on the various destinies of family connections that were all Greek to Jasper.

When Judge Lewin put down his spoon beside his empty bowl he let out another volley of words. Colonel Milliron must not misunderstand him. Had Mr. Allardyce lived he would never have moved a step towards what he liked to call a reconnaissance in force of Abington Products. But now he and a group of likeminded friends, a syndicate if you like, were ready to go the limit to steer this brilliant experiment towards the success it deserved.

"Cousin Alphonse," Abe explained, "is familiar with the Swiss mill. He appreciates our special sales angles."

"Suzy Standish, the housewife's dream." Judge Lewin kissed the tips of his fingers in a flourish like a stage Frenchman.

"Judge Lewin," said Jasper, "suppose we save time by laying our cards on the table."

"Done," said the judge.

Jasper hadn't seen him come in but already a bald young man in a dark suit stood modestly behind Judge Lewin's chair with a folder in his hand. Breakfast was cleared in a flash and papers and charts laid out on the round table. Judge Lewin perched a pair of old-fashioned gold pincenez on his nose and, freshly sharpened pencil in hand, dissected out the financial structure of the Abington companies with the zest of a surgeon at work on a cadaver before a group of medical students. Control of a few thousand shares here and a bond issue there.

He took off his glasses and looked from one to the other. "To me it is a mathematical problem, no more. . . . It will be up to you gentlemen to dictate the proper policies in all the multitudinous details of daily management."

His gray eyes, hard and clear as pebbles in a brook, were fixed on Jasper's face.

"Colonel Milliron you are a military man. Already we have rolled up the enemy's flank, but to capture the citadel we need our fifth column."

"Riverside."

"The Trojan horse," exclaimed Judge Lewin jumping to his feet.

The bald young man was deferentially shuffling the sheets back into their folder.

Jasper spoke slowly. "I believe we can do it."

"We must make it our business," Abe filled in hastily, "to see that trustees are appointed to the Allardyce Foundation who will appreciate the advantages of a reorganization."

Right now they were on their way, Jasper added, to a showdown in St. Paul.

"Gentlemen," said Judge Lewin, "I shall await your word. Meanwhile I shall make it my business and pleasure to attend to the technical details . . . You needn't bother your heads about them."

Jasper and Abe walked out through Judge Lewin's anteroom. Every seat was filled with people waiting for appointments, old ladies, grayfaced executives, sportily dressed young women, elegant graybeards: it looked like a doctor's office.

From the lobby Jasper called the Swazeys. Sylvia invited them to eat lunch at Lake Geneva. They drove out in a cab. It was warm enough for cocktails on their terrace that had a southern exposure against the tall windows of the grim Italian style villa.

"Jim," said Jasper holding up his glass for a second martini, "we have been meeting with a group of investors in Chicago. If we scrap this experimental mill we'll have a revolution on our hands among some pretty powerfully situated Abington stockholders."

Abe began to stiffen Jim up by telling him the time had come to make himself felt as chairman of the board. Jim began saying he'd never agreed with Dave Griswold for a moment.

Sylvia was remembering how she and her father had driven out with Herr Merman years ago to see a revolutionary new flour mill out on the Rhine near Basel.

"They hardly waited to put the boss in his grave before they started undoing his work." Jim pounded his palm with his fist.

As the weather continued clear the Swazeys ordered out their Beechcraft after a hurried lunch. The flight to St. Paul was smooth. Jasper and Abe and Jim were in Dave Griswold's office before five that afternoon. No need to argue about Riverside. Dave hemmed and hawed a little but in the end he admitted gruffly he guessed Boomer better reconsider his cancellation of the experimental mill. The three of them sat while Dave gave Boomer a dressing down over the telephone. When Dave set down the receiver Jasper caught the Missouri mule expression coming back into his face. You wait till next time, he must be thinking. What he said out loud was, "Take it easy boys."

It was another week before Jasper got back to Atlanta and found a free moment to call Lorna. Her voice leapt over the phone. Supper that night. Where? They had better not be seen together in any of the more popular restaurants so they picked a little dump that advertised "chicken in the rough" on the road to Lake Lancer.

She wore the same green dress she had worn the first time he met her in the elevator at the Abington Building. She was carrying the white leather handbag. There was the scent of gardenias. Jasper could tell by the soft look her eyes had and the way her lips were parted that she wanted him as much as he wanted her, but they hadn't had a chance to exchange two words, shouting to make themselves heard over the rock n' roll from the jukebox, before the counterman was hovering over their table.

The counterman was all smiles. He had recognized Suzy Standish as soon as she stepped in the door. He was a skinny-faced character with crooked teeth and dense black fur on his forearms. What could he do for Miss Standish? He wanted her to know that this restaurant used Abington products exclusively. Might he have her autograph to take home to the wife and daughters? The Suzy Standish Hour was a must in their house.

Jasper, who had wanted to start hugging and kissing her then and there, had to sit grinning like an ape while the counterman carried on about how Suzy Standish had converted him to Abington products, a wonderful line of goods. But he didn't like their cracker crumbs, really Miss Standish they ought to do something about their cracker crumbs. While Jasper fumed inside, Lorna patiently asked the man questions about what was wrong with the cracker crumbs. She even took notes. Jasper thought they never would get through talking about those damn cracker crumbs.

The man just couldn't bear to have them go. While he fried their chicken he kept pointing out Lorna to the other customers as the genuyne Suzy Standish. One woman took her picture with a Polaroid camera. She had to scribble a couple more autographs. It seemed hours before they were shut of the place.

Then they had to get caught in a traffic jam driving back into the city and Jasper had to lose a lot of time finding a parking lot so as not to let his car be seen in front of her apartment house. As a final precaution they went in the basement entrance. Even so everybody in the elevator seemed to know Lorna.

When finally Lorna's door closed behind them he had his arms around her before she could take off her hat and put down her packages. Kissing her, straining her to him, breathing in the scent of her hair—he felt ageless again.

They sat rumpled and happy on the livingroom settee eating the fried chicken out of the carton and drinking bourbon whiskey out of some beautiful cut glass tumblers she had in her chinacloset. "My this is a pleasant place," said Jasper. "I want to move right in."

On the wall opposite was an oldfashioned painting in a gold frame of a trotting horse and sulky. "Why that's Old Sam," said Jasper with a shout of laughter.

Lorna nodded. "Mr. Allardyce gave me that picture one Christmas. He said Old Sam's picture was used in their first campaigns advertising ready mixed feeds during the Grant administration. He said I ought to have it."

"From Old Sam to Suzy Standish. That's progress for you." Jasper felt all his worries dropping away as he looked laughing into her laughing face. "Lorna, if we could ever get squared away, we could have the happiest damn life together."

"Why can't we . . . I mean right now." She kissed him. "Jap we're going to be a long time dead."

"It's Harriet."

"But I thought she wanted a divorce."

"She does but on her own terms. She wants my Abington stock, not for herself but for this fornicating art museum. . . . She's hipped on being a patroness of the arts, like Sylvia and all those rich Chicago women. You ought to hear the girls on the subject."

"Jap I want to meet those girls . . . I kinda think we'll get along."

"Of course you will. Evie's getting married in June. That gives Harriet another argument."

"But I thought she was the one wanted the divorce—" Lorna's voice trailed off. Her face had the look of dismay of a child that has just dropped the icecream off her cone.

"I believe she suspects I've got somebody on the string."

"On the string . . . Boy you've got a bear by the tail."

Later that night when they were hugged tight under the covers in Lorna's narrow bed, Lorna suddenly cried out that she'd noticed he had holes in his socks. It made her feel bad. She started whispering fast with her mouth against his ear:

"Give her anything she wants Jap. . . . I really mean anything. . . . I'm making a perfectly good salary and so are you. If we decide we need a lot of dough, you're a young feller, you can step out and make it."

"Lorna it isn't money, it's leverage. I can't part with a single share. I'm in hock up to the ears to buy more."

When he kissed it her cheek was wet. He kissed her and kissed her but a chill had come between them. He got out of bed and put on his clothes. He stood over her and gently brushed her hair: "Honey I got to go to the hotel and do some figuring . . . It won't be long, honestly it won't be long. I've got some high finance behind me, a syndicate. It will be the battle of the century but we can't lose."

She squeezed his hand and he tiptoed out of the room.

Jasper and Jim Swazey and Dave Griswold nodded breathlessly to each other when they met in the control room the day they tried the first run of grain through the Chattanooga mill. It was like being on the bridge of a battleship. Through broad windows they could see the gleaming coiling shapes of aluminum ducts and struts and catwalks against the towering white concrete structure of the adjoining elevator. Phil Lorillard, unshaven and flushed, in a dirty blue shirt with a rip down the back strode to and fro in sneakered feet along a row of youthful operators who stood with their eyes pinned to dials and sheets of graphpaper unwinding under glass. Lights went on and off. Little bells rang. They pressed buttons and adjusted levers.

In the back of the room Jasper caught a glimpse of Frank

Gherkin. Frank's face was twisted into every possible expression of disgust. His skin usually so rosy had the greenish hue of a man about to throw up. Though everybody else was in street clothes Frank had insisted on sticking to his white duster and cheesecloth cap.

Of course everything went wrong. There were stoppages everywhere. Flour came out middlins where it ought to have come out high grade patent. Pipes burst. Air ducts leaked. Fuses blew out.

Wherever the repair crew went Phil Lorillard was in the lead counseling, cajoling, kidding. A low roaring through the ducts would be the sign that some process was started again. Then Phil would be seen through the transport glass tiles of the corridor wall slamming his troubleshooters on the back like the winning captain on a Little League ball team.

At last Jim Swazey began to insist that the time had come for them to go down to lunch. The more he looked at those damn dials the less he understood them. They found Jack Yates waiting at the entrance to the basement cafeteria. "Congratulations," he roared. "Phil just sent word that the classifiers are working."

"The only thing I can see that's working is your cafeteria," said Dave Griswold when he settled at the table with a tray of food. "And that's no different from any other cafeteria."

"No different?" shouted Jack Yates. "Every mouthful you men are eating was cooked by radiant heat."

Jasper couldn't help laughing at the suspicious way Frank Gherkin poked his fork into the pile of pork and beans on his plate, as if he expected to find a snake in it.

Jim Swazey was taking the philosophical attitude. Nobody could expect a complicated machine like this to run smooth the first day.

"Nobody can expect it to run smooth, period," said Griswold. Jasper had long ago given up arguing. All along the executives' table nobody answered.

"Some of us tend to forget," Jack Yates came back in a sarcastic voice intended to put every man in his place, "that we are living in the second half of the twentieth century."

Phil Lorillard's weedy figure appeared all at once smiling and teetering at the end of the table. There was a fresh smudge of grease on his nose.

"You gentlemen mustn't forget that this is a pilot operation," he said mildly. "The more sensitive a piece of machinery is the more skill it takes to run it . . . Skill comes from practice." He vanished as silently as he'd come.

As the spring days dragged on Jasper began to wonder if maybe Dave Griswold hadn't been right all along. Every time he hopped over to Chattanooga he found Phil Lorillard more haggard and absentminded than ever. At last reaching his office one hot June day he heard Phil's voice breathless on the phone. "Yesterday we ran off eighteen different grades and not a bug. We're in business."

When Jasper caught the plane north to go to Evie's wedding he had the satisfaction of knowing that the pilot mill had just run three shifts without a stoppage.

It was a beautiful June morning, blue as a robin's egg, when Jasper walked down the gangplank at the Twin Cities airport. He was feeling in the pink. He'd slept well on the flight. The stocks had gone his way for the last two weeks. The Southeastern Division was going to report a two million dollar increase in gross sales for the fiscal year soon coming to a close. He was looking forward with pleasure to the wedding. If the choice had been Jasper's Fred Jones was the man he would have picked for Evie to marry.

His good humor didn't last long. His first chore was to attend a meeting of the executors in Thurmond Anderson's office. The problem was how to fight a suit some of the cousins and nephews were bringing up to break the Allardyce will. "Just a nuisance proceeding," Thurmond announced loftily, "if the worst comes to the worst a couple of grand will handle those birds."

Courtney Cooper wasn't so sure: he made clucking noises.

Then Rasmussen came in with the news that a group of stockholders were getting ready to appear in Federal Court with a petition that the executors be enjoined against voting the Riverside stock. "Machiavelli," Abe Merman whispered to Jasper. He did not mention Dave Griswold's name. The executors were still arguing in circles when Jasper had to slip out to dress for the champagne breakfast Harriet was giving at her house for the bridal party.

On the way to the hotel he dropped by Theo Murcheson's office. Theo looked up from his desk with a thundering frown. Theo was complaining as if it were all Jasper's fault that

Harriet had dropped Rasmussen and hired herself a new lawyer, a young man named Myers, a New York, slippery, stuck up, *Harvard Law Review* and all that. He had been invited out here to give a course at the Law School, and had decided to stay and practice to astonish the hicks. Theo had met him at moot court the other night. "He assured me he was trying to avoid a scandal. . . . I don't like those kind of assurances. . . . Harriet's out for every last cent. If she can get a few more bucks by charging adultery she's going to do it. . . . What have you been doing you shouldn't, young man?"

Jasper flushed. "There is somebody I've been taking out. She's a very nice woman. Nobody knows a thing about it except the two of us."

"That's what you think. Knowing you as well as I do you've probably gone around registering as Mr. and Mrs. in every motel between here and Atlanta."

"We've been very discreet, even secretive. We'll get married as soon as the decree goes through."

"Jap you're about as secretive as a trumpeting elephant."

Jasper was already heading for the door. He wanted to get out of the office before he lost his temper. "We can talk at the reception."

"A fat chance. You'll be on the receiving line and Harriet's invited about ten thousand people. . . . Maybe she'll tell you what she's got on her mind . . . but after this, for God sake keep your lawyer informed."

Jasper was a half an hour late at Harriet's. He felt the old catch in his throat as he went in the door. The house was so filled with potted palms and assorted jungle vegetation he hardly recognized it. He found Harriet in a black lace dress lording it over a group of weirdies in the library. Her arm was around the neck of an old young man with strawcolored hair and effeminate wrists she introduced as the new museum director. Beside them lounged a blondish youth with a crewcut and a turnedup nose. "Charley Myers our legal aid." The way the fellow looked him up and down made Jasper's hackles rise. He didn't like the exchange of sharp glances, either, between the lawyer and the museum director.

Jasper found himself shaking hands with a brace of painters and a poet. Wear beards to disguise the lack of chin, thought Jasper. Harriet went on relentlessly with the introductions. There was a smoothtalking character in a checkered vest wearing what looked like a plumcolored tuxedo jacket whom she described as a lecturer. There was Doctor this and Professor that. Doubledomes every one of them. They formed a hollow square round Harriet and stared at Jasper as if he were some specimen escaped from a zoo.

"We're talking about the new art museum we're going to build," trilled Harriet in a high pitched voice with her hand on the museum director's shoulder, "and Jasper you're going to help us."

"Where are the girls?"

"In the conservatory surrounded by the dullest young men . . . Why don't you go and play the proud parent?"

Grumbling that it was the first he'd heard of a conservatory Jasper shuffled off through the livingroom. He followed the sound of youthful voices out to the old glassed-in back porch.

"Here's Dad," Evie and Maddie shouted both at the same time. They rushed up to him and each kissed him on one cheek. He put his arms around the pair of them. They looked so pretty and happy in their flouncy dresses he didn't know which one he loved most. Just hugging them made him forget all those worries.

Then there were the bridesmaids to be introduced to, and the ushers. Jasper wanted to hug them all, they looked so brighteyed and rosycheeked and cheerful. Fred Jones wrung his hand with a hard grip he liked and dragged a stocky young man with brown closecut hair and a black sparkle in his eyes up out of an armchair to introduce him as his best man.

"He's Willoughby Jenks . . . Captain Jenks. . . . Yes that really is his name," the girls all shouted together. "He's on leave from the hospital."

"I guess I ought to apologize, sir, for coming to your daughter's wedding on crutches," he began haltingly.

Maddie interrupted him. She grabbed her father's hand and put it in the young man's. "Dad this is Will. . . . He's it, if you see what I mean—"

"I hope you won't object sir," said Will with downcast eyes. "I got into a little trouble in Korea. . . . I'm really all right now, just one more set of surgery and I'll be as good as new."

Fred came up with a glass of champagne. "We understand he's in line for a Congressional Medal, sir. He darn well earned it, I know that."

Jasper drank several glasses of champagne in rapid succession. The breakfast was a whirl of young faces and pretty dresses. The groom made a funny speech and the bridesmaids and ushers recited limericks made up for the occasion. Even Harriet unlimbered enough to recite a pleasant little toast to the bride and groom. With the dessert they all sang songs. Jasper's own voice sounded particularly good to him in "Just to keep her from the foggy foggy dew."

At the wedding itself that wooden dummy feeling came on he always had at formal ceremonies. He got through it like he used to get through close order drill in the old days in the Marines, by blacking out inside.

The reception at the Country Club was worse. For three hours he stood beside Harriet shaking hands and nodding and grinning and wisecracking, playing the hospitable bear. The line of faces unreeled like ticker tape. Harriet was so busy she had only time to get in a single dig. "Jap if you would only act your age you wouldn't put yourself in such a bad light all the time."

All the way back to Atlanta on the plane next day he tried to figure that one out. To be on the safe side he asked for some airline stationery and wrote each of the girls not to worry too much if their mother made a public show of them all over the divorce: she was in the hands of unscrupulous people. In Evie's note he included a thousand dollar check to help with the honeymoon and in Maddie's another one as an engagement present. His eyes were moist when he sealed up the envelopes and handed them to the stewardess to mail.

When he talked to Lorna on the phone right after he got back to his hotel apartment at the Duke he found out what was behind Harriet's remark. Reporters for Doug Whittlesea's column had called Lorna three times at her office asking her to confirm or deny that she was being named as co-respondent in Mrs. Milliron's suit for divorce against the chief of Abington Products Southeastern Division.

Her story was she'd never heard of any divorce. She'd stuck to it. "As for myself I don't give a damn Jap," she cried with real dismay in her voice, "but think what it's going to do to Suzy Standish."

"Who's going to care?"

"All those straitlaced women who belong to Suzy Standish

clubs . . . Jap I'm in deep trouble. I'm sending my resignation in to St. Paul today. That column is syndicated in every newspaper in the country. Thank God I've got a few savings."

He was starting to tell her that she wouldn't need savings once she married him when she said good night for now dear, her doorbell was ringing, and hung up. He couldn't stand the sudden silence of his hotel room. He couldn't stand not having her to talk to.

It was that night that Jasper did all the wrong things. He simply had to talk to Lorna. He jumped in his car and drove around to her place and stepped out of the elevator just in time to find a reporter for the *Star-Post* ringing her doorbell. The reporter, an unusually brash young guy even for the *Star-Post*, recognized him instantly and muttered, "The guy with the latch key." Before Jasper knew what he was doing he'd swung on the reporter and laid him out flat on the floor.

It was only then he noticed a man with a leveled camera lurking at the end of the hall. The photographer kept on happily snapping shots while Jasper leaned over the reporter to help him to his feet. "Now you get the hell out of here," said Jasper shaking with anger. "I've been a good customer of your paper and I've got good friends on the city desk."

Mumbling that he guessed he had it coming to him, the reporter slunk away with his handkerchief held to his mouth. The photographer had already disappeared down the stairs.

Lorna was great. The minute Jasper opened the door she hugged him in her arms. "If we're not going to look like a couple of nitwits," she cried.

She shot the bolt on the door and they sat huddled on the livingroom sofa. She hated to have it happen to Abington she kept telling him. It was a grand organization and she was proud of the years she'd worked for it. All that was spilt milk now. Too late to cry. Her plan was a trip to Mexico until things blew over. Thank God it wasn't some other guy she was in this mess with.

"I'm sticking with Abington, Lorna, if you don't mind." Jasper ground his teeth. "I think I've got what it takes."

It turned out he didn't. The first intimation that things weren't going his way was a call from Larry Dale. He wanted Jasper's help to get transferred back to the Twin Cities.

Family reasons, he explained embarrassedly. The wife didn't
like segregation, the kids were razzed as damyankees in school.
Then his voice broke: "Jap you know why I can't stick with
you. . . . I got five children to educate. I know you'll understand."

"Sure, Larry, sure."

He'd hardly laid down the phone when Sylvia was in his
office. Sylvia sat bolt upright on the edge of her chair and
talked in a chill fury. She could have forgiven anything except
his trying to use his position as executor of Dad's estate to
help outside interests get control of Abington. At first she'd
thought Jim was talking through his hat but now she agreed
with him. The Hiners agreed with Jim, so did Courtney Cooper. If Jap thought they were going to stand by and see the
great industry Dad built up looted by a gang of Wall Street
kikes, he was very much mistaken.

By this time Sylvia was striding back and forth in front of
his desk, tall and gray and lean in her gray tailored suit.
She'd inherited some of the old man's lilt of authority. By
God she was a fine woman. Jasper loved her and admired her.
Without losing his temper he tried to explain that in working to modernize Abington Products, he was doing what her
father would have wanted. Sylvia wouldn't listen. "Jap, I want
you to resign as executor of my father's estate. . . . I don't
care if the court appoints a Chinaman. This used to be a
family corporation," she said as she walked out of the office.
"Maybe that's what it ought to be again."

She left Jasper musing over his polished desk with his eyes
on the brass calendar his employees had presented him five
years ago to celebrate thirty years of service. It looked in-
congruous now.

Sylvia hadn't said a word about Lorna Hubbard. She'd
never been jealous of Harriet, but maybe Lorna was different.
Maybe she'd guessed. Lorna was a little more like that girl
he'd never been able to win. Sylvia must have guessed. He
was crazy in love with Lorna. The thought that Sylvia might
be jealous was heartwarming somehow. It puffed up the little
bantam rooster that's inside of every man, he told himself.
He couldn't help a slight chuckle. He was amused at himself
and amused at Sylvia.

When Miss Lockett came in and found him sitting grinning
into the air she looked absolutely astonished. Her face had

been a mask of dismay for days. "Mr. Merman wants to see you privately," she whispered in a voice that breathed doom.

"But why announce Abe Merman? Tell him to come in." Jasper popped his eyes at her and grinned some more. "Miss Lockett, think of it as a nice cool poker game."

Miss Lockett's face crumpled. "But I've never played poker," she whimpered and ran out with her eyes spurting tears.

Abe's face was as concerned as Miss Lockett's. He intimated by an elaborate pantomime that he was worried about the possibility of some eavesdropping microphone. He beckoned Jasper over to the window where his voice would be covered by the hum of traffic from the street and grabbed him by the lapel and hissed whispers in his ear.

He was fresh from a weekend with Alphonse at White Sulphur. Alphonse had talked almost continually about Abington Products. No it wasn't that newspaper column that worried him. He thought that was a great joke: an adventure with a myth, he called it. Scandal had never hurt the film stars why should it hurt Suzy Standish? He found it piquant for a man to be involved with a woman who didn't really exist. What was bothering Alphonse was the rise in the stockmarket. "As he drove me to the airport," murmured Abe, "he talked about a merger of all the milling companies. He seemed to have lost interest in our plans for Abington."

"Hell," said Jasper, "we'll bull it through somehow."

Abe's blackbutton eyes looked up into Jasper's face out of bruised sacks of skin.

"It is impossible," he said in his elaborate way, "not to entertain the suspicion that my dear cousin Alphonse has been in communication with Griswold. Alphonse can't bear to lose, not even a little bit." Abe slunk out of the office like a kicked spaniel.

July 2nd Jasper had been slated to fly to Kansas City for a meeting of the directors of Southwestern Grain. When he checked in late at night the lobby of the Muehlbach was crowded. Faces wore a flush of excitement. Familiar faces kept churning up while he waited in line at the registration desk. Everybody in the flour business tended to converge on Kansas City round the Fourth of July. It was like the old days.

Jasper caught a faintly quizzing smile under the mustache of the old night clerk he'd known for years. With his key the night clerk handed Jasper an illustrated weekly somebody had left for him.

Jasper didn't look at it until he got to his room. Then he opened at a turnedover page.

The picture of the week.

Jasper stared at himself just clipping that damned reporter on the chin in front of Lorna's door.

"Milling Company Executive Guards Co-respondent's Door," the caption read: "Colonel Jasper Milliron who learned fighting with the Marines in two world wars defends Suzy Standish's reputation with his fists."

It was a marvelous action shot.

Oh God. He'd sue the bastards. He had to have advice. It was second nature to him to turn to long distance. First he tried to reach Lorna. No reply. Ordinarily he would have called Sylvia: there would be no help there. He put in a person-to-person call to Theo Murcheson. The operator routed Mrs. Murcheson out of bed to be told that Mr. Murcheson was on his way to Kansas City. Could be reached at the Muehlbach towards noon. Good old Theo, thought Jasper, there's a friend a man can rely on, and he went quietly to sleep.

Next morning he was no sooner out of his shower than the phone rang. It was Evie. Back from the Ozarks three nights ago. Fred had left before day on his wheat inspection. She was busy dragging around the furniture in their new house. They had to see him. Fred said was there anything he could do? They'd had trouble keeping Will Jenks from climbing out of his hospital window and going to Atlanta to shoot that photographer.

"Dad shall I dress up in riding togs and go for the editor with a horsewhip? That's what the girls used to do in the old days."

"But Evie, the guy was in line of duty," said Jasper laughing lustily. "It was a damn good shot."

"Oh Dad you're wonderful," crooned Evie. "I was afraid you'd be crushed."

Jasper ate his breakfast off the tray with considerable appetite. He felt completely outside of himself as if he were sitting up in a cloud somewhere keeping check on his own behavior on earth. He had that feeling in wartime: lying flat on his belly in the autumn leaves in a small copse of beeches when the Boche got a bead on his company with their Austrian eighty-eights, stumbling across the reef at Tarawa when they found the water was deep instead of shoal between them and the beach. "Well," he was telling himself, "it's been fun while it lasted."

On the way to the meeting in a conference room on the fifteenth floor of the Exchange Building he looked in on the grain pit. It was a busy morning. The scalpers were barking and yelping on the floor. Boys in yellow scrim shirts scampered back and forth on the catwalk in front of the giant blackboard chalking up prices. The hall, streaked with sunlight from the windows, rang and echoed and reverberated with shouting voices. Ranked heads all turned towards the electriclit weather map in one corner.

From inside the separate cloud that encased him that morning Jasper was seeing himself that young crinkleheaded Jasper in Kansas City on the Fourth of July for the first time thirty years ago, feeling the tingle of the figures changing every minute on the board, standing with the Abington buyers while they hedged their purchases—what you lose in Milwaukee you win in Chicago—following the chessgame of futures in animal feeds. He'd been crazy about the milling business in those days. By God he was crazy about it now. Wheat is king of the world, the young guys used to tell each other.

"Four inches of rain forecast for western Kansas," a stranger shouting in his ear jolted him back into the present. On the big blackboard the chalk figures flickered and changed. The straight lines said "sold."

At their tables the buyers for the milling companies sat sampling newly arrived batches of wheat. Jasper caught the scowl on one man's face. "Yellowberry." He spat some kernels out of his mouth.

"Yellowberry. I guess that's the password for today," Jasper whispered to himself: "Yellowberry."

Faces that for thirty years had been friendly turned towards him unsmiling when he walked into the conference room. Jasper stared back at them coolly. A couple of men gave perfunctory nods.

Most of them were from Abington. There were Dave and Jim and Boomer and Rasmussen from St. Paul. The meeting was supposed to deal with building new elevators to store government grain but nobody could talk about anything but Suzy Standish.

Dave Griswold's face was triumphant under the fat blank skin. Jasper had to admit that the speech he made was really eloquent, for Dave:

Suzy Standish had started as a signature at the bottom of a letter. Then she was a voice on the radio stirring millions of women to buy Abington Products. TV had made her a living person. Suzy Standish was the most valuable asset Abington Products had. She belonged to all the great complex of companies included under Abington's hospitable roof. She was as important to Southwestern Grain as she was to the Chattanooga mill or Pilgrim Foods. Southwestern Grain took the first step in preparing the product for the consumer. It was faith in Suzy Standish that led the consumer to the product.

In the Southwest and in the Southeast—Dave's eyes stared hard in Jasper's face—particularly in the Southeast their market was among homemakers, Godfearing lawabiding women: the Bible belt!

Dave's voice became hoarse with repudiation as he talked straight into Jasper's face. Any aspersion on Suzy Standish's moral character or anything that would cast ridicule and belittlement on the gracious figure that had been built up by years of patient work, by millions of dollars of careful spending by Abington's publicity and advertising staffs, meant a direct loss of sales . . . millions of dollars of sales—Dave could hardly speak for emotion—"I have a motion to make." He was out of breath.

Panting, he moved that the man responsible for this most unhappy situation should be asked to resign his directorships forthwith. Mrs. Hubbard, he added, and he spoke with all due regret, had already severed all connection with Abington Products.

Jasper felt a sudden flush of blood to his face. "Let's leave Mrs. Hubbard out of it," he snapped sharply. "Let's talk about this rationally, men. . . . We all know there isn't any Suzy Standish."

"There isn't any Santa Claus," Boomer's rasping voice answered, "but look what he does for the retail trade."

Jasper looked up and down the table. Not a smile. Not a single glance of understanding.

"I shall continue this discussion through my lawyer," he said and walked out.

Jasper found Theo just about to claim his bag from the airport limousine in front of the main entrance of the hotel. Theo looked stringy and sallow and snaggletoothed as usual. He needed a shave. They hurried up to Jasper's room. Theo snatched at the phone to tell the operator they would accept no calls, then he hung a Do Not Disturb sign on the door and pulled off his coat and lit a cigar and sat down on the edge of the bed.

For some minutes Jasper and Theo sat staring at each other without saying anything.

"Actually," drawled Jasper, "there's not a goddam thing to talk about."

"They want out," said Theo, "and after what must have happened this morning, I imagine you want out."

"Check," said Jasper.

"I should suggest retirement with full pay and the bonus. . . . After all, a contract's a contract."

"How about the Allardyce Foundation?"

"Lewin's a wizard about foundations. Lewin invented foundations."

"Then he has teamed up with Griswold?"

"What did you expect . . . if you can't beat em, join 'em. You remain an important stockholder. Jap, we can make it almost as expensive as we like for the Griswold-Lewin combo. . . ." Theo got up off the bed yawning and stretching. "I told you Jap this was going to be a big year for the Murcheson family fortunes."

"What about Jim and Sylvia?"

"You mark my words, they'll have Jim Swazey out on his ass in six months."

Jasper picked up the phone and asked for long distance. His heart was thumping like when he was a boy calling his first date. Thank God, right away, what luck, there was Lorna's voice, gentle, warm, loving in his ear.

"Lorna, that Mexican plan. It's on. How soon can you hop a plane to Kansas City? . . . Good . . . the sooner the better. . . . I'll dream up a car. . . . When you arrive at the airport call me at my daughter Evie's house Grand 1-3679. I'll be hiding out there while my lawyers clean up this mess."

"And the clever young prince carried off the pretty princess from the enchanted castle." Theo mimicked a bedtime story on the radio.

"You shut up, Theo. Did you get that number?"

Theo nodded.

"You take over this room and see what kind of a deal you can get out of Griswold. He'll be at the Exchange Building biting his nails to know what I'm going to do. . . . Call him before the son of a bitch has a heart attack."

Jasper reached for his panama. "And get the valet to pack my bags. . . . See you in church, Theo."

With Lorna at his side Jasper drove the new Chrysler slowly south along a straight cement road that cut through ripening wheat that flowed in every direction towards the horizon's rim. "Write off your losses, Mr. Allardyce used to say, that was the first rule for business success." "What losses?" asked Lorna. The car purred along through the sunny wheat. The new Chrysler was a sweetdriving car.

With a jerk Jasper came to a stop behind a black sedan parked in the shallow swale ditch. "It's one of our inspectors," he told Lorna excitedly. "Let's see what he's finding."

The still air was whitehot under the noon sun. As they walked along the fence meadowlarks flew up. A cockpheasant watched them with a beady eye from behind a budding thistle. They stood still hand in hand as he jerked his head from side to side and strutted off secure and stately in scarlet stripes through the green fringe of weeds. Meanwhile the young man from the sampling bureau was coming back towards them through the wheat. "I'd kinda hoped it might be Fred, my soninlaw," Jasper whispered, "but no matter."

The young man was dusty and tanned and ruddy with sunburn. He walked pigeontoed to avoid treading down the grain. In one hand he held a bunch of heavy bearded ears. He trailed the other behind him combing with open fingers through the dancing ears as he walked. "How are we doing?" asked Jasper eagerly as the young man climbed the fence. He showed Jasper his smudged hands. "Smut," he spat the word out disgustedly.

He reached for a brown envelope off the back seat of his car, stuffed his sample ears into it and marked down the date, the location, the variety. After he'd brushed the black streaks off his khaki pants he held out his hand and looked inquiringly at Jasper. "My name's Kennicut . . . the boys call me Spike," he began. "Mine's Milliron," said Jasper. "Southeastern Division . . . Out here for a director's meeting . . . Just nosing around."

Spike nodded wisely and told Jasper to follow along, he'd show him something real pretty.

Three or four miles down the road he stopped again. Lorna and Jasper watched him wade out into the pale glare of another field.

This time Spike came back smiling, holding up a pile of fat golden grains in his grimy palms. "See the straight clean crease." As he looked up from marking a fresh envelope his eyes fixed sharply on a white blur that was gaining outline above the horizon. "Listen," he said.

The road was silent. A few larks whistled as they flew. From the distance came the whir and clank of a combine. A column of dust hovered over the bright dancing grain that darkened to grimy gold where catspaws traveled across it under the fitful wind. "I thought so. The harvest has begun."

"So long Spike," said Jasper.

"Sometimes," he told Lorna as he switched on the ignition of the car, "I envy those young guys."

Documentary (22)

STOLEN
ANOTHER HIGHSALARIED EXECUTIVE

Are You Missing the Bus?

A message—visual or auditory—is received by a sensory organ and transmitted to the brain, where it sets up a pattern of activity in a small circuit of nerve cells.

If the message reverberates long enough in the nerve circuit, molecular changes occur that alter the form and function of the nerve cells, fixing a record of the message for a period dependent partly upon the intensity and repetition of the stimulation. If the message reverberations are too short-lived, no permanent record is fixed.

THE RACE FOR SPACE

Shoe advertising has always been something of a problem. If shoes are shown alone, there is not much appeal. If they are shown in connection with a whole human figure, the eye of the reader is drawn to the upper part of the torso and away from the shoes.

GET THE CAR THAT'S GOT THE GOODS

How Can I Justify the Purchase of a Dictating Machine?

a complete line of unique transistorized digital building block modules—and for ruggedness they are vacuum encapsulated in an epoxy resin

TWO THEORIES OFFERED AS CLUE TO ALL MATTER

New Phoneways in the Sky

The tall muscular youth was arrested as the result of a trap set for him by the police. They had the co-operation of his girl friend who was among the fifty youngsters questioned by the police yesterday morning. Two detectives accompanied the girl to their usual meeting place. They hid in two hallways. The other detectives also kept out of sight. When Serra walked to the girl the detectives surrounded him.

He was wearing a narrow striped red and gray blazer jacket. A tiny gold cross was attached to the lobe of his left ear.

ALL HUMAN SPEECH IS MADE UP OF HISSES AND BUZZES

The professor said that this theory had been tested crudely by refrigerating hamsters at varying periods after they had learned to find their way through a maze. If the cooling, which essentially halted nervous activity and so-called message reverberation, came too soon after the training, he said, the hamsters did not remember the maze.

An Answer Simple Enough

When Major General William Frishe Dean turned up alive at Panmunjom after three years as a Communist prisoner he did his best to keep people from making a fuss over him. No man could honestly claim to be ashamed of the Congressional Medal, that he admitted, but he explained that he came close to shame when he thought of the men who had done better jobs than he had without such recognition and died doing them. He kept reminding the reporters that he was a general captured because he took a wrong road:

"I lost ground I should have not lost. I lost trained officers and fine men. I'm not proud of that record," he told William L. Worden who wrote up his story for *The Saturday Evening Post*, "and I'm under no delusions that my weeks of command constituted any masterly campaign."

It puzzled General Dean that the American people insisted on making a hero of him all the same.

He described himself, with characteristic candor, as an "in-between curious kind of a general officer," who had never been to West Point, who hadn't seen action in World War I and who hadn't come up from the ranks.

As far back as he could remember he had wanted to be a soldier. He was the son of rural dentist, born and raised in Carlyle, the small country seat of Clinton County, in southern Illinois. Maybe it was on account of his mother's German blood that he was so carried away by the sight of soldiers drilling when his folks took him to the St. Louis World's Fair. He had a cornbelt childhood in the public schools; sold magazines to buy himself mailorder courses in physical culture.

As a kid he was a crank about physical fitness, weightlifting, dumbbells, pushups, chinning himself. He was an inveterate hiker.

No student, he flunked the West Point exams after graduating from highschool. The war was on in Europe but he was too young to enlist without his mother's permission.

When the family moved to California he enrolled in a prelaw course at the university. For spending money he worked as a stevedore on the San Francisco docks, as trolley conductor, washed dishes and even pounded the beat for a while as a student cop during the period when a Berkeley police chief was trying to interest college boys in the policeman's career. What he liked best about college was the students' army training corps.

He never did get a degree, but the Army had a crying need for officers: mighty few boys wanted an army career after the War to End War ended in the disillusioned peace. When Dean was twentyfour he managed to pass the examination for a commission as Second Lieutenant in the regular army.

The man was a natural born infantryman. Still a crank on physical fitness he coached athletic teams, rode, played polo. A young lady whose horse ran away when he took her out for a canter while he was stationed at Fort Douglas, Utah, ended by becoming his wife. The Canal Zone was their honeymoon. They were happy in the army life. He served as a lieutenant for twelve years, was promoted to captain at thirtyseven, to major at fortyone.

He landed in France on Omaha Beach with the 44th Infantry Division and ended the war in command of it. He liked to boast that in all the fighting up through France and across the Rhine into Germany he only lost fortyfour men captured. As a general officer he didn't believe in soldiers getting captured.

In 1947 he was military governor of South Korea, trying, through interpreters, to teach the Koreans how to run their sawedoff nation American style. Later he regretted he hadn't tried to learn more about the Koreans before he tried to do that job. At that he was known as "the walking general" because, instead of zooming about in a starspangled staffcar, he walked to his office in the morning. He was occasionally seen poking through the slums of Seoul or hiking far up into the hills to shoot pheasants. After elections, duly approved, he turned the problems of Korean selfgovernment over to Syngman Rhee and left for a new tour of duty in Japan.

One Saturday night in June 1950 General Dean and his wife attended a fancy dress party at Headquarters of the 24th

Division at Kokura. They wore the Korean costumes they had brought away as souvenirs from Seoul. The costumes were admired, but the general, who was six feet two, remembered that the robes were much too short for him. He was uncomfortable in the hard stovepipe hat of a yang ban.

Next morning the North Korean army, trained by Russian instructors and armored with Russian heavy tanks, crossed the 38th Parallel. World War III, here it comes, they told each other at Headquarters in Kokura. General Dean's troops were scattered all over the southern islands of Japan. Regiments were under strength. A bare fifteen percent had seen combat. Men were soft from occupation living, PX beer and the delicate attentions of the Jap girls they shacked up with. They didn't know where the hell Korea was and couldn't care less. While they were busy tending the refugees, military and civilian, who came out in planeloads, orders came to hold South Korea.

General Dean found himself, after a number of false starts, fumbling around in the fog on a C–45 looking for the Taejon airstrip. That highway and railroad junction in the middle of the peninsula had been picked for the hub of defense. Looked like a good place for headquarters on the map.

The fog down in Taejon was thicker than in the air above it.

Everybody was on the run. No communications. No intelligence a man could rely on. Fifth column work. At ROK headquarters slit-eyed officers were yelling Communist in each other's faces. For an American who didn't know the language it was hard to tell friend from foe.

Before General Dean had time to set up his headquarters organization the Communists had broken through down all the arterial roads. Their heavy tanks outclassed the American light tanks that had already been nearly obsolete when the fighting stopped in Europe five years before. Ammunition was short. Nobody knew the terrain. Some outfits were putting up a scrap, a few brave men selling their lives high, but nothing was holding anywhere.

It was decided to move headquarters southeast down the railroad to Yongdong. Communications were so bad General Dean decided he'd be better able to judge what was going on if he stayed a while in Taejon.

One hot July morning the general woke to the sound of gunfire. The problem that day was how to pull out of Taejon while there was still time. He spoke afterwards of the "sombre poetry" of combat. "The phrase 'fight and fall back' has a brave sound," he told Worden; and about the smells of the Korean summer morning, of ricepaddy muck and human excrement and the punky reek of smoldering thatch, laced now and then with the sharp sea of cordite. "Bone wearying" was how he described the fighting that day and the days before it.

Communist tanks were already in town.

A general's business is to give orders. Although he still had one telephone line open to the rear General Dean and his aide and a Korean interpreter were so thoroughly cut off there were no orders left to give. He decided that if he couldn't give orders he could at least give an example.

Taejon was full of infiltrators wearing the white clothes of the country people, turncoats sniping out of windows. Dean got the clerks and cooks and messengers of the regimental command together into a party to stalk tanks. Fight and fall back. In covering the retreat they accounted for a number of snipers, made unsuccessful attacks on a couple of Communist tanks they found waddling about without infantry support. The last many of the retreating troops saw of General Dean he was blazing away with his fortyfive at a tank that rumbled unconcernedly by. "Dean losing his temper" was how he explained it.

At last he got hold of a man with a bazooka who still had ammo for a wonder and crawled with him up into a plastered room overlooking a narrow shopping street. They found themselves looking down the muzzle of the cannon of a Communist tank. The general indicated a spot at the base of the cannon. The bazooka fired pointblank. A horrible screaming came from inside. Two more rounds. The tank was out of commission and the street was quiet.

The general was keeping a list that day of men he intended to decorate for bravery. (He'd been feeling a little guilty, so he said, about skimping on decorations in the European Theater.) He even had a dozen or more medals in his jeep all ready to pin on.

Dean's brave men never did get their decorations. Things moved too fast. Already it was dusk and time to evacuate what was left of the regimental post. Some light tanks sent up to relieve them were having a hard time holding their own in a firefight with the Communist armor. His troops were clumsy about taking cover, Dean reminisced sadly, hadn't played enough cops and robbers when they were kids.

The main road out was jammed with jackknifed trucks and burning halftracks. The road was under fire as far as you could see. In a squall of bullets the general's jeep roared through an intersection into a wrong road. No way to turn back.

They came on a bunch of men talking surrender under a wrecked truck. Some were wounded. Dean filled his two jeeps with the wounded and as many others as could climbed aboard. They drove careening into a Communist roadblock. Nothing to it but to take to the ditches.

Dean's aide was wounded. Afterwards Dean told of how proud he was of this Lieutenant Clarke for the way he kept the seventeen men together as they crawled through the muck of a beanfield. One of their Koreans, a welldressed one, fell into a "honey pit." Later Dean remembered waiting for dark on a riverbank and delivering a lecture about putting halizone tablets into your canteen before you drank the water.

Carrying one man too badly hurt to walk, they crossed the river at dark and climbed a steep mountain spur hoping to cut back to the road beyond the Communist roadblock. The wounded man was delirious. He drank up all the water they had and kept calling for more. At a point on the mountain, while Lieutenant Clarke was giving his little outfit a rest, Dean thought he heard water in a gully. He slipped away from the group and started to climb down. He never knew how he came to trip and plunge headfirst down the hill. He blacked out.

He must have rolled a hundred yards at least because when he came to he was lying alone on the hillside in the black night. His shoulder seemed to be broken. He was bleeding from a gash in the head. No sign of the other men.

About daybreak a Communist patrol almost stumbled over his carcass. Dean was conscious enough to hear the goatlike scamper of their feet up the stony slope. When they had gone he dragged himself into a clump of bushes where he lay all day groggy with pain.

By night he had himself in hand. His legs were all right. His head was clear. By favoring his shoulder he found that in spite of the pain he could crawl. By the time he reached the top of the ridge he was walking. All the boyish physical culture was standing by him now. He'd walk to the American lines.

He found himself, like in a nightmare, climbing handhold to handhold down a perpendicular cliff in a downpour of rain. He joined company with a young lieutenant, lost him again in a haze of weariness escaping from some Korean riflemen across a paddyfield. Day followed day. He lost track of time.

For thirtyfive days, hiding out by day in the rocky ridges and traveling at night, blarneying the country people out of a little rice now and then in the villages, he managed to escape capture. Gradually he made his way south towards the shrinking perimeter of the Pusan beachhead. He could already hear the distant rumble of American guns when his luck failed.

A pair of Koreans, named Han and Choi, whom he thought he'd secured as guides through to the American lines, led him into an ambush.

His shoulder was still agony. He was too weak from undernourishment and scurvy and dysentery to put up much resistance when fifteen home guards jumped him on a moonlit road and trussed him up like a calf and dragged him off to the Communist police in the nearest town. Still he tried to fight so hard they would shoot him: he wanted his children to know he had put up a fight to the end.

On account of the language difficulty he never really knew whether his guides had intended to betray him all along or whether they couldn't help themselves. They are said to have been paid five dollars for his hide.

Anyway there he was, an American major general locked in an L shaped cage in which he could neither stand up or lie down in a smalltown police station, a prisoner of war of the Communist Koreans.

Defeat. Captivity. This was like no other war in the nation's history. No more could any American general boast about how few men he'd had captured. All over Korea Americans were surrendering.

These were the kids who'd been soaked in wartime pros-

perity while their elder brothers manned the amphibious
landings and the desperate beachheads and the floating bases
and the great airstrikes of World War II;

raised on the gibblegabble of the radio between the family
car and the corner drugstore and the Five and Ten.

Nobody had ever told them anything
except to get more and do less.

Nobody had ever told them that to be an American meant
anything more than to look at the comics and to drive around
the roads in a new automobile

obtained on easy monthly payments
and to reach for packaged foods out of the frigidaire;

and particularly the army hadn't explained to them what
they were doing in this lousy country that was all steep hills
and muddy fields

that smelt of shit,

helping one bunch of gooks fight another bunch of gooks
that had a hellofalot better tanks

and seemed to know what they were doing. (United Nations; what the hell was the United Nations? Wasn't that a
building in New York?)

General Dean had been proud of how few of his men
surrendered in the European theater. He felt ashamed enough
squatting in that little cage, a prisoner: he'd have felt worse
if he'd known that four days after the fighting started

a captured officer
of his own 24th Infantry Division

was broadcasting enemy propaganda over the Communist
radio.

After the stalemate and the exchange of prisoners
across the 38th Parallel, army authorities went to considerable
trouble—statistics were collected, reports compiled, books
written—to discover

why,

out of seven thousand one hundred and ninety army men
captured,

thirteen percent became out and out creatures of the Communists and roughly one third collaborated in some way or
other with the enemy. They were the "progressives."

There were so many informers that not one single man

made good his escape from a prisoner of war camp (and you ask why the prestige of our nation has sunk so low in the world).

They'd all had some schooling but no one had taught those poor kids that spirit, the little spark of God in every man, is what keeps man alive in adversity. The Communist indoctrinators were able to appeal to a sort of ignorant idealism that is the dead shell of the protestant ethics our fathers lived by. Idealism without ethics is no compass.

"One of the most difficult problems for a prisoner is maintaining his judgment," General Dean told Worden.

For judgment read sense of right and wrong.

No one had told these kids that right and wrong was the inner compass that points true north. When army discipline broke down they fell to pieces, each poor devil by himself. They didn't help each other the way the Turks did or the Marines. They didn't take care of themselves. If you can't help yourself you can't help the next man. They wouldn't eat the gook chow. Two thousand seven hundred and thirty let themselves die in captivity. Of the survivors two thirds confessed to the army investigators they had "played it cool."

Thirteen percent told the enemy nothing, wrote no confessions, joined no study classes, memorized no Marxist litanies. They were the "reactionaries." They had tough sledding but they came out best in the end,
and with honor.

Fiftyyearold General Dean with a broken shoulder and an infected foot, suffering from dysentery and every disease that fatigue and underfeeding brought in their train, would definitely have been described as a "reactionary." Dean had spirit enough and to spare.

For thirty years Communism had been building a technique, using everything from the thumbscrew and the rack to the latest psychological methods of the scientific laboratories,
and dark and cold and solitude and starvation
to kill God's spirit in man. They tried threats and misery on Dean; they tried rational argument; they tried luxury;
but still Dean talked back.

Torture? No they didn't torture him, not a bit.

He was taken first to a modern sort of penitentiary (he'd inspected it himself as military governor). The commandant suggested kindly that he must go on the air to explain to his family and friends that he was safe, that they were treating him with the deference his rank deserved, and incidentally that the Communists were being welcomed as brothers by the Koreans of the south.

No. Dean wouldn't go on any radio.

The commandant asked him whether if they turned him loose he would continue to fight.

Dean said that if his country gave him a chance after the mess he'd made of his command he'd try to do better next time and kill a lot more Communists.

Torture? No they didn't torture him, not a bit.

He was taken north and put in the hands of a certain Colonel Kim who was learned in the techniques.

It was Kim's business to try to make Dean sign a propaganda petition. At first Kim tried good food and pleasantries. He even sent in a doctor to attend to Dean's dysentery. He offered him a pleasant country house and all the whiskey he wanted to drink and the assurance that he wouldn't be tortured.

Dean said he didn't drink whiskey.

Colonel Kim's geniality faded. He took to waking Dean up in the middle of the night.

About the time of the Inchon landing there was a break. Dean was hurried into Pyongyang the Communist capital and interrogated by the Chief of Security about the American plan of maneuver. He insisted on a written answer. Dean wrote it out with stiff fingers:

> Fortunately I do not have the information you seek. But even if I did I wouldn't give it to you, because by so doing I would be a traitor to my country. So help me God, William F. Dean.

He was sent back to Colonel Kim. The real interrogation began. It was winter by that time. Day after day and night after night they made Dean sit on a hard chair in the light summer suit they'd given him when they took away his uniform. His infected left foot had swelled so he couldn't bear a shoe. He had lost so much weight that sitting on the hard straight chair was agony. He had to sit on his hands. Sitting on his hands made them swell up almost as much as his foot. The interrogations seemed to be heading towards his trial as a war criminal. Colonel Kim and another Kim and a Ph.D. worked in shifts.

The room was cold. The temperature about 33°. Colonel Kim complained because Dean's teeth chattered. Colonel Kim who wore a heavy overcoat said it wasn't cold at all. To prove it he made Dean strip down to his shorts. Day after day they went on keeping him awake, starving him, freezing him, using oldfashioned third degree methods. The only breaks were when Dean had to go running to the latrine.

No they didn't torture him. Not a bit. Colonel Kim interspersed his interrogation with references to the torture to come. At last Dean could stand it no more. Afraid he might tell something under torture in his wornout state he managed to steal the revolver off a sleeping guard. When the Koreans jumped on him from all sides he couldn't get the revolver to fire. Dean was sorry for the poor guard, a simple fellow who had been nice to him. He was led away and probably shot for falling asleep on duty.

Somehow the desperation of Dean's act impressed his captors. Colonel Kim was seen no more. There was no more talk of torture. Doctors visited him. He was kept warm. His food became fairly decent.

By that time MacArthur's army was sweeping north. Ill as he was Dean was hurried in trucks and jeeps up to the Yalu and across into Manchuria for safekeeping as the Korean Communist army broke in pieces.

On that trip Dean could relax a little. Everybody was too busy to interrogate him. He wasn't treated too badly, now that the Americans seemed to be winning.

Dean began to make observations. Already he had observed with some interest that sitting motionless stripped to the skin in extreme cold, his body, even in its weakened condition, somehow managed to retain a little warmth.

His guards were enemies but they were sometimes friends. He became interested in what he described to Worden as "the manysided, kind and cruel, inventive, clever, stupid, resilient unpredictable Korean character." Maybe getting to know these people was worth what he was going through. It would never have happened to an uncaptured general.

After the Chinese victories rolled back MacArthur's advance he was spirited from place to place. He had an idea the Korean Communists were trying to keep him out of the hands of the Chinese. He wasn't mistreated but he was never allowed out of doors. Months passed cooped in tiny rooms. He had no reading matter. They wouldn't let him play the local form of chess his guards played. To keep from losing his mind he squared numbers and did square roots and kept track of the flies he killed. His biggest day he killed 522.

He began to be cozy with the Communist Koreans. A number of his guards were training to be officers. He became interested in their careers and helped them with their homework. He learned all he could about their Communist theory and practice.

"The most important discovery to me," he told Worden, "was that the ordinary Communists who guarded me and lived with me really believed that they were following a route that would lead to a better life for themselves and their children. . . . It was easy for us to say they were mistaken but not so easy to explain to these men of limited experience just why their ideology must fail. . . . We can't convince them with fine words. We've got to show them something better. We must have an answer simple enough for the dullest to understand."

At last after three years Dean was exchanged with the rest at Panmunjom. The first Americans he saw were gaunt prisoners in a column of trucks. "Hi General Dean!" they yelled. "Hi General! We didn't know we were waiting for you." The Yankee voices sounded wonderful to him.

Soon afterwards with unaffected dignity, with perfect candor, he was telling his story to the world's press assembled at Freedom Village. Somehow in everything Dean said, in everything he did while he was a prisoner there had appeared that answer simple enough for the dullest to understand.

The American people were right to make a hero of him.

Documentary (23)

CHINESE MESSES FEED 400,000,000

CITY DISCOUNTING STRONTIUM FEARS

Says It Would Be Foolish to Stop Drinking Milk

IT'S VERY COOL AND DREAMY
IN A TEENY WEENIE BIKINI

From her lofty pinnacle as reigning movie queen
and one of the world's most envied women, Lana
Turner, rich and beautiful, reached down into the
back alleys of Hollywood to surrender her heart to
the strange and mysterious John Stompanato.

Ruby Cooled to 425 Below Zero

"I am writing this letter as a last resort. I don't dare sign
my name. I might wake up at the bottom of the Erie Canal."

Some came by rowboat and others in skindiving
equipment, he said, and policing the airport, which
has an eighteen-mile perimeter, under such conditions was impossible. He said that the converging
of thrill seekers had been caused by radio and television reports of the possible disaster and added,
"No police force in the world could have kept back
the crowds."

SAWGRASS URGED FOR NEWSPRINT

Easy Ownership Plan

"If you get a blade between your hand and the
pole, it will cut you to the bone, with a jagged gash

that takes long to heal. The nose and face suffer
much."

THE MAN IN THE CONVERTIBLE KNOWS HOW
TO ENJOY THE BETTER THINGS IN LIFE

> Evidence makes it reasonably certain that the an-
> cestors of the group had to pass through a stage of
> existence underground as deaf, half-blind and legless
> burrowing lizards.

"Is this what I fought for in World War II? Is this the world
my children are growing up into?"

INVESTIGATOR'S NOTES VII

They offered the investigator a seat at a white enamel
table in their bright new kitchen in a shady suburban street.
They took him right in like a member of the family. They
both looked so young it was hard to believe they'd been married five years, seemed more like brother and sister. Both came
from Italian families, with dark eyes, even white teeth and
dark hair that curled. There was an eager competent look
about the pair, a clean and welldressed wellfed look, as if
they'd been clean and welldressed and wellfed all their lives.
They wore good collegiatelooking clothes.

It was the young man who got up from his chair to fetch
the investigator a can of beer and reached into the big new
shiny refrigerator for a loaf of long Italian bread and some
cheese and salami. She sat there watching him as if opening
the refrigerator door was the cleverest thing any man had
ever done in this world. When he started to talk her eyes
were fixed on his face, her mouth a little open with an amazed
expression, as if she were watching him do the highwire act
at the circus.

In highschool he'd been crazy about politics, elections,
mock conventions, and stuff like that.

She interrupted: he was an honor student and earned a trip
to Italy on a scholarship.

In the union, it was a little like highschool politics, he went on, laughing, only they played for keeps. He worked in an aeronautical plant. A big local, at one time they had fourteen thousand employees. He operated a drill press on the third shift. During the war he'd been a parachute rigger in a service squad with the Army Air Force.

When he came back from the service the people in his department elected him shopsteward. They were under the Auto Workers. Dues were two fifty a month, initiation fifteen bucks, though the top rate was only a dollar fortyfour. A guy couldn't make money without overtime. With top employment the union took in thirtysix thousand a month. That meant eighteen thousand to the International, a lot of money.

Way back in organization days—he had a quiet smiling way of explaining things; you could see that this was the kind of fellow who wouldn't have trouble getting elected anywhere— the workers in this particular plant had been divided between the Square Dealers and the Ububs. The Ububs had gotten Walter Reuther's benediction over a glass of milk in a diner. He laughed. The International sent in some recordings of evidence pretty bad for the Square Dealers, he himself sided with the Ububs. A lot of them were old schoolmates. When he was elected shopsteward, he told his people to make up their own minds.

Some people didn't like Walter Reuther. People admired his fighting spirit, a gogetter, but a lot of people just plain didn't like him. So far as he knew Walter was straight and so was the regional office of the International. The trouble was in the local.

In the elections they went through all the forms but the president and the plant chairman and the group in the office managed to rig 'em just the same.

Sure they had voting machines. The voting was in the lunch hour and after each shift, in a big tent outside the plant. Twentyfour voting machines were lined up like in a penny arcade at an amusement park. The trouble was you didn't have to sign your name when you voted. It was the plant chairman who gave out authorizations to vote and you might have a stack of them in your pocket. Next shift you'd come back and vote again.

The other system was: people would save up union cards of men who'd left the plant for some reason or other. They'd vote first under their own name then under some other guy's name, maybe he was dead. The challenger had a hard time checking because the administration kept all the records.

"They never would let us get in the Honest Ballot Association to take charge of an election."

Well for a lark a few years before, this young shopsteward and some friends decided to give 'em a little opposition. They put up a slate of candidates and got thirtytwo hundred out of eight thousand votes. They were sure they had more support than that in the plant so they charged the election was fraudulent.

They got up a letter of protest.

Every man who signed that letter of protest was suspended by the union. The checkoff saved them from being fired. According to the Taft-Hartley Law so long as they paid their dues they couldn't be fired. That was when they started this Vanguard group, to keep the opposition together so that they wouldn't be picked off separately.

Some of them were fired by the company at that. There was a colored fellow, one of the best men they had, he'd been a committeeman for nine years and still he got fired.

"You can't tell me there isn't collusion between the personnel department and the union officers, I know it's a hard thing to prove but what happened tells the story."

This young shopsteward who was talking, he'd been hauled up before a kangaroo court and suspended for conduct unbecoming a union member. Then the president of the local brought suit for libel against all the men who signed the protest. Another colored fellow was fired, he had to join the Ububs and crawl to get his job back.

The Vanguard group they hired them a lawyer but the lawyer doublecrossed them. The union officers had all the money; the International paid half their legal expenses. This lawyer was disbarred later for swindling. He was a sweet talking man but he had a little streak of larceny in his heart.

"Well we got ourselves a new lawyer, an honest Italian lawyer." He was talking loud now. His wife was nodding her head emphatically. "He got us a court order to produce the books of the local. The local president pretty near went to jail for refusing to produce the books. We did get in a CPA to look at them. He found defalcations, but we haven't been able to do a thing about it. Not yet."

He let his voice drop. The procedure to fight election fraud was too cumbersome and costly, he explained in his patient smiling way. It took four or five years of battling in the courts and by that time everybody had forgotten what the stink was about in the first place. If there was collusion with management the guys who asked embarrassing questions could be fired for small infractions. They'd pick 'em off one by one.

The industry was up against hard times. There had always been seasonal layoffs. Well the independents guys got laid off first.

"The shopstewards have too much power. I ought to know. I'm one myself." He grinned with a flash of teeth. "Money's passed under the table for seniority. There's a kind of superseniority the shopsteward can hand out as a bonus. When thousands of people are being laid off a man'll do almost anything to keep his job."

For the first time there was a worried frowning look on his face. His wife looked as if she were ready to cry. He stretched and yawned and sat staring down at the table for a while.

"I'm the kind of guy that likes to get along with people," he burst out suddenly smiling again. "Those people made me mad." He threw back his head and showed all his white teeth in a laugh. "The madder I get the harder I'll fight. We're organizing to fight this thing just like in the old days when they were organizing to start the first unions. You just watch the headlines."

He jumped to his feet. "Here I been talking too much . . . How about another can of beer?"

The Great Taxicab War

Will Jenks let his cheek brush Maddie's as he leaned across her to fasten her seatbelt and whispered thank God that was over.

Golly it was a relief when he heard the plunk of the outside door closing and the feathered props began to turn. The warmth of her seeping through the blue tailored suit made his fingers tingle. Maddie's round face looked tired under her black bang but there was still a flash of jet when her eye met his.

Wasn't Dad awful? Maddie groaned. Will hadn't figured on two mothersinlaw, she was sure of that. By the time the plane was airborne and grumbling towards Miami through the night sky they were thanking their stars that neither of them had tried to get married to somebody else. Not with those parents. Nobody else in the world would have understood.

The stewardess had dimmed the lights. They tipped back their seats and stretched out hand in hand whispering in spurts under the sound of the motors. Now that they had made a safe getaway it all struck them funny.

Will had wanted to be married at Hollow Lane Meeting which his family had attended for generations but some of the elderly Friends had let it be known, in that inimitably unspoken Quaker way they had, that since Miss Milliron was an Episcopalian it would hardly be suitable for him to take her in marriage until she had been received as a member, and nobody needed to tell him how long that might take; so they had been married in Dad's front parlor by a feeble old whitehaired Unitarian who stuttered. Then Maddie's dad had to bring along that television queen he'd just married with the ink hardly dry on his divorce and Maddie couldn't ask her own mother to stay away, now could she? And Colonel Milliron had covered his embarrassment by getting drunk as a coot to the illconcealed disgust of Will's old man who was a frantic teetotaller and not a bit well besides. And there was Maddie's mother stalking about stiffnecked as a giraffe. If Fred and Evie could only have been there they could have helped handle the parents, but at the last moment Maddie'd had a wire from Kansas City that both they and the babies were down with the measles and couldn't come. That had been the final blow.

"Will I never could have gotten through it without you," sighed Maddie and that struck them even funnier and they laughed till they fell asleep.

It was still night when they tumbled out of the plane at the Miami airport with two hours to wait for the Nassau flight. They sat mumbling and blinking in the harsh electric light of the airport café sleepily trying to choke down some breakfast. What a way to start a honeymoon. The next time they got married they'd do it right, they joshed each other. They were so sleepy they didn't have much laugh left in them.

All Will could think of was how much he wanted bed, bed with Maddie.

The time seemed endless before their flight was called, but from the moment the plane took off into the marbled dawn over the sea: blue, then Gulf Stream purple streaked with spume, then clear blue again and green and amber over coralheads and milky over great shallow banks here and there blotched by a haphazard strip of low land mislaid in an immensity of sea and sky, the hours began to race.

Will tried to hold on to every second but Nassau went by as fast as a technicolor travelogue punctuated by a few daiquiriflavored kisses behind the hibiscus in the hotel garden where they lunched, and they were off again in a little English plane with a chatty Londoner for a pilot to the island Joe Finch had lent them where they were left alone with two cartons of groceries in a sunscorched bungalow under the palms. The only population was landcrabs and lizards.

Alone on an island with Maddie. Hot dickerty damn. Will had been dreaming of it for months. In hospital that was all he thought of. Will had planned endless unimaginable lovemaking but for all he could do, now that it was real, it was over so soon. The little details of life kept crowding in, getting meals and burying the garbage and tinkering with the radio and swimming till they were waterlogged, staring their eyes out through the panes on their diving helmets at the thousand-colored fish that lurked among the seafans and the sponges under the coralheads; and before they knew it, it would be night and they would eat and drink together by lamplight and roll into bed drugged with sunburn and salt air and exercise and before they'd had time to enjoy the marvelousness of each other, sleep would blot them out.

Maddie turned out to be a right good simple cook except that she declared she didn't know how to clean fish and didn't intend to learn. The only argument they had was about Will's swimming out too far along the reef with his fishspear among the sharks and the barracuda. But that wasn't really an argument; and, of course, Maddie was right. From the beginning she started to look out for Will first. The motherly little-girl-with-a-doll look that came over her face when she rubbed castor oil over the crisscrossed scars on his crippled carcass knotted him all up inside. There was so much of the surgeon's needlework showing on his legs and left hip he'd been ashamed to have her see him without his clothes, but now, every time he made her happy with his lovemaking he got back a little of the joy in the smooth sturdiness of his own body.

Their life on Joe Finch's island had hardly begun before it was over. The damn cockney pilot turned up on the airstrip a day early with the story that there was a norther brewing and if he didn't take them now it might be a week. It gave them an extra day to roam around the candycolored streets of Nassau but with a swim on a beach and a few drinks and a couple of meals to the sound of calypso drums, the day was gone in a flash and there they were homeward bound to Miami.

While they waited for the takeoff Maddie said seriously, in a tone she intended to have listened to, that they'd proved to her satisfaction that what he needed was plenty of sunlight and swimming to straighten out his crippled leg. He answered that they'd try to go back once a year.

"Twice a year," said Maddie.

"Maddie let's just go back, period."

Home in Chestnut Hill, Will thanked God he and Maddie had had their island. It was a miserable raw sleety March. Dad had never been the easiest man in the world to get along with, but now he was really feeble, and querulous. He'd failed since the wedding. It was heartbreaking to see him, stooped and shaky, puttering around the house.

It was hard on Maddie too, taking care of the big bleak stone house full of unfamiliar furnishings gone to dust and mildew in the five years since Mother died. They had to stay. There was nobody else in the world to take care of Dad or the business since Chattie had married a viceconsul assigned to Indonesia and brother Lewis had been killed in a car crash while Will was in Korea. It wasn't Will's idea of a good time selling tombstones either, though he liked the crabbed old stonecutters, Italians mostly, who worked for them, but he did his best. It was the old family business and a good one and he had to stick to it at least while Dad lived. "Never mind," he would whisper to Maddie and nudge her when he caught her looking glum, "we'll climb out of the graveyard one of these days."

The day after Dad's funeral was a Sunday. It was a glorious

October morning. Will felt in no mood to go to meeting. Maddie was in the fourth month of her second pregnancy and still felt pretty sickish now and then. Since Chattie and Ned Weaver, who had been using up their hardearned leave, poor devils, to help with Dad's last agonies, were staying in the house, they could take care of the baby. Maddie hadn't had an outing for weeks. To freshen her up a little Will decided to drive her over to her father's. The Millirons had just settled into a farmhouse they'd recently bought out in Bucks County near Providence Forge. Will, who had a great respect for the old gentleman's business sense, wanted to talk to Colonel Milliron about what to do next.

Driving out towards Doylestown on the broad highway full of Sunday cars gleaming in the mellow sunlight, Will started explaining to Maddie—she knew all about it anyway; she always knew what he was thinking—that he just couldn't see them wearing out their lives like Dad in Chestnut Hill. Hell no. The world was too damned exciting. The time had come to make a break. Tombstones—he knew he ought to call them memorials—just weren't his meat. He wanted to get into a business where a man didn't have to have his mouth full of mashed potatoes all the time.

Will had been all over the state selling memorials that summer. "I just don't get a bang out of it Maddie." Undertakers gave him the creeps, of course he oughtn't to call them that, not even in fun. Dad had accumulated a fund of good will among the morticians of the whole Philadelphia area. That was the only real asset the firm of Monroe, Jenks and Co. had in this world. He could feel it being frittered away. Those folks knew he didn't have the proper attitude. He could tell the way they looked at him at the state convention. The time to sell out was now, particularly as Chattie was home and she'd have to decide about her half interest.

Maddie said hadn't they better wait till the new baby was a little further along. "No we can't wait," whined Will.

Fillingstations, used car lots, luncheonettes, stranded farmhouse gardens full of dusty dahlias and chrysanthemums flitted by under the telephone poles on either side.

There was something else he had to tell her. Will was talking in an even tone with his eyes fixed on the road ahead, giving an occasional glance back through the side mirror, because he was going just a mite over the speed limit. "Maddie I do the damndest things."

It was this girl in the office, the one with sandy hair and bangs. Something kinda smoldering about that Lee Matson, cheekbones too high, a little busty maybe, but she was a good worker and a perfectly nice girl; he couldn't fire her just because he had a letch on her, now could he? To tell the truth when he first saw her he felt Lee looked something like Maddie, only blond. Mother used to say that Satan found some mischief still for idle hands to do. Will just didn't have enough to do in that damned office, sitting there all day waiting for customers to call. One day he'd happened to brush against Lee when they were getting their coats in the little cloakroom off the hall and before he knew it she was pressed up against him and he was kissing her. He kissed her good and hard. She hustled off and neither of them had ever exchanged a word about it, before or since.

Minutes went by. Will kept his eyes on the road.

Then Maddie said she'd taken him for better or for worse hadn't she? But he had felt her stiffen on the seat beside him.

"Whew I feel better," he cried out. No real harm done yet he went on soothingly. If that was the kind of guy he was he didn't want to spend his life struggling with that sort of stuff. He had to get into a business that was really full time. Now did she understand?

Maddie started to explain, in the voice of an old woman worldweary with experience, that things like that happened to most men while their wives were busy having babies. "But most men aren't Will Jenks." She gave his cheek a little quick pat.

They made a lot of wrong turnings before they found the Millirons' farm. At last after asking at every fillingstation in Providence Forge they blundered into a driveway that had the name Milliron on it. The newly metaled road led up a steep hill. At the top Will could hardly find a place to park among the piles of bricks and flagstone and tiles and contractor's litter. A Chrysler and a Buick already occupied the unfinished carport. He finally did squeeze his car in next to the cement mixer.

Lorna met them briskly at the open front door with a paintbrush in her hand. She called them her darlings. Her hair was done up in a blue polkadot scarf and she had a smudge on her nose. She looked out at them with real affection in her big gray eyes. Will thought she was the happiestlooking woman he'd ever seen.

Lorna hugged them both with her free arm as they slid in the door and led them in across the concrete floor of the hall half laid with quarry tiles. She was saying she knew what a sad time they had been having, she had wanted to go to the funeral, just out of inlaw solidarity, but Jap had absolutely had to go into New York to meet his partner Mr. Merman just in from Atlanta. The new firm was going great guns. Sure he knew, Will shouted boisterously, Merman, Milliron Associates, Industrial Consultants. A free consultation, that was what he was coming for.

Colonel Milliron and his partner Mr. Merman were sitting with drinks in their hands on a puttycolored davenport in the new livingroom in front of a broad window. Jap Milliron's skin showed ruddy under his closeclipped crisp gray hair. He looked remarkably fit for a man of his age. "Ain't this sumpen?" he cried jumping up to kiss his daughter. "Lorna dreamed this up out of a broken down stone barn."

He spread out his arms to include the grassy terrace outside, and, through a clump of silvertrunked beeches, a view of wooded hills dense with yellow and crimson and russet leaves tumbling in steps down into the valley of the Delaware. The Jersey hills beyond were really blue in the October noon. "Pretty nice," said Will.

"One hour exactly from the Empire State Building," said Mr. Merman smiling and bowing and crinkling up his little black eyes like a tame muskrat.

Lorna was taking charge of Maddie like a trained nurse. She led her off into the only finished bedroom to lie down until lunch was ready. The colonel fetched Will an oldfashioned while Mr. Merman murmured condolences about his father's death. They couldn't have been nicer.

Will sipped his drink. "If you were a young man with maybe a hundred thousand to invest what kind of a business would you start?" he asked abruptly.

Colonel Milliron spoke right up. It would have to be a service industry.

Mr. Merman said to invest it in blue chips and go to Europe and live on the interest.

"What the hell would I do all day?" asked Will, and besides a man couldn't raise a family on five thousand a year. He and Maddie were planning on six.

"The more the merrier." Colonel Milliron slapped his knee. Then he looked Will up and down as if he were his commanding officer. "Will, what did you do in the army?"

Will said he ran a transportation pool down at Pusan until he asked for combat duty. He waggled his game leg and tapped it with his cane. Maybe that hadn't been the best idea.

The colonel gave a deep understanding laugh. "Son, those are things a man can't help . . . Believe it or not, there's still money to be made in trucking in spite of the Teamsters . . . Beauty parlors, filling stations, shopping centers, taxicabs. A whole lot of upandcoming new cities have outgrown their taxicab service."

"I believe that Cousin Alphonse," put in Mr. Merman, "controls some companies that build and operate taxicabs . . . Should I call him to ask his advice?"

The colonel made a face. His neck flushed. He said sharply that Abe would have to get the telephone connected first. Evidently he didn't like to hear about Mr. Merman's cousin Alphonse. He hastened to tell Will that he'd read something in Barron's about a GI Cab Company on the rocks out in Duquesne. Duquesne was a big city and had only two hundred and fifty cabs. "Abe, that's probably another of your cousin Alphonse's monopolies."

"Touché . . . touché," said Mr. Merman smiling his concave smile.

At that point Lorna came out with a cardtable announcing that the casserole was ready. While the colonel leaned puffing over the cardtable to open it he told Will to give him a ring at his office in the morning. He'd get some details.

Mrs. Merman, a short stocky little woman who Will thought had the same muskrat look as her husband, was already hovering over them with a tray of plates and glasses. Lorna followed with the casserole in a Mexican terracotta dish. They had French bread with garlic in it and Beaujolais wine. It turned out to be a very jolly lunch.

On the way home Will kept saying that thank God he liked his inlaws, particularly Lorna, she was a peach. "You'd like Mother too," said Maddie sadly, "if you got to know her with-

out Dad. . . . Will," she cried out abruptly, "whatever happens
let's not get divorced."

"What do you think I married you for?" said Will.

The next week business suddenly picked up. It was three
months before Will had a chance to go out to Duquesne.
Meanwhile he'd had a certain amount of rather unsatisfactory
correspondence with a lawyer who signed himself attentively
yours, Hawthorne B. Shook.

Will found "Attentively yours" at a desk in a hive of other
lawyers in a nondescript officebuilding in Duquesne's second
best downtown street. He was a narrowfaced smallish man of
uncertain age with moist brown eyes set a little too close to a
crooked nose. He had a long blue jaw. He wore a checked
tweed jacket with a tancolored vest. There was a faint air of
the racetrack about him. Right away he called Will by his first
name and acted as if he'd known him all his life. "Frankly"
was one of his favorite words, frankly this and frankly that.

"Frankly, Willoughby, though I know I shouldn't be saying
it since I've been appointed by the court to liquidate these
assets for the benefit of the creditors, I don't know if I want
to see you go into this thing. Frankly an upandcoming young
fellow like you may be better off right where you are."

Will kept asking to see a statement of the assets and liabilities of the Swiftservice Cab Company. Instead Hawthorne B.
Shook wanted to know who had put Will up to being interested in cabs in Duquesne. Will finally took him out to
lunch at the best hotel he could think of and fed him a number of martinis. His manner became more and more confidential but he still didn't loosen up on any figures.

By this time they were calling each other Will and Haw.

Frankly, Will, Swiftservice Cabs had been started by the
finest bunch of returned GI's a man would like to see, full of
enthusiasm for public service, and private enterprise and
everything like that, but they just didn't understand what
they were up against. Disinterested parties had tried to tell
them the facts of life. Haw screwed up his face and let his
voice drop to a whisper. Frankly Haw himself had tried to
explain the situation to them. His lips almost touched Will's
ear. Would they listen? No . . . . They just didn't have what it
took. When the going got tough they ended up, just as he told
them they would, with a petition in bankruptcy.

Will said he couldn't understand why a booming city like this, in the middle of one of the densest industrial regions in the country, with dozens of busy towns only a few miles apart, couldn't support three or four cab companies.

Haw leaned back in his chair and stared in Will's face with one eye halfclosed. "Look at him I bet he still thinks it's the stork."

He slapped Will's shoulder and sprayed his face he laughed so hard. "Don't mind me Will. I'm just being open and aboveboard, frankly that's my greatest failing."

When they shook hands in the hotel lobby, Haw held on to Will's hand for a long time. Frankly Will this had been a very pleasant experience, but frankly he couldn't see that it could lead to much in a business way. In a personal way now he hoped it might lead to a happy association. Maybe Will would come to the races with him one of these days. He had connections. He knew he oughtn't to bet but it was only yuman.

He waggled Will's hand up and down and stared in his face out of watery eyes.

Then suddenly he threw himself back as if a new light had struck him. Will was a yuman being wasn't he? Well Hawthorne B. Shook was a yuman being too.

Will found himself nodding like a porcelain Chinaman.

At first Haw thought: this young man was trying to make a fast buck, but as a yuman being why didn't he have as much right to make a fast buck as the next yuman being? As a yuman being, he, Hawthorne B. Shook, revered and respected every other yuman being.

Now if it was a question of this young man, with public spirit on his heart, bringing in capital to help develop the great future of one of the industrial centers of the American Ruhr, if Will was bringing in capital and was willing maybe to spend a little money on the side, then he Hawthorne B. Shook would give him every assistance; within the bounds of his obligations to other parties, understand? As a yuman being he could do no other.

He rolled his eyes to heaven. If he hadn't had his hat in his hand he certainly would have taken it off.

Will had managed to get his hand loose. He let a little of his peeve get into his voice when he said he wouldn't be interested unless he received a report on assets and liabilities in the next mail. "Nobody wants to buy a pig in a poke."

Of course not, of course not, Will mustn't get him wrong.
Haw had meant no offense by his frankness. He had to be
that way.

He cocked his head to one side. "Now if you want to find
out why the GI's failed you just make me an offer for Swiftservice Cabs."

He put up his coatcollar and slammed on his hat and darted
out into the sleety drizzle.

Will was ready to spit with vexation. He turned back to the
phonebooths in a recess in the lobby and looked up cab
companies in the yellow pages. Redtop was all over but even
after he found the number for Swiftservice tucked away without any advertising there was no answer. He got his coat and
hat from the checkroom and stumped out into the raw afternoon.

As luck would have it there was a battered green cab
marked Swiftservice just trundling past the door. Will signaled
the driver. He slowed down but didn't stop. Will had to sprint
to catch him as he turned a corner beyond the hotel.

"Sorry sir," said the hack driver, "but the cop would have
given me a ticket if I'd stopped at the hotel."

"How come?" asked Will out of breath.

"As you probably know if you live here, this here's a
monopoly town. Where to sir?"

"First I want to go to the terminal of your cab company. . . .
I'm sightseeing, a special kind of sightseeing. I got a couple of
hours to kill before my train."

The hackdriver hunched up his shoulders.

"Lovely day for it," he said as the cab sludged through a
pile of slush into a side street.

When he reached a section where traffic was scanty the
hackdriver, a stocky man with a broad forehead under a mess
of untidy brown hair, drove up to the curb and stopped. He
flicked up the flag on the meter and turned and looked inquiringly at Will out of blue eyes set wide in a square bulldog
face.

"Excuse me sir," he said, "but if it's information you want I
might be able to give it to you. All you'll find at the garage is
a mechanic and he don't know nothin', particularly about
cabs."

Will explained that he represented a group from Philadelphia that might be interested in reorganizing the Swiftservice Company. He figured this town could use a little competition in the cab business.

It sure could said the hackdriver. Will asked how come he was driving one of their cabs. He'd been told the company was broke and had suspended operations.

Well it was this way, said the hackdriver, a buddy of his had made a fix with a mug they called Frank Stellato—though he didn't think that was his real name—to let a few hacks operate as independents. What Frank said went. "The gangsters need a cab themselves sometimes."

When Will tried to ask more questions the hackdriver clammed up. Will figured he thought he'd talked too much already. He asked him to drive around town and show him where the hackstands were. He tried to draw him out about rush hours, traffic problems and stuff like that. At the end of a street he caught sight of a sign over a garage entrance and suggested as tactfully as he could that maybe it wouldn't hurt if he stuck his head in.

Ranks of beatenup green cabs filled the concrete garage. The floor was slippery with spilled oil. No mechanic in sight. The only occupant was a rat that scuttled under a pile of discarded tires in one corner.

Will still had an hour before traintime when they got back to the depot. He asked the hackdriver if he wouldn't drink a beer with him in the saloon across the street. The hackdriver said it would cost him money because the busy time was beginning. Will said maybe he could take care of that. "You keep your money," said the hackdriver grinning, "and I'll buy the beer."

When they settled in a booth the hackdriver began to ask questions himself. He was a nice intelligent fellow, a veteran of the Southwest Pacific. When Will dropped the remark that he'd been out there too as a kid and had collected this damn limp he had in Korea the hackdriver suddenly opened up.

There was good money in hacking in this town. The trouble was the shakedown, cops, politics, crooked from a to z. Assets? He didn't know. Mostly headaches. The terminal garage couldn't be worth much. The one asset Swiftservice Cabs had was good will. Folks were fed up with the lousy service they got from Redtop. When Will told him what business he was in the hackdriver laughed like he'd split. "If you get

mixed up in hacking in this town you may need one . . . and
I'm not kidding."

At the door of the saloon they shook hands. "My name's
Willoughby Jenks."

"Mine's Terry Bryant."

Will came home full of enthusiasm for Duquesne.

"Maddie it looks to me like a goldmine. That crooked lawyer's trying to scare me off . . . The other cab company has
him fixed to keep out competition. They give lousy service.
Properly operated hacks will have a walkaway."

Whenever he sat down at his desk in his father's old walnutpaneled office Will fell to dreaming of taxicabs. He sent Lee to
the public library to look up everything she could find about
public transportation. It was a way of getting her out of the
office. Weekends he traveled around the country inspecting
taxi services. He searched out cab companies in the stockmarket reports. He heckled old Josiah Bramble, who had been his
father's lawyer and didn't want him to sell out of the family
business, until finally the old man let young Josh Bramble
find an honest Duquesne lawyer named Bennett Little to
handle Will's dealings with the receivers. Meanwhile Will
started dickering with a mortician in Chestnut Hill who
wanted to buy into the tombstone firm. It all took more time
than Will could ever have imagined.

When Will found he'd need bigger capital than he could
raise himself he thought of Joe Finch. Joe, who had been his
roommate one year at Haverford, was one of the heirs of the
Ludlow Pickles fortune.

To tell the truth Joe wasn't very bright. In college he got
along tolerably well because he just copied Will in everything.
As an intercollegiate boxer he was tops. The trouble was he
did everything the coaches told him to do and they let the
poor guy fight himself silly. The Olympics ruined him. He
stood up to a much stronger man and only lost the bout on
points, but he took a terrible beating.

After that Joe just never could make up his mind about anything, except when he was drunk. That was how Joe bought
that island where Will and Maddie spent their honeymoon.
Joe just woke up one morning and found he owned it. It was
that way with his wives. He'd find himself in bed with a new

blonde and being a wellmeaning sort of fellow he'd take her out and marry her and she'd hurry to the nearest lawyer and divorce him and go off happily with a chunk of the Ludlow Pickle money.

When Will got Joe to the telephone from some sort of a dance at the Bellevue-Stratford Joe thought Will was offering him a job. Sure he'd like to drive a cab . . . For some time he'd been looking for nice clean healthy outdoor work that would keep him out of mischief.

Joe hurried into the office next morning all enthused. Will's little secretary was in a flutter when she ushered him in. She and Joe were giving each other the eye already. Huge and mild as a panda Joe sure looked the amateur Olympic champion with his blond crew cut and his broken nose. Will introduced him as an old college friend. Will could see right away that Joe was going to date her: it would be a relief if Joe did, because Will felt guilty about the girl. He went through tortures when he was alone with her.

Joe was so disappointed he nearly cried when Will broke it to him it was his money he wanted instead of his services. Will had to think fast to keep him from storming out of the room in a pet. "Looks like I might need you for a bodyguard, Joe."

When Joe turned, blinking a little the way he did when he was trying to understand something, Will hastened to explain that they'd be in for the fight of their lives if they went into the taxicab deal. He was taking a calculated risk. They'd be up against some mighty tough elements.

Joe's face brightened. He started shadowboxing an invisible enemy. Sure he'd come in. Sounded like a good deal. He made Will fill out a check for him to sign before it slipped his mind.

Months went by. Dealings with the receivers were inconceivably slow. There were all the complications of reorganizing the company. Hearings on renewal of the franchise of the old GI Swiftservice Cabs dragged on and on. Martha was four and little Jasper was already toddling before the time came for Will to drive Maddie out to Duquesne to look for a place to live.

Since everything in Dad's old house was packed up to move, as the morticians who were buying Will's share of the business were planning to use it for a funeral home, it had been arranged that the kids—both of them towheads at this stage and a handful—would stay with their grandfather at Providence Forge. Everybody called Colonel Milliron Gramps now and he loved it.

They left the kids playing jackstraws with Lorna one steamy summer morning and drove through alternate sun and thundershowers out the turnpike west. At sixtyfive miles an hour the air felt fresher. In their excited state it was like visiting a foreign country for the first time. Old barns with hex signs and silos, wooded hills, railroad bridges, gleaming industrial plants, grubby steel and mining towns all looked new to them. "We're in too deep to back out now," Will exploded happily as he drove down Duquesne's main street. "Maddie we got a coon up a tree."

As soon as they checked in at the hotel Will called Bennett Little. Bennett had left his office but Will found him at home. Bennett said it was damn lucky Will called, he'd been trying to get him all over, the hearing was set for 9 A.M. "Looks like somebody was trying to catch us off our guard."

"Have you done all your homework?"

"Sure," said Bennett.

"I'll be there," said Will, "and with bells on."

Next morning Will met Bennett at the information desk of the courthouse building and they went up in the elevator together. Bennett was a tall pale quiet broadshouldered man with an abstracted manner. This morning his expression was more preoccupied even than usual. "Fireworks Will," he said glumly. "Expect to see some fireworks."

Will had hardly stepped in the door of the courtroom where the hearing was scheduled before Hawthorne B. Shook was pumping his hand. "Frankly Will"—he wagged his head—"I'm afraid you're going to take a beating . . . You can't say I wasn't open and aboveboard with you, now can you? Right now I want to introduce you to one of our more prominent citizens and a great yuman being, Mr. Wilfred H. Bass, the president of Redtop Cabs."

Will found himself shaking the hand of a plump whitehaired man with a dimply pink face.

"Mr. Jenks your ears must have rung many times," Mr. Bass said in a quavering voice. "My old friend Haw Shook here never tires of singing your praises."

Haw Shook, breathing hard, dragged Will into a corner by the lapel. Haw and Mr. Bass—"Frankly now Will" . . . "Confidentially my boy"—started talking into each other's ear about how they hated to see a nice young man like Will waste time and money butting his head. into a stone wall. Mr. Bass couldn't have been more fatherly. Haw's eyes were wet. It was Will's interests they had at heart. Redtop had controlled the situation in Duquesne for thirty years now. Labor, city hall, the police department were all for Redtop. Through the tie-in with the nationwide Halloran system Redtop had competitive advantages no other concern could meet.

Will found himself suddenly eloquent. He told Mr. Bass he appreciated his concern but why wasn't there room for both of them? Competition would bring better service and better profits. He was planning such an advertising and publicity campaign that people around here would be so taxiconscious there would be room for both cab companies. Everybody would benefit by competition. He believed in competition. A city like this ought to have three or four services. Will was so carried away by his own words he hardly noticed the expression of disgust on Mr. Bass's kindly features.

Haw Shook looked like he'd burst out crying. "Frankly Will," he began with a shake of the head.

Mr. Bass was purple in the face. "That will never be, young man. We shall put you out of business first." He turned down the corners of his mouth and walked away.

It was a rougherlooking crowd than Will had expected, but after all taxidrivers . . . Will tried to hide his limp as he worked his way through to a seat beside his lawyer at the counsel table. Bennett sat frowning into the papers neatly arranged on the table in front of him. Without turning his head he pointed out the various characters in the room.

Hardly moving his lips he whispered that the three baldheaded men were the Ruckeyser brothers, worked for Redtop in the legal department. Bennett called them Meenie, Minie and Moe. Somebody from the Chamber of Commerce, a couple of men from the Mayor's Committee, representatives of outoftown cab companies. "I even see friendly faces."

At the same moment Will spotted the hackdriver he'd drunk beer with the day he'd made up his mind. He tried to grin at him but he couldn't catch his eye.

Bennett gave Will a nudge with his elbow. "His nibs himself, boss of the Redtop local." A big greasyfaced dark man
in a black and white checked suit had just plunked himself
down in the front row. "Frank Stellato," whispered Bennett.
"He wears all those rings just in case he's forgotten to bring
along his brass knuckles. It was his stable of pluguglies that
put the old GI's out of business. It is to Mr. Stellato that we
are indebted for the distinguished character of this assembly.
You wouldn't think that a nice kind old gentleman like Wilfred
H. Bass would have a mug like that on his payroll."

A group of bulky men with blank faces occupied a table on
the platform. The hearing was called to order. People started
coughing and scraping with their feet.

Right away Meenie began to drone out reasons why the
franchise should not be renewed. Then Minie chimed in and
was echoed by Moe, but by that time people from consumers'
associations and the chamber of commerce began calling for
better service. Bennett let them all talk and then he read off a
list of towns of comparable population that had three or four
cab companies, and better service and cheaper rates. He read
the pertinent parts of the state laws and the city ordinances
and left Meenie, Minie and Moe without a leg to stand on.
Proceedings were adjourned in plenty of time for lunch.

Will turned anxiously to his lawyer.

"Well?"

"They can't refuse you the franchise," Bennett said quickly.
"It's what happens then has got me worried."

While they were waiting for the elevator a big scowling ape
in a blackleather jacket with a greasy white silk handkerchief
round his neck, whom Will had seen sitting next to Frank
Stellato, swaggered up and pointed a thick dirty finger in
Will's face and growled out of a corner of his mouth: "If you
know what's good for you you'll leave town while you can still
walk."

"See what I mean?" said Bennett.

Will and Bennett met Maddie for lunch over at the hotel.
Maddie was raving about the lovely house she'd found standing all by itself on a hill with a wonderful view, with a garden
for the kids to play in, but Will was too preoccupied to listen
very carefully. He was hungry as a dog. He ate up his own
plate of Long Island scallops and half of Maddie's and then

ordered some more. He was trying to figure things out as he ate.

When they had finished their dessert Bennett Little suddenly spoke out. "Mrs. Jenks, I don't want you taking any isolated house on a hill and particularly I don't want you bringing the children. . . . Your husband will be safer in a hotel for the present."

"I don't understand," said Maddie with an angry flash in her eye.

"I know what we're up against," Bennett went on in his expressionless voice. "If you are counting on police protection you won't get it."

Maddie bristled all over. If Will thought she'd let him stay here all by himself he certainly was mistaken. For one thing— she crinkled up her eyes—she couldn't trust him out of her sight.

Will flushed red.

"The guys'll quiet down when they find I mean business. Don't worry."

From the day the board reported favorably on the renewal of the franchise Will and Maddie didn't have time to worry. It was like being in combat all over again only this time Will gave the orders. He was in his element. He arranged himself an office in a little cinderblock building in the yard while repairwork was still going on in the garage and repairshops. That was his GHQ.

When he had trouble hiring a secretary Maddie took on the job. She kidded him that she did it just to keep an eye on him. The idea that Will was a sad rake seemed to amuse Maddie no end. They took a small suite at the Hotel Clermont and flew back to see the kids every weekend.

The Millirons were crazy about having Marty and little Jap at Providence Forge. The kids couldn't have been in better hands. It was tough on Maddie being away from them all week. It was tough on Will. They agreed that since they were in this they were going to stick, for the duration. I've been in two wars Will would say, and this is the third one.

For weeks they weren't out of the office except to sleep. Maddie kept the books. They wrote all their own advertising.

They got up releases for the press. Part of the time they didn't have a girl to answer the telephone. People were scared to work for them, even in the office.

They had trouble getting reliable drivers. Half of the men who applied for jobs turned out to be stoolies for Frank Stellato. Will was just about to take a mechanic with a particularly honest face on as foreman of the repair shop when Maddie happened to look out of the window and saw him getting ready to pour a bag of brown sugar into the gastank of one of the new cabs that had just been delivered.

"Publicity, Maddie," Will declaimed. "The only way we can fight these people is to have everything happen in a goldfish bowl."

Will didn't get very far with the press with the incident of the bag of brown sugar but when he paraded ten new green cabs through the downtown district, each with a neat little silhouette of a swift on the door and a hired soundtruck in the lead playing "The caissons go rolling along" the local papers couldn't ignore him entirely. Besides he took full page ads playing up his crusade to give the community better transportation at cheaper rates.

In his releases Will took high ground. His fight for competition was a fight to preserve the free enterprise way, the American way. His cabbies were the minute men of honest competition. Every hour over one of the local radio stations he had the announcer declaiming "Follow the sign of the swift," and girls' voices singing:

> If you want a safe ride
> And comfort beside
> Swiftservice cabs so modern and clean
> Will give you swift service
> Like you never have seen.

By spring Will had spent a lot of his and Joe Finch's money but he had eighty cabs on the street. In his publicity he hammered on the two way radio installed in each cab. No other Duquesne taxi service (meaning Redtop) had two way radio or uniformed drivers.

Courteous service paid. Operations began to show signs of profit. People were following the sign of the swift. Maddie began asking a little wistfully if it wouldn't soon be safe to start housekeeping and give the children their own home.

They had reached the point of househunting again when one wintry morning Maddie and Will drove up to the terminal bright and early to find a picket with a sign *Swiftservice Unfair to Organized Labor* barring their way in. It was a man named Ross who had been driving a cab for them for several months. When Will leaned out of his car to ask the man how come, he said that Local 987 of the Hackers Truckers and Longhaulers International Union was striking for recognition as a bargaining unit.

"But what about the union we got?"

"They voted last night to affiliate with the Truckers."

"Like hell they did."

About half the drivers said nobody had consulted them. Christmas was coming on. This was the biggest week of the year and they were going to drive. All the same, calls piled up unattended. Somebody brought in the news that the Redtop company had managed to install a radio receiver in their garage which was intercepting the Swiftservice calls. In the middle of the damndest snarl you ever saw who should come stomping into the office but Frank Stellato himself.

This was the first time Will had seen him close to. Frank didn't look quite so big and mean as he remembered him. He had tremendous shoulders but his legs were weak. He had a curious black stare as if his eyes didn't move from place to place very easily. He reeked of violet shaving lotion. Must have just come out of the barber chair. His big jowls were blue from a close shave. His greasy black hair was slicked down. He'd put on a clean pink and white striped shirt for the occasion. He sure looked pleased with himself.

"I guess I don't need to tell you who I am," he said showing his even white teeth in a grin.

Will looked him up and down and asked what could he do for him.

"All you need do is close up this dump and go home." Frank's big neck puffed pink and his shoulders swelled under the padding of his camelshair overcoat. "Then when we get good and ready our negotiatin' committee'll bring you a contract to sign."

Will said quietly that first Frank would have to prove he

had enough of the employees signed up to be certified by the state labor board.

Frank began to curse and swear and use foul language about what Will could do with the state labor board.

Will got up from his desk and said he didn't want this kind of talk in front of the girls in his office and led the way downstairs. Frank followed him bawling and threatening.

As they walked down the narrow stairs into the garage Frank let his voice drop to a confidential grumble: Didn't Will understand that the only reason he hadn't been bumped off already was that nobody had made it worth anybody's while? . . . Well all he needed was to give a little more trouble and somebody would make it worth somebody's while.

On the garage floor several hackdrivers began to cluster around. They hadn't voted for no strike they were saying. Frank raised his voice and started yelling at Will. "So you refuse to bargain collectively with your employees?"

He waved a list of names on a yellow paper under Will's nose but he wouldn't let him see it.

At that moment a cab drove in with a shattered windshield. Frank listened greedily while the driver told of having a brick hurled at him and how his passengers had gotten scared and left the cab and in the excitement he'd forgotten to make them pay the $1.75 that showed on the meter.

"What was I tellin' you?" shouted Frank. "If you think you're too goddamn smart to bargain collectively, you'll damn well have to take the consequences."

Will stood right up to him. "Who said I wouldn't bargain collectively?" He kept his voice down. "You just prove you have a majority of my employees."

Frank stalked out. At the entrance he turned and shouted back, "I'll show you you son of a bitch"—his voice broke—"in ways you won't like."

There's something weak about that guy, Will said to himself.

He put on his best kidding manner and turned to the excited men crowding around him. "I'm sure glad he smiled when he said that. I sure wouldn't like to mix it up with that big bruiser."

His heart was pounding so hard in his chest he was afraid some of the men would hear it. He made a fist and held it up just to prove to himself his hand wasn't shaking.

Back up in the office he leaned over Maddie's desk and whispered in her ear that a run-in like that was good for you now and then. It sure made the old adrenalin flow. All the same he spent his lunch hour down at City Hall with Bennett Little getting a permit to carry a gun.

That evening when he stepped out of the hotel entrance on his way to drive his car around to the parkinglot after supper, he heard a curious plunk. Something had gone over his head that he thought was a bullet from a small pistol with a silencer on it.

He stepped back into the lobby and called the nearest policestation.

The police captain who came around in a patrolcar was polite but skeptical. Now couldn't it have been a backfire on an automobile, he kept suggesting.

Will said he'd never heard anything that sounded less like a backfire, but he had to admit he couldn't show the place the bullet had hit. After poking around in the dark for a while the police captain went away. For a few days Will did notice an extra cop posted outside the hotel when he came home nights.

Will never told Maddie about this little incident but after that he made a point, when they left the terminal or the hotel, never to let Maddie step out into the street ahead of him. He left their car in dead storage and told Maddie they'd better use cabs for a while. That same night he put in longdistance calls to various low dives from Florida to Maine to try to find Joe Finch. Joe had staged one of his disappearing acts. "Just tell Joe I need him in Duquesne," was the word he left.

That weekend Will and Colonel Milliron had fun practicing with an automatic on a target they set up in the little grassy valley back of the house.

When Will and Maddie walked into the hotel lobby just from the airport Christmas night Will noticed a sturdy blue-eyed man in a blue business suit whom he thought he recognized sitting in one of the leather armchairs. When Maddie went to the desk to get the mail and their key the man got to his feet and walked over to Will.

"Mr. Jenks I don't know if you remember . . . I was the cabbie that drove you around that first day."

"Sure sure," said Will grinning hurriedly. "Tell me your

name again. I ought to know it. You're driving one of our cabs.
I didn't recognize you out of uniform."

"Terry Bryant."

Will motioned him into the little dimly lit lounge off the
closedup bar.

"I bet you wish you'd stayed in your old business," said
Terry as they sat down.

Will laughed: "I must be crazy; but I kinda like this sort
of life. Maybe I'm kidding myself."

"I guess I ought to have my head examined too," said
Terry. "Never again I used to say. Last time I messed around
with a labor union I lost a good job and five years seniority.
I got a wonderful wife and a girl and a boy in school and two
little ones in kindergarten. I know I oughtn't to take any
chances. I ought to just go along with Stellato and his system."

"Terry," said Will, "I'm in business to make money as much
as the next man, but hell; it's on account of your kids and my
kids we've got to fight this thing."

"Some people just can't learn," said Terry laughing.

Then Terry went on to tell Will what had happened. Frank
Stellato had invited twenty or thirty of the Swiftservice hackdrivers around to the Redtop local and filled them up with
beer and hamburgers, paid for by Redtop incidentally, and
highpressured them into going on strike. That guy could be
persuasive when he wanted to. Damn fools it was the suckers
who drove for Redtop who ought to be striking. They hadn't
had an improvement in contract for the last nine years, not
since Frank had gone on old Bass's payroll. Except for the
gangsters Frank had sent in to louse up the service, the drivers
who put down their names already wished they hadn't. They
were beginning to suspect that all he wanted to do was put
Swiftservice out of business.

Terry rose to his feet.

"I just wanted you to know," he said.

Will thanked him and said to tell the boys he was all for
a clean union. He'd give them better terms than any damn
labor leader could think up and any time the men wanted to
hold an election with secret ballot under the supervision
of some third party he was ready to cooperate. One more
thing Terry could tell the boys: he'd just put in an order for
fifty more cabs.

Will was beginning to yawn. The kids had gotten him up

at five that morning to open Christmas presents. He couldn't keep his eyes open. He stood there yawning and smiling.

Terry Bryant was explaining soberly that any union they joined would have to be part of a powerful organization or they wouldn't get protection. He wasn't quite the idealist he'd been when he was a young fellow. He'd already talked to an organizer for District 60 of the Associated Mine and Mineral Workers. Dues would be high but he thought they'd get a fair deal. "But will you please tell me," he asked as Will walked with him to the street entrance of the hotel, "why it has to be me?"

Maddie was already in bed. "There's one great guy," Will whispered as he slid in under the covers beside her. "Maddie we're going to do all right."

Next morning two thirds of the drivers reported to work, but when the tank truck arrived with gasoline the trucker wouldn't cross the picket line. To keep the cabs rolling Will had to send to the bank for cash and let the men buy their gas at fillingstations at retail rates. Ruinous. The streets around the terminal were crowded with pickets. Stranger pickets. There were damn few faces Will had ever seen before.

That night Will got in touch with an oil company depot over in Glastonbury where they promised him as much gasoline as he wanted. Will and Maddie were just about to step into a cab to go over to see what could be done to run the blockade when Joe Finch came driving up in an open red Mercury roadster.

"Kids," he announced, "I've sworn off drinking."

He and Lee Matson were going to get married but she wouldn't marry him unless he got psyched. He guessed he needed it all right. He'd been working at it for a month. It was like cramming for college exams at a tutoring school only harder. "Now what the hell's goin' on around here?"

Will told Joe he'd soon find out and made him drive them over to Glastonbury. The tank trailer was waiting in a back lot. Will took the precaution of hanging gunnysacks over the license plates so that the pickets wouldn't know where the truck came from. With Will pointing out the turnings they led the gasoline truck along side streets and unlighted alleys back

into Duquesne. About a block from the terminal a string of
cars jammed with pickets caught up with them.

Will made Joe swing his car across the street to block it
while the driver of the trailer backed into the entrance. It took
a long time. Will noticed that there were men with baseball
bats posted inside the gate. Must be Terry Bryant's work.

Two cops turned up. To Will's surprise they didn't say a
word to him about blocking the street. Instead they went
inside. Leaving Maddie with Joe in the car Will ducked in
after them to see what they were up to. One cop had pulled
off the gunnysack and was laboriously copying down the
trailertruck's license numbers while the other gave the driver
a rough time.

Since when was it illegal for an oil company to deliver gas
to a customer? Will asked them. The cops shrugged their
shoulders, both at the same time, then mumbled something
about orders and walked off. They looked alike. Maybe they
were brothers. When Will got back to the car Maddie told
him one of the cops had handed a slip of paper to a man
standing beside the lamppost at the corner. Will looked. It
was Frank Stellato.

The streets quieted down after the truck went home empty
and Joe drove Will and Maddie back to the hotel. Up in their
parlor, over beer and sandwiches, they planned out how to
defend the ballotboxes in the election under the State Labor
Board that was coming up next week. Will was convinced
Frank never would let them get away with it without a fight.

For Joe's benefit he drew a map of the terminal on a sheet
of paper, showed him the side doors he was going to have
walled up so that there would only be the yard entrance and
the garage entrance to defend. The balloting, to be supervised by•a man from the State Labor Board, a representative
of the Honest Ballot Association and Bennett Little, would
take place in a little building they used for storing tires in
the middle of the yard. His office would be the CP. He could
see the whole yard from the outside window.

"They may try to climb over this wall. If they do we can
pick them off one at a time. If they try to rush one of the
main entrances we'll meet them in mass formation."

Joe sat staring at Will's pencilmarks with his face all
wrinkled up and his eyes blinking. "Gosh Will I won't be able

to remember all this stuff . . . When the time comes you just tell me who to hit."

Things were bad during the next few days. Service was spotty. Half the drivers didn't show up. Cabs kept breaking down for unexplained reasons. Customers had read about the picketing in the papers and were afraid to call Swift-service. The manager of the oil company Will had bought his last load of gas from called up to say that the regional labor council was threatening him with picket lines around his distribution points unless he took back the gasoline he'd delivered. Will had to let him come in and pump it back into the trailertruck. The pickets sure cheered when they saw the gasoline carted away. They didn't know that Will had managed to convince the driver, with a ten dollar bill, that his pump had broken down before the tanks were completely dry. The only thing that cheered Will up, looking down into the garage through the inside window of the office, was the sight of Terry Bryant and his friends buttonholing the drivers as they brought in their cabs.

The day set for the election dawned cold and sodden and gray. Joe turned up early at the hotel wearing a grubby sweatshirt. He had his hands taped up under his mittens. When, after bolting some breakfast, he drove Will and Maddie into the terminal, they found cops holding Frank Stellato's boys off from the entrance. "That's Bennett's work," said Will. Bennett Little had managed to get an injunction from a local judge against interference with the election, so the police were having to go through the motions.

Nobody seemed to have much fight in him. The cops stood around in their long overcoats puffing steam into the raw air and flapping their arms to keep their hands warm. The pickets, pushed back to the pavement, had to keep jigging up and down to keep their feet from freezing. When Will pointed out their red armbands he whispered to Joe that Frank had given them out so that they wouldn't slug each other in the scrimmage. Joe grinned. He said he was relieved. "This way I can tell who to hit."

Terry Bryant spotted Joe for a pug right away, and took charge of him like a trainer. He had the huskier drivers drilled like a squad of Marines. Some of them had baseball bats and quite a few had brass knuckles. They took it for granted Joe was a pug Will had hired as a bodyguard. Nobody dreamed he had any stake in the business.

To Will's great surprise the voting passed off quietly. After half a dozen young gorillas who'd never worked for Swiftservice in their lives tried to sneak in past Terry's guards and were given the bums' rush for their pains, the boys with the armbands settled down to singing and jeering from the sidelines. None of the drivers was even jostled on his way to the polling booth.

Around noon there was another effort to infiltrate in the wake of a wrecking car towing in a cab that had had both front tires slashed. Joe Finch met this one singlehanded. Before they knew what had happened to them three of the intruders were flat on their backs on the concrete floor. It did Will good to see the happy look on Joe's face as he walked modestly back to his post in the ring of guards round the polling place. "Good boy Joe," they all shouted.

There still might have been real trouble if the snow that had been sifting through the streets all afternoon hadn't turned by nightfall into the wildest blizzard in five years. The cops and Frank Stellato and the pickets with red armbands all disappeared in a swirl of snow driven by a fiftymile gale.

After the polls were closed and the ballotboxes had been taken up into a small private office for the count, Will and Maddie sat at their desks listening to the news of the snowstorm over the radio. School buses stalled. Travelers stranded at railroad stations and bus stops. Hospitals disrupted. Highways blocked with abandoned cars. Below zero temperatures. More snow to come.

Will jumped to his feet in the middle of it. "Maddie, this is the break we've been waiting for. . . . If we can keep our hacks running we've got it made, and we'll be performing a public service besides."

He settled down to the telephone to argue his drivers into twenty-four hour duty. It wasn't too hard to convince them. Most of them were so sore at Redtop and the Truckers they hardly needed the bonuses he offered to bring them out. Whenever he saw a group of men gathering in the garage, he threw open the inner window and made them a speech about how this was Swiftservice's great opportunity.

When Bennett stepped into the office to announce in his mournful drawl that District 60 had won the election hands down, Will looked up at him blankly. He was just about to ask "What election?" when he caught himself and smiled. He grabbed Bennett's hand and shook it. "Bennett don't you worry so. Things are going our way."

Right away he forgot all about Bennett and the election. The blizzard was the big thing now. He was calling all the nearest dealers to corner their supply of chains and snowtires. It would all cost money. "Hell," he called out to Maddie, "it costs money to make money."

Meanwhile Maddie on another line was getting hold of hotplates and coffee percolators and supplies for a luncheonette she was setting up in the dispatcher's office beside the main gate. Inside of an hour she had hot soup and hamburgers and coffee and doughnuts for every driver who turned up hungry.

About midnight Terry Bryant brought in the news that Redtop had closed down. A friend over there had called him on the phone. The Redtop drivers had been kept so busy trying to gum up the election over at Swiftservice that their cabs were stalled in drifts at half the hackstands in town.

Will and Maddie grabbed hands and did a little dance around the office. Will lost no time calling the city desk of the *Duquesne Despatch* to let them know what was going on. If they needed transportation he would furnish it. At intervals Maddie discreetly fed them human interest items. A stranded family with three small children rescued from a lonely bus station, a doctor transported to a hospital for an important operation, sick people hurried to clinics when the ambulances stalled.

Neither one of them took off their clothes for two nights. Occasionally they got a few winks of sleep on a pair of army cots in Will's office. Joe Finch ran errands through the snow, as contentedly as a St. Bernard dog. Every time he came back wet and half frozen he'd kick the snow off his boots and cry out "Boy this is fun!"

The biggest moment was when Will heard that Wilfred H. Bass himself, stranded at the Elks' Hall where he'd been playing billiards with a party of friends, had to call a Swiftservice cab to get home. Will always told everybody that was what caused the heart attack that carried off Mr. Bass a few days later.

The snowstorm couldn't last forever. The sun shone. Sidewalks were salted. Snow plows cleared the streets. Trains and buses started running again and so did Redtop cabs. With the first mild day Frank Stellato's blue Mercury appeared again in the streets around the terminal and an occasional picket turned up to yell scab at a driver, but the Truckers' picketing had lost its steam.

Will and Maddie were worn out. They hadn't seen the children in two weeks. They took an extra long weekend at Providence Forge which they mostly spent in bed asleep. Will was so drowsy at Sunday dinner he hardly listened when Colonel Milliron started to tell him he'd been hearing another side of the Duquesne taxicab war. That relative of Abe Merman's, whom the colonel described as a four dimensional financier with a bet on every horse, called Abe up from Chicago and kept him hanging on the phone for three quarters of an hour asking him questions about Will and how he was managing to finance Swiftservice cabs. All Abe had been able to tell him was that there was Ludlow money behind him.

Will woke up at that. "Why's he so damned interested?"

Colonel Milliron said, "Search me." All he knew about the man was from his own experience. "He thinks he's Superman," put in Lorna making a sour face. Colonel Milliron went on, in his above the battle storytelling vein, to say that Judge Lewin had proved an inconvenient customer to handle when he had his knockdown and dragout fight for control of Abington. That was before Maddie and Will were married. Judge Lewin was one of those peculiar characters, not too uncommon in the world of pure finance, who were likely to be found on both sides of any contest. "Don't ask me how they do it. If I knew I'd be running Abington Products instead of telling other people how to manage their industries."

The Redtop cab companies all over the country, he explained in a slow careful drawl, were subsidiaries of the Halloran Corporation which manufactured cabs as well as operated them, Will must know that. Halloran's profits came from making the subsidiaries pay through the nose for cars and spare parts.

"Hot damn," cried Will, "that's what poor old Mr. Bass was trying to tell me the first day."

Of course Will had known it right along, but he'd never taken it too seriously till the colonel put it so plain.

The story worried him more than he let on. His drawer was full of bills. Interest charges overdue. He needed to raise more capital. He knew Joe would come through, but Joe had just staged one of his disappearances. If disappearances were not a standard feature with Joe, Will told Maddie as they drove to the airport after dinner, he'd have been worried as hell. When Stellato's gang found out who Joe was they sure would try to do him in or snatch him for ransom or some goddam thing.

The weather was good and the afternoon plane got them into Duquesne on time. A flock of messages at the desk at the hotel gave them plenty more to worry about. Vincent Collins, their traffic manager, had walked out after collecting his pay Friday afternoon and not been seen since. A driver, Ed Meiggs, had been waylaid and slugged Saturday night answering a call to a lonely freightyard down by the river. When he came to he found that somebody had driven his cab out onto a point of rocks and set it afire.

The next day was spent in calling the police commissioner, offering rewards for the apprehension of the arsonists, trying to stir up editorials in the press of Duquesne and the adjacent towns. Before they went home that night Will had typed out a five page story explaining how the Halloran interests were strangling the growth of Duquesne by their monopoly of transportation through Redtop Cabs.

Maddie drew a cartoon for it showing a boa constrictor with a head labeled "Truckers' Union" crushing a small taxicab in its jaws. The scaly body labeled "Halloran" was wrapped around a female figure labeled "Free Enterprise."

"By gum, Maddie that ought to have the Guggenheim reward. Damned if I won't send it in."

Will gave her a hug. What a wonderful girl I've got for a wife, he was saying to himself.

Corrupt Labor joins with corrupt Management to strangle Competition, was the caption he wrote under it.

He rushed it over by messenger to the *Despatch.*

The managing editor called up himself to explain in a confidential apologetic tone that it was a dandy cartoon but he couldn't exactly use it, no not even as a full page paid advertisement. Powerful interests. He hemmed and hawed. Libel. Will must understand.

"Damned if I understand," said Will hanging up. "I'll print it myself for a throwaway."

Will kept a stack of them on his desk to stick into every letter that went out. "If people only knew about these things they'd do something about them," he kept saying.

He stirred up Bennett Little to look into the wording of the Sherman Act to see if there weren't some way it could be made to apply to the situation in Duquesne. He wrote out appeals to the state labor board and the utilities commission. He presented petitions to the state legislature. He wired a congressional committee in Washington asking for an immediate investigation. He wrote a long letter to the President of the United States.

He rented a mimeograph machine so that everything he sent out could be distributed as a release to every newspaper in the region. "Persistence Maddie," he said when she began to keep tabs on what his campaign was costing. "Remember what Calvin Coolidge said. Persistence is the real road to Success."

They were at their desks from eight in the morning to twelve at night.

About the only immediate response to all this activity was a telephone call from Hawthorne Shook. Will's old buddy couldn't have been more cordial. "Long time no see." Didn't Will ever take a day off? Frankly Haw had been expecting to run into him at the Country Club or the races. Well frankly Will's cabs had chalked up a reputation in that snowstorm. Everybody was talking about it. Haw had been basking in reflected glory. Hadn't he been just a teeny bit helpful in the matter of the franchise?

Will couldn't remember that he had but he didn't like to come right out and say so. After fifteen minutes of beating around the bush, Haw blurted out an invitation to lunch next day. Frankly Haw had a proposition to transmit. Will asked if Haw would mind if he brought Bennett Little along. Haw sure laughed at that. Frankly that was a good one. But why not? Bennett was a yuman being wasn't he?

Will hurriedly told him yes he'd come and managed to ring off. He was calling Bennett to tell him of the engagement when Terry Bryant came into the office.

Will had offered Terry the job of traffic manager a few

days before and Terry had asked for time to think it over. "Sit down Terry," said Will.

"I was worried, Mr. Jenks, about whether I ought to stick with this union local, now that we've got it started, but I've talked it over with Tasha. She's my wife, and she says it's the opportunity we've been waiting for all these years."

He'd enjoyed driving a cab, but a man couldn't drive a cab all his life. There was just one assurance he wanted. Will wasn't getting ready to sell out to Redtop, now was he? Terry's friends over at Redtop had reported that that was the story going around there.

Will jumped to his feet. He'd be damned if he'd sell out to anybody. He'd promised that, cross his heart and hope he might die, he said laughing. Terry laughed too. All right, that was all he wanted to know.

When Will met Bennett before lunch next day, Bennett had the same story. Will shouted that everybody seemed to know more about his business than he did.

It might not be a bad idea, Bennett suggested in his quiet way; Will sure had proved his nuisance value.

"Hell no," said Will.

At lunch Will let Haw and Bennett do the talking. It took a long time but Haw finally admitted frankly that a syndicate had frankly approached him to find out frankly what the price tag might be on Swiftservice Cabs.

Right now he didn't have anything to sell said Will. A few years from now he might have something it would be worth while buying into.

Haw seemed miffed and muttered that, frankly, it was just a feeler. Bennett suggested they keep in touch. Will thanked Haw for a very nice lunch.

That night two more cabs were burned. It was the same story each time. A cab got a call to an outoftheway location. When the driver stopped to pick up what seemed to be a fare a bunch of men swarmed into the cab, mugged him from behind and pulled a gunnysack over his head. Then they trussed him up with rope and dumped him out in a back lot. While he was doing a Houdini act trying to get loose they drove the cab off and burned it.

Will demanded police protection, but whenever a cop went along on a cab naturally nothing happened. They couldn't put a cop on every one of his hundred cabs. Police headquarters got tired of sending out patrol cars on false alarms. The drivers were getting edgy.

Will, with a loaded gun in his overcoat pocket, took to going along whenever a cab left the terminal for a suspicious-sounding location. Nobody ever bothered the cabs when he went along. Even so Maddie put her foot down. Will's place was in the office directing operations.

One blustery March morning Will unlocked the heavy steel-bound door he'd had installed at the foot of the office stairs just in case Frank and his friends should try to pay him a surprise visit. He ran up the steps two at a time. By gum his leg was stronger every day. His face was blazing from the cold wind. He was rubbing his hands. He was feeling good. Not a picket in sight.

He was all primed to tell Terry about a proposition a dealer down the street had made him to furnish some spare generators they needed. "Say Terry," he called when he sat down at his desk. No answer came from Terry's cubbyhole. As Maddie was home at the hotel with a cold there was nobody in the office but the girl at the switchboard. She said in an offhand way that Mr. Bryant had gone out on a call, would be back in half an hour.

Like hell he had. Will went storming downstairs to the dispatcher's office. There he found one of the drivers, a skinny yellowfaced young colored man named Warfield who had only recently been hired. He said Mr. Jenks he'd felt feet walking across his grave when that call came in and Mr. Bryant got his Irish up and took that call himself. His cab was number 116. Mr. Bryant had surely been hasty. Warfield's face was gray. His hand was shaking so he kept dropping his cigarette.

Will took the mouthpiece from old Ed the radio operator and pressed the button on the transmitter. "Come in one one six."

Amid all the shortwave racket Terry's voice came in saying he was all right. He'd be careful as hell. Wasn't it broad daylight? The call was to the corner of Memorial Drive and River Road. Plenty of traffic on Memorial Drive.

Voices of other drivers registering calls filled the air.

"Come in one one six."

Terry's voice was saying he could see his fare, looked like a girl in a raincoat standing at the corner . . . over.

"Come in one one six . . ." Terry's voice saying "Okeydoke." Static drowned it out.

Come in one one six. No answer. Every other cab was on the air but one one six.

After about ten minutes Warfield couldn't stand it any longer. "Mr. Jenks let's go see. I'll drive you." They jumped into an offduty cab. Warfield drove down Memorial Drive to River Road. It was a region of gas tanks and freightyards. Nothing in sight. Back at the terminal no word from one one six.

Will called up the nearest police station. A cab and driver were missing. Not much cooperation. They'd heard that story before.

Will called up Captain Fairwether of the State Police traffic patrol. Captain Fairwether was civil. He had a pleasant voice. He'd broadcast the description of the cab and the driver. He'd report.

Then it was up to Will to call up Mrs. Bryant and tell her that her husband was missing. A little girl answered the phone. Will's throat knotted up. Suppose it was Marty hearing that her daddy was missing. "Mommie," called the little girl.

Will hadn't met Mrs. Bryant. She had a nice quiet practical kind of a voice with a trace of some kind of a foreign accent. She listened carefully to what Will had to say. Her only sign of emotion was a quick sucking in of the breath. Will kept explaining that it had happened before. None of the drivers had been badly hurt. Terry would turn up any time now.

"Some people," Mrs. Bryant said, "don't have good luck."

That was all she said.

Will was all broken up. He felt it was his fault. He had to talk to Maddie. He got Warfield to drive him over to the hotel. On the way Warfield said he wasn't scared any more. Mr. Bryant was a mighty fine man. If those gangsters at Redtop hurt one hair of Mr. Bryant's head, he'd know who to go for when the cutting started. He didn't believe in fighting, nor cutting, nor razors, but he knew how to use one.

Who should Will find sprawled on the couch in their little parlor talking over his shoulder to Maddie who was in bed

in the bedroom but Joe Finch. Joe looked awful. His skin
was yellow and he had blue bags under his eyes.

"Never again," he was telling Maddie. He wouldn't have
done it this time if he hadn't been nervously upset. It was this
doc Lee had made him go to. The doc kept hinting around
that the trouble with Joe was he'd been in love with his
mother, as a little teeny child, could you beat that? Wasn't
that enough to put a guy off his rocker? Malarkey. That doc
he didn't know Joe's mother. Nobody could love Joe's mother.
Hadn't she proved it by having five divorces?

That damn doc had shaken Joe up so he'd had to have a
few drinks to steady his nerves. One thing he regretted. He
oughtn't to have done it because the doc was a little guy. Joe
had had a few drinks and then he'd gone back to see that
doc just to argue with him, but instead of arguing he'd let
him have it, as gently as he could, see?—Joe wasn't any
sadist—one little uppercut right on the button. That doc he
went out like a light.

Joe had a talking jag on all right. Will had a time to get
him to shut up long enough to tell Maddie about Terry
Bryant.

When Joe heard Terry's name he began to pay attention.
He got to his feet and made Will tell him all over again what
had happened.

He stood blinking and frowning in the middle of the room
and made Will tell it a third time. Then he asked where the
adhesive tape was and went into the bathroom to tape up
his hands.

Joe said he knew exactly what to do, but he had to have
transportation. He didn't have a driver's license right at the
moment, the damnfool cops had complained about the way
he drove his car.

Will said this boy Warfield was waiting with a cab.

"Thanks Will," said Joe. "Terry's a great feller Will," said
Joe. He seemed suddenly perfectly sober. "I'm going to have
a little talk with that guy."

"Wait a minute," said Will.

"See you in church," said Joe and was out the door and
gone.

After Joe went Will walked up and down the floor with his
teeth clenched. He oughtn't to have let Joe go. He ought to

have seen to it Terry Bryant didn't go out on that cab. There were times he told Maddie when everything a man did turned out wrong.

"What more could you have done?" asked Maddie. "Didn't you fix Terry up with a job in the office?"

"It's the wife and kids I'm thinking about," said Will. "Suppose it was us."

"If you're planning on me being a widow," cried out Maddie, "all I can say is, Will Jenks, I renege."

Maddie was up out of bed and bustling about the room getting her clothes on when the phone rang. It was Captain Fairwether of the State Police reporting that the cab had been found in eight feet of water in Back River. Looked like the cab had been rolled down a hill back of the Blighsville dump. A wrecking truck was pulling it out. The operator wanted to know about the insurance coverage. No, no body had been found, not yet.

Will called one of his own cabs and he and Maddie spent the rest of the afternoon talking to Captain Fairwether at the State Police Barracks about ways and means of getting a body out of Back River. Captain Fairwether was a stout grayhaired grayeyed little man, fond of the sound of his own voice. Dragging rivers for bodies seemed to be a hobby with him. Will kept trying to convince him that Terry had been pulled off that cab before it was pushed in the river but Captain Fairwether wouldn't talk about anything but dragnets and grappling lines. He talked learnedly about how long it took for the gases of decomposition to bring a body to the surface. He was planning to write a book on the subject.

Maddie was on the edge of tears. Will was snapping his fingers with impatience as he tried to convince Captain Fairwether that Terry was lying trussed up in a back lot somewhere between Blighsville and Duquesne. "In that case," concluded Captain Fairwether, without a trace of interest in his voice, "he's out of my jurisdiction . . . That's a problem for the local police."

Meanwhile the sergeant at the switchboard had been putting in calls to the various precincts. At last the Duquesne Police Commissioner's office reported that a man who might be the missing cabdriver had been picked up for a drunk by a routine patrol. Identified by chauffeur's license as W. Terence Bryant, of 6164 Heightstown Avenue. Since he seemed incoherent the police surgeon had sent him to the General Hospital for observation.

Captain Fairwether was real disappointed. Will and Maddie were in a fever to get out of his office. He stood between them and the door explaining to Will he sure would let him know next time he had to drag for a body. He employed methods that possibly weren't employed elsewhere. He knew Will would be interested. They had a time getting away from him.

On the way to the hospital they stopped by to pick up Mrs. Bryant. She was a short stoutish woman with large brown eyes fringed with black lashes. She wore a blue and white checked scarf on her head. There were gray streaks in her black hair. Her stubby hands showed how much work she'd done all her life. She had very little to say except would they mind if she brought the children? She didn't want to go without them.

The children's eyes were big with fright. The older boy and girl, nine or ten or so, had brown eyes with long lashes like their mother's, though they were already taller. The two little ones had blue eyes like Terry. They were cleanly dressed and very quiet. Will was struck with the look the whole family had of standing together against the world. Maddie told Will afterwards that the Bryants had an air of being accustomed to misfortune, somehow. Mrs. Bryant was taking it for granted that her husband would die.

"It's the children," she told Maddie as they went up in the ether smell of the elevator at the hospital. "It's the deprivation for them. He was such a wonderful father to them."

They found Terry lying unconscious on a rolling cot in the anteroom to the accident ward. The hair had been shaved off the top of his head which had the frail look of a bare skull under the bandages. His face was calm. He lay flat on his back with closed eyes. The frightening thing was the heavy irregular snorting noise he made when he breathed. A flustered orderly drove them all out into the hall. No they couldn't see the doctor. The patient was on his way to the operating room.

The caseworker at the desk in the waiting room said the injury was down as a severe concussion. Prognosis reserved. That was all she knew.

Will told her the details of the Swiftservice hospitalization plan and insisted on a private room. He felt deadly tired. His game leg ached. There was nothing more he could do.

Maddie tried to give Mrs. Bryant a little consoling hug but she didn't seem to notice it. She sat in an armchair with the children huddled about her staring into space. All their eyes were looking in the same direction. They didn't even say "Good night."

Back at the office it was a relief to be caught up in the usual Saturday night bustle. Wilkerson seemed to be doing all right as acting traffic manager. There was the normal number of mixups, breakdowns, flat tires. No sign of pickets.

Will and Maddie had hardly settled at their desks before they heard heavy steps on the stairs. With Warfield in the lead a group of drivers filed in. Jim Kron did the talking.

Mr. Jenks, he said, he had to apologize for taking time off in the middle of the rush hour, but they had done something that had to be done. They couldn't have done it without Joe Finch but if they'd waited till later Joe would have been too damn drunk to be any use. He'd picked that driver off that Redtop cab like you'd pick an apple off a tree. Mr. Jenks would have been right proud of his man Joey. They'd done their best not to hurt the guy but they'd tied him up and set him in the corner of an alley and told him he could tell his boss after this it would be driver for driver and cab for cab.

No, the man couldn't have recognized nobody. Joey had pulled a bag over his head.

One of the boys stayed to stick around with Joey to see he didn't get into no trouble until he got drunk enough to take him home to bed.

"But what happened to the cab?"

They all started laughing. Mr. Jenks didn't need to know about that. He'd hear about that when he tuned in on the ten-thirty news. It would do Terry Bryant good if he heard it from his hospital bed.

And they all filed out.

Before going to bed that night Will managed to get a fellow he knew who was an intern at the General Hospital on the phone. The intern said he'd check with the recovery room. A couple of minutes later he called back. Severe brain

damage from a fractured skull. Terry Bryant died on the
operating table at 10:30 P.M.

Nobody could have been more surprised than Will to find
that the burning of a Redtop cab that Saturday night brought
the Duquesne taxicab war to an end. On fine days one elderly
picket still did park a battered old Pontiac with an UNFAIR
sign on it across the street from the entrance to the Swiftservice terminal. The picket got to be quite friendly with
Will's drivers. It was his livelihood he explained apologeti-
cally, how else could a man make thirty dollars a week without lifting a finger? When Will asked him what had happened to Frank Stellato and his blue Mercury, "Gone to
Miamah," he answered with a significant drawl, "for his
health."

Will threw everything he had into making a big thing of
Terry Bryant's funeral. If people could be made to realize
that Terry Bryant had died for freedom, like the Americans
who stood up against the redcoats on Bunker Hill or who
held out in Bataan against the Japanese, his death wouldn't
seem so senseless and unnecessary.

Will wrote a letter titled "Your Kids and Mine" which, under the usual disclaimer of responsibility for the sentiments expressed, the *Duquesne Despatch* screwed up its courage to
print. Here was a man who had chosen death rather than lose
his liberty. It was up to us to keep our country a decent place
for our kids to live in, even if we had to give our lives to do it.

The international press service covered the funeral in the
Catholic cathedral and photographers for the weekly news
magazines swarmed all over the cemetery during the in-
terment. Will's letter was reprinted in a box on editorial pages
all over the country. A United States senator read the last
few lines in the course of a speech on labor legislation and
requested that the whole of it be printed in the *Congressional
Record*. A few days later the *Duquesne Despatch* got into
the act by opening a subscription for the education of the
Bryant children.

The resulting publicity, plus the fact that with the coming
of summer Will put into service the first airconditioned cabs
in the country, gave a great boost to Swiftservice profits.
Everybody in Duquesne talked about Will Jenks's success.

Only Will and Maddie knew what a load of debt and interest charges they had to carry.

Just at the moment when they needed Joe Finch's money most Joe up and married Lee Matson, at that young woman's urgent insistence, and flew her down to his island in the Bahamas on his new private plane. Before they left, Lee, who really was quite a nice girl, called Will up long distance and told him that she'd thought it best to put the Trust Department of the First National Bank in charge of what was left of the Ludlow fortune before it was all frittered away. She had to think of the children. "Children?" asked Will.

Well it was only a third of a one yet, Lee answered pertly. Then suddenly she said in a rush of words, "Lord how I wish the father was you," and hung up.

Will dropped the receiver as if it had burned him. He blushed. Of course Maddie, looking up from her desk across from his, had to catch him sitting there red as a beet. That kidding look came into her face. "Will, I hope she doesn't claim that you're the proud parent."

"They've turned over Joe's finances to the First National Bank of Woodside . . . some trust deal for the children to come. . . . Those old fogies will never put money in cabs . . . oh hell."

Maddie got to her feet and let her hand drop on Will's shoulder. He mustn't forget what Dad had said: when they needed fresh financing to consult with him.

She had hardly said the word "financing" when the buzzer was going again on Will's desk. Maddie listened frowning while Will tried to wriggle out of accepting some invitation. Then he said, "All right, at the main entrance to the clubhouse at two."

When he hung up Maddie said she knew who that was. Will made a face. It was frankly Haw Shook. "He may have a new offer. Maddie it may be providential."

"Don't you commit yourself to anything until you talk to Dad."

"You mean if we have to deal with the Halloran Corporation Abe Merman's connections may be better."

"Sure." She gave her head a toss. "It's a lovely afternoon; why don't I go to the races too?"

"Haw said to come alone."

"Will, are you sure it isn't a trap?"

"With the police still on the trail and a ten-thousand-dollar reward posted and all the unfavorable publicity Redtop and the Truckers got? They wouldn't try any rough stuff in a public place like a racetrack."

"Will you call me every few minutes?" Maddie sidled up and rubbed against him like a cat. "I mustn't be worried Will. It's the case of Lee Matson all over again, only this time"— she had her face close: her eyes were full in his—"we are sure who the father is."

Will said golly he'd been so busy he forgot she'd gone to the doctor's yesterday. He gave her a hug and a kiss and ran downstairs and told one of the cabbies to drive him out to the Fair Grounds.

It was a hazy blue afternoon. A big crowd of men and women in summer clothes sweating and smoking and rustling dopesheets and newspapers was streaming from the paddock to the stands and lining up at the parimutuel windows. Through the shadow under the stands Will had a glimpse of bright patches of jockeys' colors against the sunny green grass in the middle of the track.

Haw Shook, his panama hat tipped back on his head, was waiting for Will at the clubhouse turnstiles. He slipped a pass into Will's hand. Delighted to see him. Now if Will was interested, frankly, he whispered with his lips against Will's ear, the word was Evergreen Boy.

"Never gamble," Will said cheerfully. "Just brought up that way." He sure would enjoy seeing the horses run.

There was something else Will would be interested in seeing. Haw led him to a table stacked with beerbottles.

A heavy man sat at the table looking out over the track. The broad back in the houndstooth jacket, the slick black hair, the pink neck; it was Frank Stellato.

Haw lifted a beerbottle.

No, Will said, he never drank in the afternoon. Just brought up that way.

Will's hands were cold. He folded his arms and sat with his fists clenched in his armpits. That's what it feels like to have your flesh creep he told himself.

Without turning his head Frank had started to talk through the cigar in the corner of his mouth. His eyes were fixed on the starting gate where most of the horses stood sleek and quiet but a couple of them, already in a lather, were nervously jigging on their slender crooked legs.

Frank was saying he wanted Will to withdraw that reward. He was afraid it would make the cops pin the job on some poor innocent hackdriver. . . . He didn't know nothin' about what had happened to that organizer for District 60 but he was sorry it happened. With all these reactionary enemies of the working man in Congress stickin' their noses into other people's business it was too bad. That organizer was just tryin' to make a buck like the rest of us. He'd have made a good thing of that local if he'd lived. The boys hadn't meant no harm. They just meant to burn the cab. They were gettin' a nice bonus for every Swiftservice cab they put out of business. He'd caught hell all down the line. The International had bawled him out for bein' bad public relations.

The horses had started. The people at the tables rose as one man.

Frank kept his eyes on the horses but he didn't stop talking. He wanted Will to know Will wasn't in no danger no more. The International was goin' to suspend his charter if there was any more rough stuff and the characters who said they were goin' to make it worth his while weren't goin' to make it worth his while no more. All this laborbaiting McCarthyism had scared the piss out of these characters and they weren't puttin' up no more dough. He just wanted Will to know he didn't have to carry that gat around nor hire no more brokendown pugs like that big Joey. . . . Say that was a foulup wasn't it?

Well what did you know? He poked Haw with a big beringed hand. Evergreen Boy won by a nose.

"First time in a dog's age I ain't lost money off one of Haw's hot tips. . . . Take these to the ten dollar window for me Haw."

Frank shoved a batch of tickets into Haw's hand. Haw moved off obediently to the parimutuel window.

When they were alone Frank turned his head and gave Will one of his sudden black stares.

"The less that bastard knows the better. He'd sell his own mother for a lousy buck. I didn't have nothin' to do with it see? That girl she got in the car and her business was to talk a blue streak so that this cabby couldn't get a chance to report his position. Then when he was makin' change for a sawbuck these guys came out from behind a billboard and jumped him. They didn't mean to bust that organizer's skull in but that organizer was too strong for 'em. He put up a terrible fight and it was broad daylight and they had to quiet him down fast with a piece of lead pipe."

It was just accidental manslaughter in any court in the land. That was why Frank wanted Will to withdraw his reward. Some guys would perjure themselves from hell to breakfast for ten grand. Will wouldn't want an innocent man to get framed?

Haw came hustling back with a big wad of bills. The smile on his face and the cringe in his shoulders made Will think of a dog retrieving a stick for his master. It made Will feel just a little sick he told Maddie afterwards. He got to his feet. Well he had to go back to the office. He appreciated what Frank had told him. He'd think it over, he said.

All the beerbottles on the table jingled when Frank Stellato stood up and faced Will. "No hard feelings, boy." While he rammed the bills in his pocket with his left hand he held out his right. "Shake," he said.

Will shook Frank Stellato's hand. Immediately he slipped away between people crowding forward to see the start of the next race. "I wished I hadn't," he told Maddie when he got back to the office, "but just at that minute there was something appealing about the guy." He let himself drop glumly into the chair by his desk.

After a while Will looked up from going over a stack of letters commending him for his courageous stand.

"Damn," he cried, "it's hard to know how to do right."

Maddie stared back at him out of big black troubled eyes.

When Will and Maddie drove up the hill to the Millirons' stone house at Providence Forge that Saturday night every window was lighted. An extra maid they'd never seen before took their coats. "Gramps is having a party," shouted Marty and little Jap as they tumbled out giggling and jumping and cavorting into the hall. "And we're not invited."

Abe Merman stopped Will on the stairs as he was hurrying up to change his clothes for dinner after a quick drink with the colonel and Lorna. The little man was all of a fluster.

"Will," he said hastily, "Judge Lewin"—he cleared his throat—"a favorite cousin of my wife's, is coming to dinner tonight. . . . That doesn't mean that we approve of them. He's very fond of Berta, but your fatherinlaw found him rawther sticky as the British say. You have heard us speak of him many times. My impression is, though my information is not certain, that he has recently acquired control of the Halloran Corporation." Abe Merman's voice dropped to a whisper. "I don't need to tell you to be careful. Let Bennett Little attend to the details." He smiled up into Will's face. "Anyway it will be an experience."

"Thank you, Mr. Merman."

Abe Merman's bruised eyes, with their benevolently self-deprecating expression, followed Will admiringly, Will felt with some satisfaction, as he stumped up the stairs.

By the time Will and Maddie had dressed and put the kids away, Marty with her teddybears and Jap with his sixshooter, the guests were all assembled on the terrace under the big beeches, festooned with a string of Chinese lanterns that lit up with festive flecks of pink and yellow and green and purple, light smiling faces and women's bare arms and eyes and men's white shirtfronts clustered around the marble café tables. Everybody wore his best bib and tucker. People had an animated right on their toes look.

Judge Lewin, tall, oliveskinned, steelyhaired, with sudden ways of moving and sudden spurts of conversation, dominated them. His profile was so sharp that when part of his face was in shadow it looked like a paper cutout. He'd brought a lady with him whose mascaraed eyes never left his face, a Mrs. Jubilirer who made Will think of a drawing of a Gibson girl in one of the yellow spotted oldtime magazines he used to read in the attic at home.

It was a warm night with a moon. There were no mosquitoes but junebugs buzzed and blundered around the lights. Lorna was looking unusually handsome in a yellow silk dress. Will's fatherinlaw was the cheerful redfaced attentive host, affecting the just-off-the-range bluff old rancher's manner that was his style at parties.

Waspwaisted Mrs. Jubilirer had a daughter with her, a skinny yellowhaired girl in her late teens named Pat. The only member of the party Pat had eyes for was Stan Goodspeed, Lorna's adored nephew whom Will had heard tall stories about but never met. Stan looked about sixteen and full of mischief. He had a curl to his hair and full lips and a

glint in his eye. When they said hello he gave Will an impudent onceover and looked for a second as if he were going
to ask him a question. Instead he turned away. For the
benefit of Pat Jubilirer, he was playing man of the world.

Judge Lewin didn't pay much attention to Will either, but
Will could see he was inspecting Maddie carefully. There
was a connoisseur's look in his glassy gray eyes when he examined the women. He seemed to be checking them for points
like a racetrack character watching the horses being led
around the paddock.

They had a lot of first rate wine with dinner at a long
table in the diningroom that opened through screened french
windows onto the terrace. Everybody got very talkative. Will
kept his mouth shut and listened. He was trying to rank up
questions in his head he wanted to ask Judge Lewin if they
ever did get a chance to talk business. Before he had found
time to straighten out his ideas he found himself distracted
by an argument between the Mermans and the judge.

For the benefit of the young people present Judge Lewin
had embarked on an encomium of the study of mathematics.
Mathematics was the learned language of today. As Latin had
been the key to culture and power in the Middle Ages, mathematics was the expression of the mind of today's élite. Without calculus a man was a mere peasant, a helpless clod fit only
to be exploited by political demagogues.

"What's the use of splitting your clever little head with
math," Will heard Stan whisper tittering across the table to
Pat, "when any calculating machine can do it better?" Pat
tittered back.

"But Alphonse," Berta Merman was smiling up from her
plate at her tall cousin, "here's what worries me. Perhaps
you can explain it. Our own dear Einstein, one of the kindest
gentlest most innocent men who ever lived, invents a formula
out of pure mathematics and before you can turn around your
delightful intellectual formula has turned into a hydrogen
bomb that any mad politician can use to destroy mankind.
. . . Suppose Hitler had had it?"

"*Sub quadam specie aeternitatis*," said Judge Lewin in
unctuous Latin. "In the sight of God in other words it is the
fact that Einstein's formula is true that is divine. The truth
is above good and evil. Didn't Spinoza speak of mathematics
as the intellectual love of God?"

"Spinoza was a good citizen and a good republican," said Abe.

"His philosophy is the foundation of modern atheism. That's why the Communists admire him."

"He spent his life with Christian monks," Abe insisted.

"He was virtually a Christian in his life," added Berta.

"Sentimentality, my dear friends," said Judge Lewin, letting the words hiss through his teeth. "By God Spinoza meant nature, the essence of the universe, exactly what I mean by mathematics. Take my own life, I do not consider myself an evil man, yet my business, my hobby, my science is that special little section of arithmetic known as finance . . . insignificant from the point of view of great minds like Einstein's or Spinoza's, but still a sort of poor relation of mathematics. When I assume control of a corporation through the use of my own private skills, I have to consider it a problem in pure finance. I can't be bothered with what it takes or what it sells. I can't be distracted by worrying about administration, who gets fired from what job, all the grubby little lives involved. . . . I leave that sort of thing to my public relations men. As you know Berta, I'm as softhearted as mush. I'd never sleep a wink."

"Alphonse," said Berta with her sweetest fuzziest smile, "sometimes I think you are a very wicked man."

Judge Lewin laughed dryly. "Perhaps. I try not to be. But personal kindness in life has nothing to do with mathematics, that investigator of the nature of the universe which is communion with God in the highest sense of the word. The hydrogen bomb destroys life but the knowledge that built it transcends life. That is what Spinoza meant by God."

Stan must have drunk too much wine on top of the cocktails. "I can't stand this," he shouted all at once. He jumped to his feet and shook his hair off his forehead. He gave a wild glare round the table. "If it's God to kill all the people in the world I say to hell with it."

He burst out through one of the french windows and went streaking off across the terrace. Pat ran after him. In a second she was back almost tearful. "He's running off down the hill through the underbrush," she whined in a singsong. "I called but he wouldn't come back."

Lorna led the ladies fluttering off into the livingroom for

coffee. Will found himself facing Lewin across the table while Colonel Milliron was sloshing brandy about in heated snifters and Abe Merman was searching in the sideboard for a particularly good box of cigars he had left there last weekend.

"Abe," Colonel Milliron blurted out more redfaced than ever, "I always knew you were a man of many hidden talents but I never knew that the expounding of Spinoza was one of them."

"Abe and Berta gave me a rough time," said Judge Lewin with his dry laugh. "It's a pleasure to find people who'll stand up and argue their convictions. People are often afraid to stand up to me . . . and with good reason." He laughed again. "And who is the little whippersnapper who struck the final blow?"

"That's Stan Goodspeed," said the colonel. "He's the black sheep of Lorna's family."

"His comment provokes thought."

Looking remarkably like some kind of odd eagle, with his white shirtfront, black shoulders and pearly gray vest, perched at the end of the table with his sharp beak over the brandy snifter, Judge Lewin was quiet for a while. When Will, puffing on one of Abe's Havana cigars, sat down beside him he spoke up abruptly.

"Do you know young man, you've been giving my friends in Duquesne a whole lot of trouble."

"I certainly hope the sort of people who have been giving me trouble in Duquesne aren't friends of yours, Judge Lewin."

"You have a going concern, but your financial situation is weak. Were this sort of thing in my line I might point out that fresh capital would allow you to develop your plans."

"We've made out on our own up to now."

"The Ludlow Pickle money," said Judge Lewin staring right at him. "No more where that came from."

"We've shown a profit consistently now for six months," said Will staring back.

The judge let his voice drop to a confidential drawl. "Why wouldn't the civilized thing to do be to merge your two warring cab companies, under the present administration of Swift-service you understand? Redtop of Duquesne will show losses that might be attractive to you taxwise."

"That's the kind of monopoly I've been fighting," said Will.

"Sentimentality," hissed the judge and leaned forward with

his hands on the table. He got to his feet. "But as I told you these details are not my affair. Perhaps even Nationwide Redtop would benefit from youthful energies."

"I should insist on a free hand in purchasing, traffic, personnel."

"My dear fellow this is not in my province." Judge Lewin started teetering on the balls of his feet. He picked up his untasted brandy glass and gave it a final sniff.

He surprised Will with a sudden warm very personal smile, a smile just for him.

Then he turned to his host. "Colonel Milliron this has been a delightful evening but we mustn't forget we have an hour's drive back into town." He headed for the living room. "Girls . . . Agatha, Patricia," he called. The others trooped after him. He was clapping his hands at the Jubilirers. "Hurry my dears or Cinderella's Lincoln will turn into a pumpkin."

"Well?" asked Maddie when at last they were alone up in their own room pulling off their sweaty evening clothes.

Will let himself drop frowning on the edge of the bed.

"Maddie . . . It's hard to know how to do right."

Maddie yawned. "Let's sleep on it, Will," she said.

Documentary (24)

WHEN YOUR WIFE GOES OFF ON A TOOT

9 EUROPEAN MONKS
CARRY ON IN CANADA

every second about twenty of them flash through the body of every person on earth. Yet, after some solar flares—about one in five—something cuts their intensity by about one-third

TONIGHT YOU WILL SLEEP IN LONDON

shapes are slimmer, that's why everything in the windows looks better than you do. There's a new set of refreshed blends and patterns

A HELICOPTER IS A TRUCK
IS A BUS A COMPANY CAR

All else fails: Chicken Farmers Try Hoffa

The king of the disc jockeys was throwing a ball
so I decided to ankle along. There must have been
a thousand more cats than they had seats for. They
started off with cool numbers but pretty soon they
speeded up. As the music got warmer so did the
cats. They started climbing out of their seats, running up and down the aisles screaming to their buddies. One kid dressed in a leather jacket and para-
troop boots stood up in his seat and started to wave
his arms. Four cops tried to take him out. Before
long twenty or thirty kids had pitched in to help him
and everybody else was yelling like crazy and tossing
things at the cops.

TO MOST PEOPLE IT LOOKS LIKE ANOTHER
HUMDRUM DAY BUT NOT TO YOU

a swarm of motorcyclists descended today on this
quiet California town, breaking windows, tearing
down signs, wrecking buses in an orgy of vandalism
that drove the inhabitants to take refuge in their
homes

The Sinister Adolescents

James Dean the motion picture actor was no relation
to William Frishe Dean the general. About all the two had
in common was that they both came from the Middle West.
They represented different generations. Very.

There is nothing much deader than a dead motion picture
actor,

and yet,

even after James Dean had been some years dead,

when they filed out of the close darkness and the breathed-
out air of the second and third and fourth run motion picture
theatres where they'd been seeing James Dean's old films,
they still lined up:

the boys in the jackboots and the leather jackets, the boys
in the skintight jeans, the boys in broad motorbike belts,
before the mirrors in the restroom
to look at themselves
and see
James Dean;
the resentful hair,
the deep eyes floating in lonesomeness,
the bitter beat look,
the scorn on the lip.

     Their pocket combs were out; they tousled up their
hair and patted it down just so;
made big eyes at their eyes in the mirror
pouted their lips in a sneer,
the lost cats in love with themselves,
just like James Dean.

     The girls flocked out dizzy with wanting
to run their fingers through his hair, to feel that thwarted
maleness; girl-boy almost, but he needs a shave. . . . "Just him
and me in the back seat of a car."

Their fathers snort, but sometimes they remember: "Nobody understood me either. I might have amounted to something if the folks had understood." The older women struggle
from their seats weteyed.

with wanting to cuddle to mother (it's lack of motherlove
makes delinquents) to smother with little attentions the poor
orphan youngster,

the motherless, brotherless, sisterless lone wolf brat strayed
from the pack,
the poor mixed up kid.

     The pressagents told us James Dean lacked parental
love, that he was an orphan, a farmboy who couldn't get
along at school, a poor mixed up kid from the blacksoil belt
in Indiana. (He never could quite get rid of that Hoosier
twang.)

. . . Hoosier ghosts of forgotten Penrods, crackerbarrel reveries . . . *the thoughts of youth are long long thoughts . . . for I was once a barefoot boy . . . Life on the Mississippi . . . The Arkansas Traveller* . . . Hundredyearold Huck Finn drifting with runaway Jim downriver on their eternal raft. . . . The young used to be comical in America. . . .

"I'm a serious minded and intense little devil," the movie magazines quoted James Dean as saying, "terribly gauche and so tense I don't see how people stay in the same room with me. I know I wouldn't tolerate myself."

The teenagers approved: "Everything he said was cool."

In midcentury America the barefoot boys are all shod in loafers.

The Hoosier farmboys have no cows to milk before day, no wood to chop, no horses to currycomb or oats to measure out into the manger, no coaloil lamps to fill, no chores: "If it's housework let Mother do it"; no chapter of the Bible to read every day,

no roaring preachers to remind them from the pulpit every Sunday that good is Heaven and bad is Hell,

no examiners to ask hard questions;

only perhaps an occasional package to carry out from the A&P, or maybe the family car to wash

before driving down to the drugstore for a coke and a cigarette of some advertised brand, and a comic book; (nothing in midcentury America is less comical than a comic) diagramming murder and mayhem and rape, tirelessly strumming on the raw nerves

for kicks.

Kicks are big business: the sallow hucksters needle the nerves. Through radios drumming rock and roll and blurred girls crooning on TV

they hammer on the wracked nerves:

buy,

buy speed, buy horsepower, buy chromium, buy happiness in a splitlevel ranchhouse, elegance in shocking pink lipstick, passion in a jar of Parisian perfume,

or that portable transitor set

you can take along on your vacations

so that even beside the thunderous ocean, or camping out

in some hidden intervale green in a notch of the hills, you'll
never be free
     from the clamor of salesmen.

     Why not resentful? There's more to life; the kids
knew it. Their fathers won a war but weren't men enough to
keep the peace, they let the pundits and the politicians whee-
dle them into defeat; they let the goons pilfer their pay-
checks, too busy watching TV to resent oppression . . . (Freedom what good is it? Let's have social security
     and welfare and tailfins on our cars
     and packaging)
There's no cellophane can protect the glory of life when
you've lost it; the kids knew it.

     Even in success James Dean was resentful. This kid
had talent. That's how he differed from the general run of
drugstore cowboys. The critics said he had the makings of a
great film actor. He won awards. Even after he was dead the
audience voted him the best actor of the year. James Dean
was resentful, we were told,
     because he came from a broken home. "My mother died on
me when I was nine years old. What does she expect me to
do? Do it all myself."
     His father married again. An aunt and uncle raised him on
their neat farm in Fairmount, Indiana. He was a moody boy.
He was terribly nearsighted: He did poorly in his studies,
     but in highschool he played baseball, basketball, led the
track team and excelled in dramatics. They gave him a medal
for the best all around athlete senior year.
     His elocution teacher took a fancy to him. She spotted the
talent. She coached him in parts in school plays and had him
win a statewide contest in public speaking
     reading THE MADMAN, by Dickens.
     When she induced him to enter a national contest held out
in Colorado, the judges passed him over. He resented that.
He never forgave that poor teacher.

     His father went to work as a dental technician in LA.
After young Dean graduated he went out to stay with his
father and stepmother. Farmwork wasn't his idea. A boy with
talent is too sensitive to work on the farm. His father set him

up to a course in physical education at a junior college. Then
he switched to prelaw courses at the U of C. His schoolmates
didn't appreciate him. He got into a fight with his fraternity
brothers and dropped out of college in a huff. He didn't take
to that kind of schooling;

but when a fellow he knew started to study acting with a
retired motion picture performer, James Dean tagged along;
he panicked the class acting the part of a pinetree in a storm.
Now he knew he wanted to be an actor.

He hung around LA, broke most of the time, working as an
usher in movie theatres, getting an occasional part as an extra
on the lots, or a bit on TV,

dreaming and yearning and hungry,

eating cold spaghetti out of the can.

Dirty shirt, never a haircut, needed a shave, the grubbiest
guy in town. Sometimes he got a job parking cars in a parking
lot to earn the two bits he needed for a hamburger and a cup
of coffee.

At last he made a break for New York, rode East all
the way on the bus. He had a friend with TV connections.
For a year he hung around Broadway with the outofwork
actors.

"New York is vital, above all fertile," he told the reporters
later. "I fit to cadence and pace better here." He developed
a lingo.

out of tearoom talk about bebop and Bach,

and stale shards of Freud, sex treatises in paperback, cap-
tions dubbed in on Cocteau's films, explanations tacked on the
wall beside the paintings of Miro at the Modern Museum,

existentialism,

and scraps out of French translations sold under the counter:

"Include me out"; selfexpression.

In the drab summer desert of New York, James Dean
lacked friends; he lacked girls, he lacked dough;

but when the chance came he knew how to grab it: a young
director took an interest, invited him out sailing on a sloop on
the Sound—farmboy turned deckhand—gave him a part in a
show which immediately flopped;

but he'd been seen on the stage. Next he played the blackmailing Arab in a dramatization of André Gide's *Immoraliste*. He walked out on the part, the play closed, but he'd been seen by people who knew show business: rave writeups: he was an actor.

They took him on to study at the Actor's Studio. The Actor's Studio was celebrity's lobby in those days. That year Marlon Brando was the artistic idol of the screen. Directors saw a young Brando in Dean (the hepcat school, sideburns and a rat's nest for hair, leather jackets, jackboots and a motorcycle at the curb. These are tough guys, delinquents; but sensitive: Great God how they're sensitive). Elia Kazan hired him to play a sinister adolescent: "Live the part," Stanislavski told his actors.

Dean did just that. He was obstreperous as hell. "I can't divert into being a social human being," he snarled at the reporters through the butt that dangled from his lip, "when I'm working on a hero who's essentially demonic."

Demonic, but lovable under it all.

The sinister adolescent was box office. Long before the picture was released he was besieged by Hollywood agents, promoters, feature writers, photographers.

       He wanted to have it known that he was crazy about racing cars. Speed was how to die. Artistic. He made up his own mobiles, was planning to be a bullfighter: *Death in the Afternoon.* "Cool," echoed the teenagers. "Everything he said was cool."

In Hollywood he went on playing the parts he played on the screen: He would keep Hedda Hopper, the Eleanor Roosevelt of the motion picture press, waiting two hours for an interview,

then he would turn up in a torn dirty sweater and riding breeches out at the knees. He quarreled with his friends. He walked out on dates. He drove his directors crazy by being late on the lot. Wouldn't rehearse. He pouted and sulked. Sometimes they couldn't get a word out of him—"A wary suspicious loner," one director called him. Another was more forgiving: "Just a boy on the rise."

He was always nice to his fans though, the teenage crowd. He was just one of the gang with the night watch; the young wouldbe actors who hung around the early morning hamburger joints on Sunset Boulevard. Three glasses of beer made

him woozy, he never cared to drink liquor; so he chain-
smoked cigarettes and drank cup after cup of coffee right
through till it was day. No wonder he couldn't sleep and
turned up late and blearyeyed at the studio. *Rebel Without a
Cause*.

The teenagers saw themselves in James Dean. Everything
he said was cool.

Already he was beginning not to like it much if people didn't look up when he slouched into the Italian restaurant
where he ate his meals. Wasn't he James Dean?

He was handy with the mambo drum. His bachelor actor's
home was loud with hi-fi. He had to pick an isolated location
so that the neighbors wouldn't complain about the rock and
roll. In quiet moods he liked to be seen at night spots with
another celebrity. He played around with the girl who'd made
a name for herself up and down the Coast playing Vampira
on TV, the ghoul who gave people right in their own homes
their daily creeps,

like a Charles Addams cartoon. (No romance, said their
friends,

and how she was real warmhearted underneath and understood his resentments.) He told her everything.

A few days before he died she sent him a postcard picture
of herself posed beside an open grave. "Come join me," it said.

An actor had to have a hobby to satisfy the public
relations staff. Dean owned a horse but racing cars was his
personal bid for publicity. He'd won a race for novices at
some meet. His racing, the public was told, gave the producers fits. He was quoted as telling them that speeding was
a glorious way to die. (Life couldn't be all social security and
safety first. The kids knew that. It was glory a man had to
have.) Some friend furnished him with a St. Christopher
medal, but the studio, so it was said, had written it into his
contract that he wasn't to race a car until the picture he was
working on was ready for release.

The last day of September he was free from that
clause. There was to be a meet at Salinas. Instead of taking
his white Porsche-Spyder with the 130 painted on its side
over to the track on a truck like most of the contestants he

had to drive it over himself. His German mechanic went along.

A photographer followed in a stationwagon.

He wanted to feel her speed.

Already at Bakersfield a traffic cop gave him a ticket for doing sixty through a forty mile zone.

The sun was setting. It was nearly dusk. He wanted to feel her speed. He was making seventyfive, eighty, a hundred— accounts differ—when near Paso Robles on the empty highway he collided head on with a car turning in from an intersection,

a Ford driven by a young man named Donald Turnupseed.

James Dean was killed. The steering wheel went right through him; Turnupseed and the mechanic were hurt but recovered.

Dead at twenty four:

"James Dean can't be dead," the girls told each other, "he's in hospital undergoing facial surgery." It would take a long time but some day they would see him slouching out onto the screen again.

People paid fifty cents a head to see the wreck of his car.

In LA the clairvoyants and psychics did a land office business interviewing James Dean in the spirit world. Some interviews were printed. "Everything he said was cool," the teenagers said.

At Warner Brothers the requests for photographs, which had merely been average, went up by the time he'd been dead a year to seven thousand letters a month. Everybody from his grandmother to the waiters at the Italian restaurant was interviewed by the motion picture press. The pulp merchants sold oneshot lives of him in hundreds of thousands of copies. Bronze heads and plaster masks were marketed in bulk. One popular item was made of a plastic supposed to feel like human skin when you stroked it.

The teenagers found it hard to believe that James Dean was dead. There he was right on the screen when they saw his old pictures. The promoters had been struggling hard to blow up the story that millions wouldn't believe he was dead, but when they released a picture on his life nobody went to see it. James Dean was dead sure enough.

Documentary (25)

FLY NOW PAY LATER

Now's the Time to Get Away, Change the View, Break the Routine, Watch the Sandpipers Do the Scurrying

US PLANS PAYLOAD TO LAND ON MOON

it is a private world of rare and beautiful birds:—the roseate spoonbill, snowy egret and reddish egret, ibis, pelican and the great white heron. Lurking in quiet places are manatees or seacows, alligators and the nation's only crocodiles

JAPANESE CIRCUS IS A SIGN OF SPRING

Included are a variety of shadow checks besides the classic solids.

IT TAKES A LOT OF PUSH IN THE RIGHT PLACES TO PUT A PROGRAM INTO SPACE

Indicted in Sale of Smut Records

National Guard Troops with loaded carbines moved in early today to help break up a riot of teenagers. The mob had flouted police authority and milled through a business section near the ocean beach for more than four hours. The riot stemmed from efforts of the police to stop a group of youths from racing their cars on ramps leading to the beach and from signal lights on the city streets. Instead of dispersing the youths slashed the tires of two police cars and started throwing rocks. They seemed to have an idea a teenager had been arrested and kept calling "Bring him back, Bring him back."

GET RID OF THREE O'CLOCK COBWEBS

If this one doesn't make you want to travel you already live where all the fun is.

Tomorrow the Moon

"If he didn't mean for me to pick 'em up why did he have to leave his credit cards laying around on the bathroom floor? I certainly didn't mean to take 'em. I meant to give 'em back all the while but they never gave me a chance. 'Here are your credit cards, Uncle Jap,' I was planning to say, 'You dropped 'em on the bathroom floor,' and to give him a dirty look and a sneer.

"It's his own damn fault. Why did he have to leave 'em laying around if he didn't expect me to pick 'em up? Or did he do it on purpose just to see what I'd do?

"No he didn't. Drunk that's why. He let 'em fall out of the inside pocket of his jacket because he was drunk, the cards and a small wad of bills. He was good and drunk. Gets drunk every night, the old soak, and if I get so much as enthusiastic over a can of beer, he lectures me on the evils. He must have wanted a son awful bad and it's too late now, so the crazy clod takes it out on me with his little peptalks.

"I meant to show all that in my tone of voice and the way I looked him in the eye when I gave him back the credit cards. I'm Stan Goodspeed and I'm not taking a thing, I meant my look to say. But they never gave me a chance to slide in a word. Too damn busy listening to themselves gibblegabble about how they were going to blow up the world with their nuclear friction, or whatever the screwy name is they have for it.

"They say teenagers are screwy but it's the adults who are really nuts. At teenage parties we have a nice happy violent time getting rid of our frustrations. We have fun. But these damned adults, all the poor clods do is sit there beating their brains out over their liquor. It was that egghead way they just sat there, drinking sips out of their drinks with their little fingers crooked, smiling like it was all just too cute to blow up the whole entire goddam human race, that got me started. That's nothing to smile about.

"I know I'm emotional. Maybe I ought to take tranquilizers. I've been going slowly crazy ever since I came from that lousy school. They had it in for me at that school right from the beginning. That housemaster hated my guts from the time he first set eyes on me.

"I don't blame Aunty she's just so soft on him she does anything he says. Imagine sending Stan Goodspeed to a dump where they won't let you go out for a little relaxation Saturday nights. The nerve of them to expect a kid to go to bed at half past ten. I'd just have laid there getting more and more frustrated. They must think I'm chicken. One thing I sure showed those masters I wasn't. They acted all the time like they thought a guy ought to be scared pissless of them. Not Stan Goodspeed. Not while there is a taxicab left in the world.

"Now to be real truthful—a kid oughtn't to lie to himself—I didn't exactly mean to give the bills back. Uncle Jap never would miss a couple of skins. Let him worry about where he dropped them. Shit I don't know what I meant. It all just got in my hair. That's what. Sanctimonious talk about how blowing up the human race was the love of God. Why can't they say what they mean?

"And soninlaw sitting there with his eyes on that old square's face like he was in church listening to the Lord's Prayer. That old square thinks he's God Almighty. I used to think Will Jenks was the greatest man in the world, a single-handed superman fighting the gangsters for everything that was on the level. If he told me to stick my hand in the fire I'd a done it. I went down on my knees to beg him to let me drive a cab for him. I'd have given my life for him like that crazy clod Terry Bryant. If he'd let me fake my age and drive a cab for him I wouldn't be all frustrated and disturbed like I am. A kid gets to the point where he has to have action.

"Maybe I'm neurotic but it gave me the cold creeps to sit there and see Will Jenks sucking up to that old square just because he needs money to put in his screwy taxicabs. It's crazy. Will Jenks a brownnose. Made me ashamed of myself for belonging to the human race. If I hadn't walked out on 'em I'd have puked, I'd have thrown up all over Aunty's silver lamé tablecloth or whatever screwy material it's made of.

What did they expect me to do? Take it till I upchucked over the table and that girl staring at me with the come hither eyes, she was a dog if I ever saw one.

"When I ran off down that hill I was all excited. I didn't know what I was going to do. I just ran on down, tripping and stumbling through the bushes till I got a stitch in my side. What was the use of getting all out of breath and sweaty? What was there to get chicken about? None of 'em was going to come after me. All too wrapped up listening to Money Bags.

"They couldn't care less. Except Aunty. I'll write Aunty saying not to worry.

"So I started to walk on quietly down the road into Providence Forge. I had to play this one cool. Here's where I'd begin to live it up. So I walked along through the misty mild moonlight night listening to those screwy whippoorwills and smelling the sexy sweet honeysuckle that made me want a playmate real bad. Take it easy. Playmate coming up. Play this one cool. 'Stan, don't you do anything foolish,' I kept telling myself.

"As luck would have it there was a bus marked Philadelphia standing right in the busstation. I hopped right in. The bus was full of kids coming home from some screwy picnic. The girls were all dogs so far as I could see. They looked up at me as if to say 'Now what's his racket?' But I didn't mess with them. My racket was to get far away fast. So I just sat there with my eyelashes over my eyes looking over the literature that came with Uncle Jap's credit cards. That's how I got my big idea.

"When the busdriver asked for my ticket before he started I tried to get away with a hardluck story about how I'd lost it down a drain in the busstation but he wouldn't fall for that one so I had to use some of Uncle Jap's hardearned folding money to pay my fare into town. That left me fourteen dollars and a quarter. May sound like a lot of dough but it was just peanuts for what I was planning.

"As the bus went zooming along through the moony summer night I sat there studying Uncle Jap's signature on the credit cards. He had his Jasper Milliron written in kind of a shaky immature round hand. Isn't it a sign of immaturity for an old clod like that to sign his name like a kid? Maybe that's what's wrong with Uncle Jap. Maybe that's what attracted

Aunty. Aunty's too full of motherlove for her own good. If he weren't immature he never would have stuck his neck out and got all messed up trying to tangle with one of the biggest milling concerns in the country over some kind of screwy new machinery. Why can't he get hep? Aunty always said that if he'd kept his mouth shut and let things ride, he'd a been chairman of the board to this day. Of course Aunty thinks he's wonderful, always was crazy about dead cats. It's immaturity accounts for his drinking.

"Copying Uncle Jap's signature wouldn't be forgery, indeed it wouldn't. Didn't he tell me once he wanted to adopt me as a son? I had a time shaking that one off. 'Let's let it ride,' I said. 'That's OK Uncle Jap,' I said.

"So I sat there reading about how to charge services including *food, drink and room accommodations at the finest restaurants, night clubs and hotels* (I was getting hungry and sleepy just reading it) *in major cities and resort areas throughout the country,* (and I sure won't be alone) *auto rentals* (safety fast, that's what the ads say) *through the world's leading auto rental agencies; motel accommodations, interstate liquor package* (yeah man!) *and retail liquor charging where the state law permits* (I'll buy me a case. Won't make me mad) *gasoline and repair services at more than three thousand affiliated stations from coast to coast, gift and florist shops in major cities throughout the world; air, sea and rail transportation and other travel facilities and men's* (just watch for that bleeding madras jacket) *and women's clothing stores* (women's! Wait till the chicks see what I can buy 'em on credit) *and much more.*

"What do they mean by 'much more'?

"Did I need a tranquilizer? Just play it cool, Stan Goodspeed, I kept telling myself. And I sat there in the bus telling myself that if I didn't do anything foolish and kept moving fast enough the bills would never catch up. Maybe they would blow the screwy world up before the bills came in at that.

"If the worst came to the worst I'd just explain to Uncle Jap that I wasn't costing him any more this way than if I'd stayed home and gotten all frustrated and disturbed so he'd have to take me to a psychist or whatever the screwy name is of those nut doctors they take disturbed kids to. Why there was a kid in school whose parents paid some analyzer twentyfive dollars an hour for years and years to have him analyzed, and they still do.

"Then the bus stopped and all the kids got out and right away everybody was gone. I almost chickened out all by myself walking around in the empty lonesome glare of the downtown streets. I knew I couldn't get me a real plush pad without luggage at that time of night so I just walked down to the Thirtieth Street station and sat there in the waitingroom. I sat there all night reading the ads out of a wad of slick paper magazines and smoking pack after pack of cigarettes. I guess I musta smoked four packs. The more I smoked the more I thought. 'Play it cool Stan Goodspeed,' I kept telling myself.

"First I had to have my story in case they questioned how come I had this credit card. I'd say I really was Jasper Milliron Jr. and the crazy clods had left off the junior, but it was all in the family and Dad would be good for it anyway. Then I had a kinder second string yarn about how my dear Uncle Ben had died and left me all this jack, his entire fortune come to think of it, but I couldn't get my hands on any cash, natch, and had to live off my credit cards till the estate was settled. I wasn't going to do like that kid I read about in the paper who did great on his credit cards but got snagged by the cops because he cashed a check and it bounced.

"So there I sat hazily dreamily thinking about how I'd find me a playmate with kinda sultry blond hair and beautiful big bubs all a lovely even tan in a cabaña built for two on some beach on the Coast. Or why not Lake Tahoe on the way? And then Honolulu? Honolulu was the place to go, but not alone. A girl on a beach. A girl. A girl.

"It would have almost turned into a wet dream if a big cop hadn't scared me out of a year's growth. When I looked up from my glossy paper mag with my eyes batting, there he was standing over me and saying this was a waitingroom, it wasn't no dormitory for runaway teens. I opened my eyes wide. Just to show I was in the groove ('Keep your shirt on my good man,' was in my tone of voice) I told him I'd gotten in late on the bus from school and was waiting for a morning train to New York. I gave him Merman, Milliron Associates as my dad's address and all that. And then I showed him all this rich identification and told him I didn't get me a pad at the Bellevue because I was so late it didn't seem worth while to blow in all that dough for such a short time because I was saving my pennies to buy me a Grumman Gulfstream for a private plane. The crazy clod just about took off his hat. He called me Sir. Can you beat it?

"Stan Goodspeed, this is going to be cool.

"First thing a kid needs is to be nicely dressed, not too snazzy but casual, like the beachnik togs and wash and wear nantril fiber slacks they advertise in the slick paper mags, and airplane luggage to go with it. If I get past the first couple stores the way I wowed that flatfoot bugeyed, I'll be all set. Then I buy my airplane tickets and drive me a U-Drive It car from one of the world's leading auto agencies. Jeez how I love the kinda sweet sharp rubber varnish leather smell of a new car. Why don't some of those perfume companies put out a perfume smelling of Chrysler Imperial right off the floor? You could sprinkle it over some playmate before you worked her. Say why not hire me a car and pick up some chick on the way to the airport? Yeah man.

"By that time it was daylight. With my mags in a bundle under my arm I walked around outside the station. A beautiful pink early light made everything look out of this world. My tongue was black from smoking all those cigarettes but I couldn't care less. This was going to be Stan Goodspeed day.

"All I had to do now was wait for the stores to open strolling around in the lovely sunshine. I didn't want to spend any more hard money than I had to but I did have to go to the terminal drugstore and buy me a safetyrazor. Cash was going to be my toughest problem. I knew that the sky was the limit on credit but if I got snagged it would be for lack of two bits to slip to a bellhop. Still I had to wear a shining face. I went to the men's room moving fast and keeping my eyes to myself to keep out of the way of the lurking homosexuals and shaved and patted down my hair and cleaned up good.

"At nine thirty I tried my first store. I'd already spotted it an hour before by a little sign, 'Credit Cards Honored.'

"The crazy clod was so anxious to make his first sale he didn't check on a thing. Was I tense? While he was writing up the bill for me to sign the guy noticed I was all of a sweat. I told him it had been the night before the morning after but he wasn't trying to pin anything on me. All the crazy clod was trying to do was sell me some screwy new deodorant to stop tension odor. Can you beat that?

"The man in the luggage shop was wackier yet. I thought he'd kiss me when he figured out the amount of the bill. Couldn't he send the suitcases around to the hotel? No I'd pick 'em up on the way to the airport. I was catching a jet to the Coast. I talked big but he sure ate it up.

"I was just walking into the U-Drive It place when I stopped dead in my tracks. I remembered my driving license. Sure as hell they'd want to see it and it read Stan Goodspeed. Thinking ahead like that showed I was in the groove. Nothing to it but to spend cash money on a taxi. I never did mind spending money on taxis. Meanwhile I had to waste two nickels on the phone to make me a plane reservation. The clod at the other end of the wire was apologetic as hell because he couldn't put me on a jet right there. I'd have to fly to Washington and change. Nonstop to San Francisco. This was the life. I hopped into a cab. Restaurants, nightclubs, hotels in the major cities and resort areas, affiliated stations from coast to coast, men's and women's clothing stores, gift and florist shops throughout the world, here I come.

"And much more?

"A handsome outboard cruiser sleeping two with the famous fiberglas hull that never needs scraping, sanding, calking or painting; a sports compact deluxe convertible featuring nimbler handling, that easyriding zoom; a pad for indoor-outdoor living, airconditioned, soundconditioned with builtin appliances and luminous ceilings; an easy to operate aerodynamically advanced private plane for fast cool clean direct nonstop travel, a cosmic butterfly powered by parabolic mirrors, a spin out beyond the stratosphere in a supersonic spaceliner. Why not?

"And much more . . .

"Stan Goodspeed's throwing a ball. . . . Yeah man."

Sendoff

Musing midnight and the century's decline
man walks with dog,
shuffling the roadside gravel where sometimes we used to
find among the quartzy riverpebbles,
spent arrowheads of the Powhatans.

Overcast blots the stars. Not even a glimpse of impudent
Echo, America's toy balloon the radio man said go out and
see. The fall's too late for lightningbugs, only a chill hint here
and there of a glowworm in the wet grass.

The dog trots eager, sniffing the night, proud of her man's
steps behind. The man,
    shamed drags beaten strides, drained of every thought but
hatred
    of the tinpot pharaohs whose coarse imprecations
    the impartial transistors have been dinning in his ears. Evil
is indivisible. By hate they rose to flashbulb glory and the roar
of cowed multitudes, police sirens shrieking how great the
leader, how little the led: the abject mike ever waiting to
receive
    the foul discharge of their power to kill. The lie squared,
the lie cubed, the lie to the power of x deals death like a
tornado. By hate they live. By hate we'll see them die. We've
seen them die before. The hate remains
    to choke out good, to strangle the still small private voice
that is God's spark in man. Man drowns in his own scum.
    These nights are dark.

In the light of the carriagelamps on the brick steps of the
sleeping house back home the man pauses for a last breath of
the outdoor air; the dog's nose nuzzles his hand. She bows,
wriggles, cavorts, goes belly up, eyes rolling in frantic appreci-
ation:
    walker on hindlegs, hurler of sticks, foodgiver, builder of
shelter, toolmaker, creation's lord, initiator, master of Yes and
No;
    wagging dog-Shakespeare her tail declaims:
    Oh paragon of animals.

On the best-seller list for more than
50 weeks at $6.95. NOW ONLY **95¢**

THE
MAKING
OF THE
PRESIDENT
1960

THEODORE H. WHITE
author of THE VIEW FROM THE FORTIETH FLOOR

CARDINAL EDITION GC•953

If your bookseller does not have this title, you may order
it by sending retail price, plus 5¢ for postage and handling
to: MAIL SERVICE DEPT., Pocket Books, Inc., 1 West 39th
Street, New York 18, N. Y. Enclose check or money order
—do not send cash.

Published by POCKET BOOKS, INC.